THIEF OF THIEVES ™

CREATED BY ROBERT KIRKMAN

ANDY DIGGLE
WRITER

SHAWN MARTINBROUGH
ARTIST

ADRIANO LUCAS
COLORIST

RUS WOOTON
LETTERER

JON MOISON
EDITOR

ARIELLE BASICH
ASSISTANT EDITOR

SHAWN MARTINBROUGH
ADRIANO LUCAS
COVER

THIEF OF THIEVES, VOL. 6: "GOLD RUSH."
ISBN: 978-1-5343-0037-8
PRINTED IN U.S.A.
First Printing

Published by Image Comics, Inc. Office of publication: 2701 NW Vaughn St., Ste. 780, Portland, OR 97210. Image and its logos are ® and © 2017 Image Comics Inc. All rights reserved. Originally published in single magazine form as THIEF OF THIEVES #32-37. THIEF OF THIEVES and all character likenesses are ™ and © 2017, Robert Kirkman, LLC. All rights reserved. All names, characters, events and locales in this publication are entirely fictional. Any resemblance to actual persons (living or dead), events or places, without satiric intent, is coincidental. No part of this publication may be reproduced or transmitted, in any form or by any means (except for short excerpts for review purposes) without the express written permission of the copyright holder.

For information regarding the CPSIA on this printed material call: 203-595-3636 and provide reference # RICH – 720309.

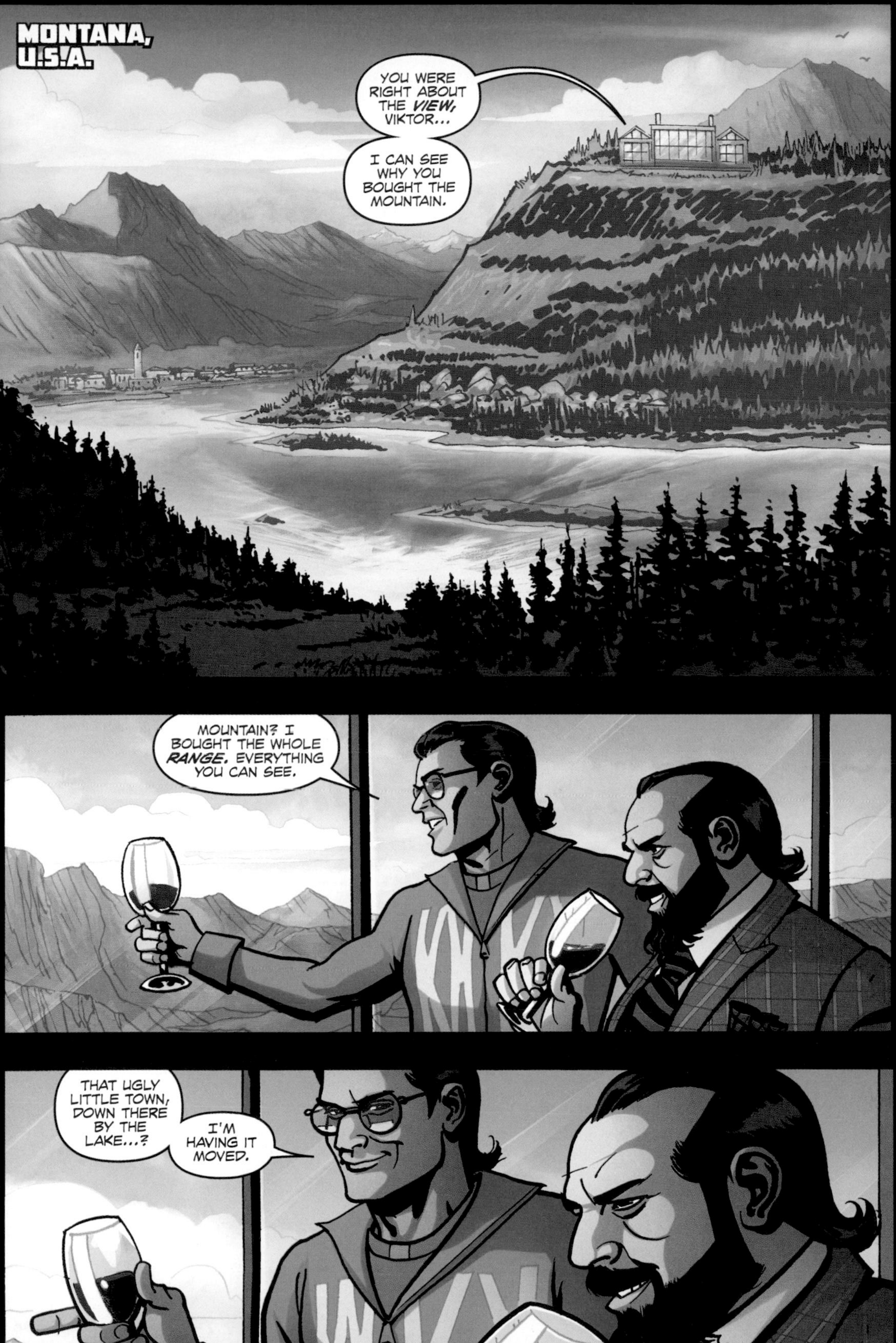
MONTANA, U.S.A.
YOU WERE RIGHT ABOUT THE VIEW, VIKTOR...
I CAN SEE WHY YOU BOUGHT THE MOUNTAIN.
MOUNTAIN? I BOUGHT THE WHOLE RANGE. EVERYTHING YOU CAN SEE.
THAT UGLY LITTLE TOWN, DOWN THERE BY THE LAKE...?
I'M HAVING IT MOVED.

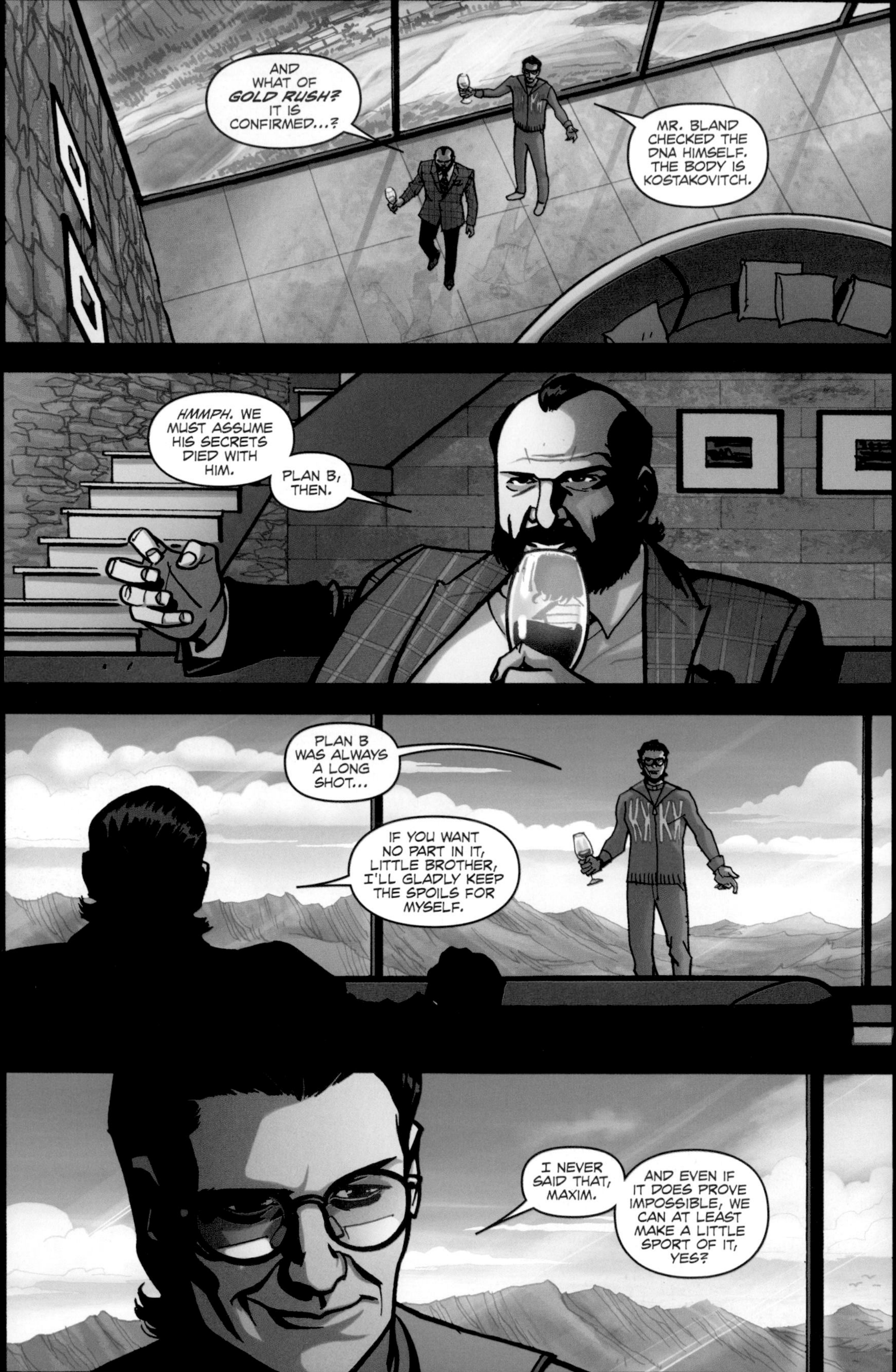
AND WHAT OF *GOLD RUSH?* IT IS CONFIRMED...?
MR. BLAND CHECKED THE DNA HIMSELF. THE BODY IS KOSTAKOVITCH.
HMMPH. WE MUST ASSUME HIS SECRETS DIED WITH HIM.
PLAN B, THEN.
PLAN B WAS ALWAYS A LONG SHOT...
IF YOU WANT NO PART IN IT, LITTLE BROTHER, I'LL GLADLY KEEP THE SPOILS FOR MYSELF.
I NEVER SAID THAT, MAXIM.
AND EVEN IF IT DOES PROVE IMPOSSIBLE, WE CAN AT LEAST MAKE A LITTLE SPORT OF IT, YES?

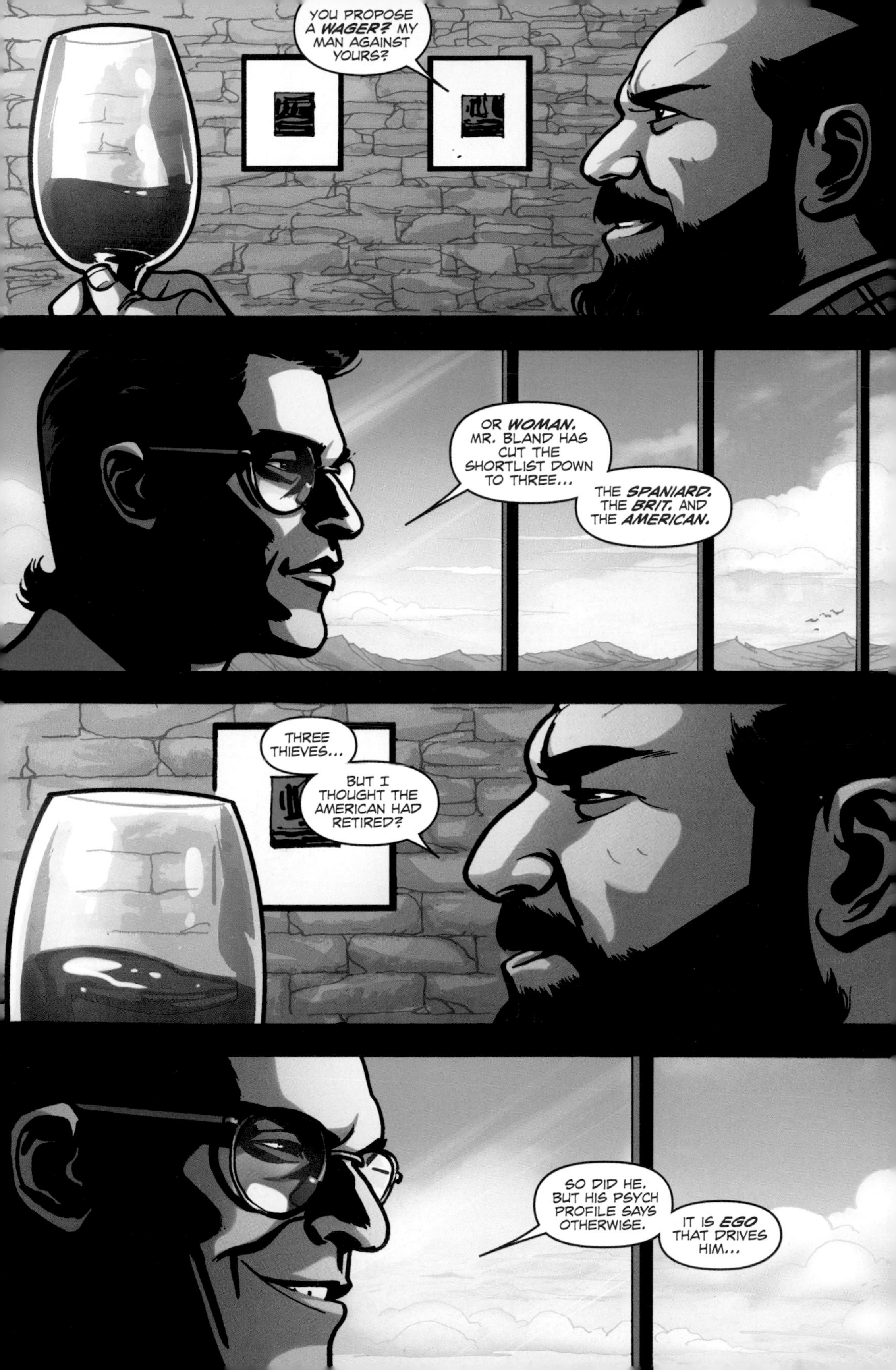
YOU PROPOSE A WAGER? MY MAN AGAINST YOURS?
OR WOMAN. MR. BLAND HAS CUT THE SHORTLIST DOWN TO THREE...
THE SPANIARD. THE BRIT. AND THE AMERICAN.
THREE THIEVES...
BUT I THOUGHT THE AMERICAN HAD RETIRED?
SO DID HE. BUT HIS PSYCH PROFILE SAYS OTHERWISE.
IT IS EGO THAT DRIVES HIM...

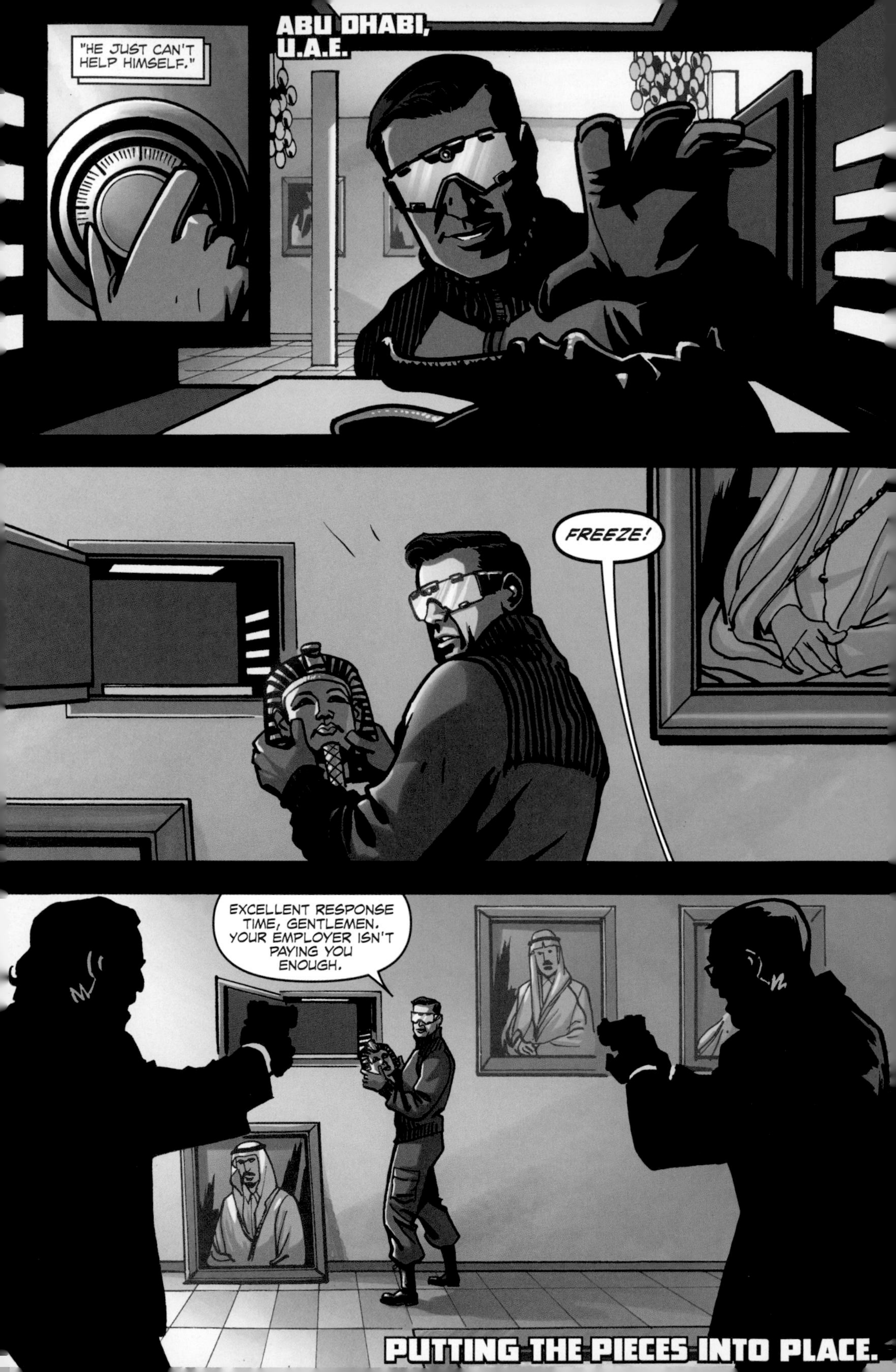
ABU DHABI, U.A.E.
"HE JUST CAN'T HELP HIMSELF."
FREEZE!
EXCELLENT RESPONSE TIME, GENTLEMEN. YOUR EMPLOYER ISN'T PAYING YOU ENOUGH.
PUTTING THE PIECES INTO PLACE.

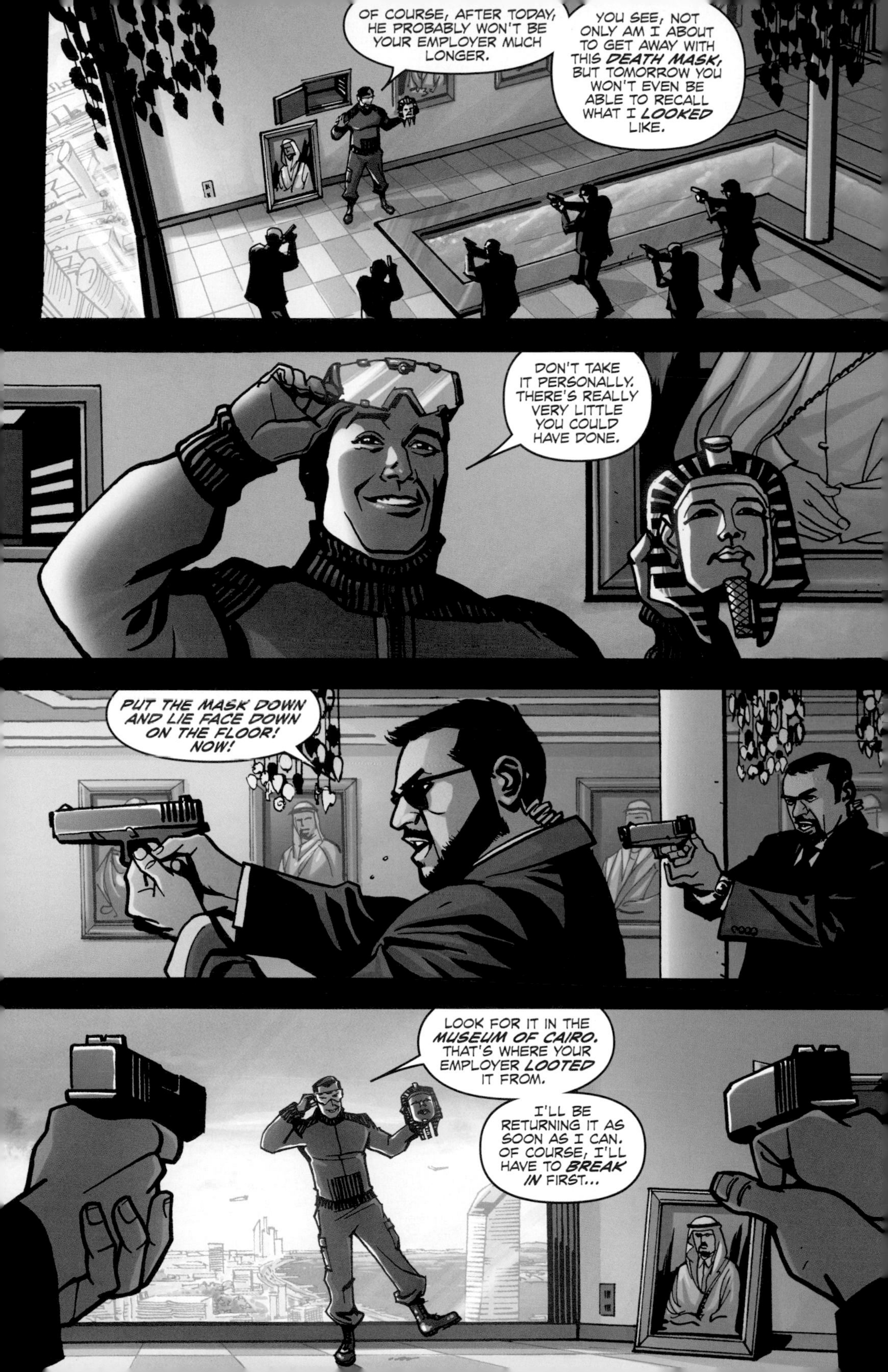

OF COURSE, AFTER TODAY, HE PROBABLY WON'T BE YOUR EMPLOYER MUCH LONGER.
YOU SEE, NOT ONLY AM I ABOUT TO GET AWAY WITH THIS DEATH MASK, BUT TOMORROW YOU WON'T EVEN BE ABLE TO RECALL WHAT I LOOKED LIKE.
DON'T TAKE IT PERSONALLY. THERE'S REALLY VERY LITTLE YOU COULD HAVE DONE.
PUT THE MASK DOWN AND LIE FACE DOWN ON THE FLOOR! NOW!
LOOK FOR IT IN THE MUSEUM OF CAIRO. THAT'S WHERE YOUR EMPLOYER LOOTED IT FROM.
I'LL BE RETURNING IT AS SOON AS I CAN. OF COURSE, I'LL HAVE TO BREAK IN FIRST...

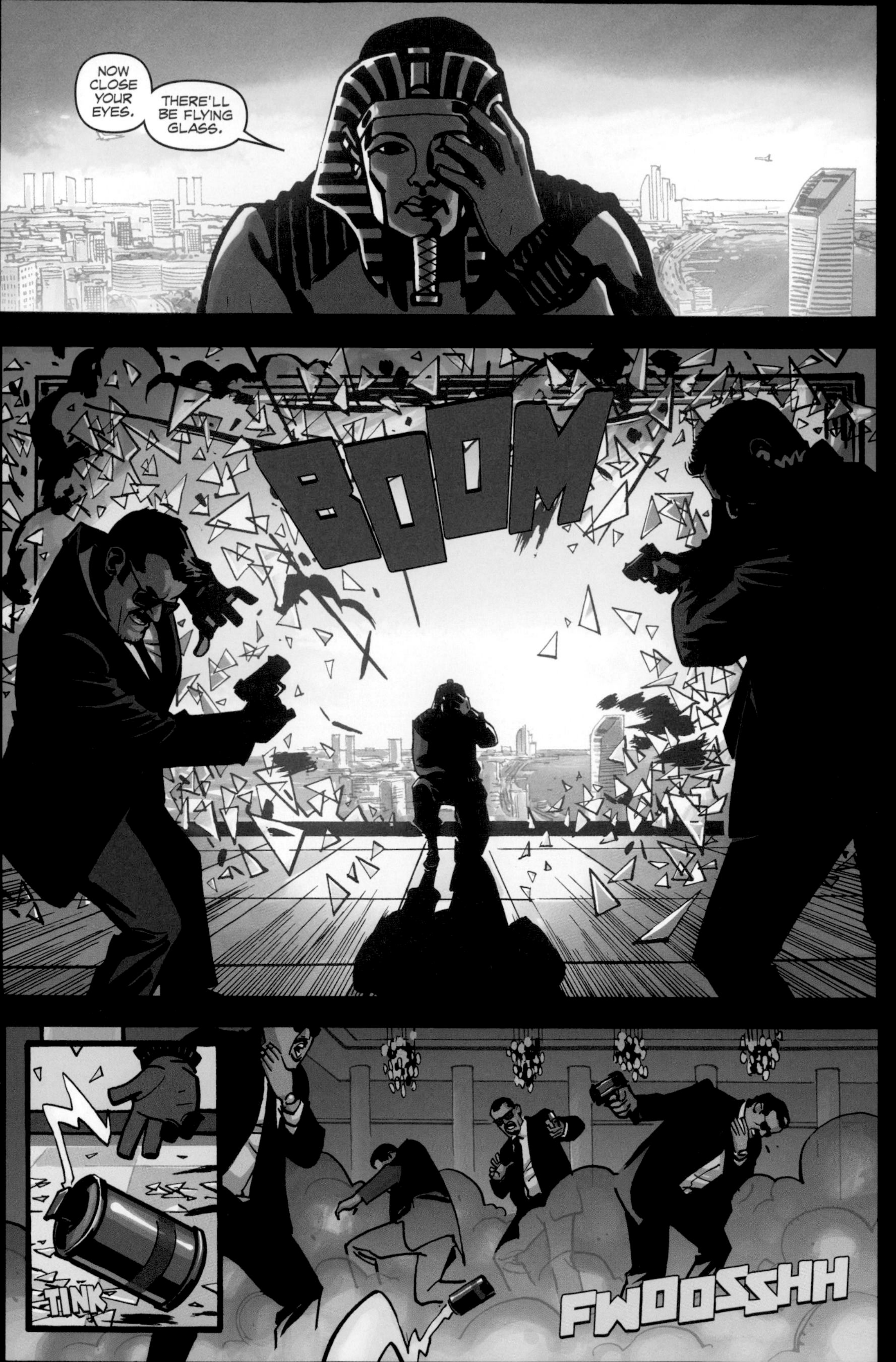
NOW CLOSE YOUR EYES.
THERE'LL BE FLYING GLASS.
BOOM
TINK
FWOOSSHH

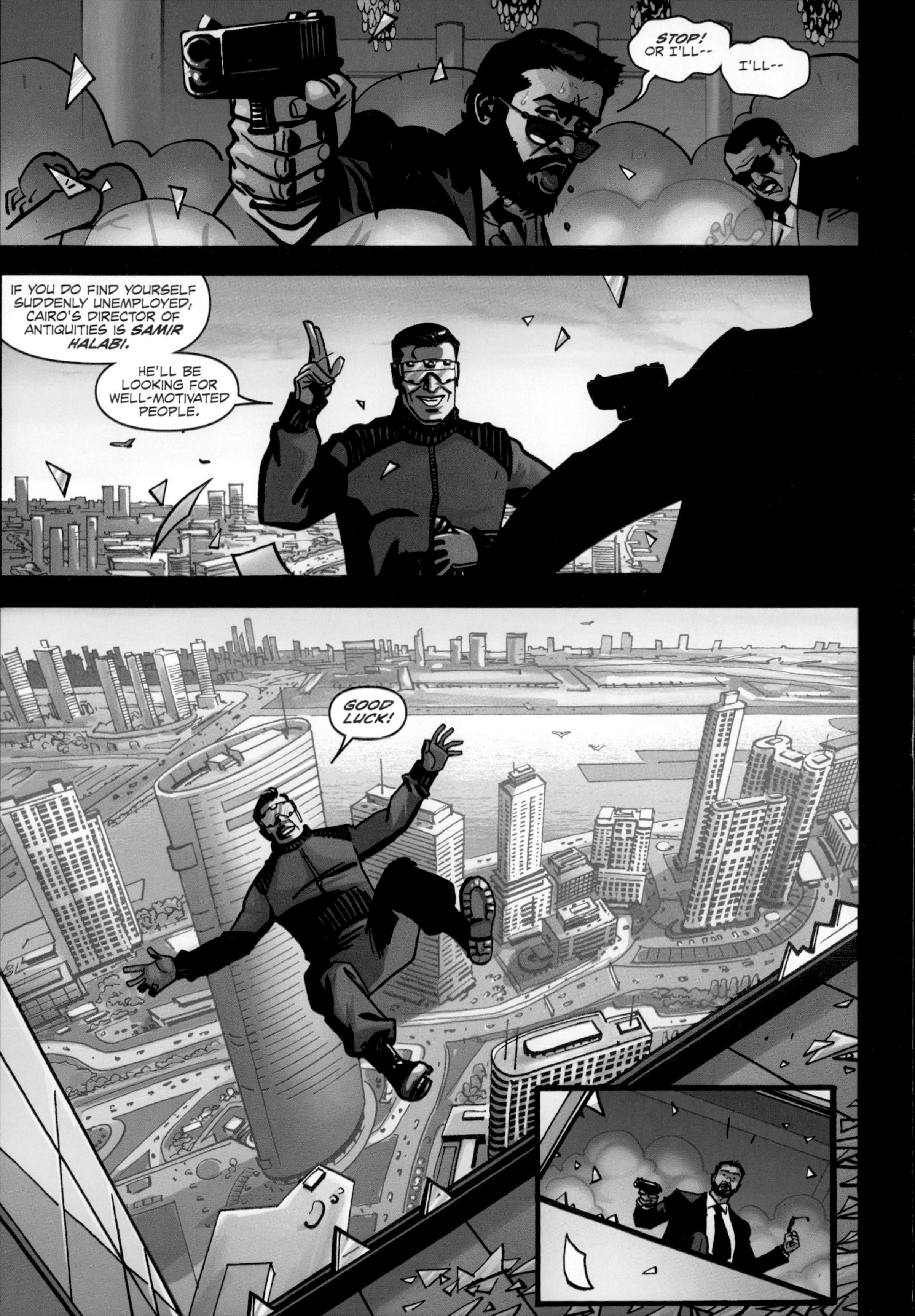
STOP! OR I'LL--
I'LL--
IF YOU DO FIND YOURSELF SUDDENLY UNEMPLOYED, CAIRO'S DIRECTOR OF ANTIQUITIES IS SAMIR HALABI.
HE'LL BE LOOKING FOR WELL-MOTIVATED PEOPLE.
GOOD LUCK!

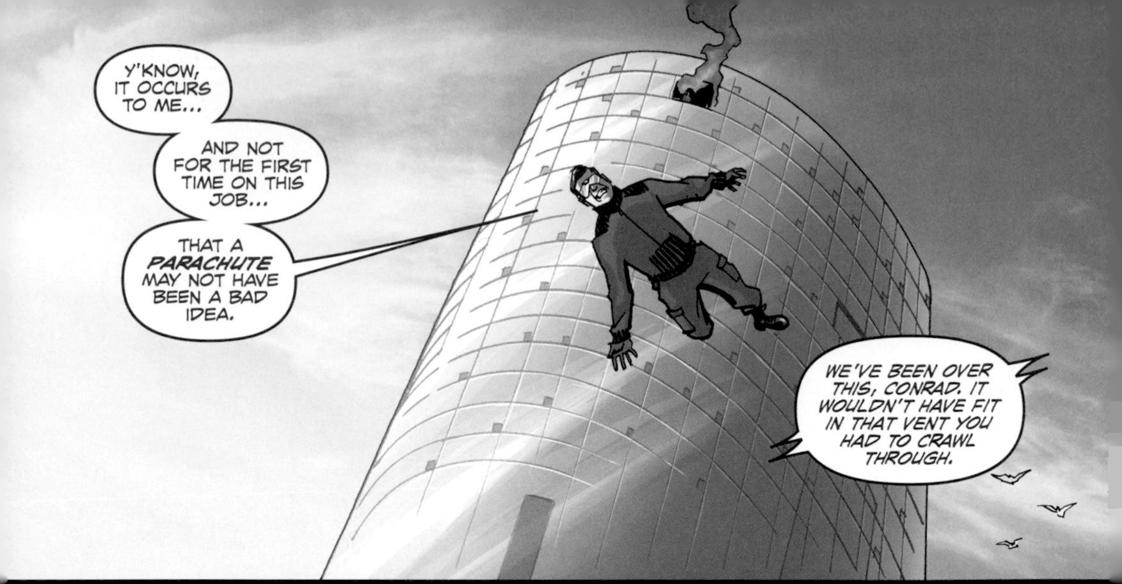
Y'KNOW, IT OCCURS TO ME...
AND NOT FOR THE FIRST TIME ON THIS JOB...
THAT A PARACHUTE MAY NOT HAVE BEEN A BAD IDEA.
WE'VE BEEN OVER THIS, CONRAD. IT WOULDN'T HAVE FIT IN THAT VENT YOU HAD TO CRAWL THROUGH.

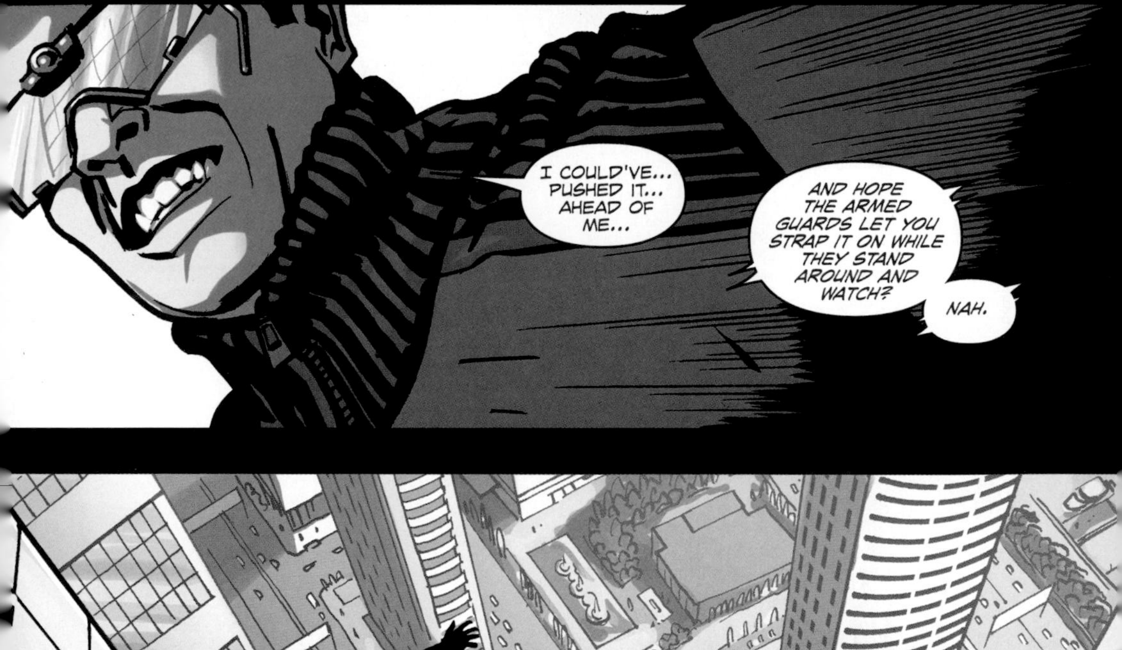
I COULD'VE... PUSHED IT... AHEAD OF ME...
AND HOPE THE ARMED GUARDS LET YOU STRAP IT ON WHILE THEY STAND AROUND AND WATCH?
NAH.

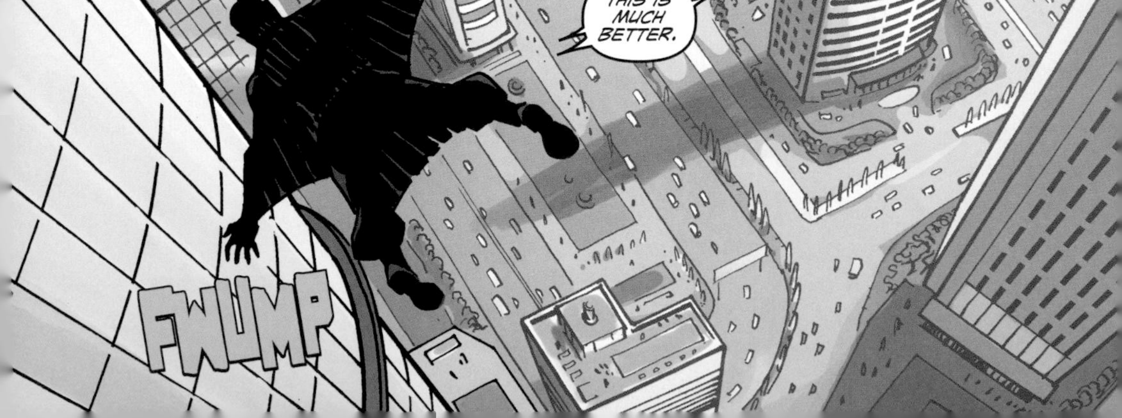
THIS IS MUCH BETTER.
FWUMP

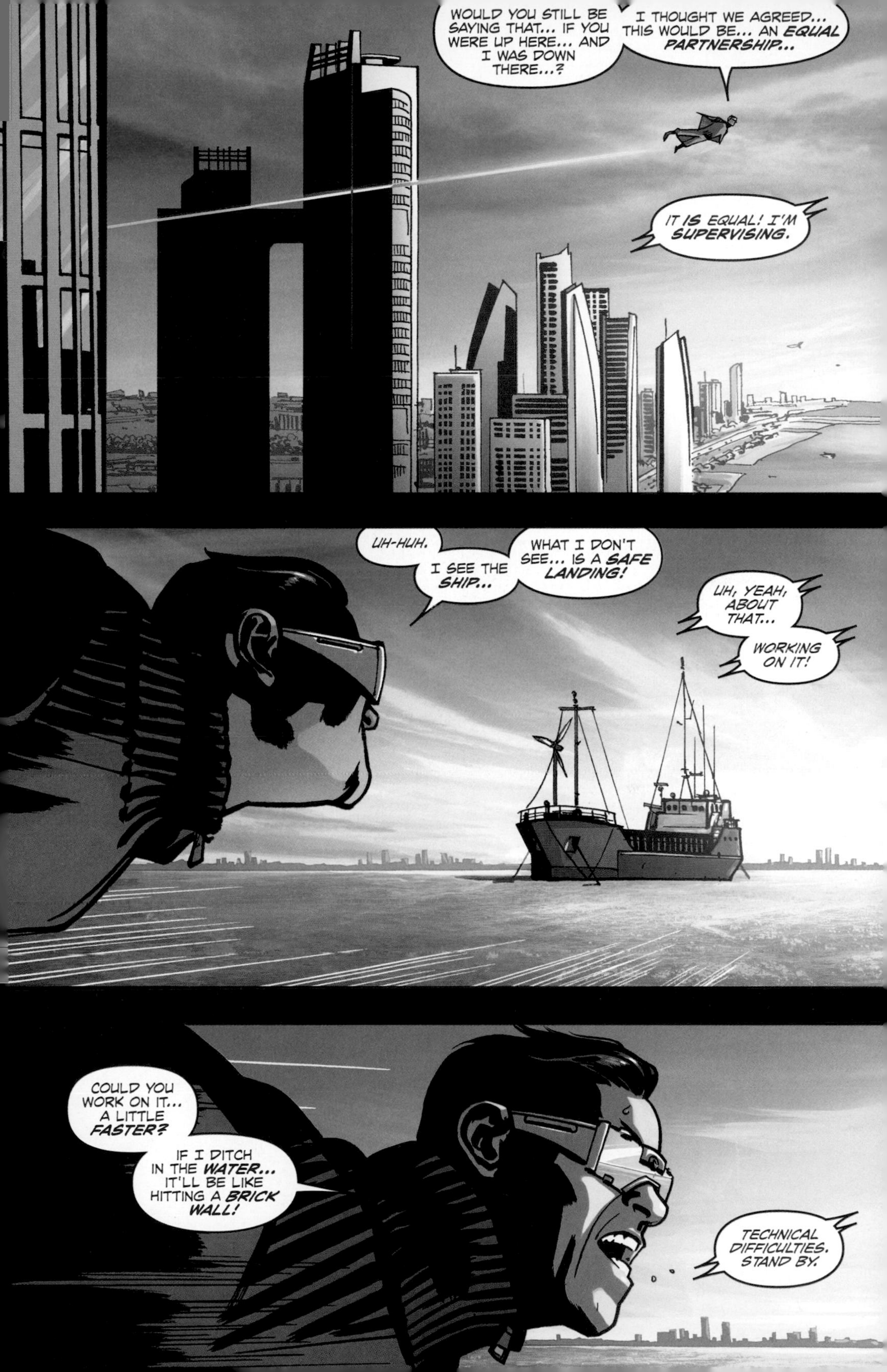

WOULD YOU STILL BE SAYING THAT... IF YOU WERE UP HERE... AND I WAS DOWN THERE...?
I THOUGHT WE AGREED... THIS WOULD BE... AN EQUAL PARTNERSHIP...
IT IS EQUAL! I'M SUPERVISING.
UH-HUH.
I SEE THE SHIP...
WHAT I DON'T SEE... IS A SAFE LANDING!
UH, YEAH, ABOUT THAT...
WORKING ON IT!
COULD YOU WORK ON IT... A LITTLE FASTER?
IF I DITCH IN THE WATER... IT'LL BE LIKE HITTING A BRICK WALL!
TECHNICAL DIFFICULTIES. STAND BY.

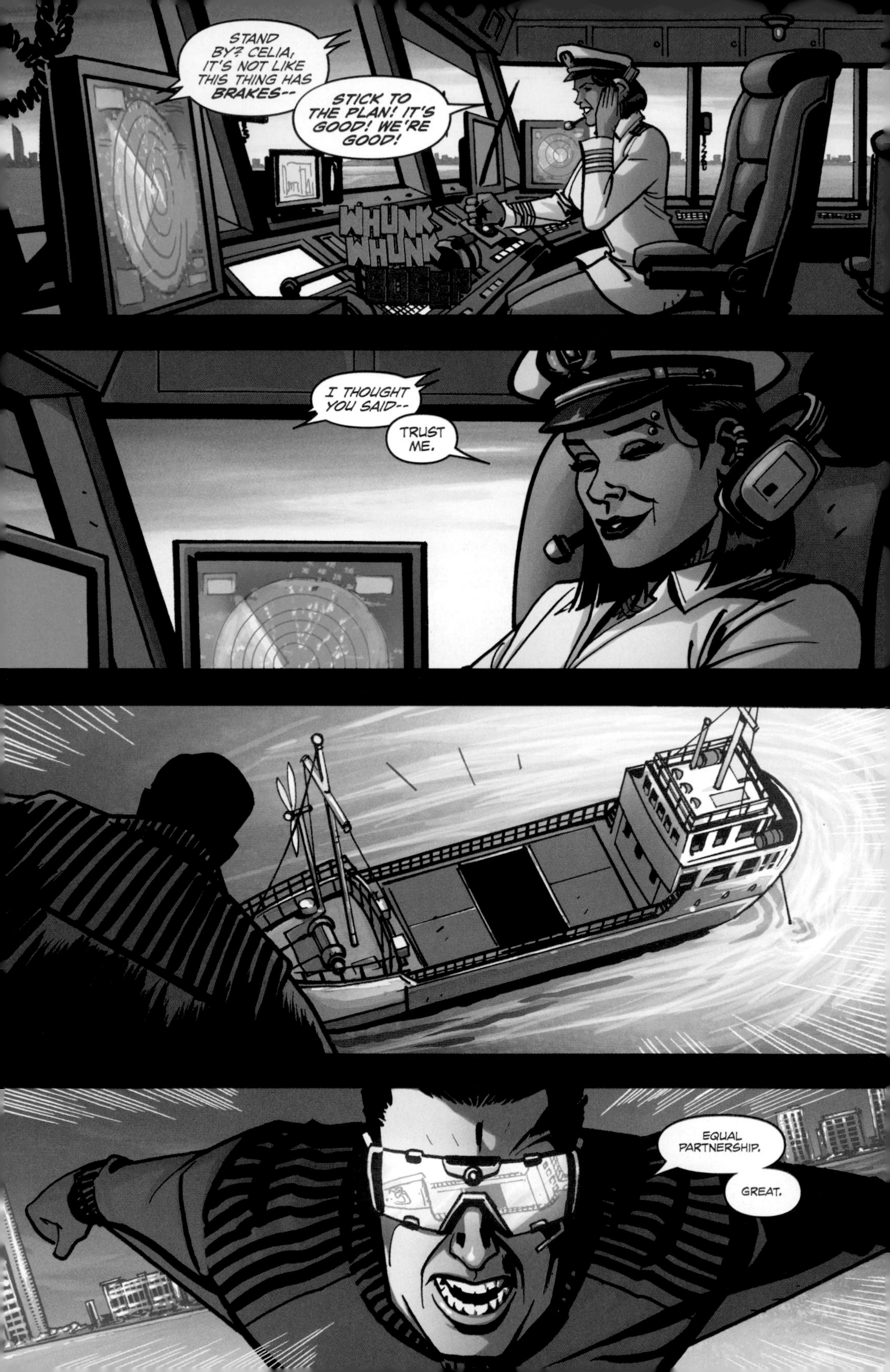
STAND BY!? CELIA, IT'S NOT LIKE THIS THING HAS BRAKES--
STICK TO THE PLAN! IT'S GOOD! WE'RE GOOD!
WHUNK WHUNK
I THOUGHT YOU SAID--
TRUST ME.
EQUAL PARTNERSHIP.
GREAT.

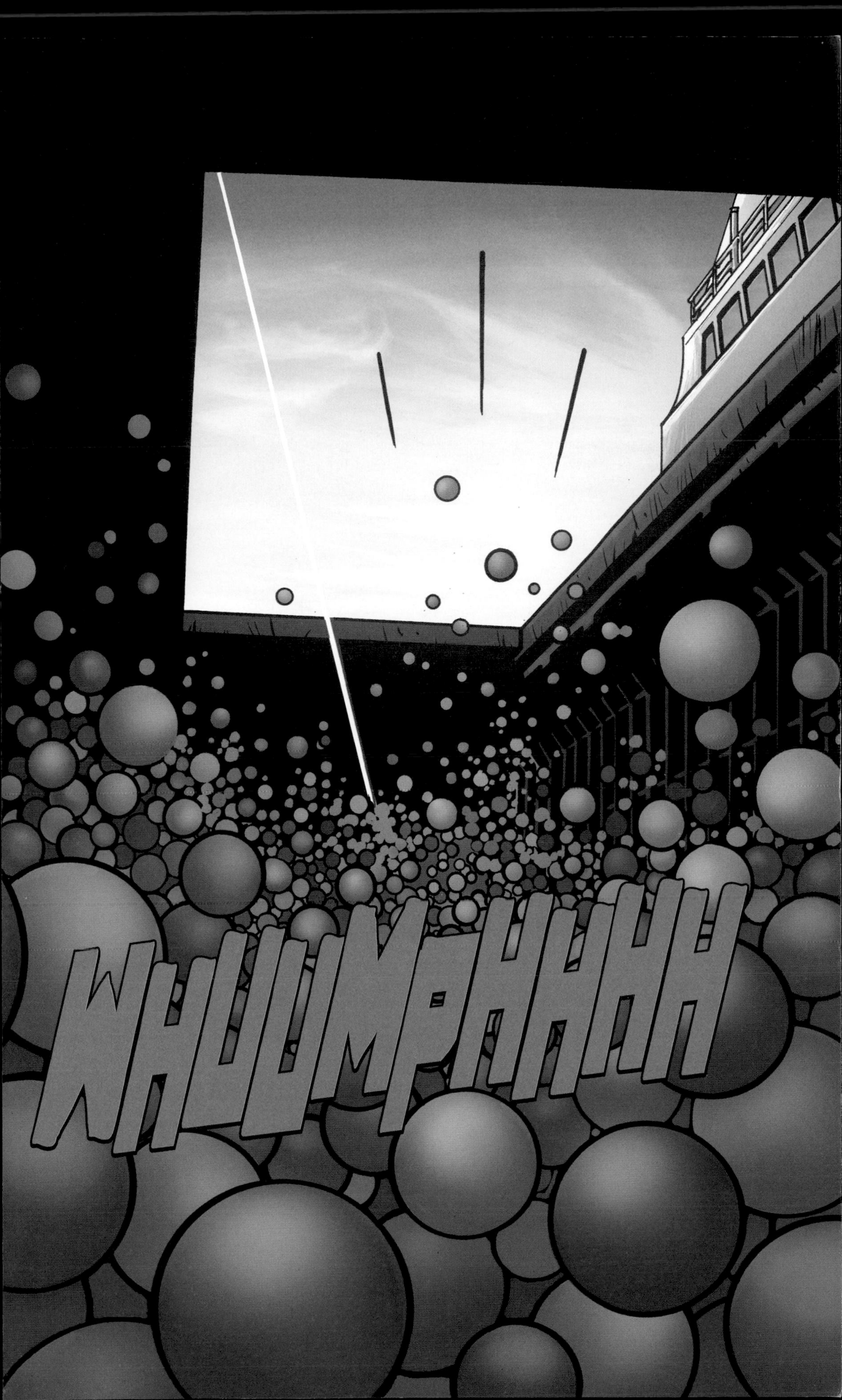
WHUUMPHHHHH

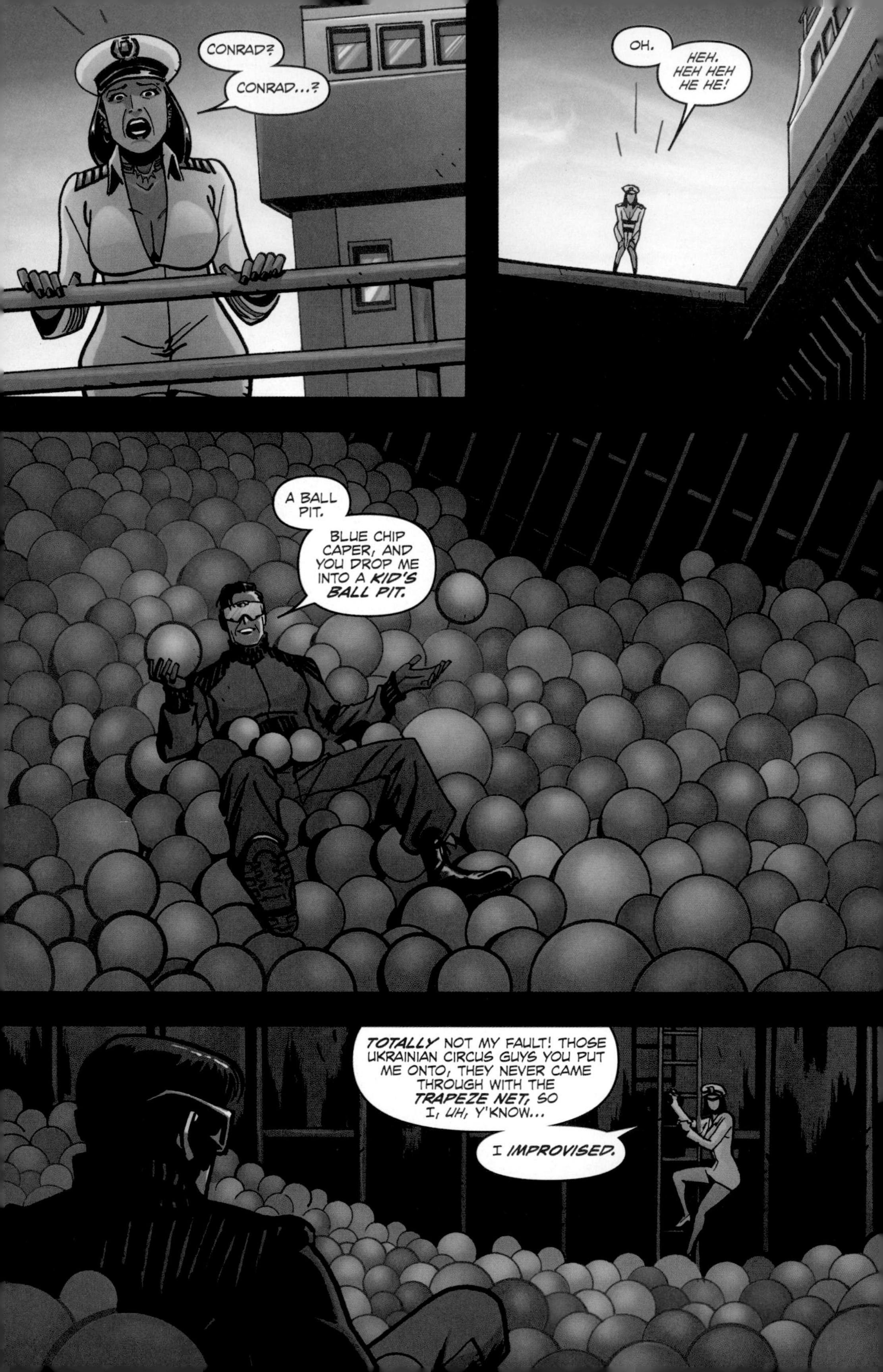
CONRAD?
CONRAD...?
OH.
HEH. HEH HEH HE HE!
A BALL PIT.
BLUE CHIP CAPER, AND YOU DROP ME INTO A *KID'S BALL PIT.*
TOTALLY NOT MY FAULT! THOSE UKRAINIAN CIRCUS GUYS YOU PUT ME ONTO, THEY NEVER CAME THROUGH WITH THE *TRAPEZE NET,* SO I, *UH,* Y'KNOW...
I *IMPROVISED.*

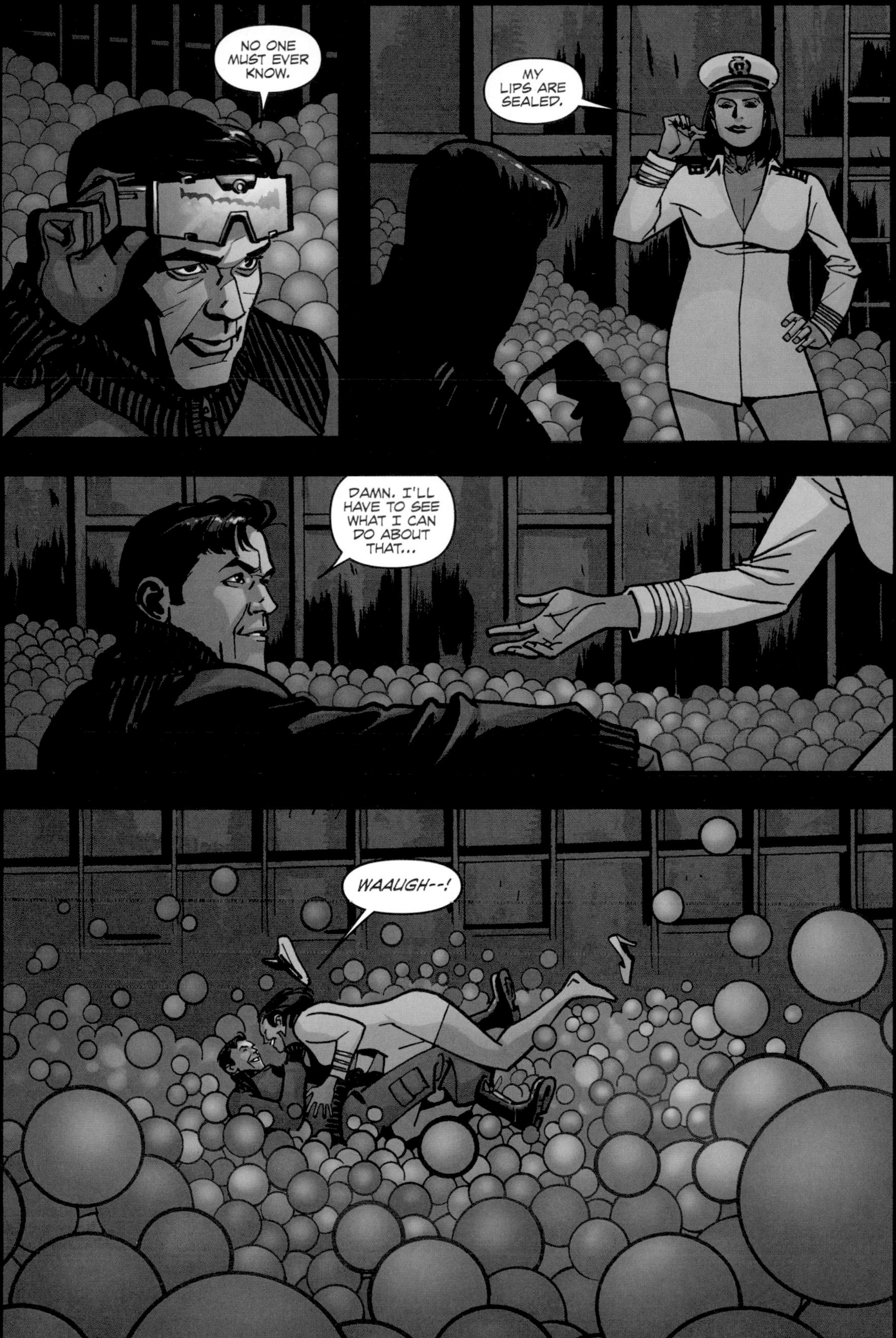
NO ONE MUST EVER KNOW.
MY LIPS ARE SEALED.
DAMN. I'LL HAVE TO SEE WHAT I CAN DO ABOUT THAT...
WAAUGH--!

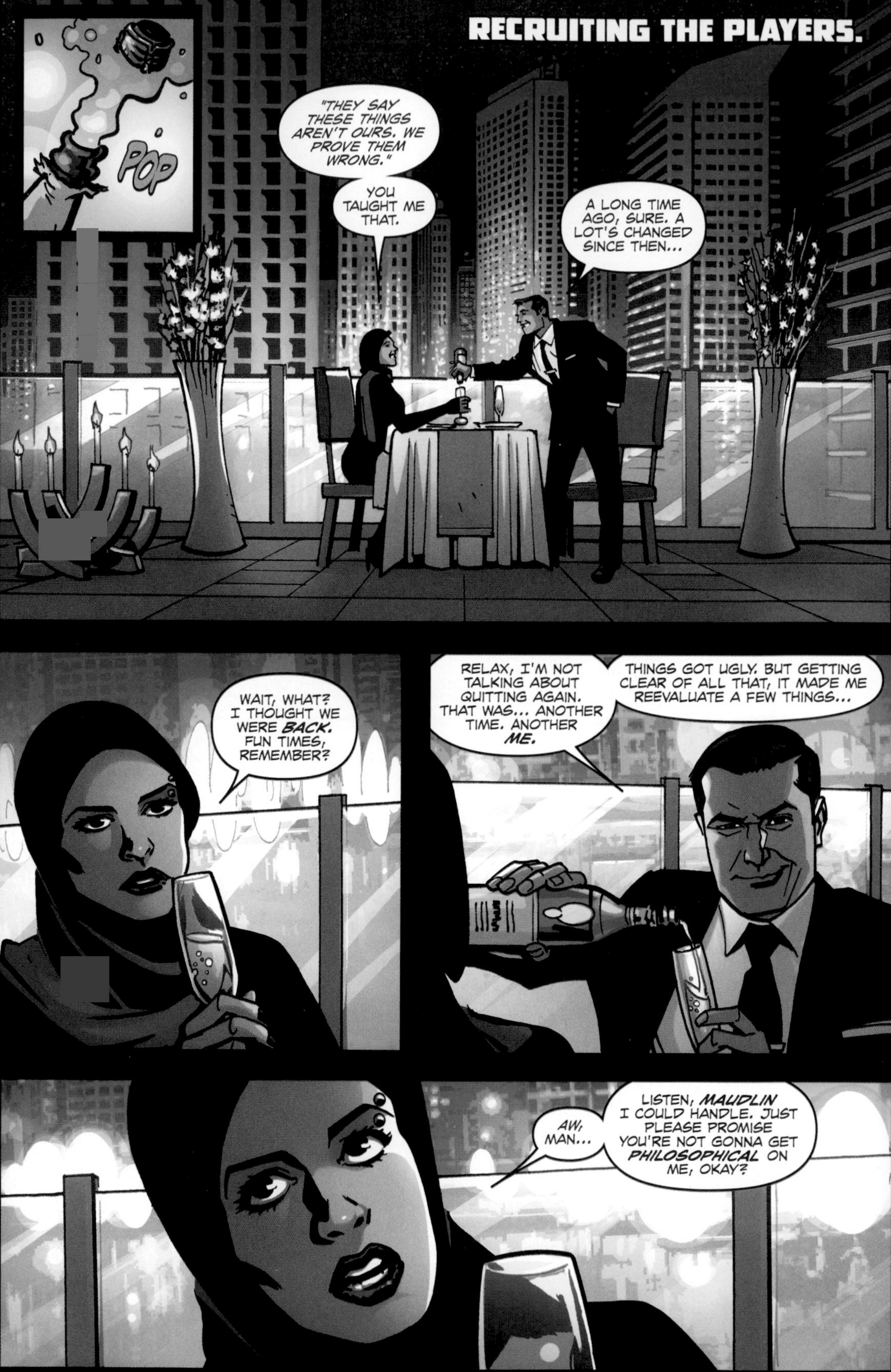
RECRUITING THE PLAYERS.
POP
"THEY SAY THESE THINGS AREN'T OURS. WE PROVE THEM WRONG."
YOU TAUGHT ME THAT.
A LONG TIME AGO, SURE. A LOT'S CHANGED SINCE THEN...
WAIT, WHAT? I THOUGHT WE WERE *BACK.* FUN TIMES, REMEMBER?
RELAX, I'M NOT TALKING ABOUT QUITTING AGAIN. THAT WAS... ANOTHER TIME. ANOTHER *ME.*
THINGS GOT UGLY. BUT GETTING CLEAR OF ALL THAT, IT MADE ME REEVALUATE A FEW THINGS...
AW, MAN...
LISTEN, *MAUDLIN* I COULD HANDLE. JUST PLEASE PROMISE YOU'RE NOT GONNA GET *PHILOSOPHICAL* ON ME, OKAY?

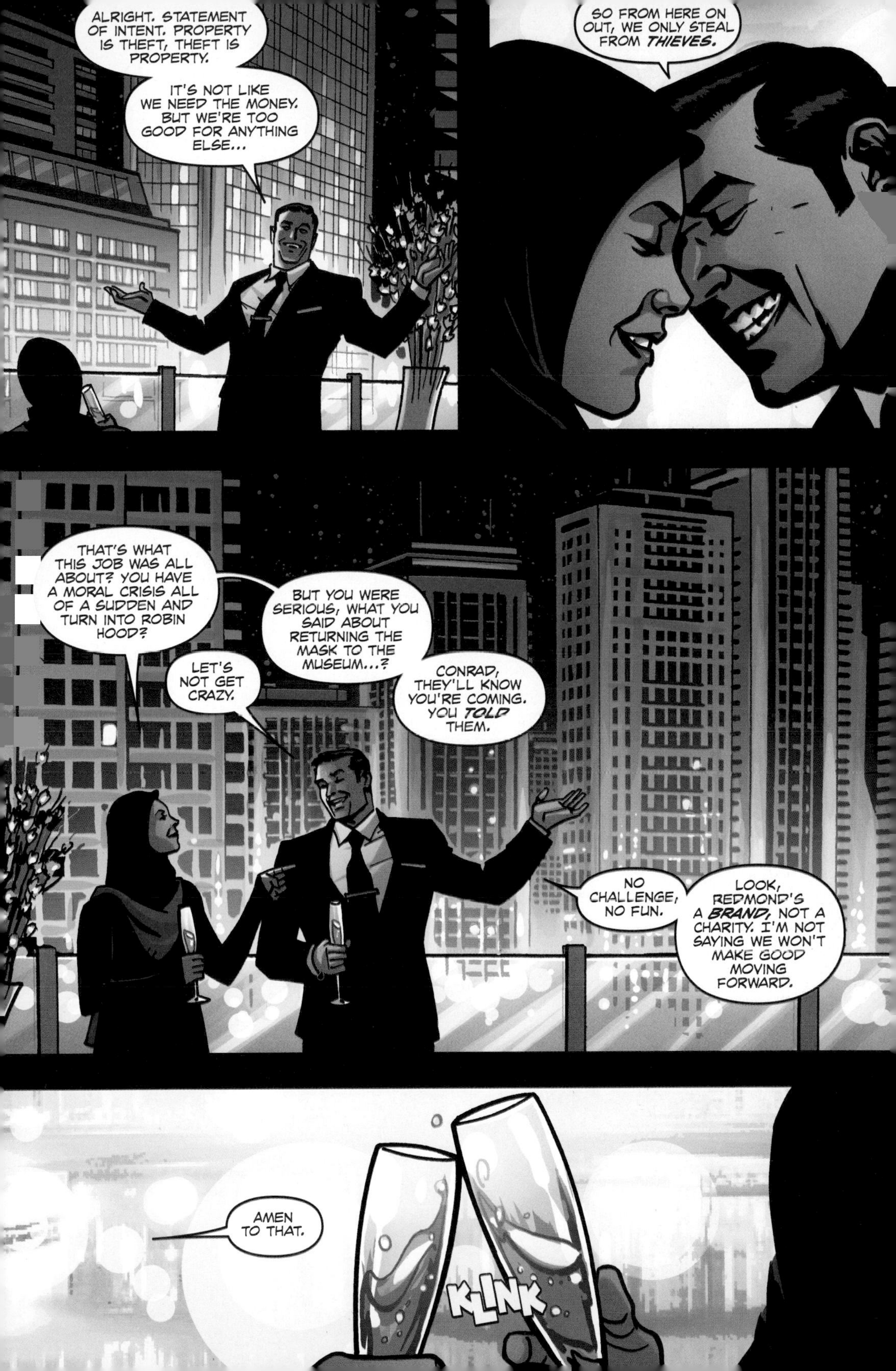
ALRIGHT. STATEMENT OF INTENT. PROPERTY IS THEFT, THEFT IS PROPERTY.
IT'S NOT LIKE WE NEED THE MONEY. BUT WE'RE TOO GOOD FOR ANYTHING ELSE...
SO FROM HERE ON OUT, WE ONLY STEAL FROM *THIEVES.*
THAT'S WHAT THIS JOB WAS ALL ABOUT? YOU HAVE A MORAL CRISIS ALL OF A SUDDEN AND TURN INTO ROBIN HOOD?
LET'S NOT GET CRAZY.
BUT YOU WERE SERIOUS, WHAT YOU SAID ABOUT RETURNING THE MASK TO THE MUSEUM...?
CONRAD, THEY'LL KNOW YOU'RE COMING. YOU *TOLD* THEM.
NO CHALLENGE, NO FUN.
LOOK, REDMOND'S A *BRAND,* NOT A CHARITY. I'M NOT SAYING WE WON'T MAKE GOOD MOVING FORWARD.
AMEN TO THAT.
KLINK

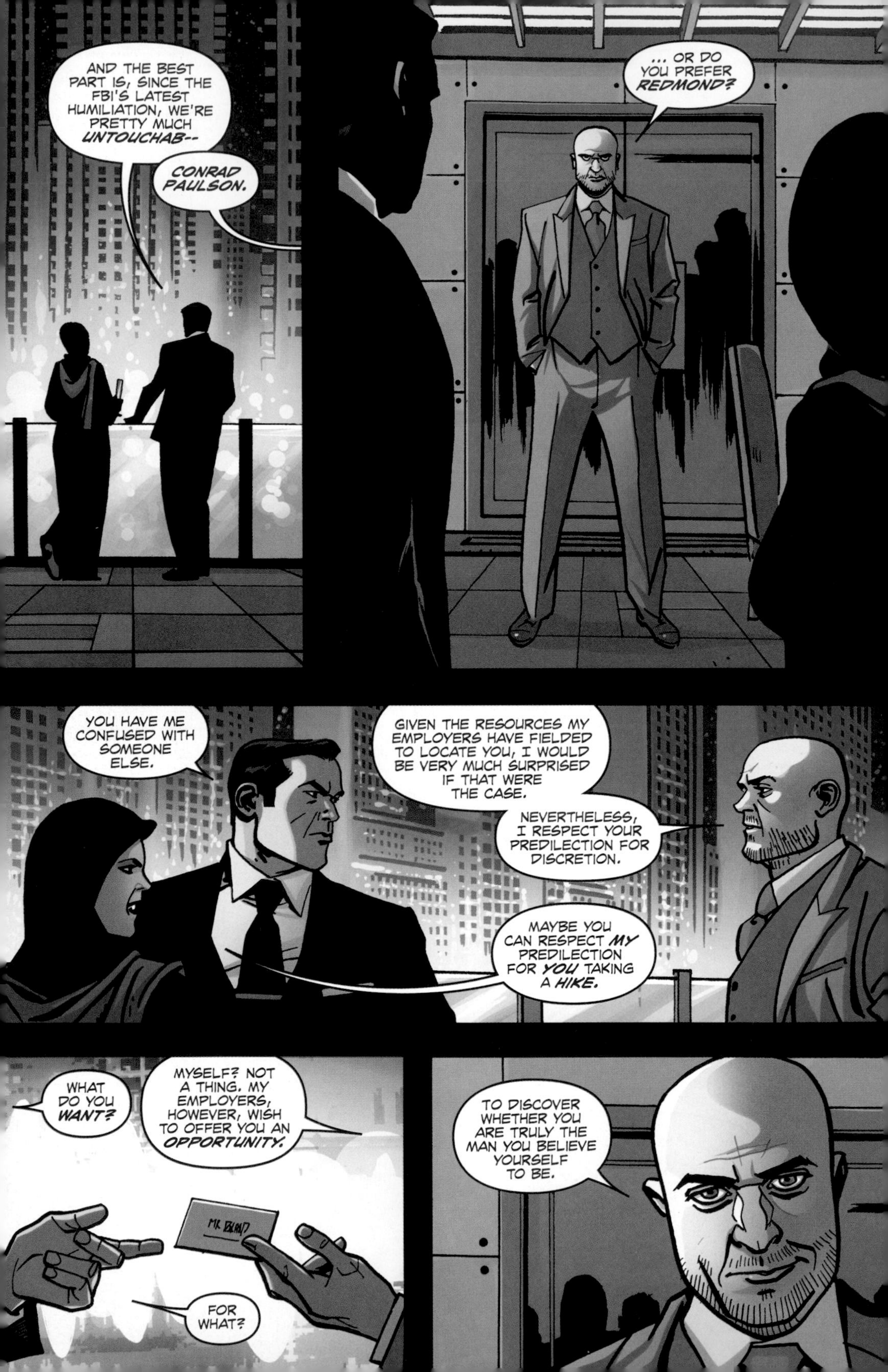
AND THE BEST PART IS, SINCE THE FBI'S LATEST HUMILIATION, WE'RE PRETTY MUCH UNTOUCHAB--
CONRAD PAULSON.
... OR DO YOU PREFER REDMOND?
YOU HAVE ME CONFUSED WITH SOMEONE ELSE.
GIVEN THE RESOURCES MY EMPLOYERS HAVE FIELDED TO LOCATE YOU, I WOULD BE VERY MUCH SURPRISED IF THAT WERE THE CASE.
NEVERTHELESS, I RESPECT YOUR PREDILECTION FOR DISCRETION.
MAYBE YOU CAN RESPECT MY PREDILECTION FOR YOU TAKING A HIKE.
WHAT DO YOU WANT?
MYSELF? NOT A THING. MY EMPLOYERS, HOWEVER, WISH TO OFFER YOU AN OPPORTUNITY.
FOR WHAT?
TO DISCOVER WHETHER YOU ARE TRULY THE MAN YOU BELIEVE YOURSELF TO BE.

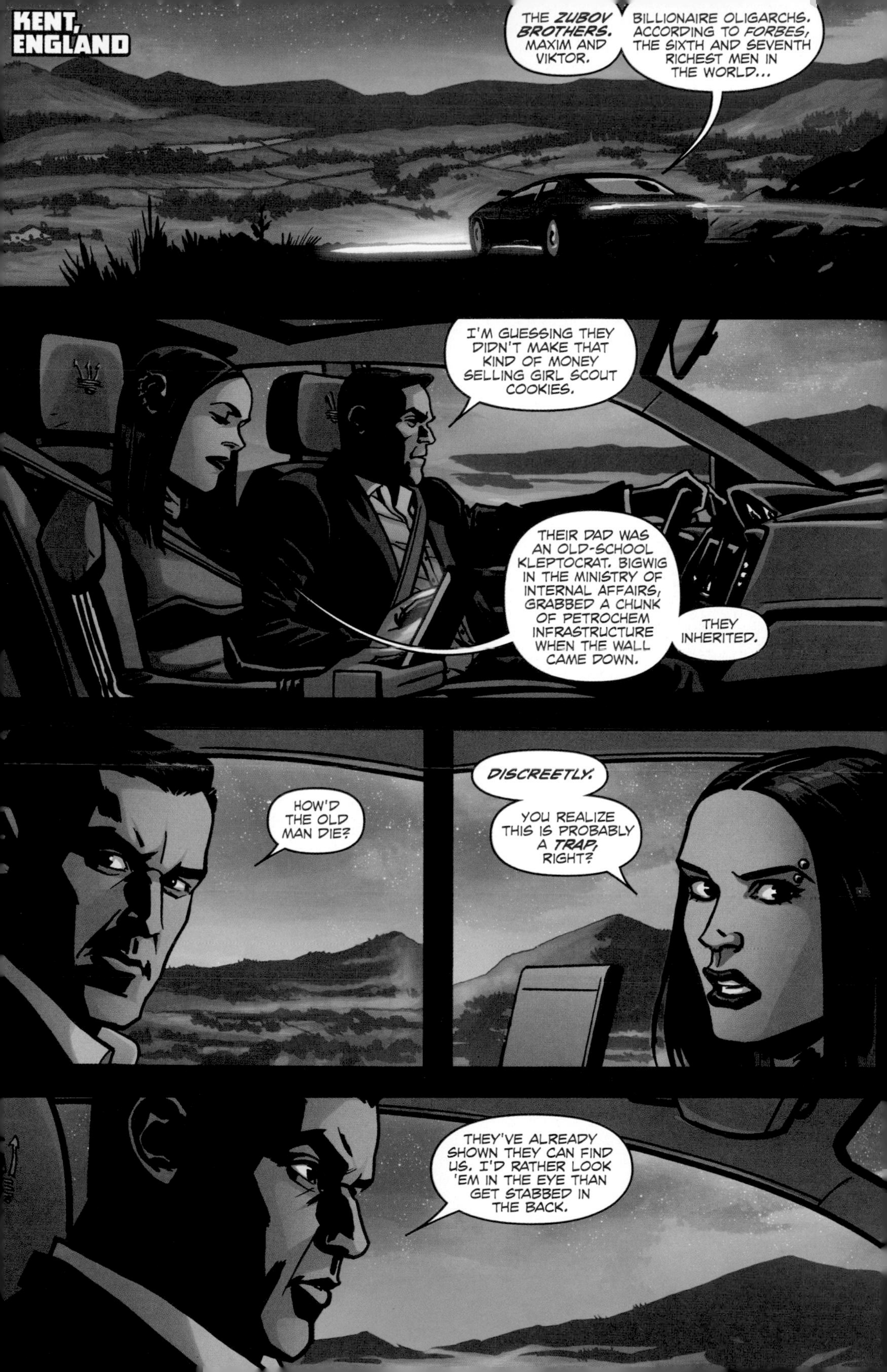
KENT, ENGLAND
THE ZUBOV BROTHERS. MAXIM AND VIKTOR.
BILLIONAIRE OLIGARCHS. ACCORDING TO FORBES, THE SIXTH AND SEVENTH RICHEST MEN IN THE WORLD...
I'M GUESSING THEY DIDN'T MAKE THAT KIND OF MONEY SELLING GIRL SCOUT COOKIES.
THEIR DAD WAS AN OLD-SCHOOL KLEPTOCRAT. BIGWIG IN THE MINISTRY OF INTERNAL AFFAIRS, GRABBED A CHUNK OF PETROCHEM INFRASTRUCTURE WHEN THE WALL CAME DOWN.
THEY INHERITED.
HOW'D THE OLD MAN DIE?
DISCREETLY.
YOU REALIZE THIS IS PROBABLY A TRAP, RIGHT?
THEY'VE ALREADY SHOWN THEY CAN FIND US. I'D RATHER LOOK 'EM IN THE EYE THAN GET STABBED IN THE BACK.

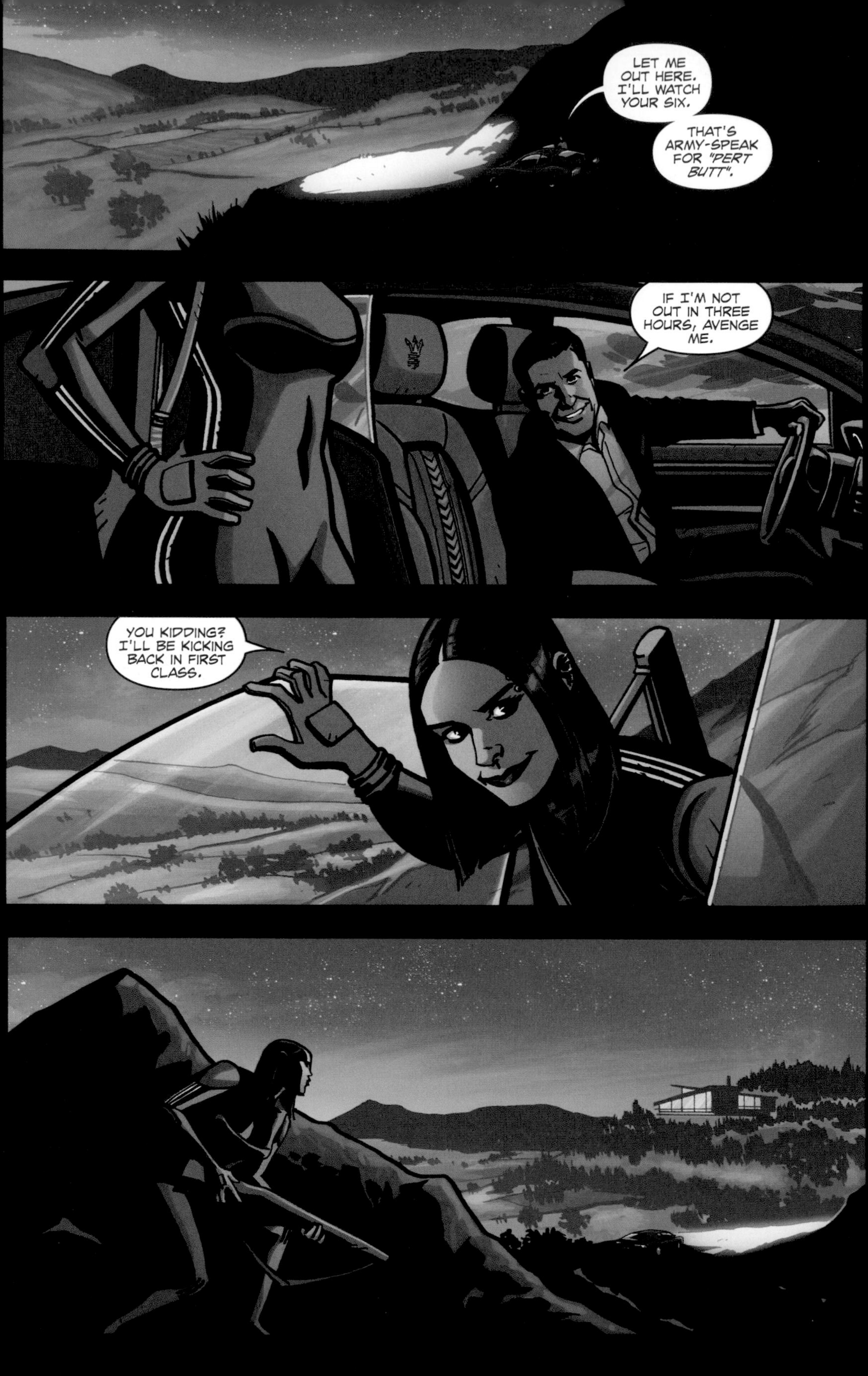
LET ME OUT HERE. I'LL WATCH YOUR SIX.
THAT'S ARMY-SPEAK FOR "PERT BUTT".
IF I'M NOT OUT IN THREE HOURS, AVENGE ME.
YOU KIDDING? I'LL BE KICKING BACK IN FIRST CLASS.

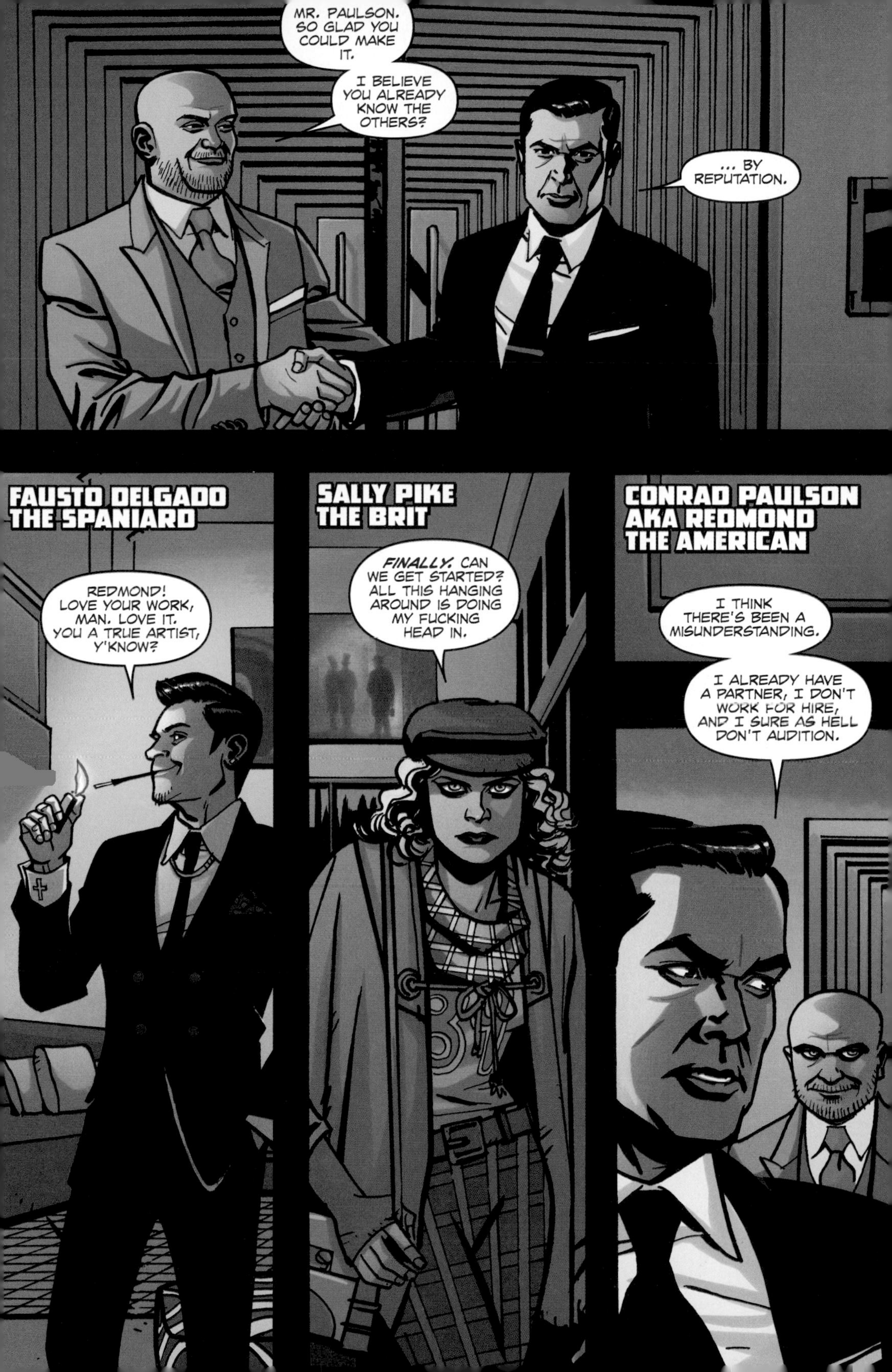
MR. PAULSON. SO GLAD YOU COULD MAKE IT.
I BELIEVE YOU ALREADY KNOW THE OTHERS?
... BY REPUTATION.
FAUSTO DELGADO THE SPANIARD
REDMOND! LOVE YOUR WORK, MAN. LOVE IT. YOU A TRUE ARTIST, Y'KNOW?
SALLY PIKE THE BRIT
FINALLY. CAN WE GET STARTED? ALL THIS HANGING AROUND IS DOING MY FUCKING HEAD IN.
CONRAD PAULSON AKA REDMOND THE AMERICAN
I THINK THERE'S BEEN A MISUNDERSTANDING.
I ALREADY HAVE A PARTNER, I DON'T WORK FOR HIRE, AND I SURE AS HELL DON'T AUDITION.

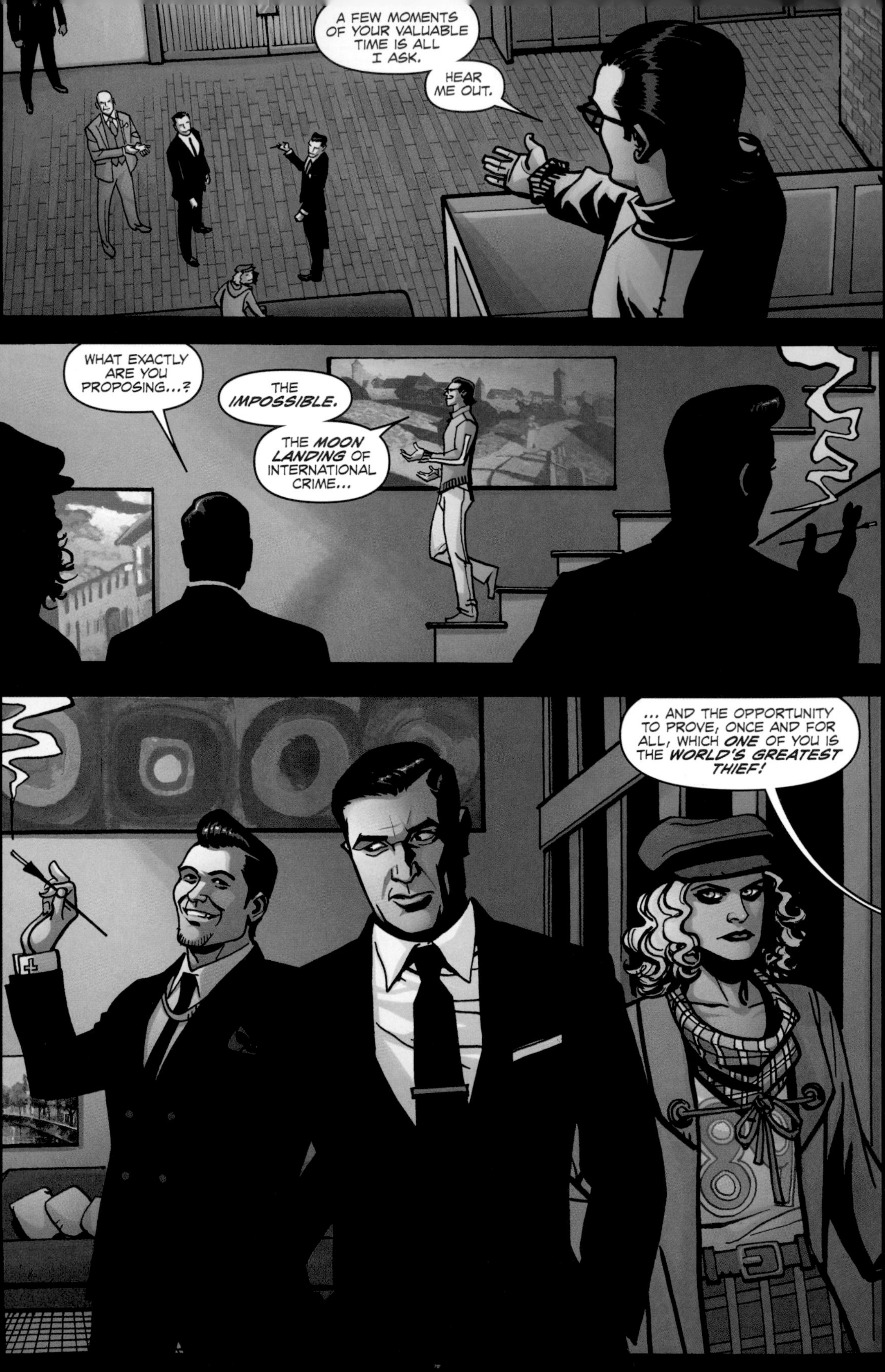
A FEW MOMENTS OF YOUR VALUABLE TIME IS ALL I ASK.
HEAR ME OUT.
WHAT EXACTLY ARE YOU PROPOSING...?
THE *IMPOSSIBLE.*
THE *MOON LANDING* OF INTERNATIONAL CRIME...
... AND THE OPPORTUNITY TO PROVE, ONCE AND FOR ALL, WHICH *ONE* OF YOU IS THE *WORLD'S GREATEST THIEF!*

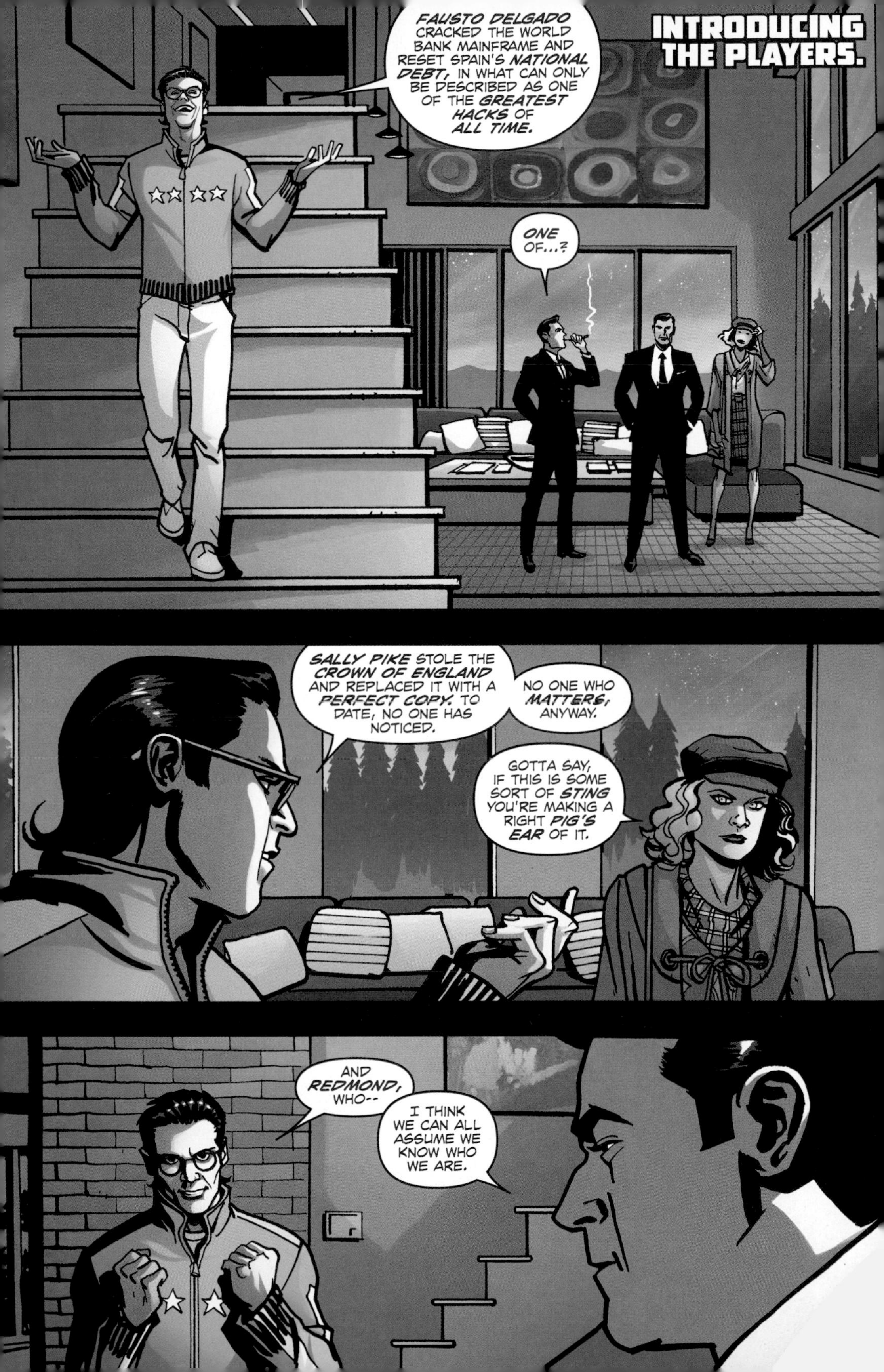

INTRODUCING THE PLAYERS.
FAUSTO DELGADO CRACKED THE WORLD BANK MAINFRAME AND RESET SPAIN'S NATIONAL DEBT, IN WHAT CAN ONLY BE DESCRIBED AS ONE OF THE GREATEST HACKS OF ALL TIME.
ONE OF...?
SALLY PIKE STOLE THE CROWN OF ENGLAND AND REPLACED IT WITH A PERFECT COPY. TO DATE, NO ONE HAS NOTICED.
NO ONE WHO MATTERS, ANYWAY.
GOTTA SAY, IF THIS IS SOME SORT OF STING YOU'RE MAKING A RIGHT PIG'S EAR OF IT.
AND REDMOND, WHO--
I THINK WE CAN ALL ASSUME WE KNOW WHO WE ARE.

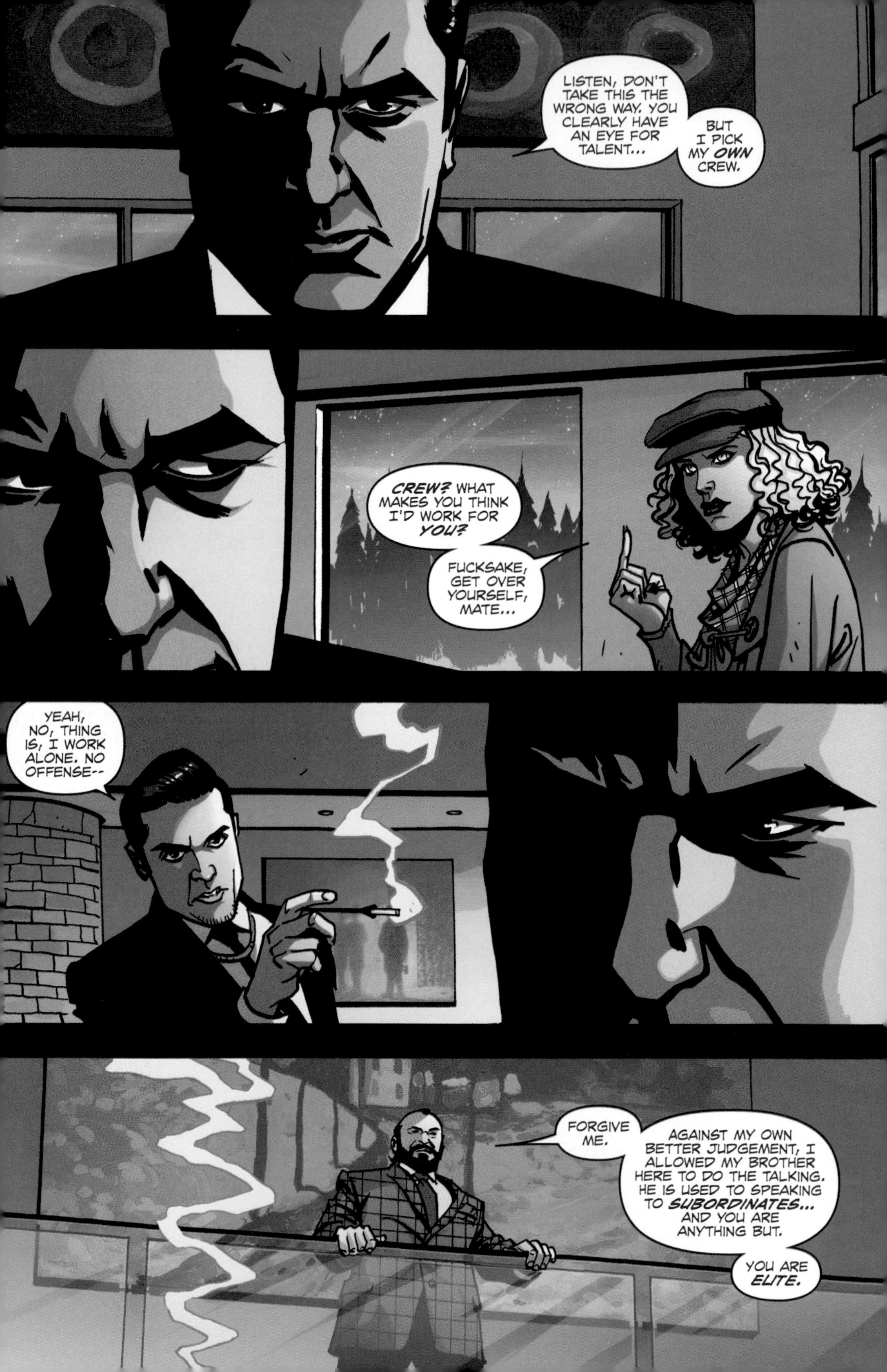
LISTEN, DON'T TAKE THIS THE WRONG WAY. YOU CLEARLY HAVE AN EYE FOR TALENT...
BUT I PICK MY OWN CREW.
CREW? WHAT MAKES YOU THINK I'D WORK FOR YOU?
FUCKSAKE, GET OVER YOURSELF, MATE...
YEAH, NO, THING IS, I WORK ALONE. NO OFFENSE--
FORGIVE ME.
AGAINST MY OWN BETTER JUDGEMENT, I ALLOWED MY BROTHER HERE TO DO THE TALKING. HE IS USED TO SPEAKING TO SUBORDINATES... AND YOU ARE ANYTHING BUT.
YOU ARE ELITE.

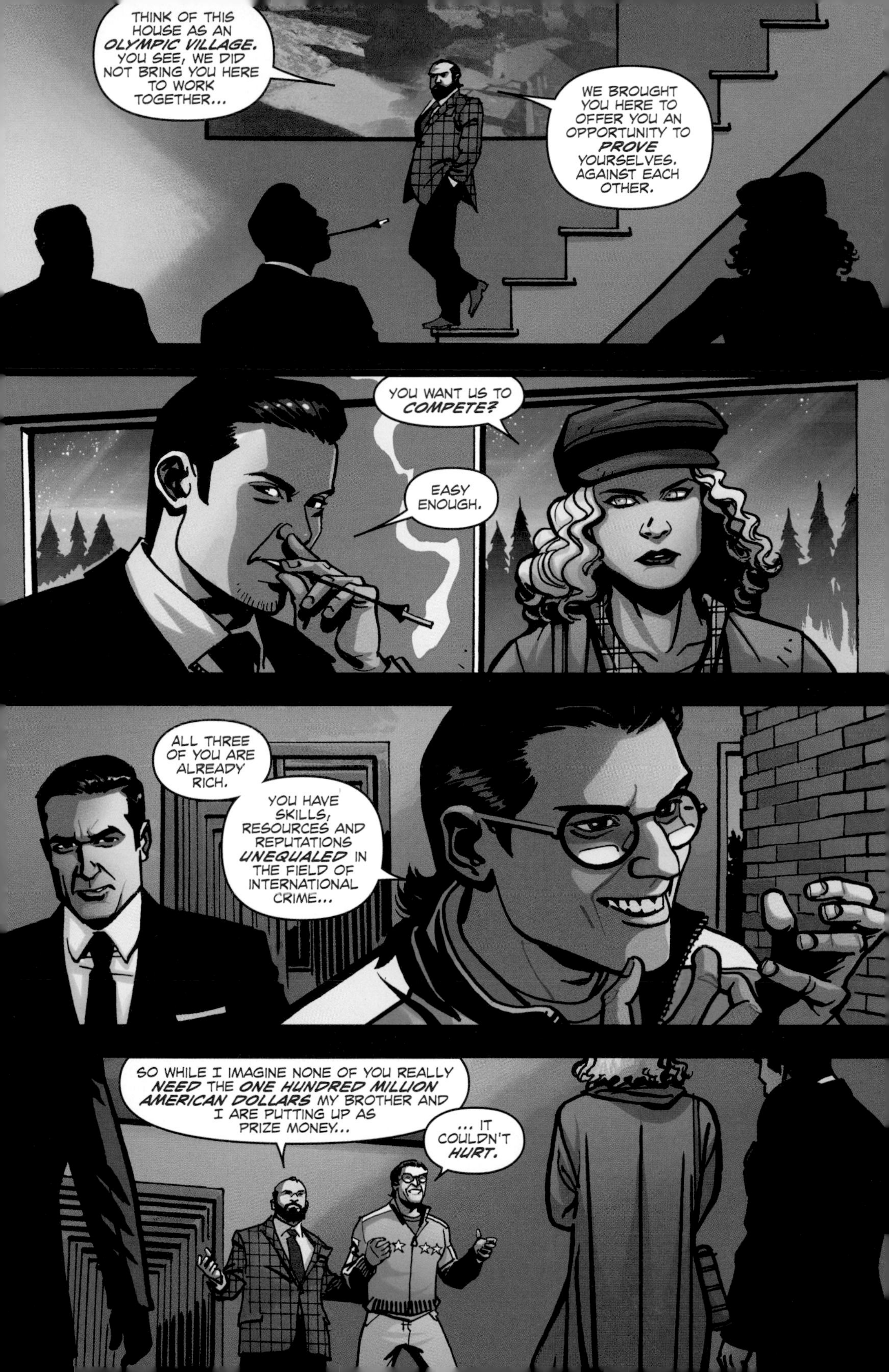
THINK OF THIS HOUSE AS AN *OLYMPIC VILLAGE.* YOU SEE, WE DID NOT BRING YOU HERE TO WORK TOGETHER...
WE BROUGHT YOU HERE TO OFFER YOU AN OPPORTUNITY TO *PROVE* YOURSELVES. AGAINST EACH OTHER.
YOU WANT US TO *COMPETE?*
EASY ENOUGH.
ALL THREE OF YOU ARE ALREADY RICH.
YOU HAVE SKILLS, RESOURCES AND REPUTATIONS *UNEQUALED* IN THE FIELD OF INTERNATIONAL CRIME...
SO WHILE I IMAGINE NONE OF YOU REALLY *NEED* THE *ONE HUNDRED MILLION AMERICAN DOLLARS* MY BROTHER AND I ARE PUTTING UP AS PRIZE MONEY...
... IT COULDN'T *HURT.*

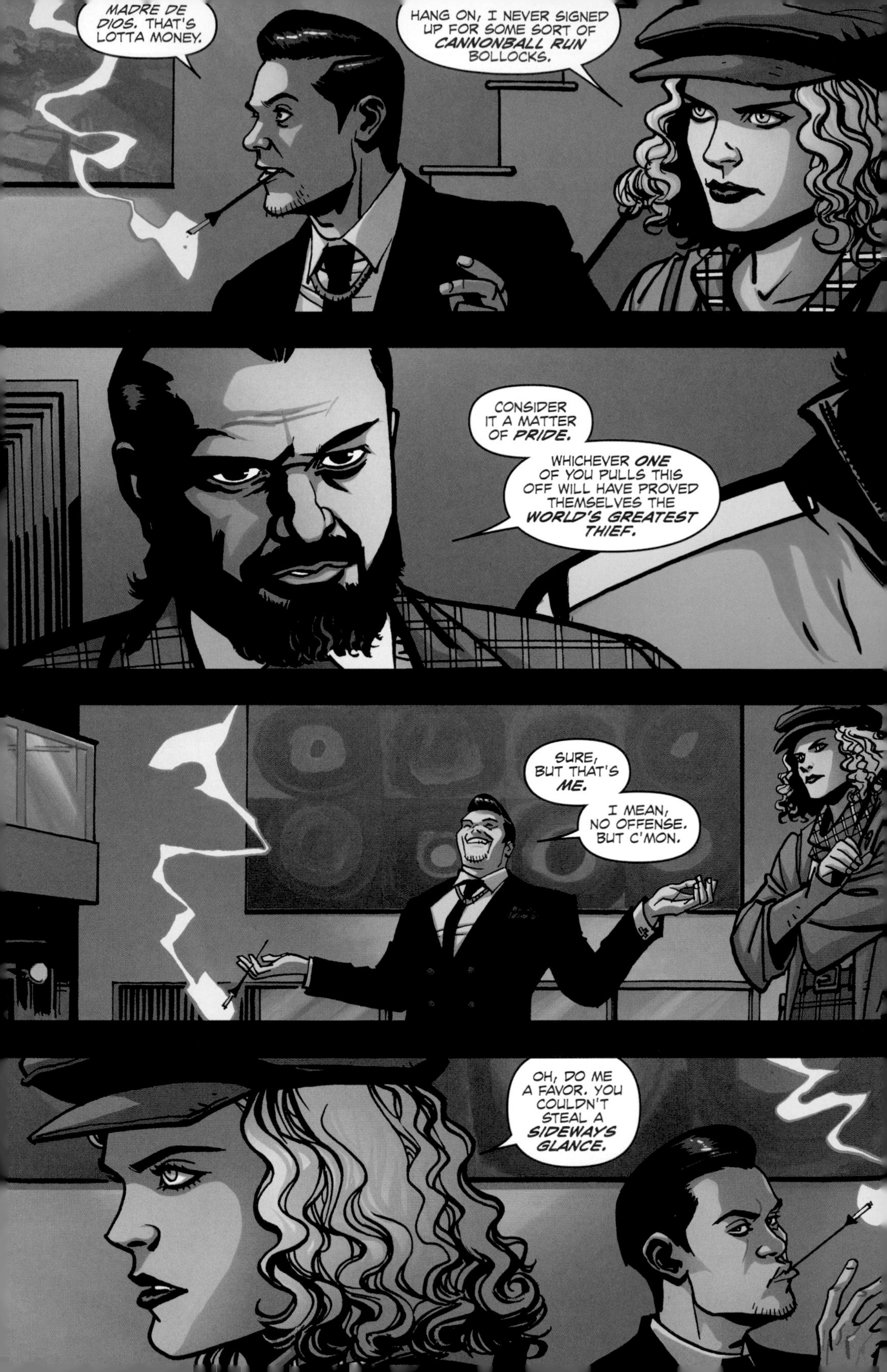
MADRE DE DIOS. THAT'S LOTTA MONEY.
HANG ON, I NEVER SIGNED UP FOR SOME SORT OF CANNONBALL RUN BOLLOCKS.
CONSIDER IT A MATTER OF PRIDE.
WHICHEVER ONE OF YOU PULLS THIS OFF WILL HAVE PROVED THEMSELVES THE WORLD'S GREATEST THIEF.
SURE, BUT THAT'S ME.
I MEAN, NO OFFENSE. BUT C'MON.
OH, DO ME A FAVOR. YOU COULDN'T STEAL A SIDEWAYS GLANCE.

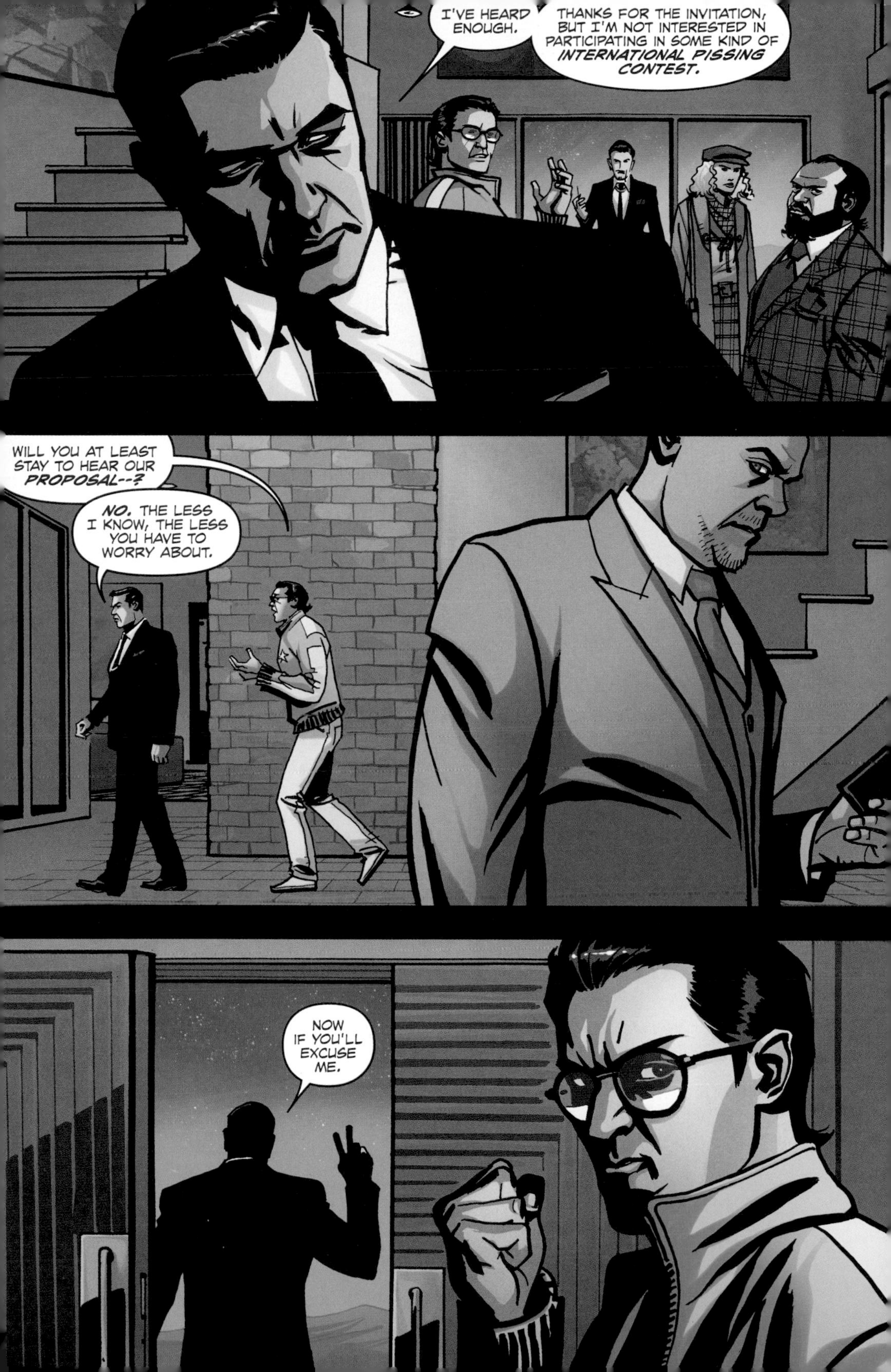
I'VE HEARD ENOUGH.
THANKS FOR THE INVITATION, BUT I'M NOT INTERESTED IN PARTICIPATING IN SOME KIND OF *INTERNATIONAL PISSING CONTEST.*
WILL YOU AT LEAST STAY TO HEAR OUR *PROPOSAL--?*
NO. THE LESS I KNOW, THE LESS YOU HAVE TO WORRY ABOUT.
NOW IF YOU'LL EXCUSE ME.

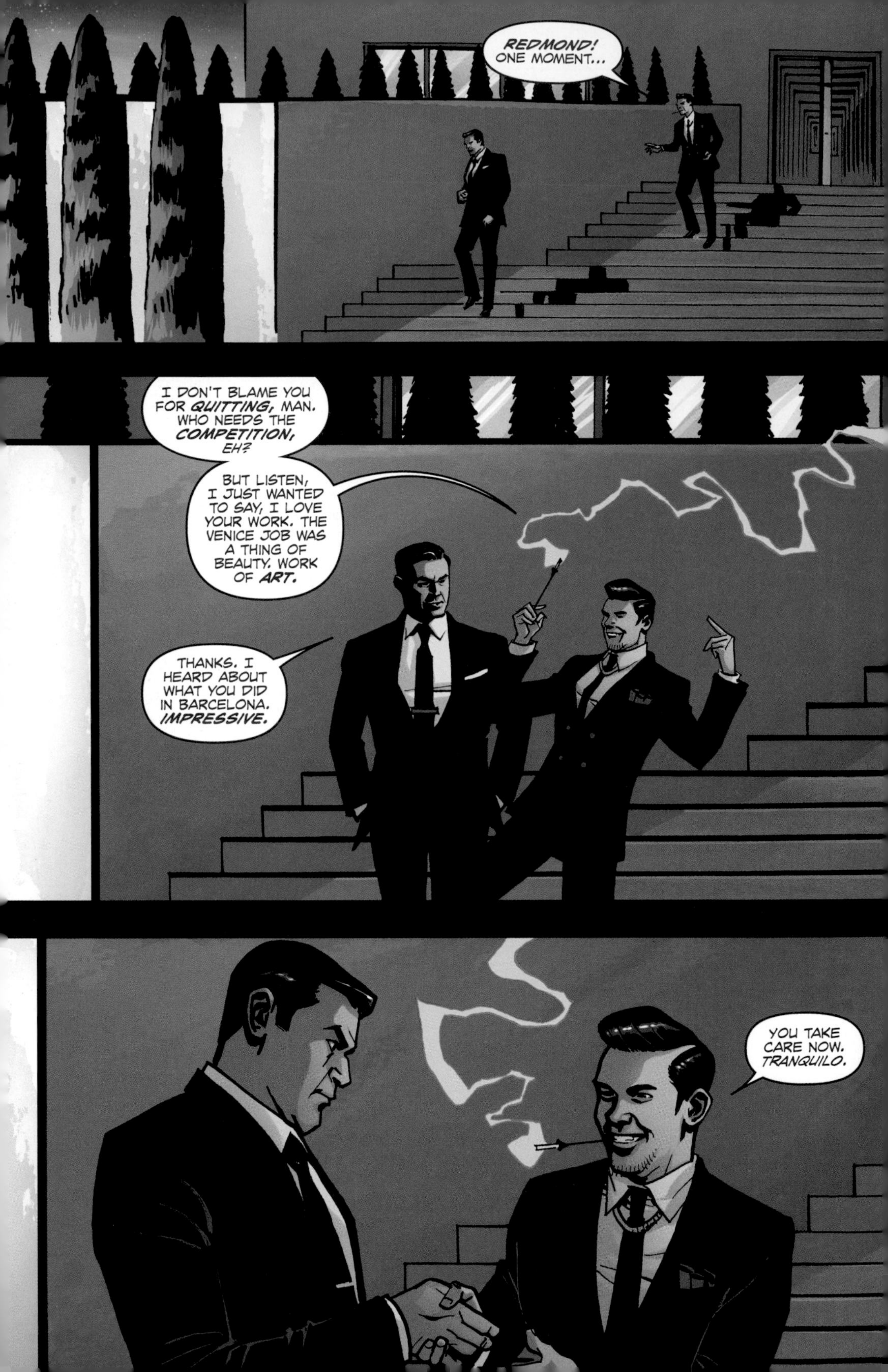
REDMOND! ONE MOMENT...
I DON'T BLAME YOU FOR QUITTING, MAN. WHO NEEDS THE COMPETITION, EH?
BUT LISTEN, I JUST WANTED TO SAY, I LOVE YOUR WORK. THE VENICE JOB WAS A THING OF BEAUTY. WORK OF ART.
THANKS. I HEARD ABOUT WHAT YOU DID IN BARCELONA. IMPRESSIVE.
YOU TAKE CARE NOW. TRANQUILO.

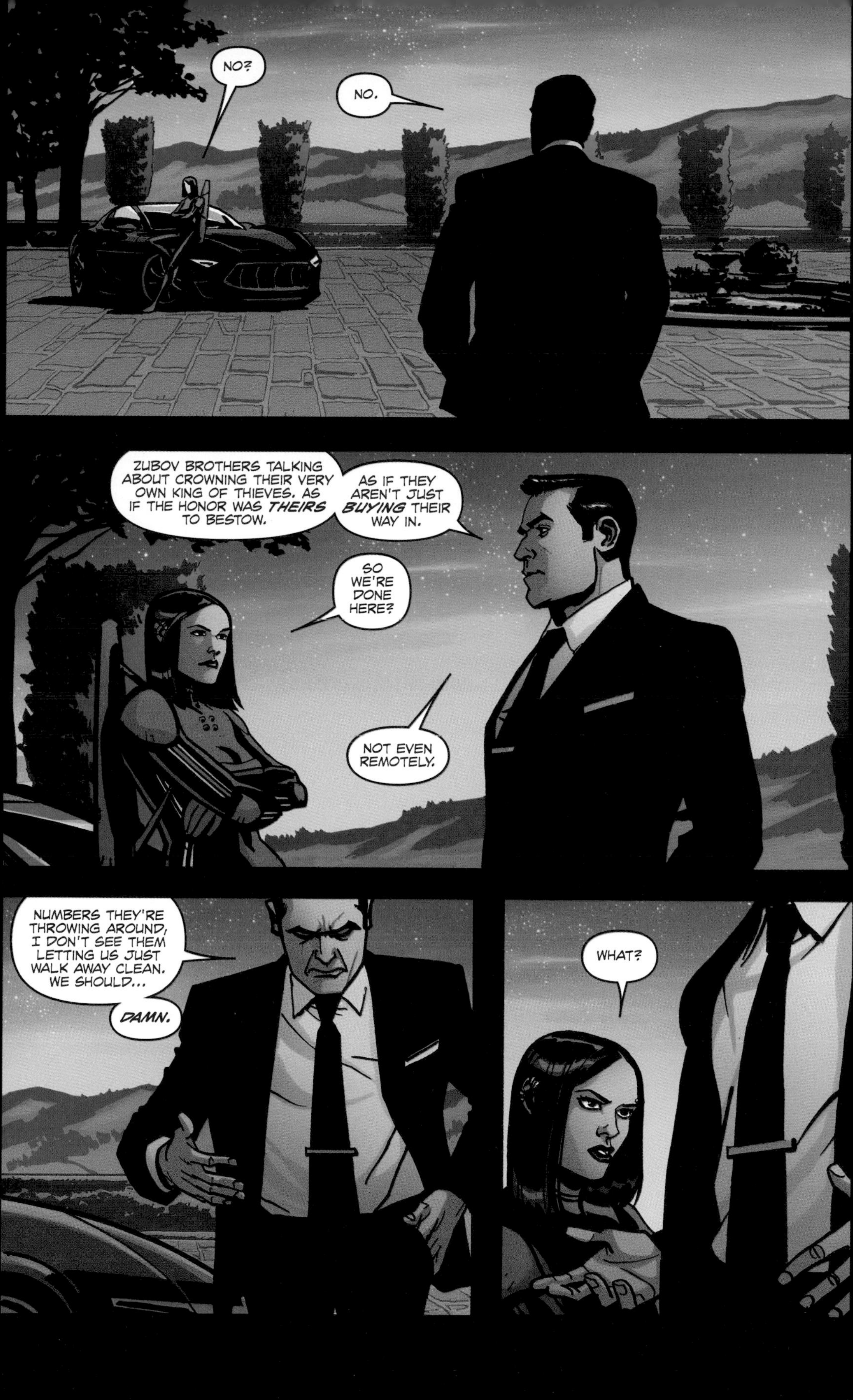
NO?
NO.
ZUBOV BROTHERS TALKING ABOUT CROWNING THEIR VERY OWN KING OF THIEVES. AS IF THE HONOR WAS *THEIRS* TO BESTOW.
AS IF THEY AREN'T JUST *BUYING* THEIR WAY IN.
SO WE'RE DONE HERE?
NOT EVEN REMOTELY.
NUMBERS THEY'RE THROWING AROUND, I DON'T SEE THEM LETTING US JUST WALK AWAY CLEAN. WE SHOULD...
DAMN.
WHAT?

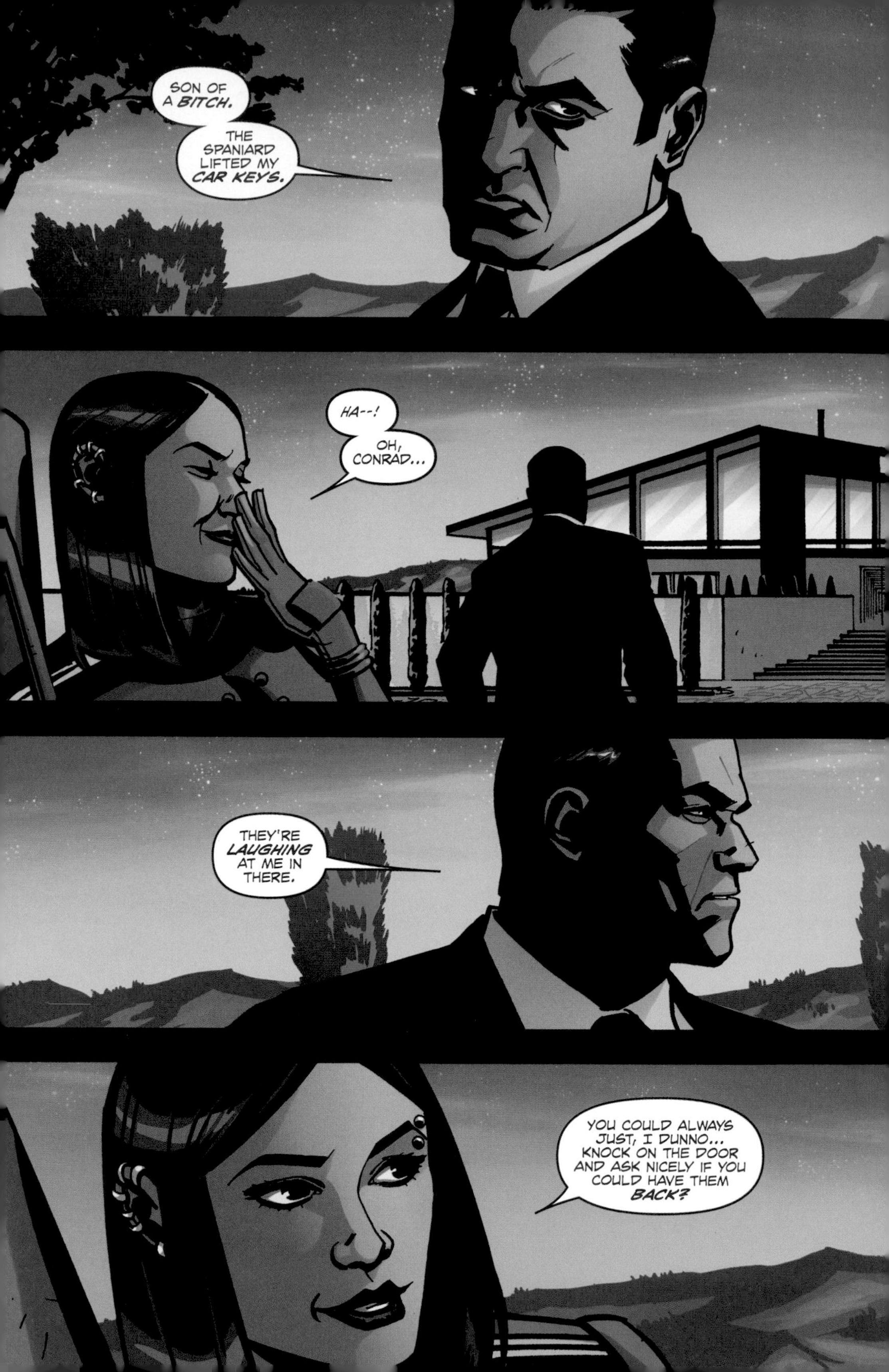
SON OF A BITCH.
THE SPANIARD LIFTED MY CAR KEYS.
HA--!
OH, CONRAD...
THEY'RE LAUGHING AT ME IN THERE.
YOU COULD ALWAYS JUST, I DUNNO... KNOCK ON THE DOOR AND ASK NICELY IF YOU COULD HAVE THEM BACK?

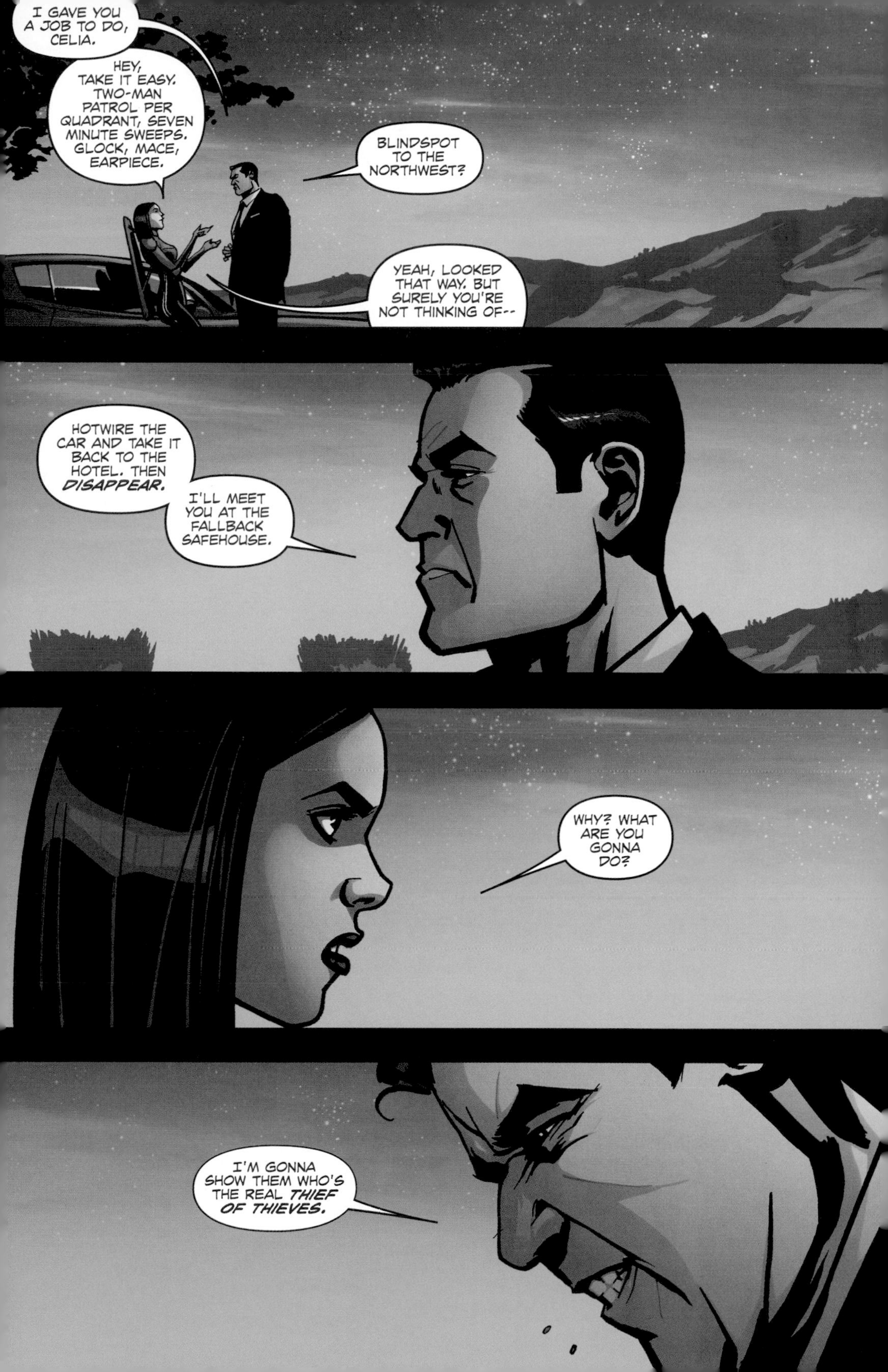
I GAVE YOU A JOB TO DO, CELIA.
HEY, TAKE IT EASY. TWO-MAN PATROL PER QUADRANT, SEVEN MINUTE SWEEPS. GLOCK, MACE, EARPIECE.
BLINDSPOT TO THE NORTHWEST?
YEAH, LOOKED THAT WAY. BUT SURELY YOU'RE NOT THINKING OF--
HOTWIRE THE CAR AND TAKE IT BACK TO THE HOTEL. THEN *DISAPPEAR.*
I'LL MEET YOU AT THE FALLBACK SAFEHOUSE.
WHY? WHAT ARE YOU GONNA DO?
I'M GONNA SHOW THEM WHO'S THE REAL *THIEF OF THIEVES.*

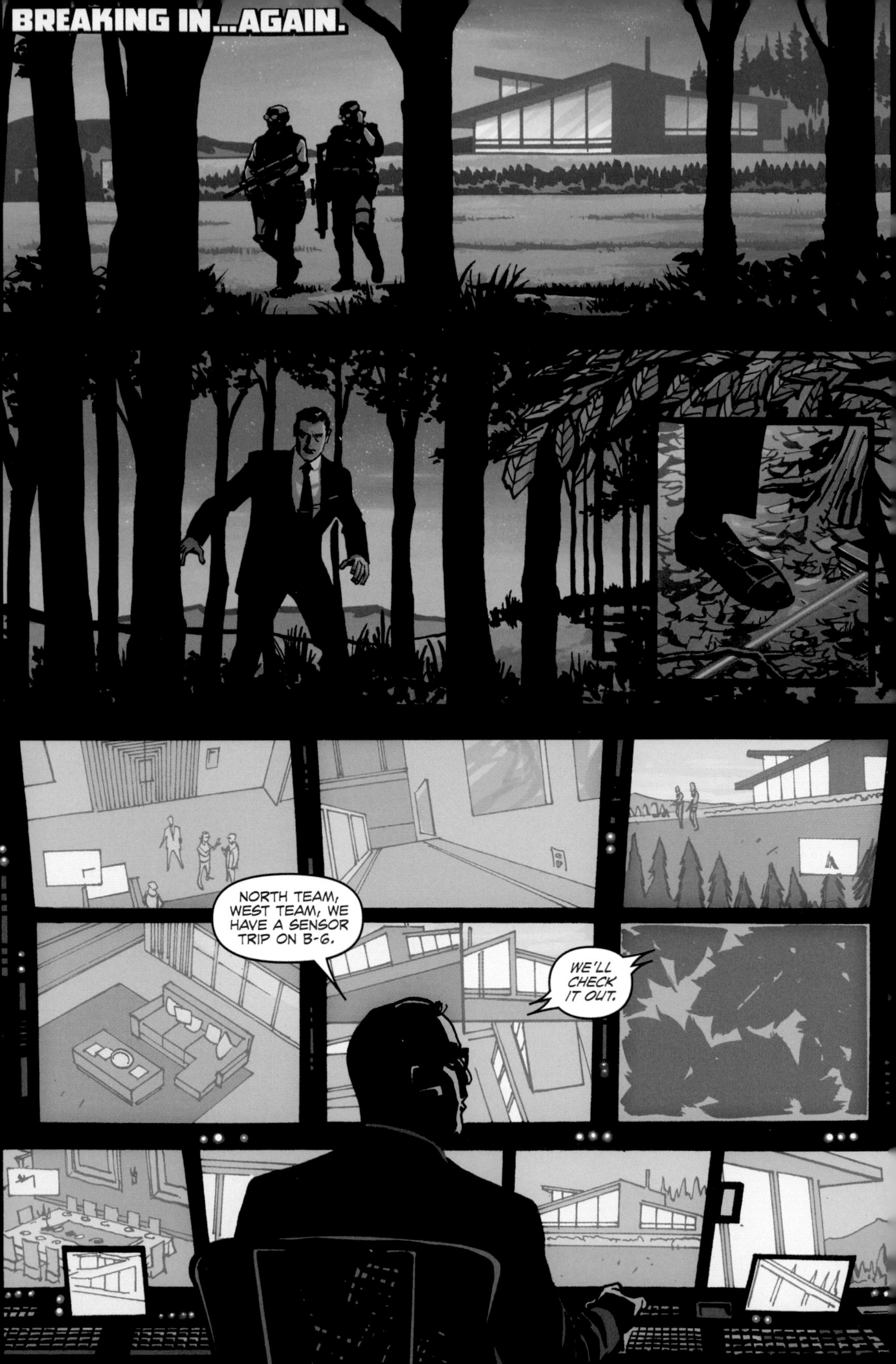
BREAKING IN...AGAIN.
NORTH TEAM, WEST TEAM, WE HAVE A SENSOR TRIP ON B-6.
WE'LL CHECK IT OUT.

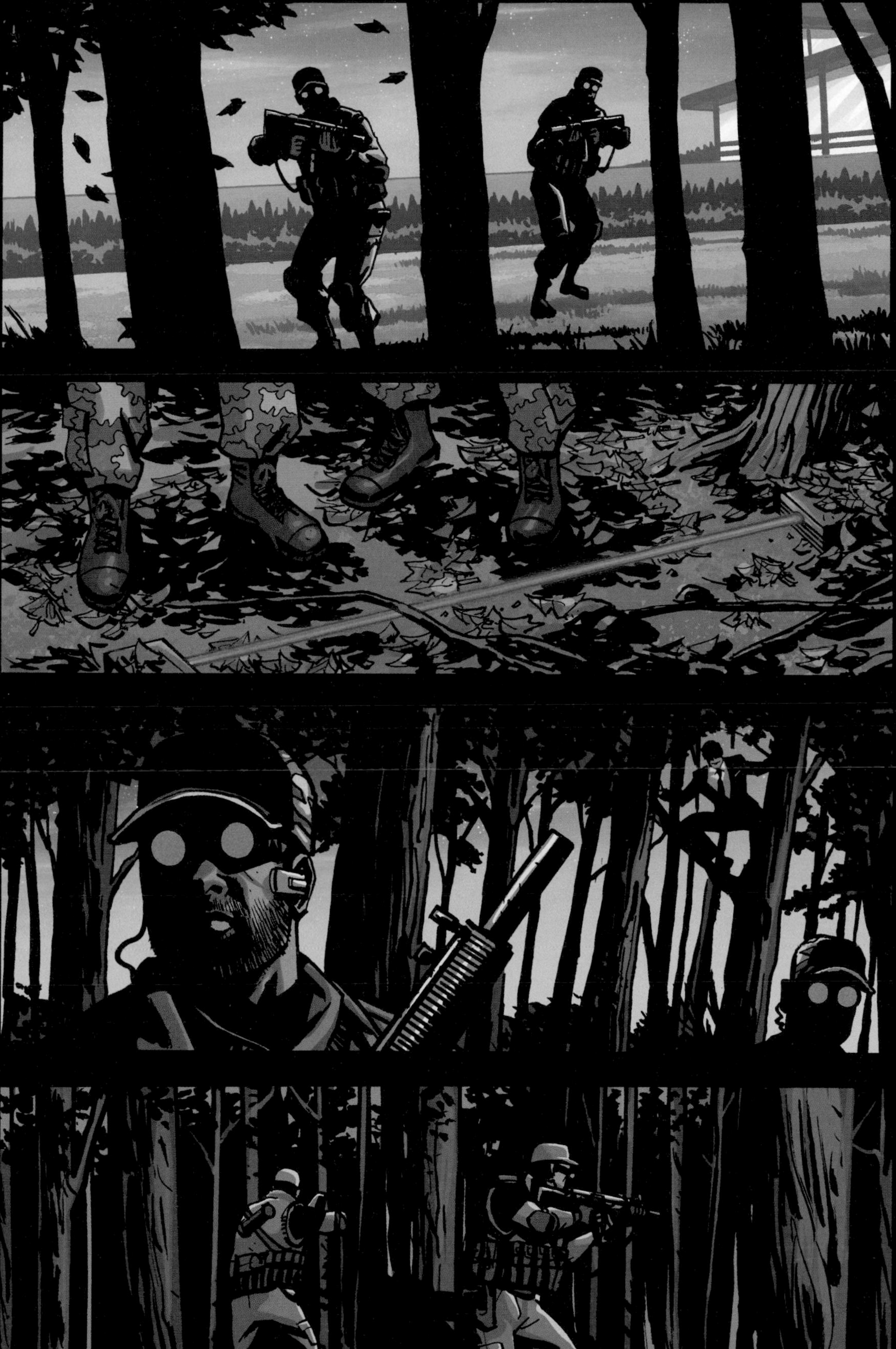

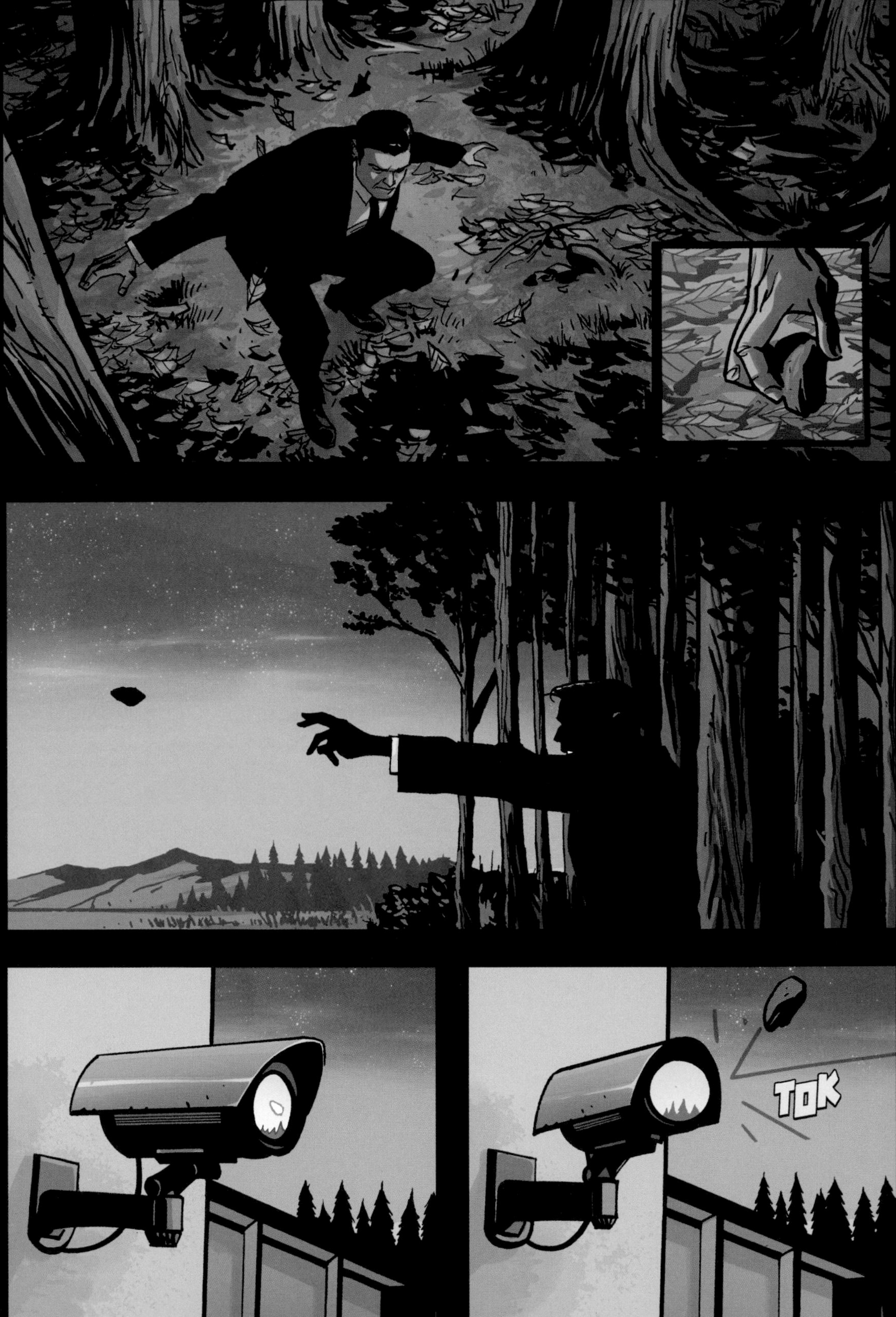
TOK

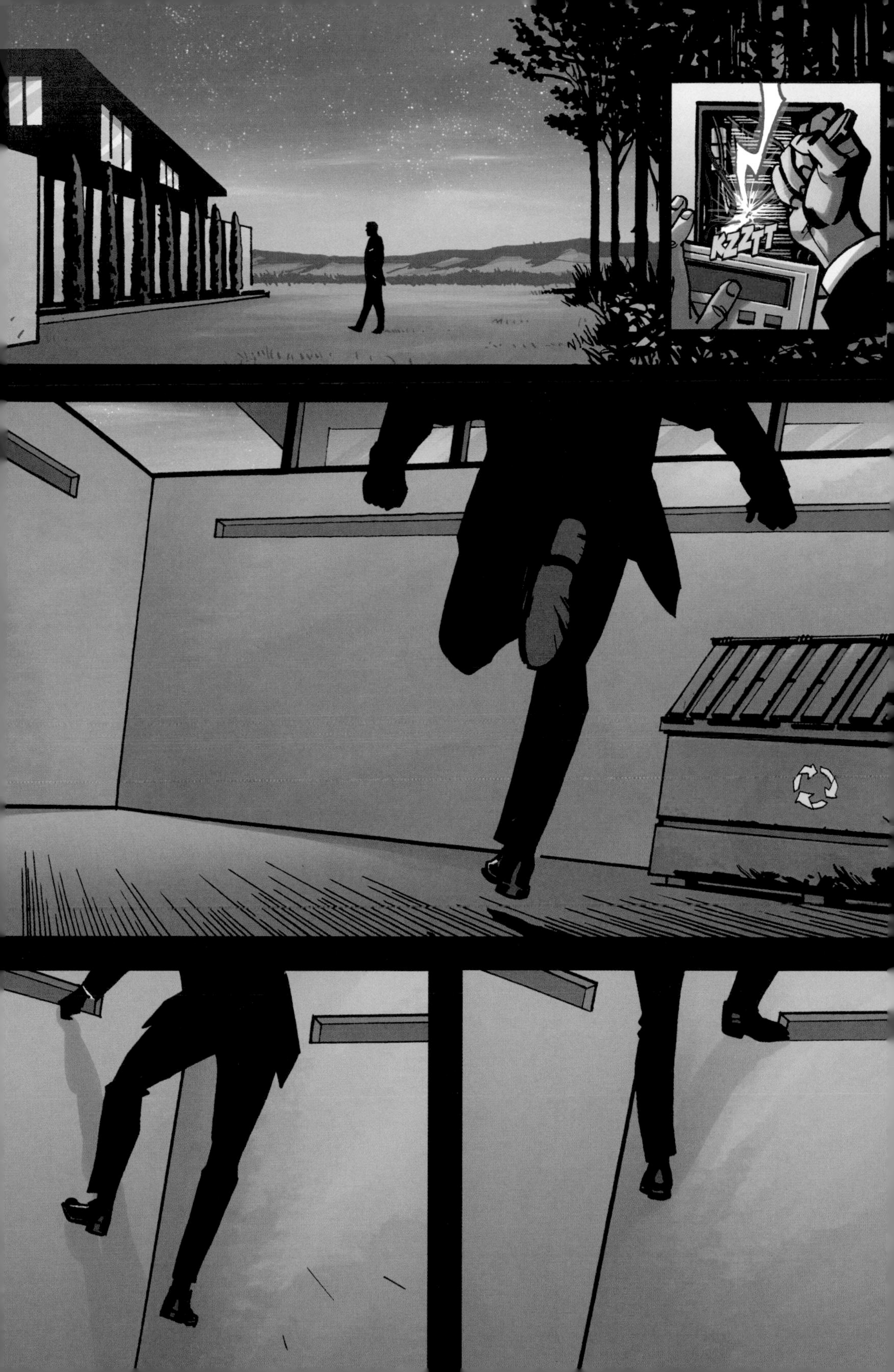
KZZTT

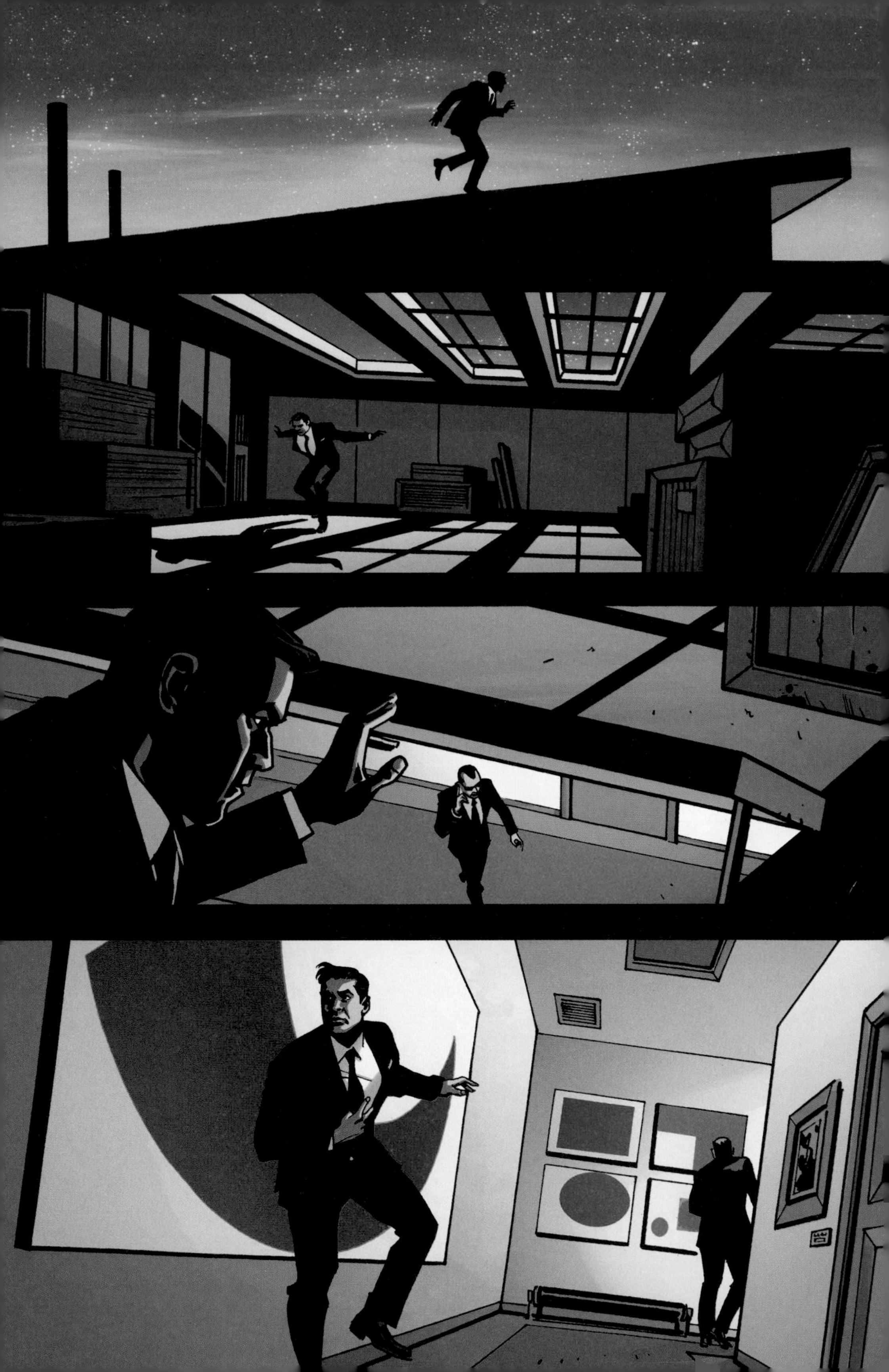

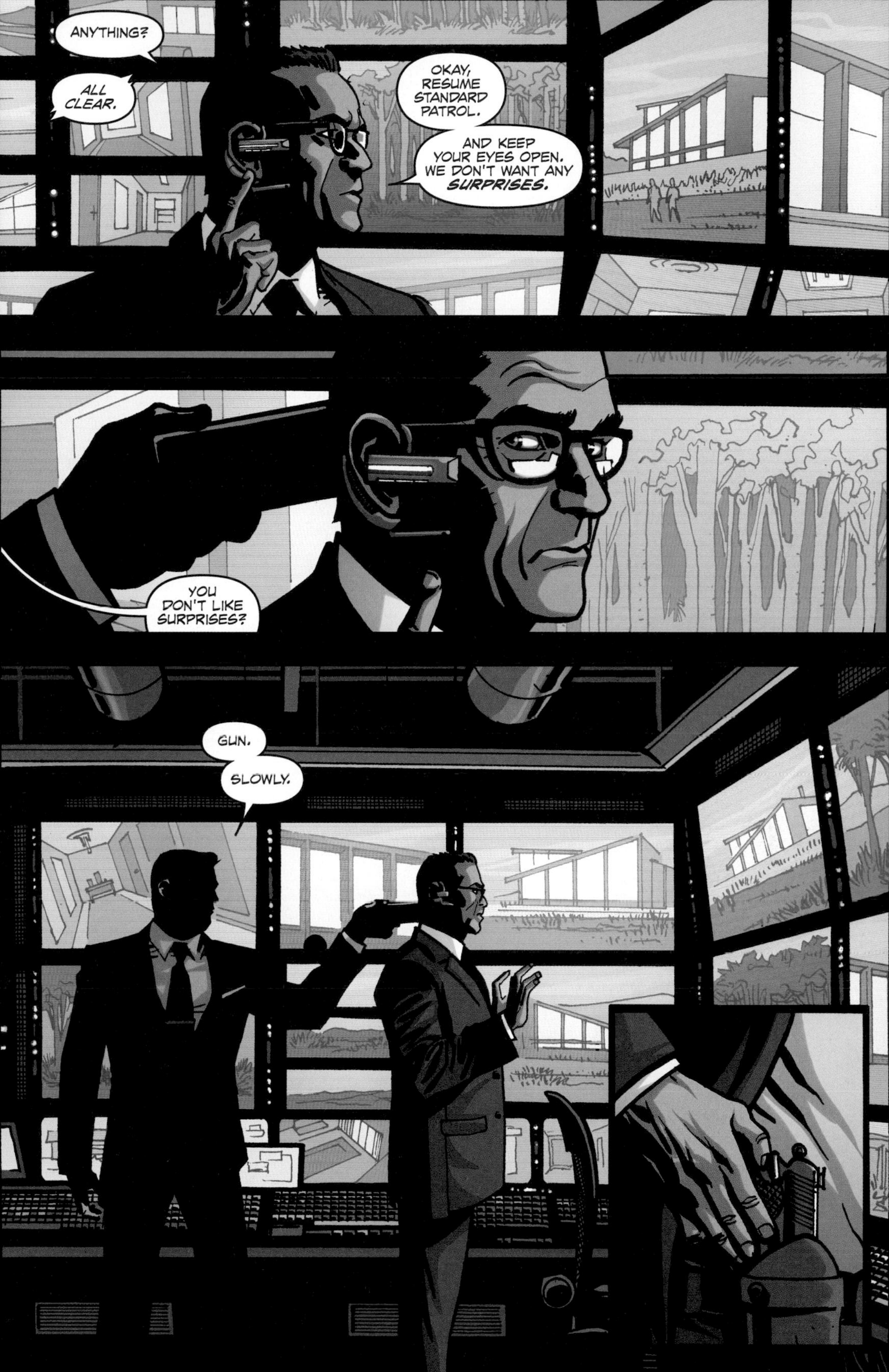
ANYTHING?
ALL CLEAR.
OKAY, RESUME STANDARD PATROL.
AND KEEP YOUR EYES OPEN. WE DON'T WANT ANY *SURPRISES.*
YOU DON'T LIKE SURPRISES?
GUN.
SLOWLY.

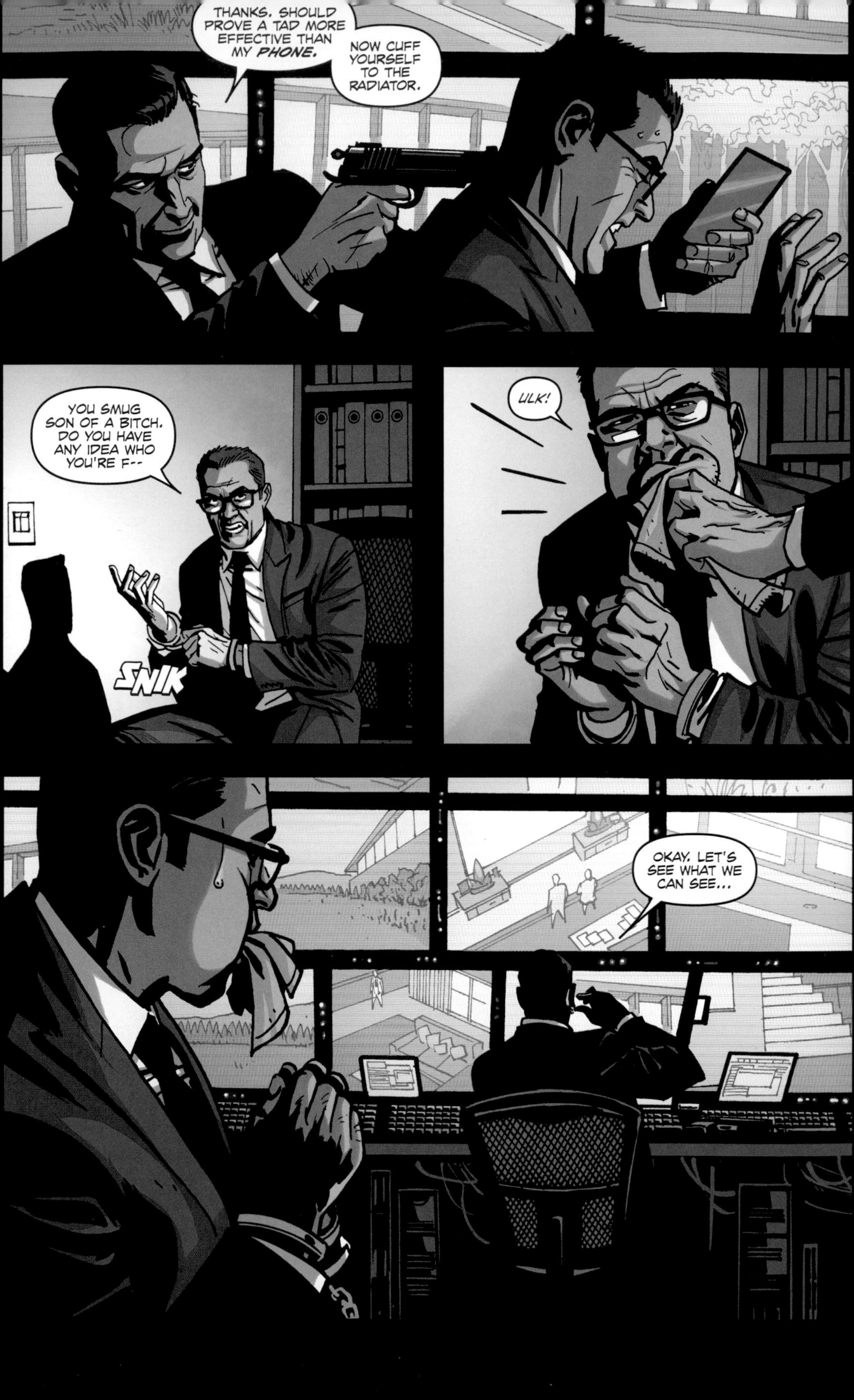
THANKS. SHOULD PROVE A TAD MORE EFFECTIVE THAN MY PHONE.
NOW CUFF YOURSELF TO THE RADIATOR.
YOU SMUG SON OF A BITCH. DO YOU HAVE ANY IDEA WHO YOU'RE F--
SNIK
ULK!
OKAY. LET'S SEE WHAT WE CAN SEE...

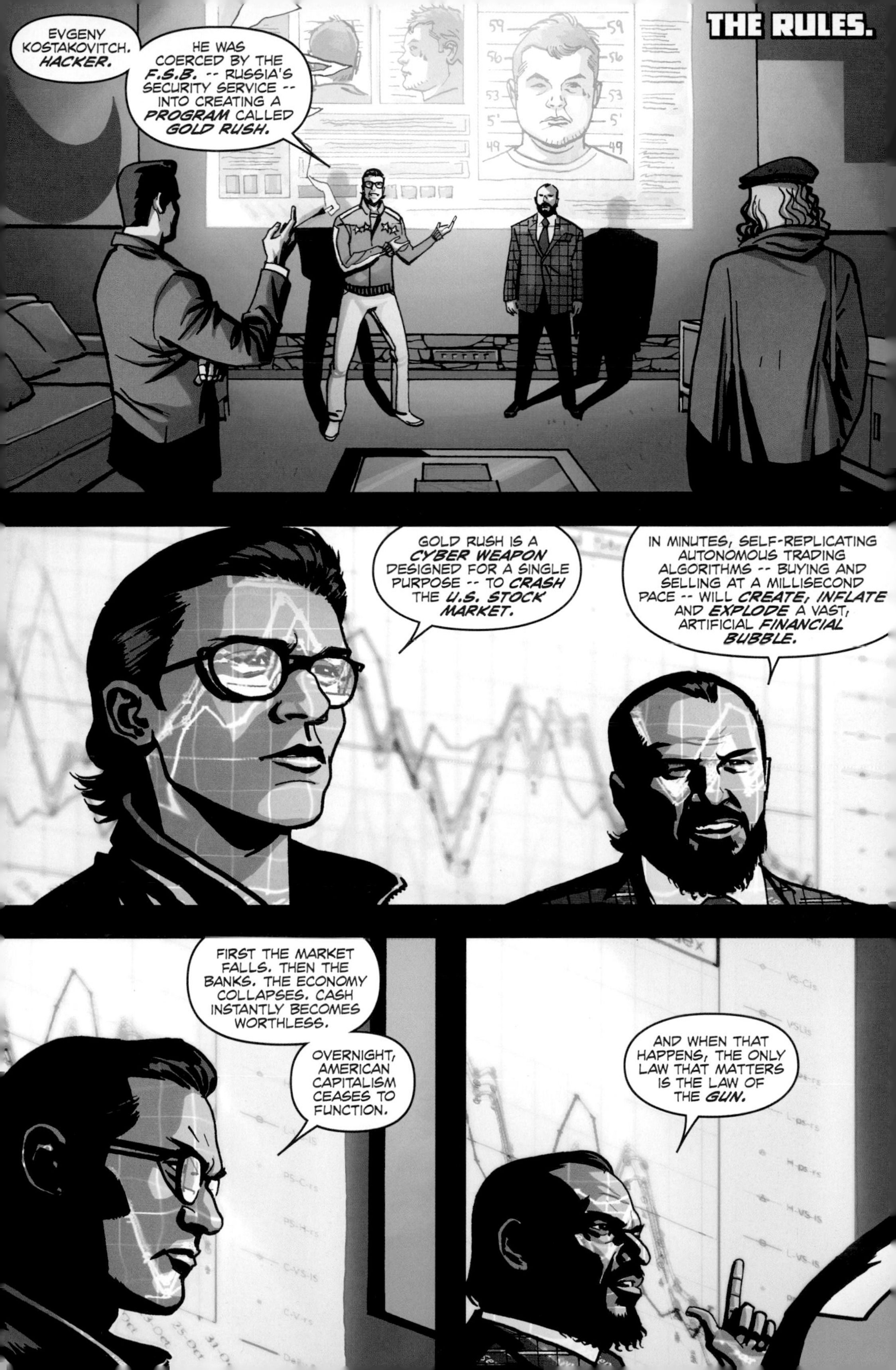
THE RULES.
EVGENY KOSTAKOVITCH. HACKER.
HE WAS COERCED BY THE F.S.B. -- RUSSIA'S SECURITY SERVICE -- INTO CREATING A PROGRAM CALLED GOLD RUSH.
GOLD RUSH IS A CYBER WEAPON DESIGNED FOR A SINGLE PURPOSE -- TO CRASH THE U.S. STOCK MARKET.
IN MINUTES, SELF-REPLICATING AUTONOMOUS TRADING ALGORITHMS -- BUYING AND SELLING AT A MILLISECOND PACE -- WILL CREATE, INFLATE AND EXPLODE A VAST, ARTIFICIAL FINANCIAL BUBBLE.
FIRST THE MARKET FALLS. THEN THE BANKS. THE ECONOMY COLLAPSES. CASH INSTANTLY BECOMES WORTHLESS.
OVERNIGHT, AMERICAN CAPITALISM CEASES TO FUNCTION.
AND WHEN THAT HAPPENS, THE ONLY LAW THAT MATTERS IS THE LAW OF THE GUN.

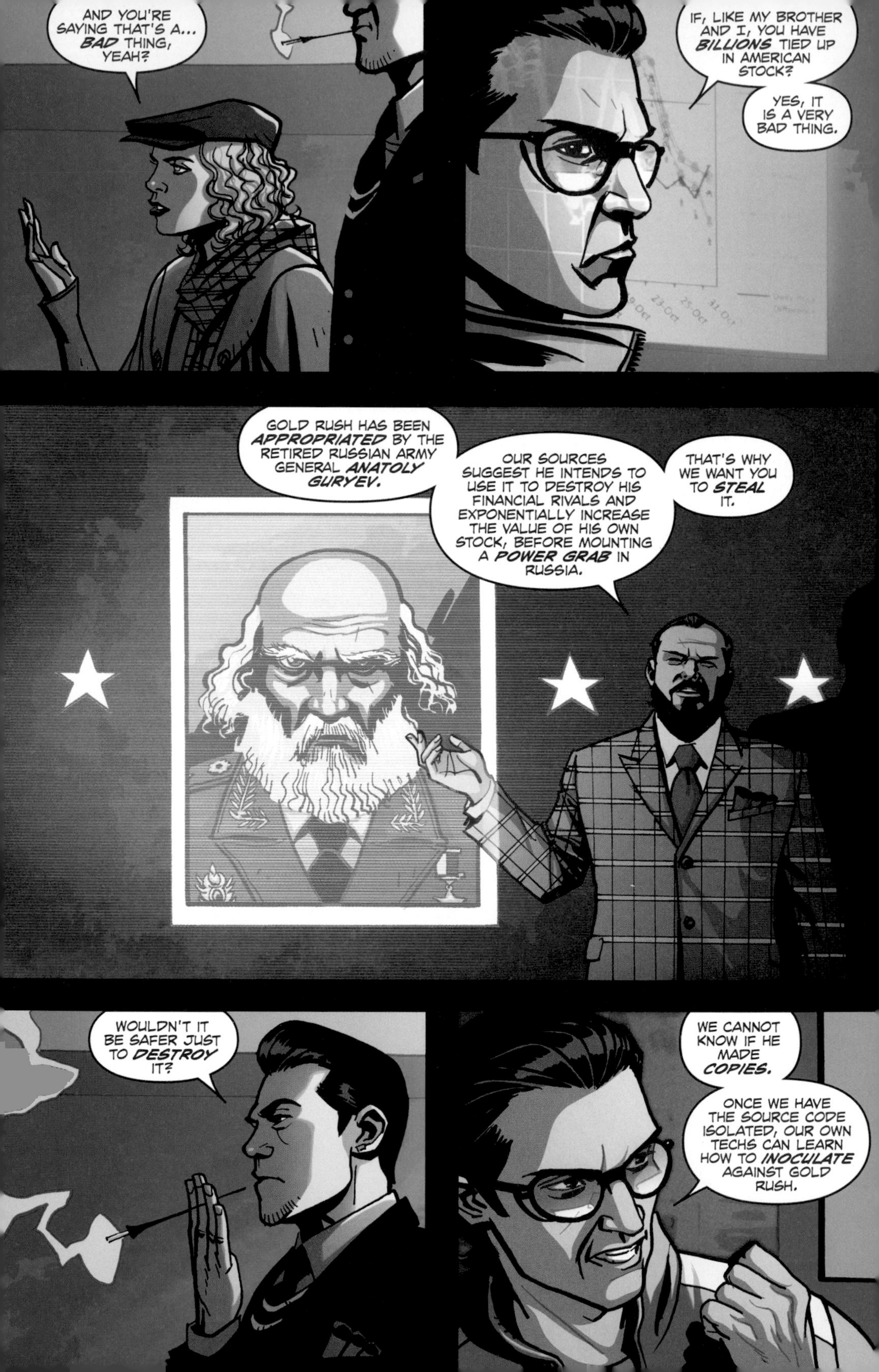
AND YOU'RE SAYING THAT'S A... BAD THING, YEAH?
IF, LIKE MY BROTHER AND I, YOU HAVE BILLIONS TIED UP IN AMERICAN STOCK?
YES, IT IS A VERY BAD THING.
GOLD RUSH HAS BEEN APPROPRIATED BY THE RETIRED RUSSIAN ARMY GENERAL ANATOLY GURYEV.
OUR SOURCES SUGGEST HE INTENDS TO USE IT TO DESTROY HIS FINANCIAL RIVALS AND EXPONENTIALLY INCREASE THE VALUE OF HIS OWN STOCK, BEFORE MOUNTING A POWER GRAB IN RUSSIA.
THAT'S WHY WE WANT YOU TO STEAL IT.
WOULDN'T IT BE SAFER JUST TO DESTROY IT?
WE CANNOT KNOW IF HE MADE COPIES.
ONCE WE HAVE THE SOURCE CODE ISOLATED, OUR OWN TECHS CAN LEARN HOW TO INOCULATE AGAINST GOLD RUSH.

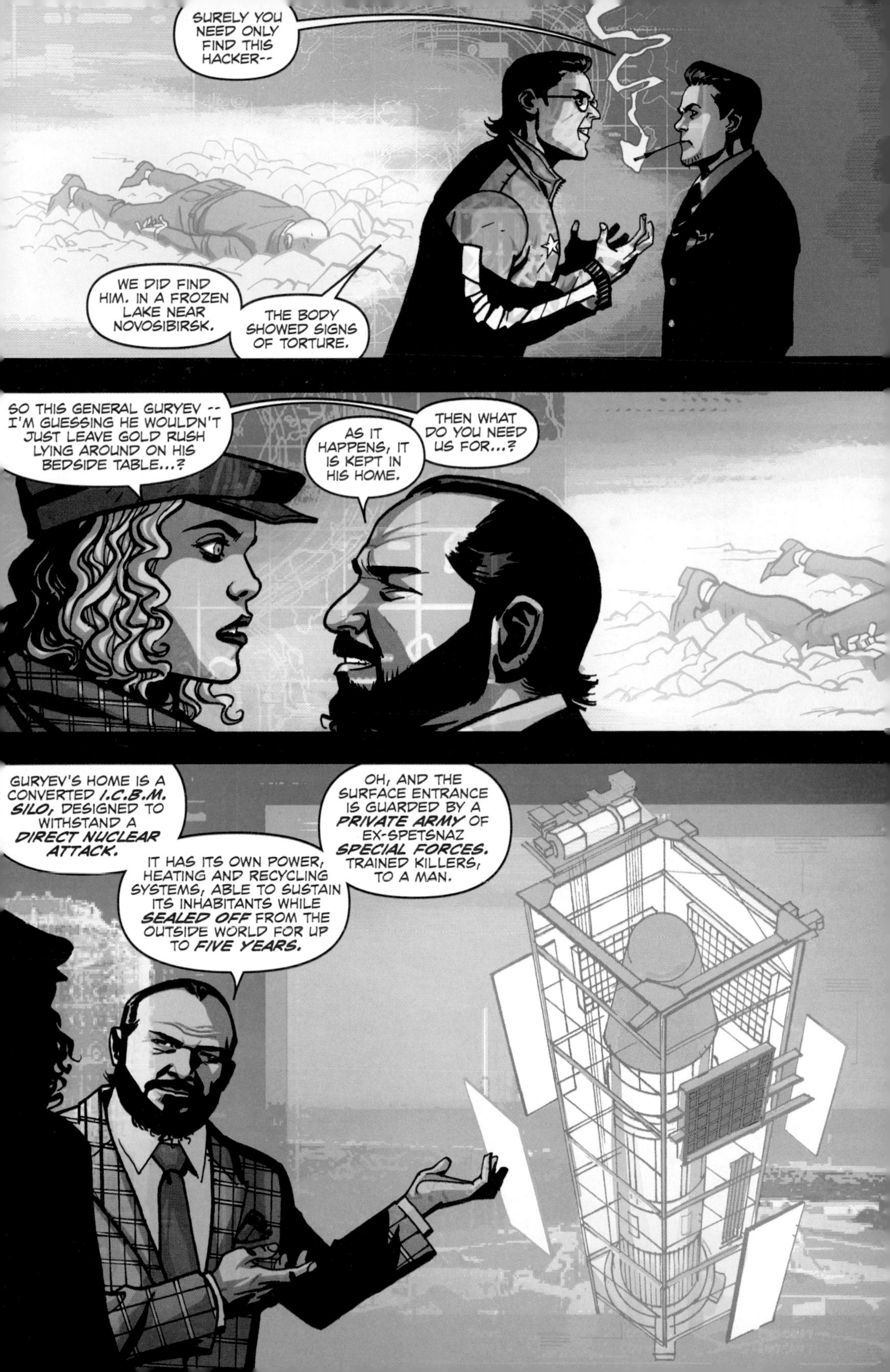
SURELY YOU NEED ONLY FIND THIS HACKER--
WE DID FIND HIM. IN A FROZEN LAKE NEAR NOVOSIBIRSK.
THE BODY SHOWED SIGNS OF TORTURE.
SO THIS GENERAL GURYEV -- I'M GUESSING HE WOULDN'T JUST LEAVE GOLD RUSH LYING AROUND ON HIS BEDSIDE TABLE...?
AS IT HAPPENS, IT IS KEPT IN HIS HOME.
THEN WHAT DO YOU NEED US FOR...?
GURYEV'S HOME IS A CONVERTED *I.C.B.M. SILO,* DESIGNED TO WITHSTAND A ***DIRECT NUCLEAR ATTACK.***
IT HAS ITS OWN POWER, HEATING AND RECYCLING SYSTEMS, ABLE TO SUSTAIN ITS INHABITANTS WHILE ***SEALED OFF*** FROM THE OUTSIDE WORLD FOR UP TO ***FIVE YEARS.***
OH, AND THE SURFACE ENTRANCE IS GUARDED BY A ***PRIVATE ARMY*** OF EX-SPETSNAZ ***SPECIAL FORCES.*** TRAINED KILLERS, TO A MAN.

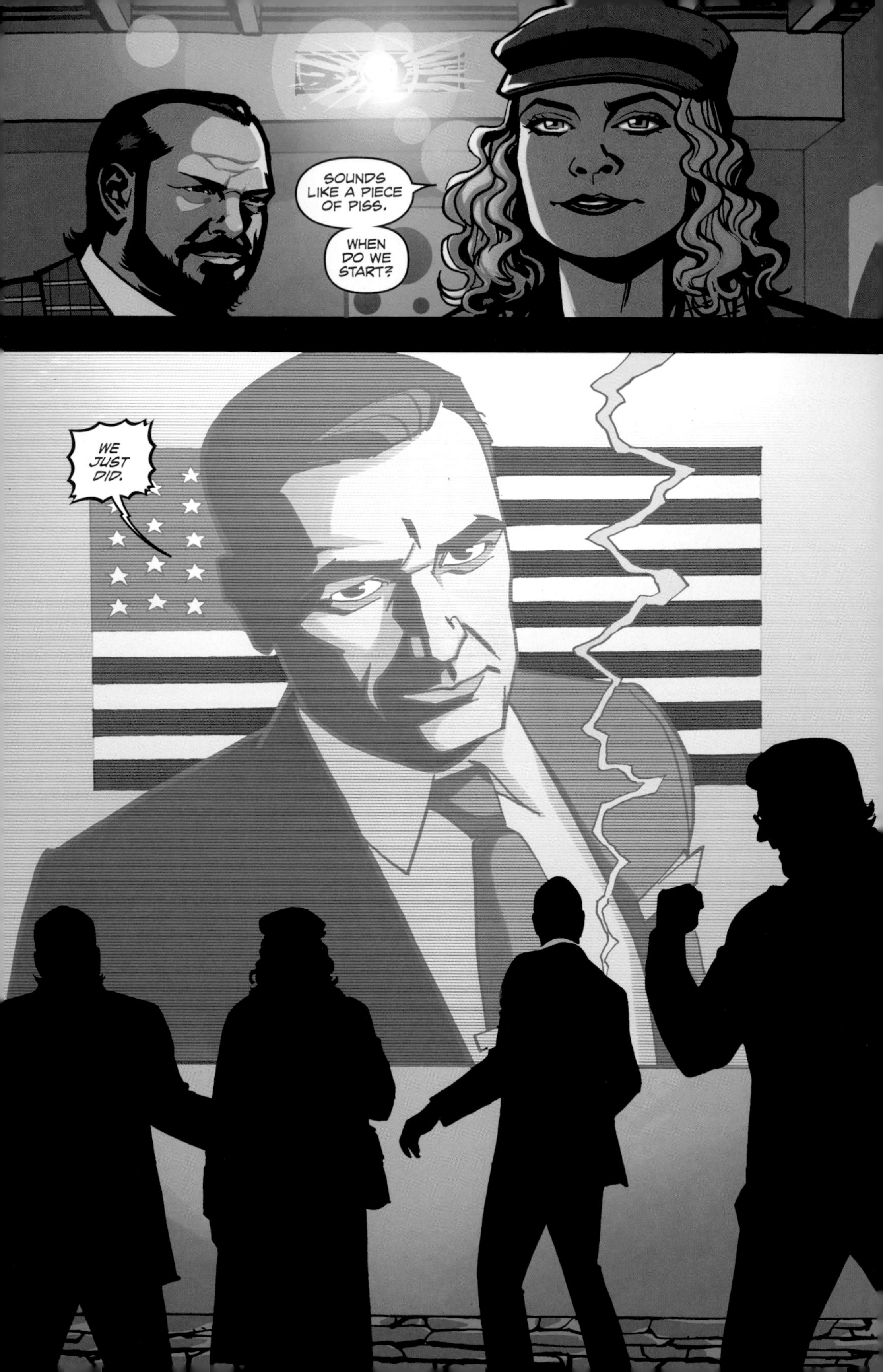
SOUNDS LIKE A PIECE OF PISS.
WHEN DO WE START?
WE JUST DID.

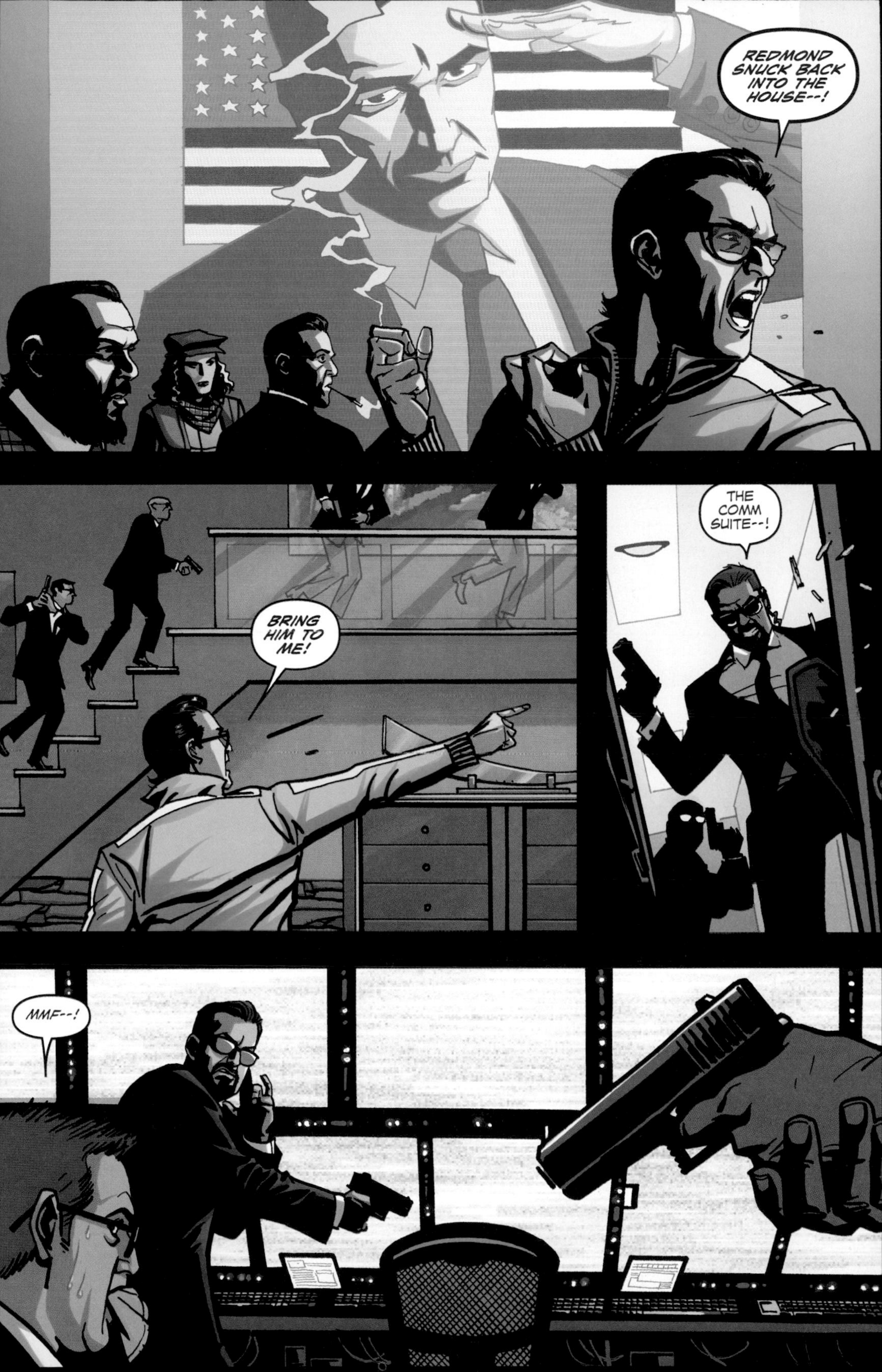
REDMOND SNUCK BACK INTO THE HOUSE--!
BRING HIM TO ME!
THE COMM SUITE--!
MMF--!

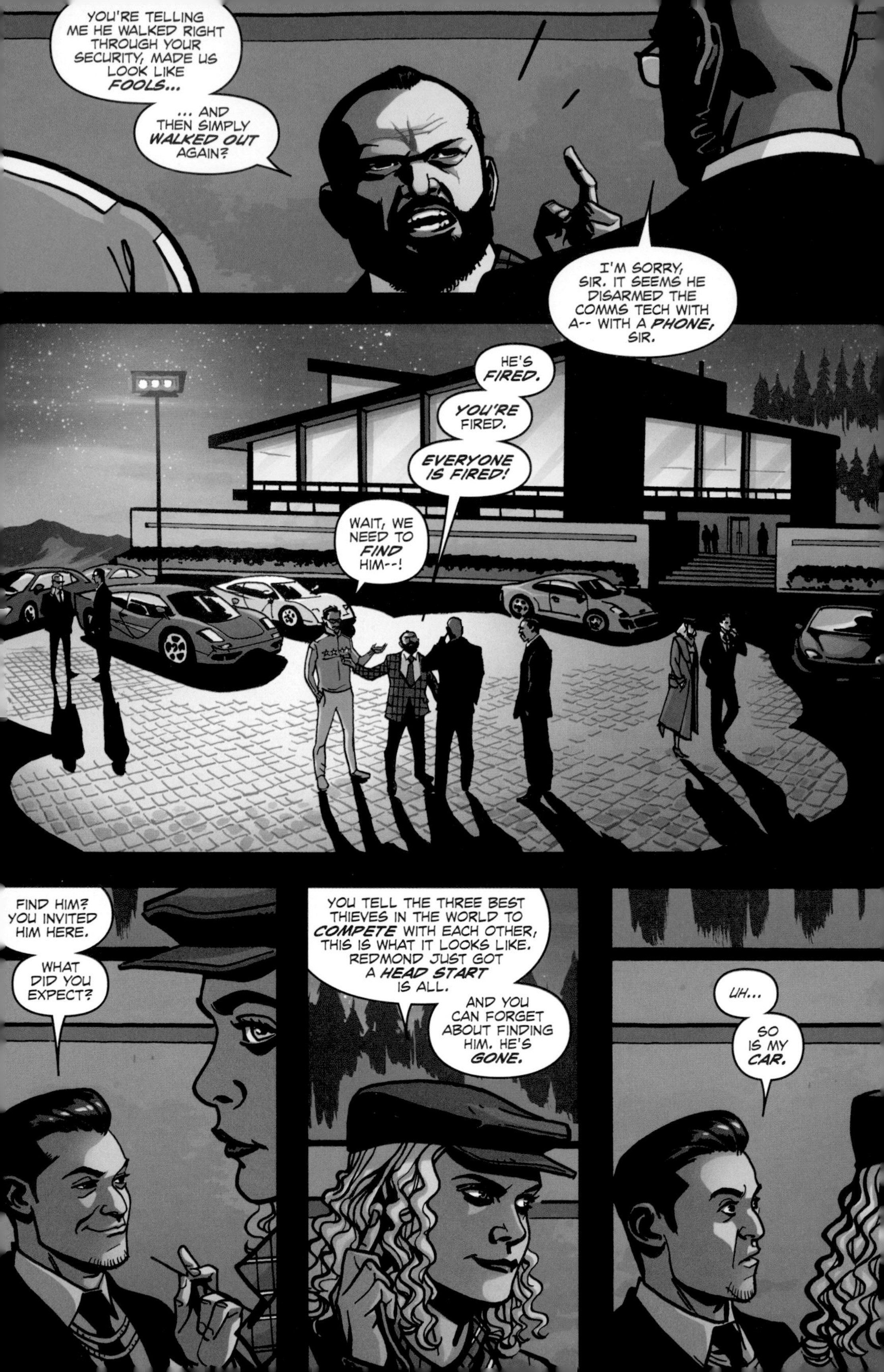
YOU'RE TELLING ME HE WALKED RIGHT THROUGH YOUR SECURITY, MADE US LOOK LIKE FOOLS...
... AND THEN SIMPLY WALKED OUT AGAIN?
I'M SORRY, SIR. IT SEEMS HE DISARMED THE COMMS TECH WITH A-- WITH A PHONE, SIR.
HE'S FIRED.
YOU'RE FIRED.
EVERYONE IS FIRED!
WAIT, WE NEED TO FIND HIM--!
FIND HIM? YOU INVITED HIM HERE.
WHAT DID YOU EXPECT?
YOU TELL THE THREE BEST THIEVES IN THE WORLD TO COMPETE WITH EACH OTHER, THIS IS WHAT IT LOOKS LIKE. REDMOND JUST GOT A HEAD START IS ALL.
AND YOU CAN FORGET ABOUT FINDING HIM. HE'S GONE.
UH...
SO IS MY CAR.

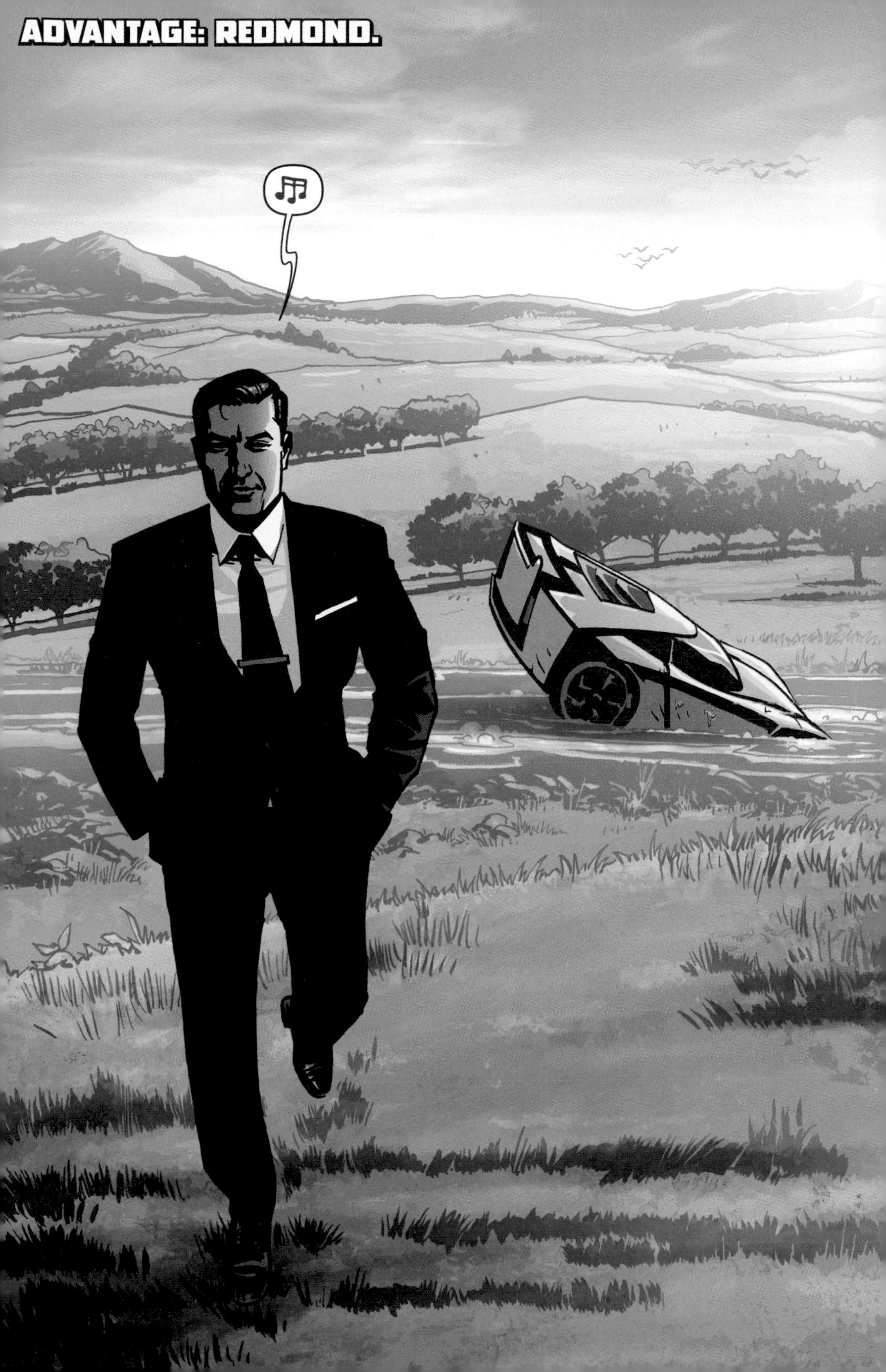
ADVANTAGE: REDMOND.

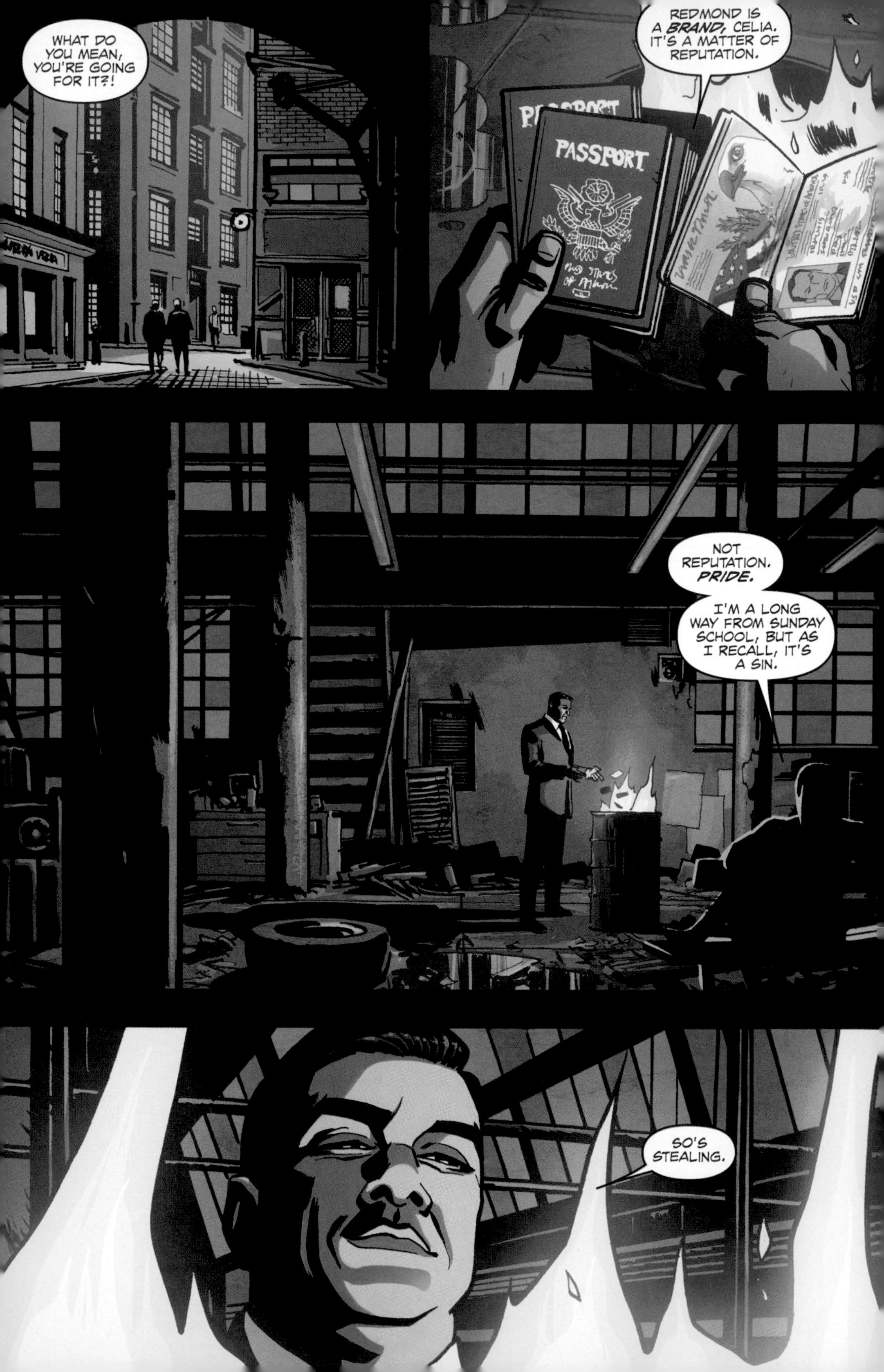
WHAT DO YOU MEAN, YOU'RE GOING FOR IT?!
REDMOND IS A BRAND, CELIA. IT'S A MATTER OF REPUTATION.
PASSPORT
PASSPORT
NOT REPUTATION. PRIDE.
I'M A LONG WAY FROM SUNDAY SCHOOL, BUT AS I RECALL, IT'S A SIN.
SO'S STEALING.

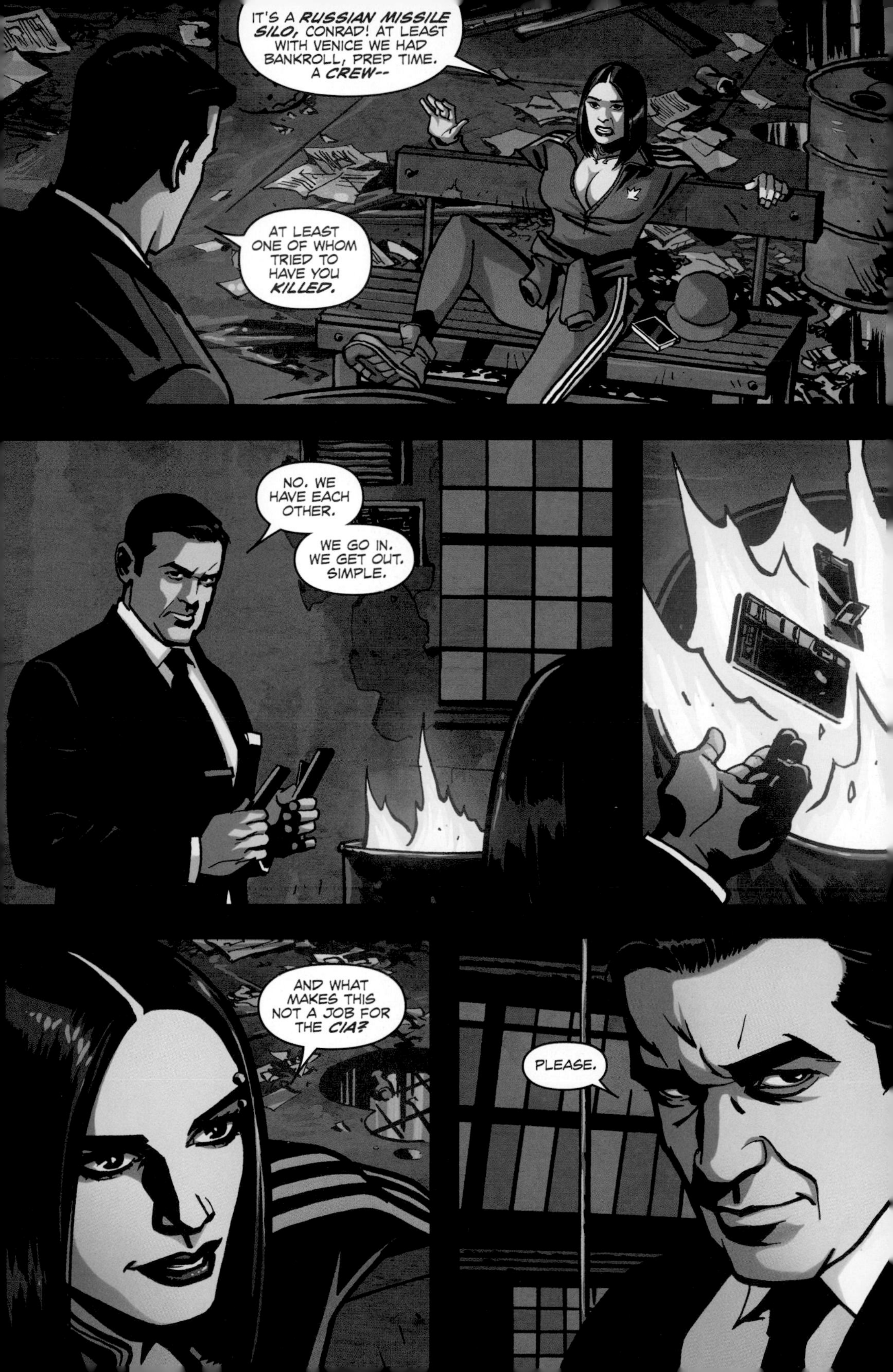
IT'S A RUSSIAN MISSILE SILO, CONRAD! AT LEAST WITH VENICE WE HAD BANKROLL, PREP TIME. A CREW--
AT LEAST ONE OF WHOM TRIED TO HAVE YOU KILLED.
NO. WE HAVE EACH OTHER.
WE GO IN. WE GET OUT. SIMPLE.
AND WHAT MAKES THIS NOT A JOB FOR THE CIA?
PLEASE.

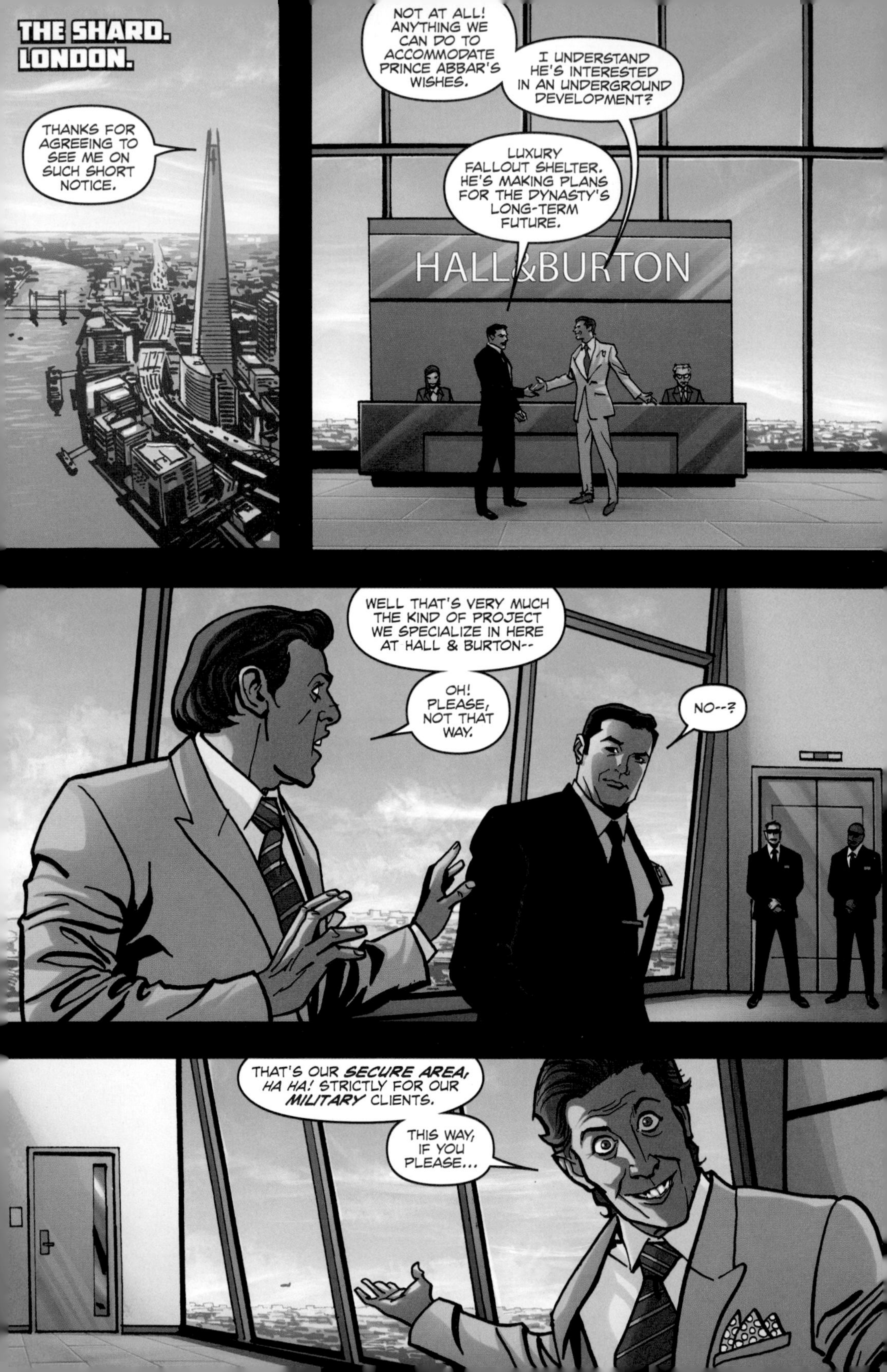
THE SHARD.
LONDON.
THANKS FOR AGREEING TO SEE ME ON SUCH SHORT NOTICE.
NOT AT ALL! ANYTHING WE CAN DO TO ACCOMMODATE PRINCE ABBAR'S WISHES.
I UNDERSTAND HE'S INTERESTED IN AN UNDERGROUND DEVELOPMENT?
LUXURY FALLOUT SHELTER. HE'S MAKING PLANS FOR THE DYNASTY'S LONG-TERM FUTURE.
HALL&BURTON
WELL THAT'S VERY MUCH THE KIND OF PROJECT WE SPECIALIZE IN HERE AT HALL & BURTON--
OH! PLEASE, NOT THAT WAY.
NO--?
THAT'S OUR *SECURE AREA, HA HA!* STRICTLY FOR OUR *MILITARY* CLIENTS.
THIS WAY, IF YOU PLEASE...

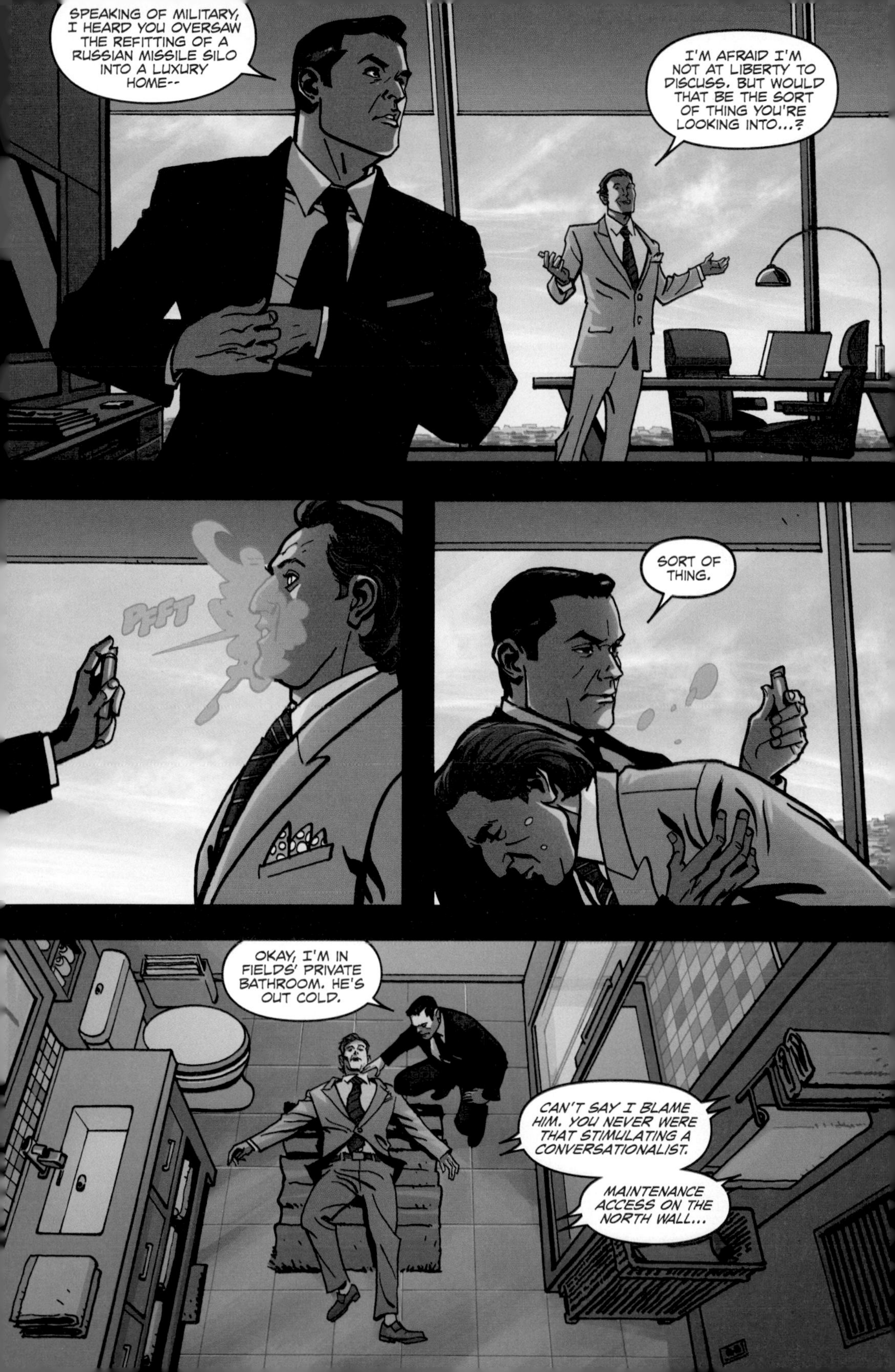
SPEAKING OF MILITARY, I HEARD YOU OVERSAW THE REFITTING OF A RUSSIAN MISSILE SILO INTO A LUXURY HOME--
I'M AFRAID I'M NOT AT LIBERTY TO DISCUSS. BUT WOULD THAT BE THE SORT OF THING YOU'RE LOOKING INTO...?
PFFT
SORT OF THING.
OKAY, I'M IN FIELDS' PRIVATE BATHROOM. HE'S OUT COLD.
CAN'T SAY I BLAME HIM. YOU NEVER WERE THAT STIMULATING A CONVERSATIONALIST.
MAINTENANCE ACCESS ON THE NORTH WALL...

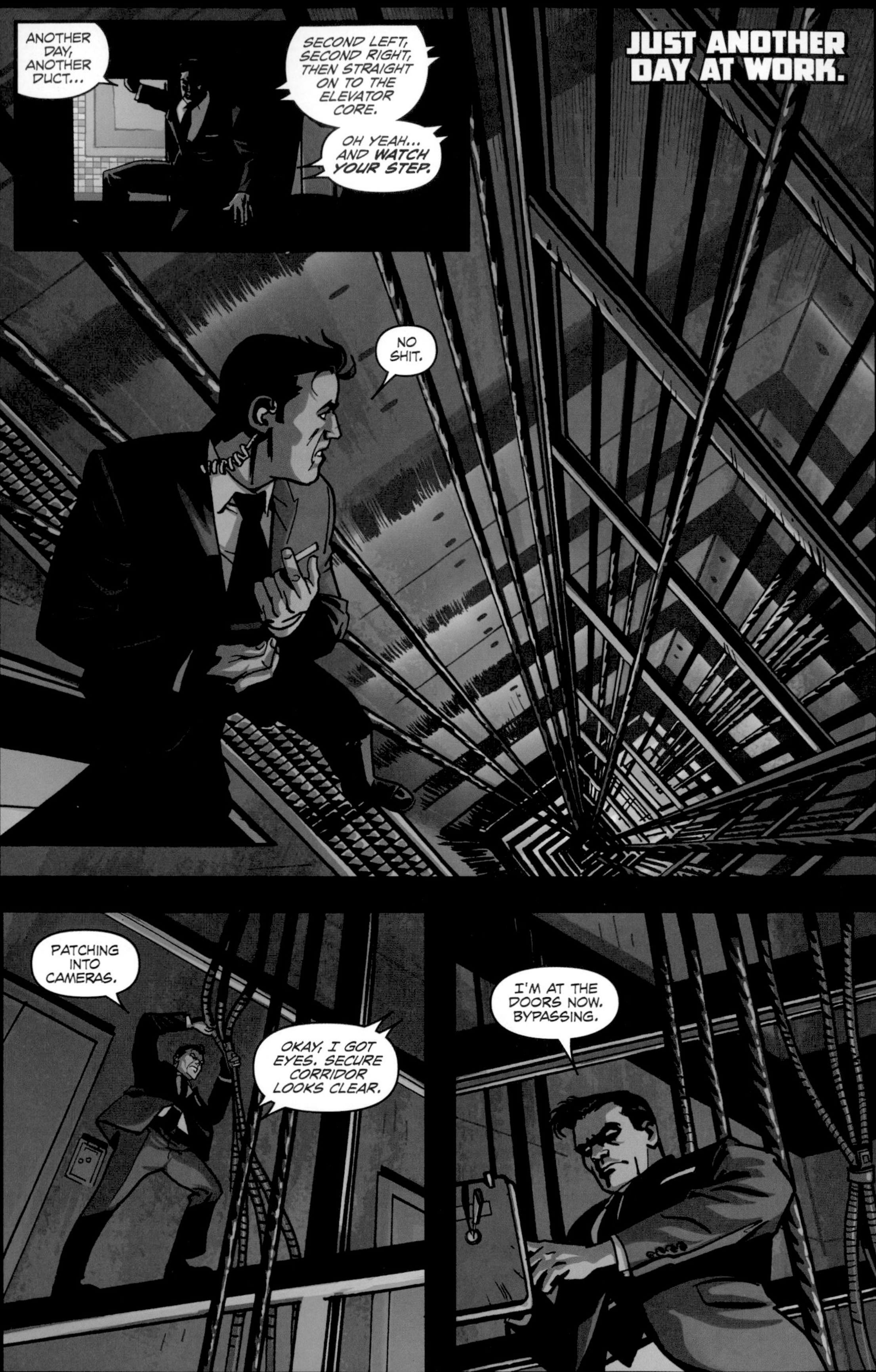
JUST ANOTHER DAY AT WORK.
ANOTHER DAY, ANOTHER DUCT...
SECOND LEFT, SECOND RIGHT, THEN STRAIGHT ON TO THE ELEVATOR CORE.
OH YEAH... AND WATCH YOUR STEP.
NO SHIT.
PATCHING INTO CAMERAS.
OKAY, I GOT EYES. SECURE CORRIDOR LOOKS CLEAR.
I'M AT THE DOORS NOW. BYPASSING.

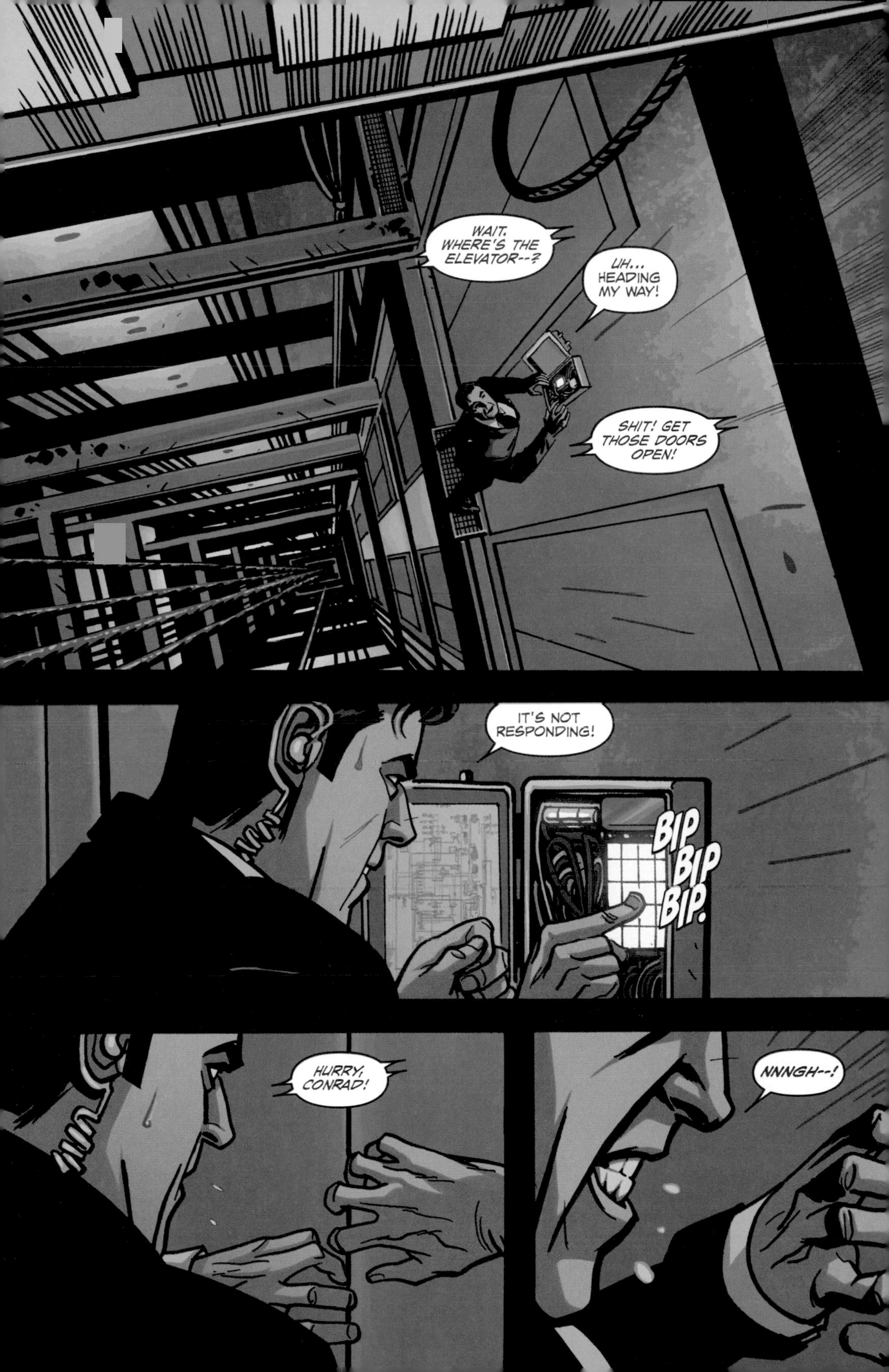
WAIT. WHERE'S THE ELEVATOR--?
UH... HEADING MY WAY!
SHIT! GET THOSE DOORS OPEN!
IT'S NOT RESPONDING!
BIP BIP BIP.
HURRY, CONRAD!
NNNGH--!

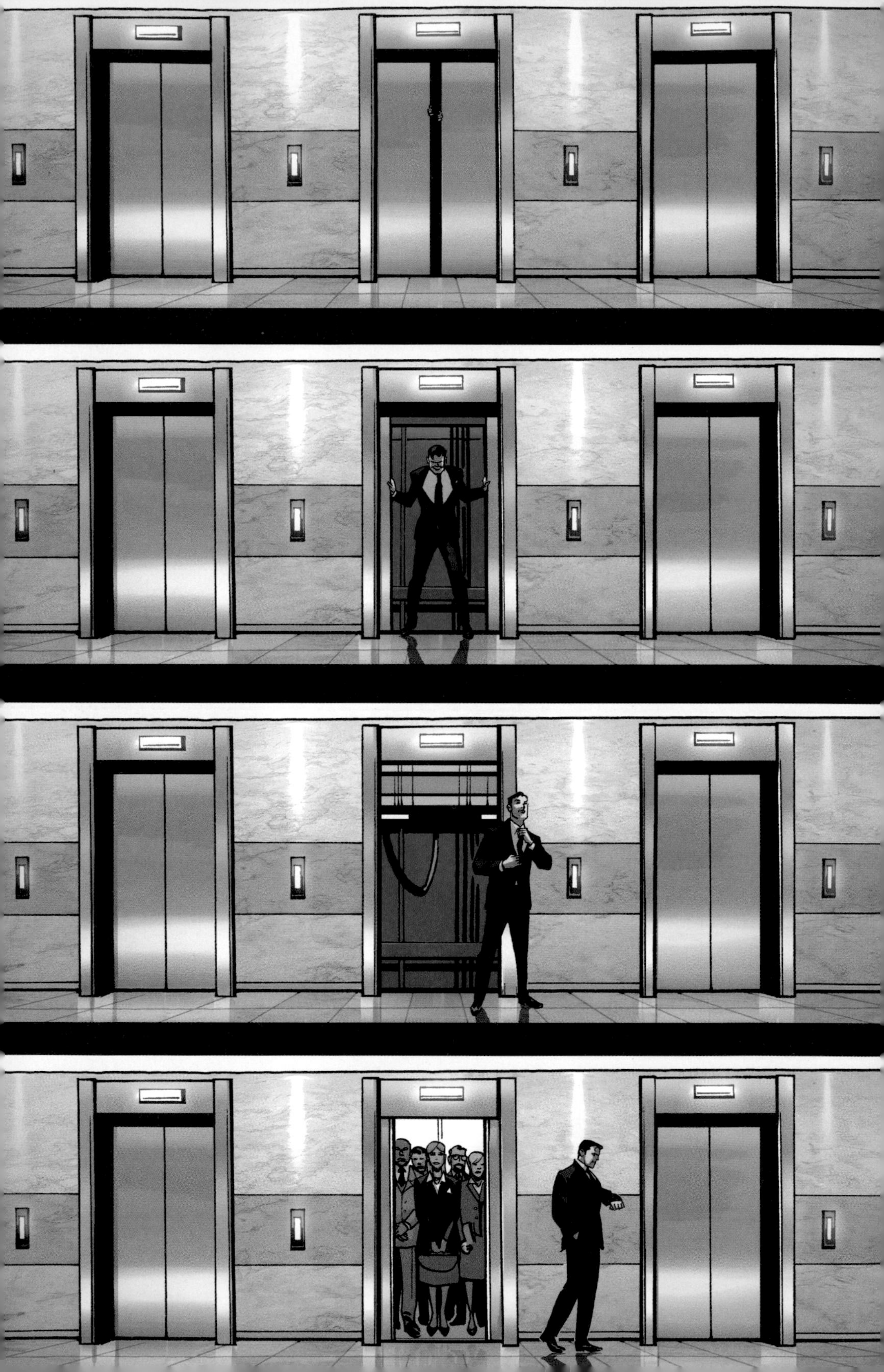

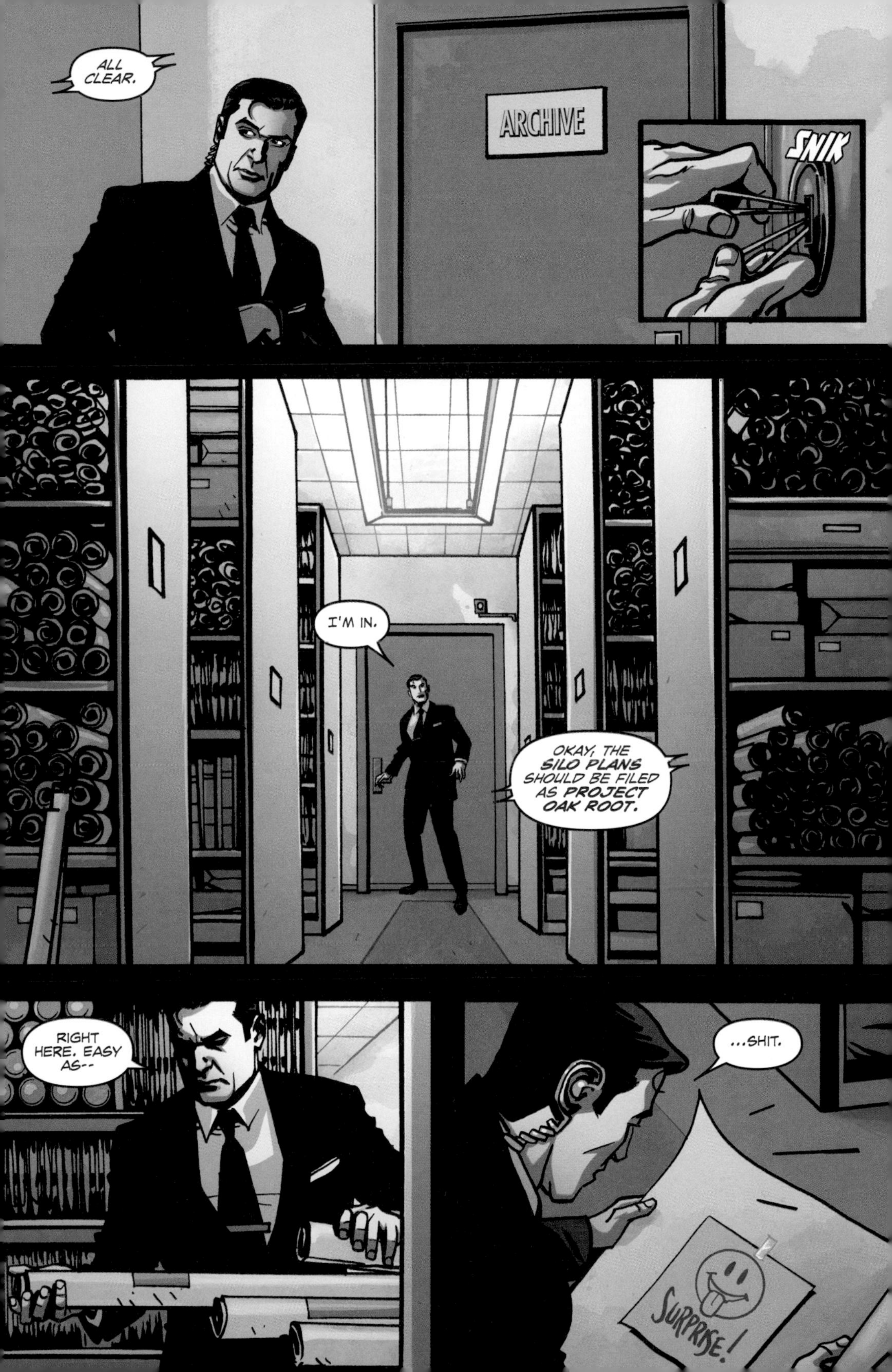
ALL CLEAR.
ARCHIVE
SNIK
I'M IN.
OKAY, THE SILO PLANS SHOULD BE FILED AS PROJECT OAK ROOT.
RIGHT HERE. EASY AS--
...SHIT.
SURPRISE!

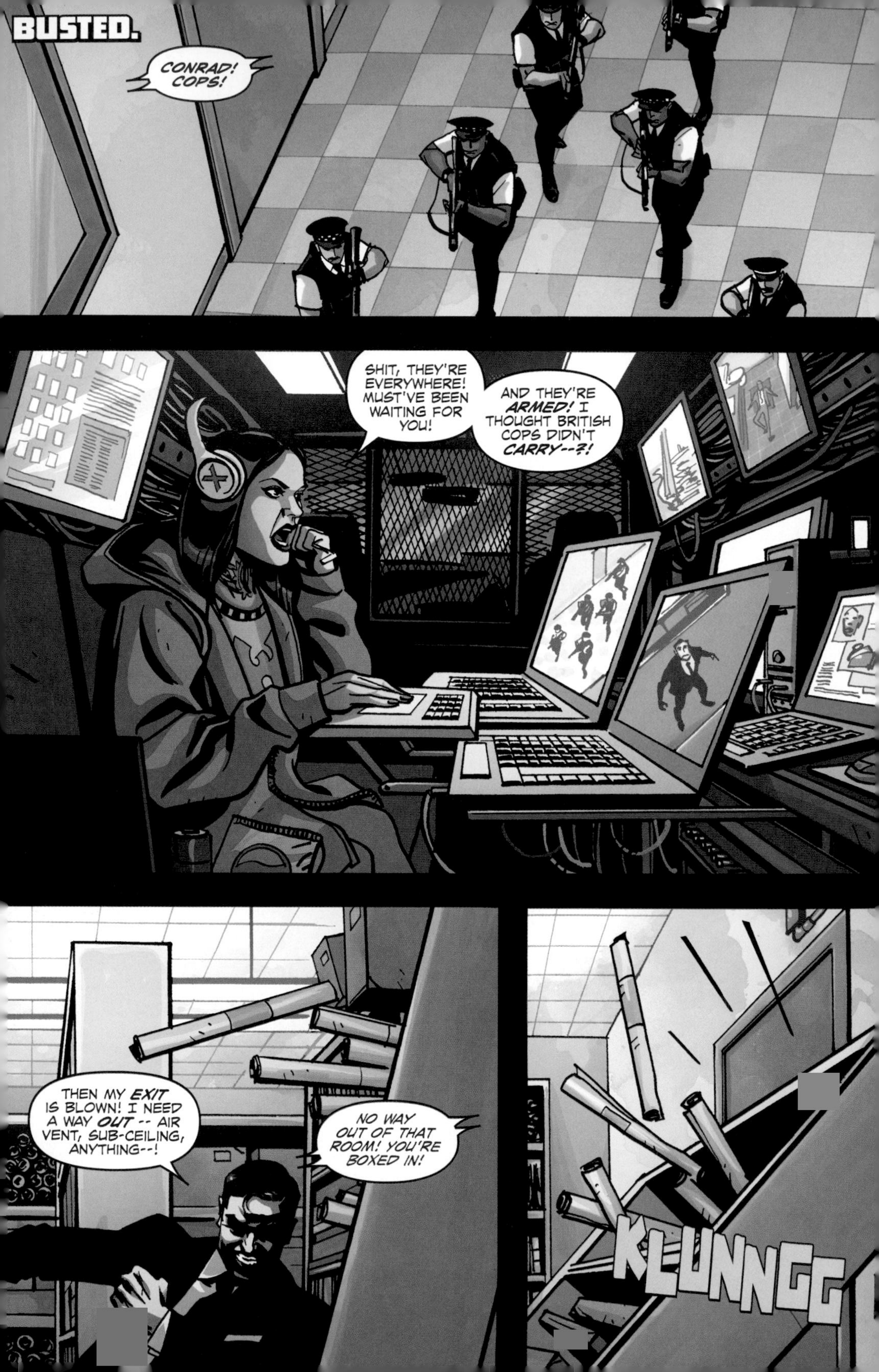
BUSTED.
CONRAD! COPS!
SHIT, THEY'RE EVERYWHERE! MUST'VE BEEN WAITING FOR YOU!
AND THEY'RE ARMED! I THOUGHT BRITISH COPS DIDN'T CARRY--?!
THEN MY EXIT IS BLOWN! I NEED A WAY OUT -- AIR VENT, SUB-CEILING, ANYTHING--!
NO WAY OUT OF THAT ROOM! YOU'RE BOXED IN!
KLUNNGG

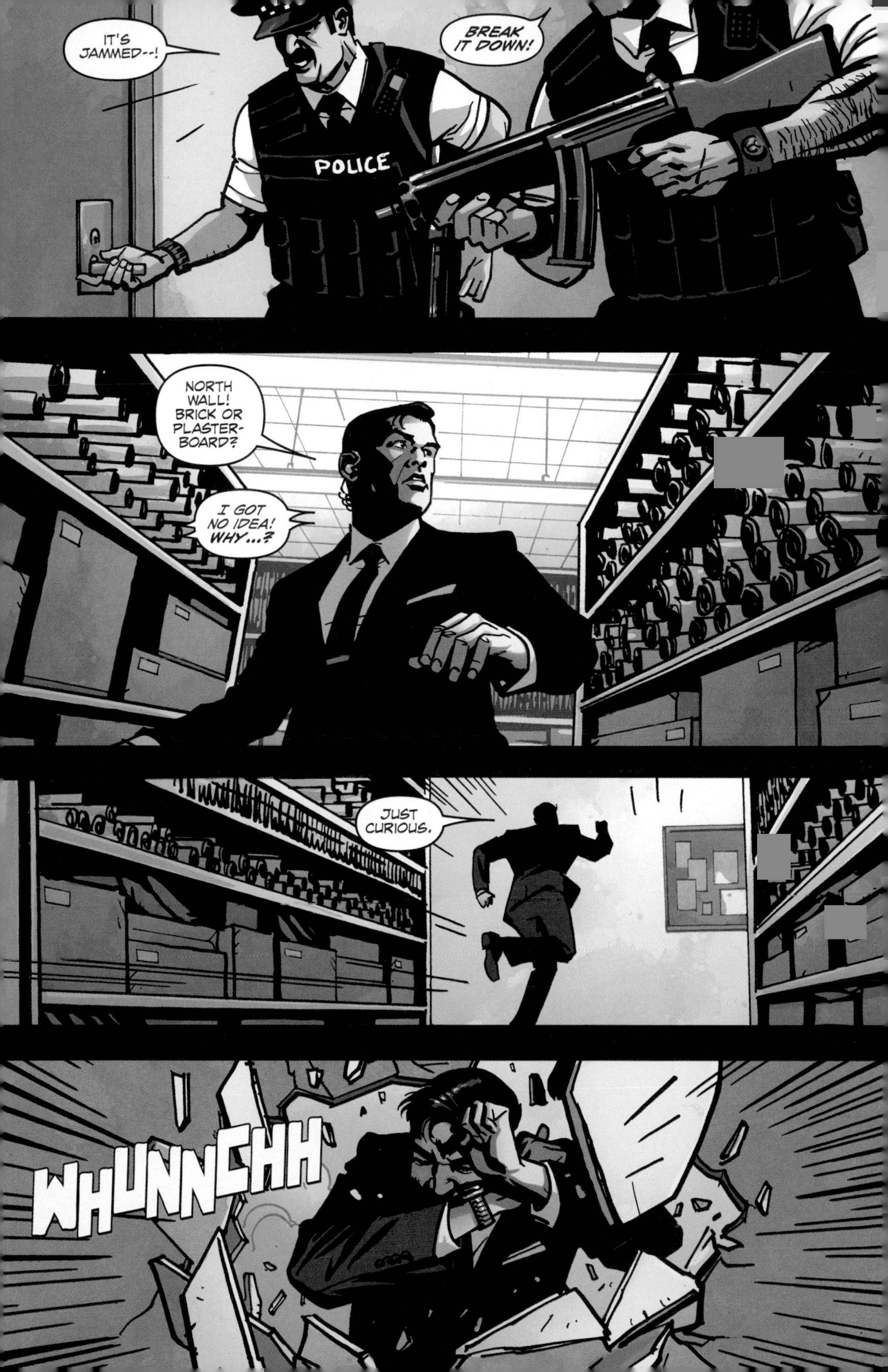
IT'S JAMMED--!
BREAK IT DOWN!
POLICE
NORTH WALL! BRICK OR PLASTER-BOARD?
I GOT NO IDEA! WHY...?
JUST CURIOUS.
WHUNNCHH

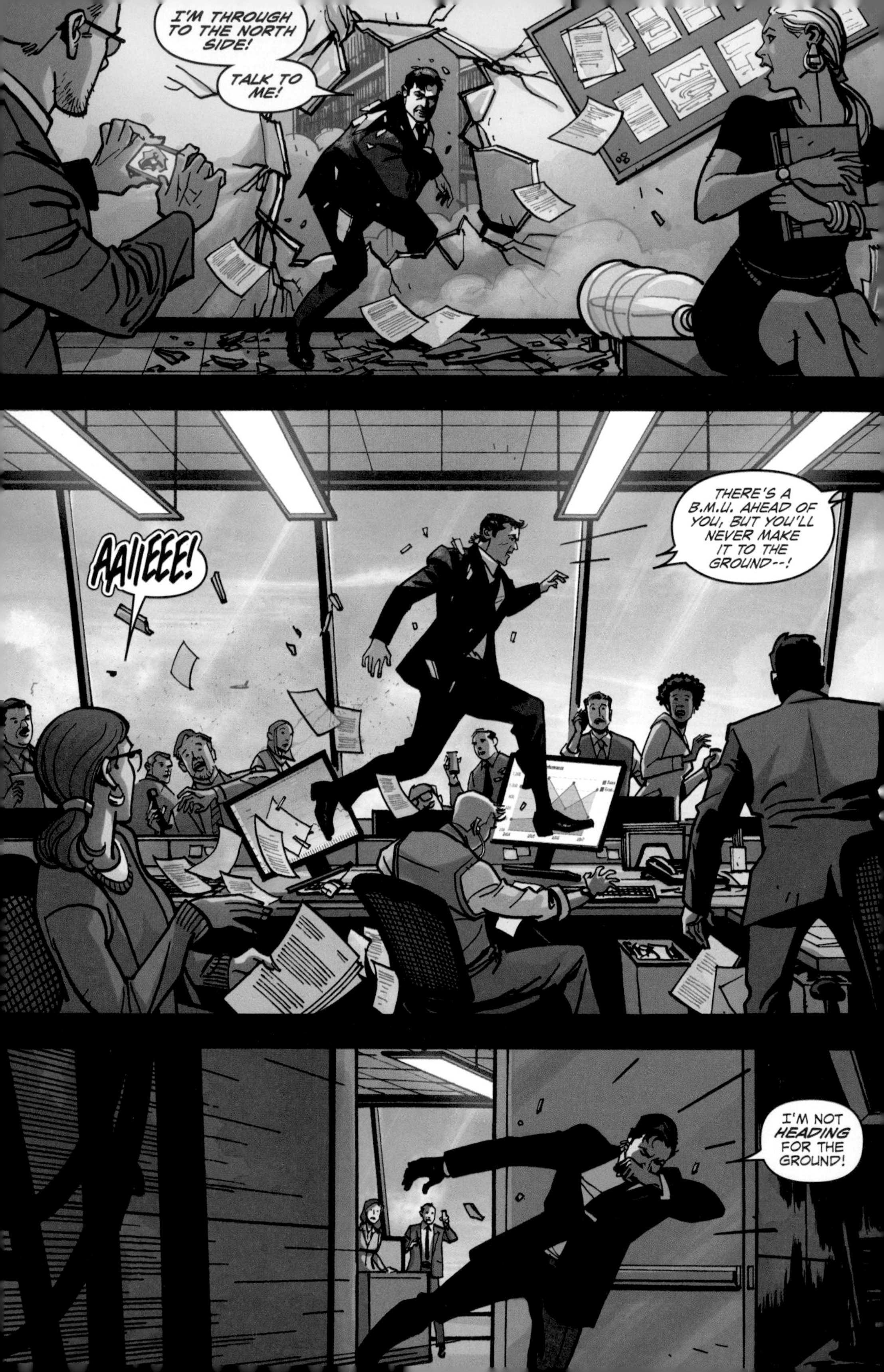
I'M THROUGH TO THE NORTH SIDE!
TALK TO ME!
AAIIEEE!
THERE'S A B.M.U. AHEAD OF YOU, BUT YOU'LL NEVER MAKE IT TO THE GROUND--!
I'M NOT HEADING FOR THE GROUND!

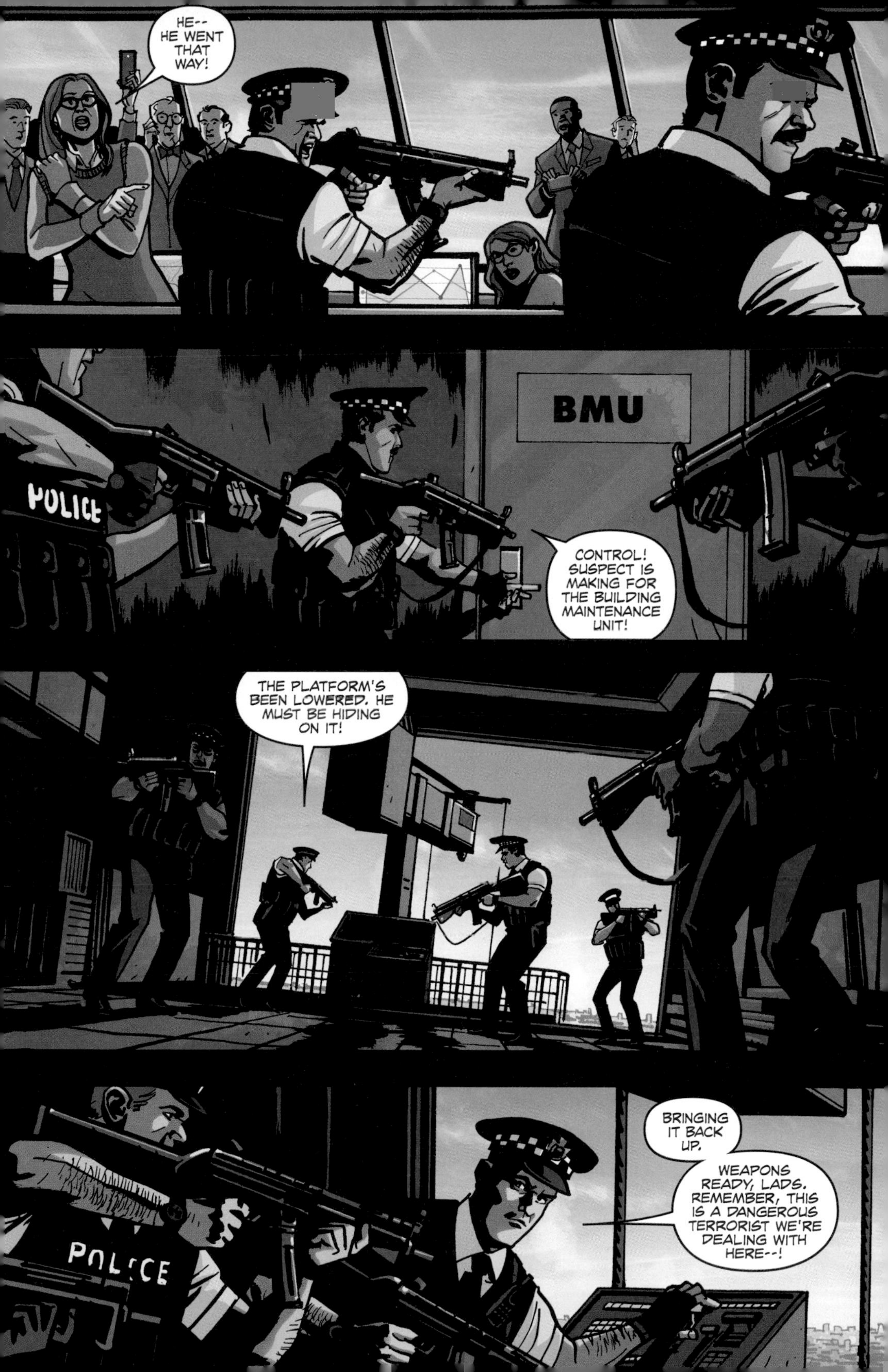
HE-- HE WENT THAT WAY!
BMU
POLICE
CONTROL! SUSPECT IS MAKING FOR THE BUILDING MAINTENANCE UNIT!
THE PLATFORM'S BEEN LOWERED. HE MUST BE HIDING ON IT!
POLICE
BRINGING IT BACK UP.
WEAPONS READY, LADS. REMEMBER, THIS IS A DANGEROUS TERRORIST WE'RE DEALING WITH HERE--!

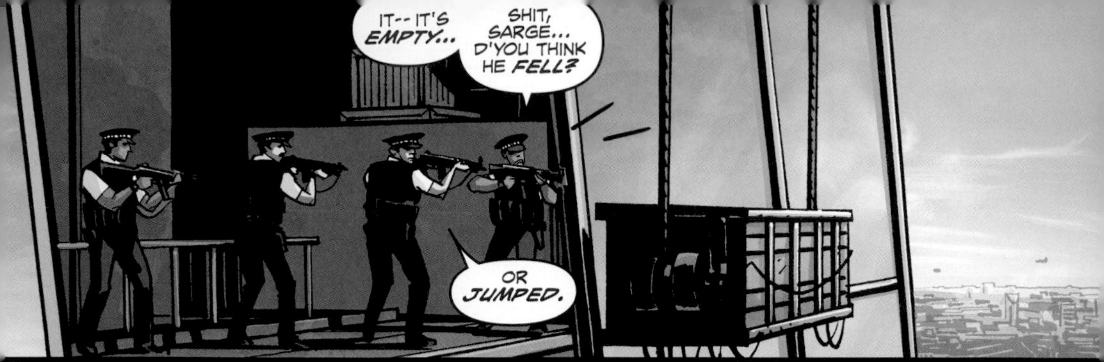

IT-- IT'S *EMPTY...*
SHIT, SARGE... D'YOU THINK HE *FELL?*
OR *JUMPED.*

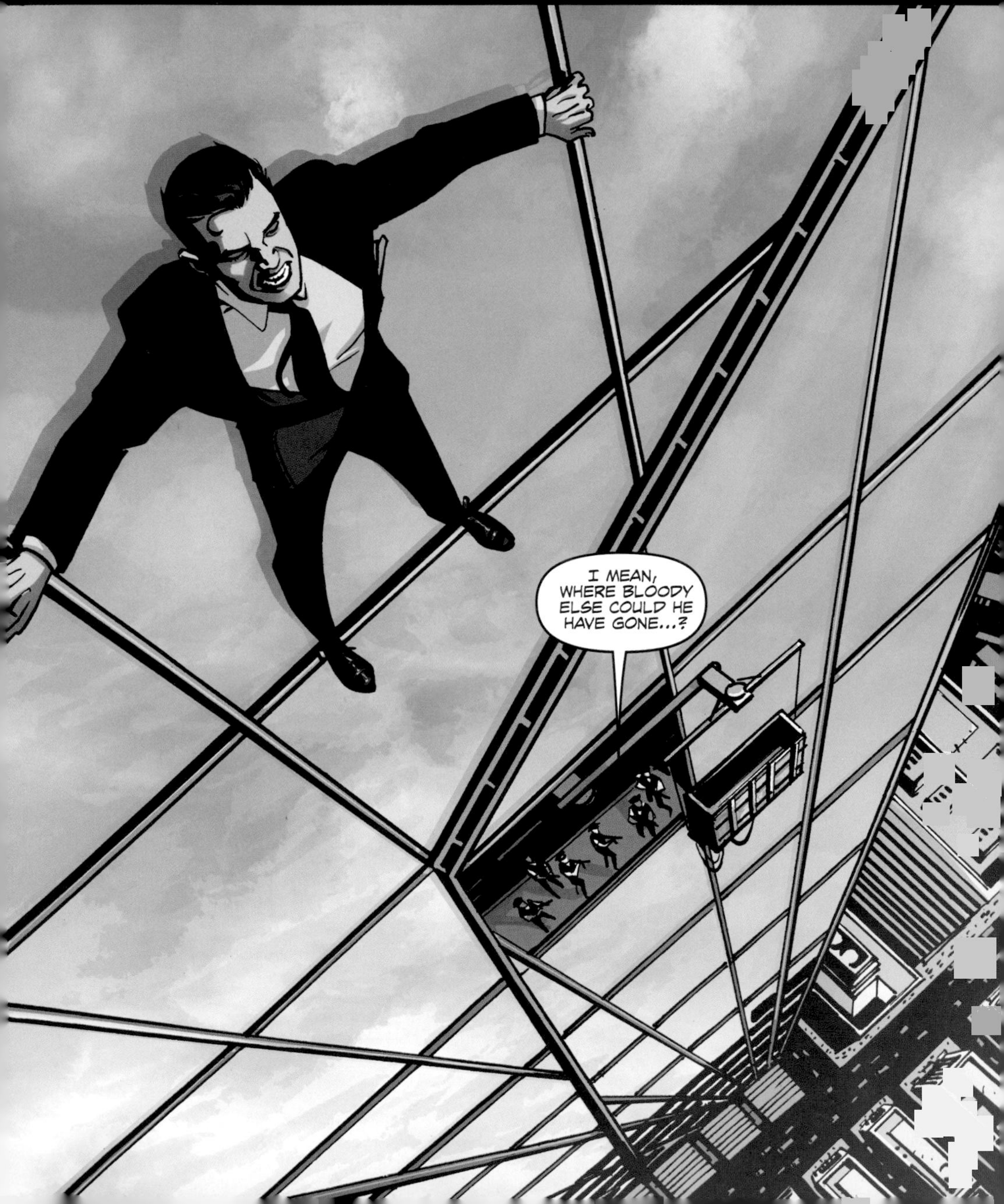

I MEAN, WHERE BLOODY ELSE COULD HE HAVE GONE...?

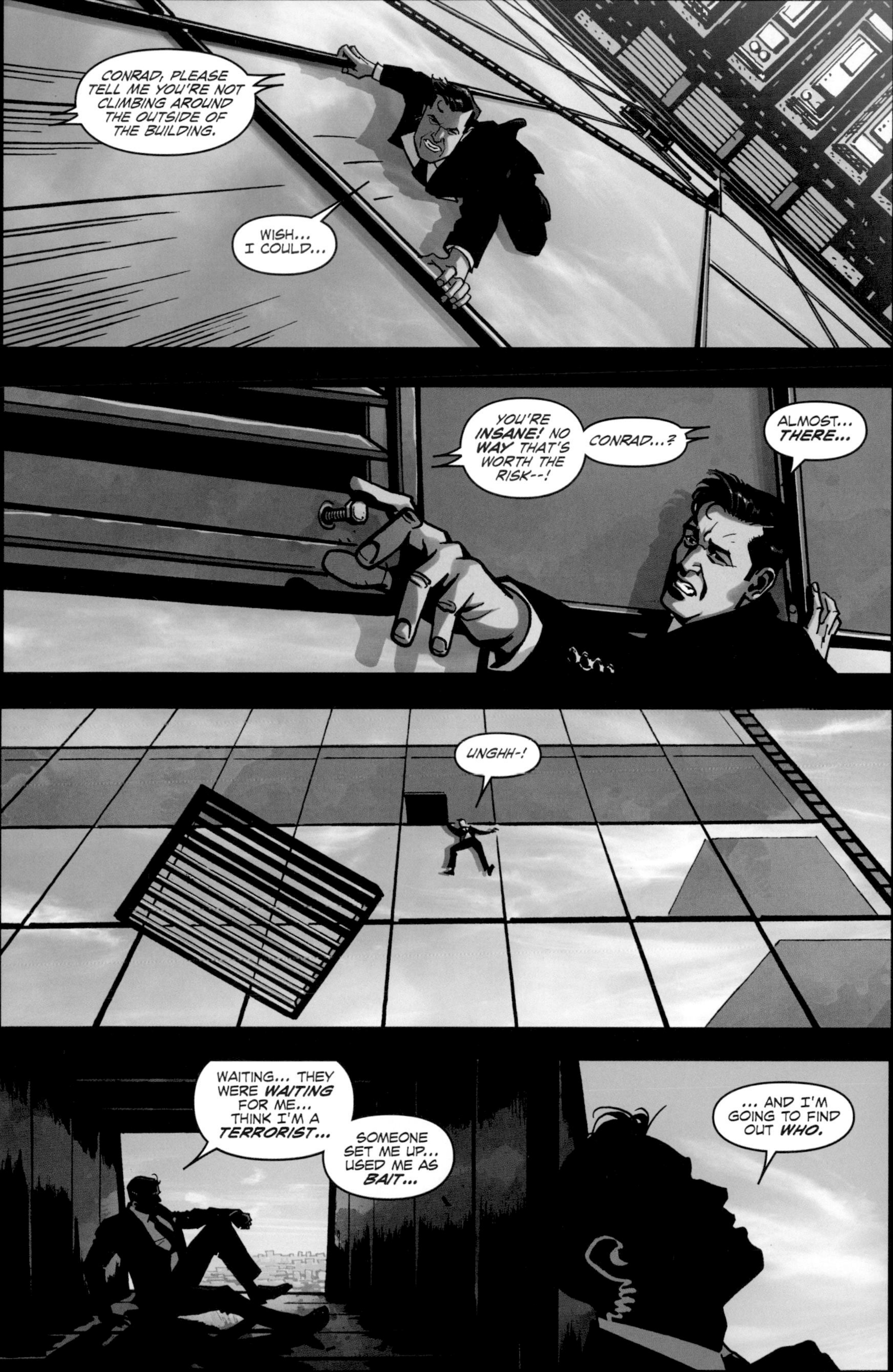
CONRAD, PLEASE TELL ME YOU'RE NOT CLIMBING AROUND THE OUTSIDE OF THE BUILDING.
WISH... I COULD...
YOU'RE INSANE! NO WAY THAT'S WORTH THE RISK--!
CONRAD...?
ALMOST... THERE...
UNGHH-!
WAITING... THEY WERE WAITING FOR ME... THINK I'M A TERRORIST...
SOMEONE SET ME UP... USED ME AS BAIT...
... AND I'M GOING TO FIND OUT WHO.

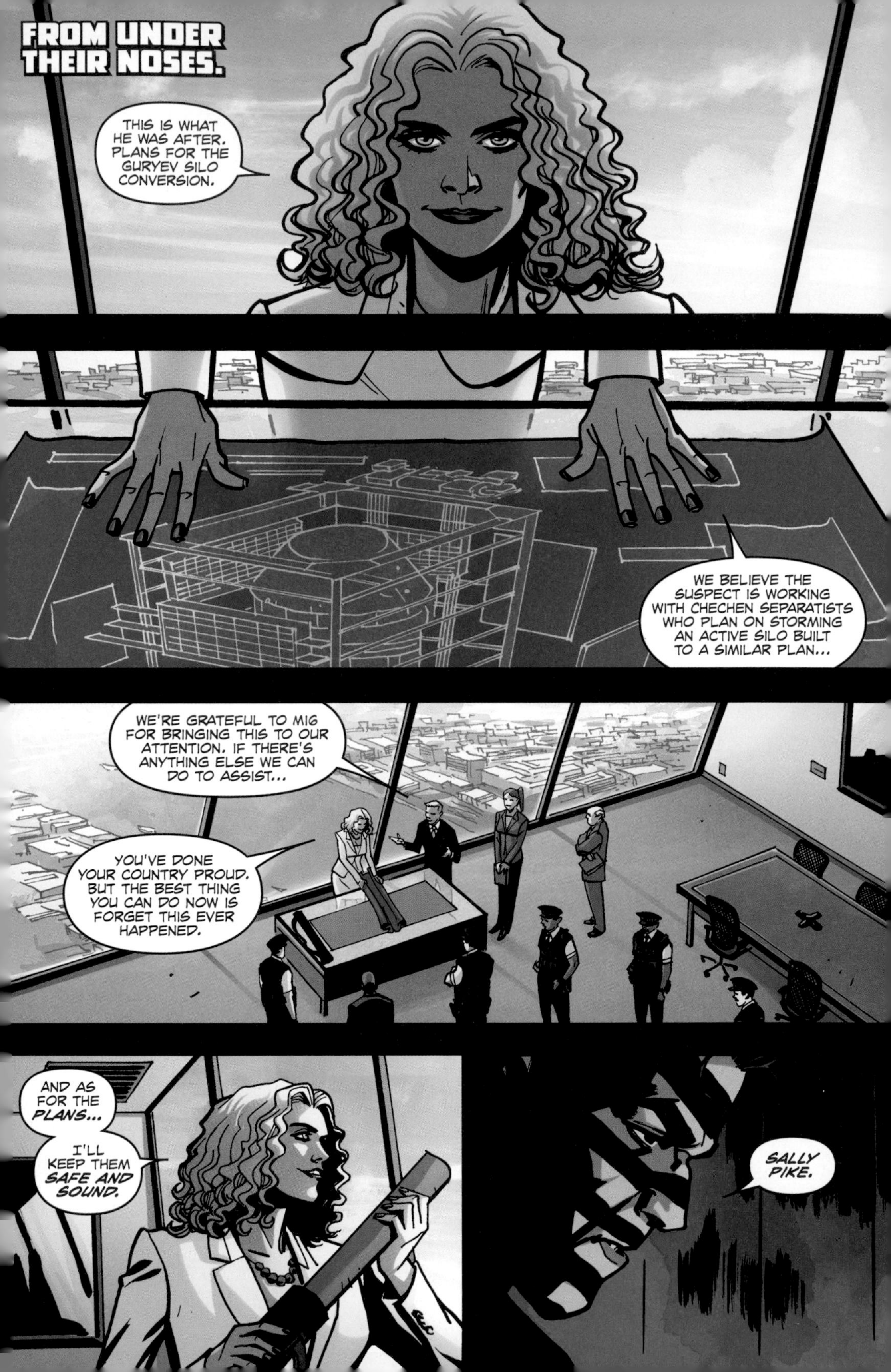
FROM UNDER THEIR NOSES.
THIS IS WHAT HE WAS AFTER. PLANS FOR THE GURYEV SILO CONVERSION.
WE BELIEVE THE SUSPECT IS WORKING WITH CHECHEN SEPARATISTS WHO PLAN ON STORMING AN ACTIVE SILO BUILT TO A SIMILAR PLAN...
WE'RE GRATEFUL TO MI6 FOR BRINGING THIS TO OUR ATTENTION. IF THERE'S ANYTHING ELSE WE CAN DO TO ASSIST...
YOU'VE DONE YOUR COUNTRY PROUD. BUT THE BEST THING YOU CAN DO NOW IS FORGET THIS EVER HAPPENED.
AND AS FOR THE *PLANS*...
I'LL KEEP THEM *SAFE AND SOUND.*
SALLY PIKE.

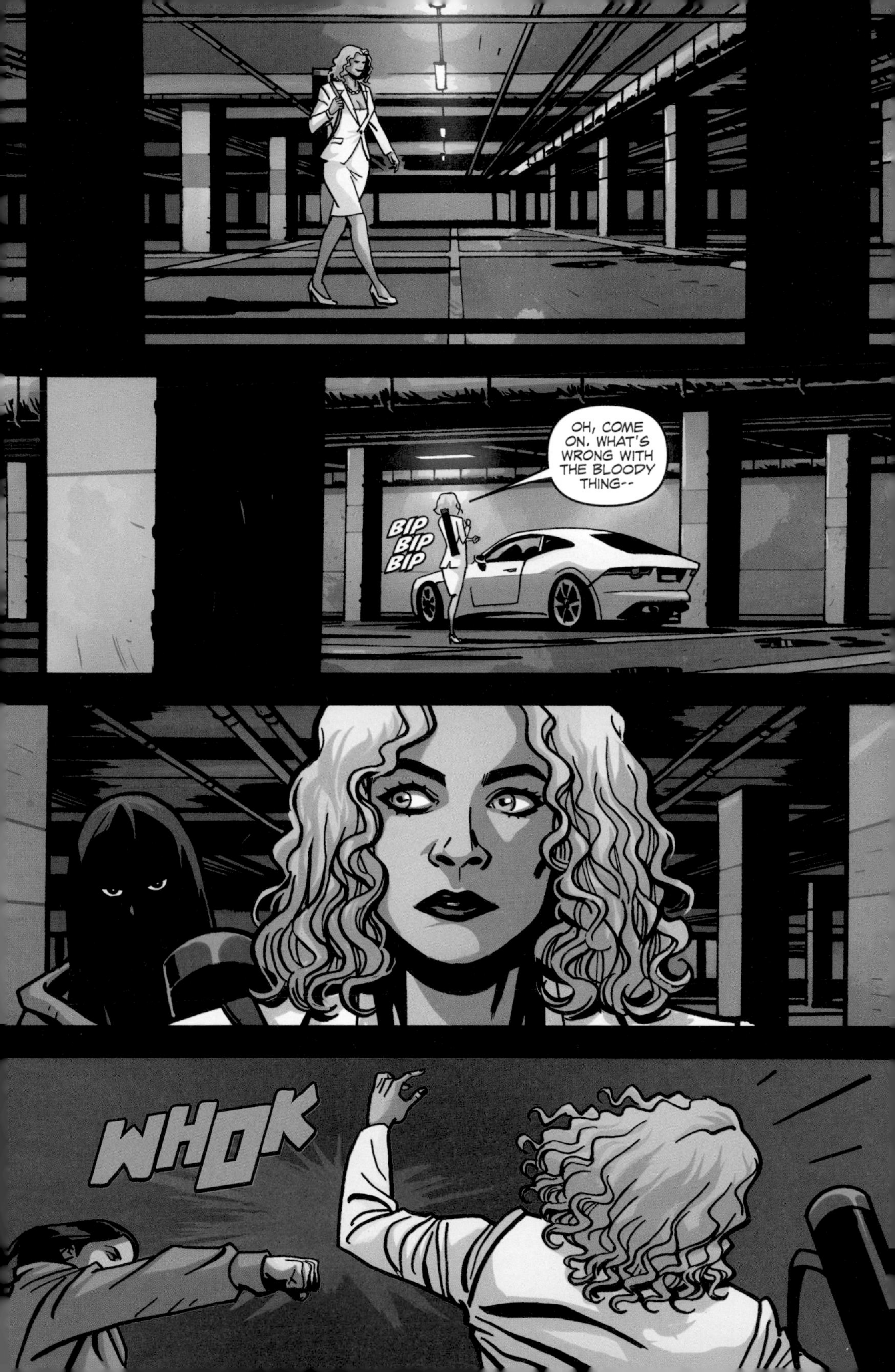
OH, COME ON. WHAT'S WRONG WITH THE BLOODY THING--
BIP BIP BIP
WHOK

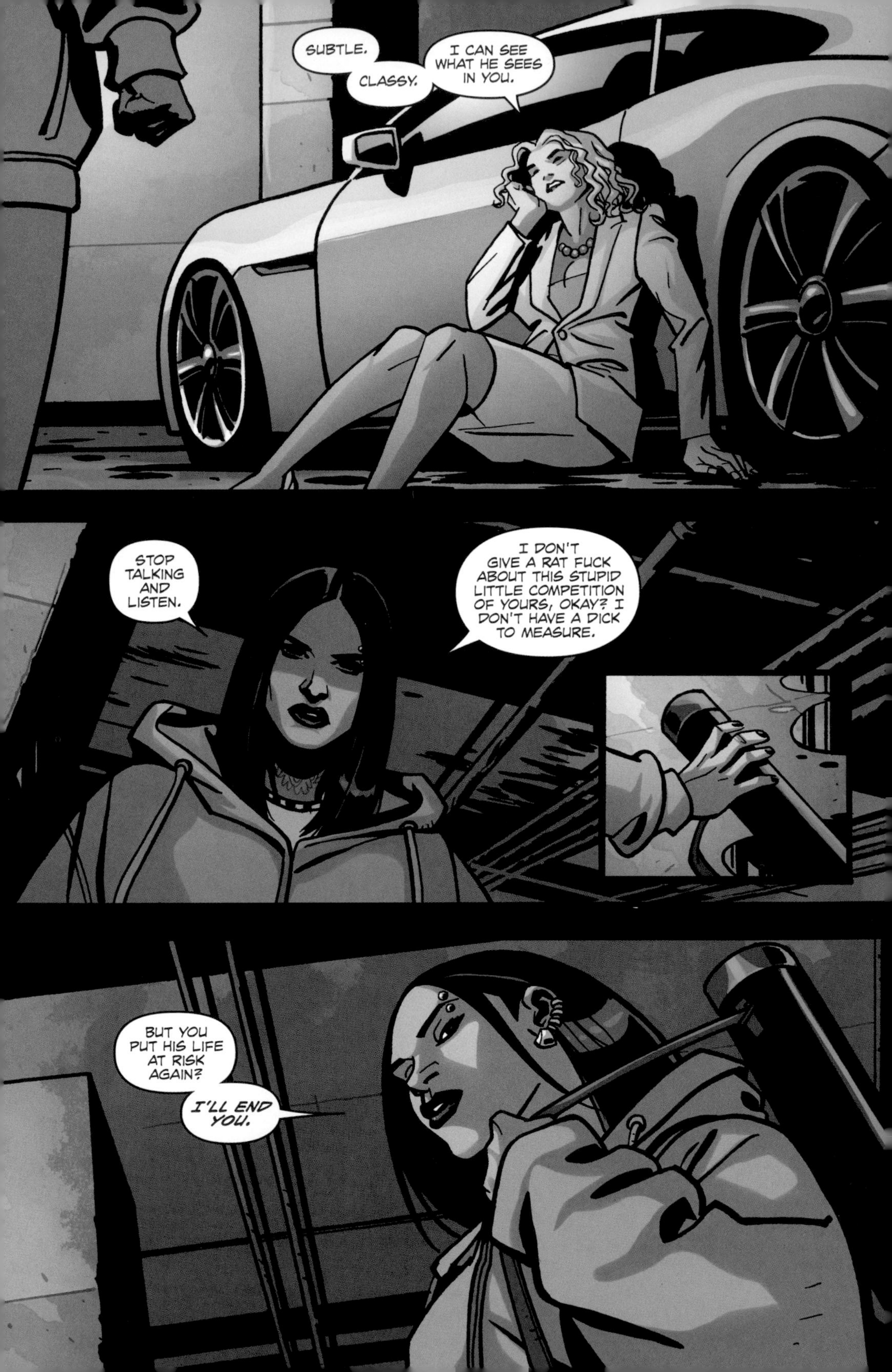
SUBTLE.
CLASSY.
I CAN SEE WHAT HE SEES IN YOU.
STOP TALKING AND LISTEN.
I DON'T GIVE A RAT FUCK ABOUT THIS STUPID LITTLE COMPETITION OF YOURS, OKAY? I DON'T HAVE A DICK TO MEASURE.
BUT YOU PUT HIS LIFE AT RISK AGAIN?
I'LL END YOU.

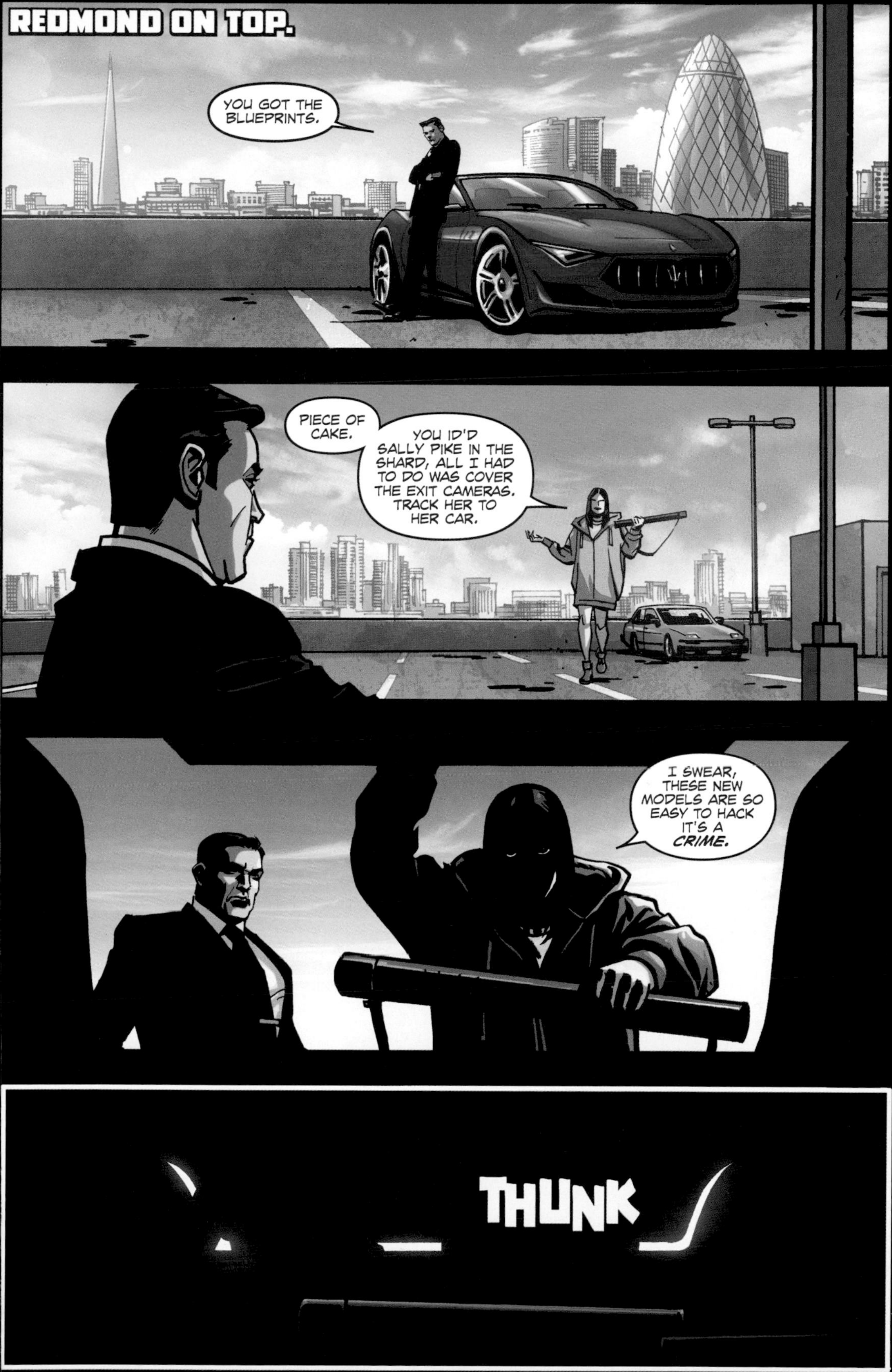
REDMOND ON TOP.
YOU GOT THE BLUEPRINTS.
PIECE OF CAKE.
YOU ID'D SALLY PIKE IN THE SHARD, ALL I HAD TO DO WAS COVER THE EXIT CAMERAS. TRACK HER TO HER CAR.
I SWEAR, THESE NEW MODELS ARE SO EASY TO HACK IT'S A *CRIME*.
THUNK

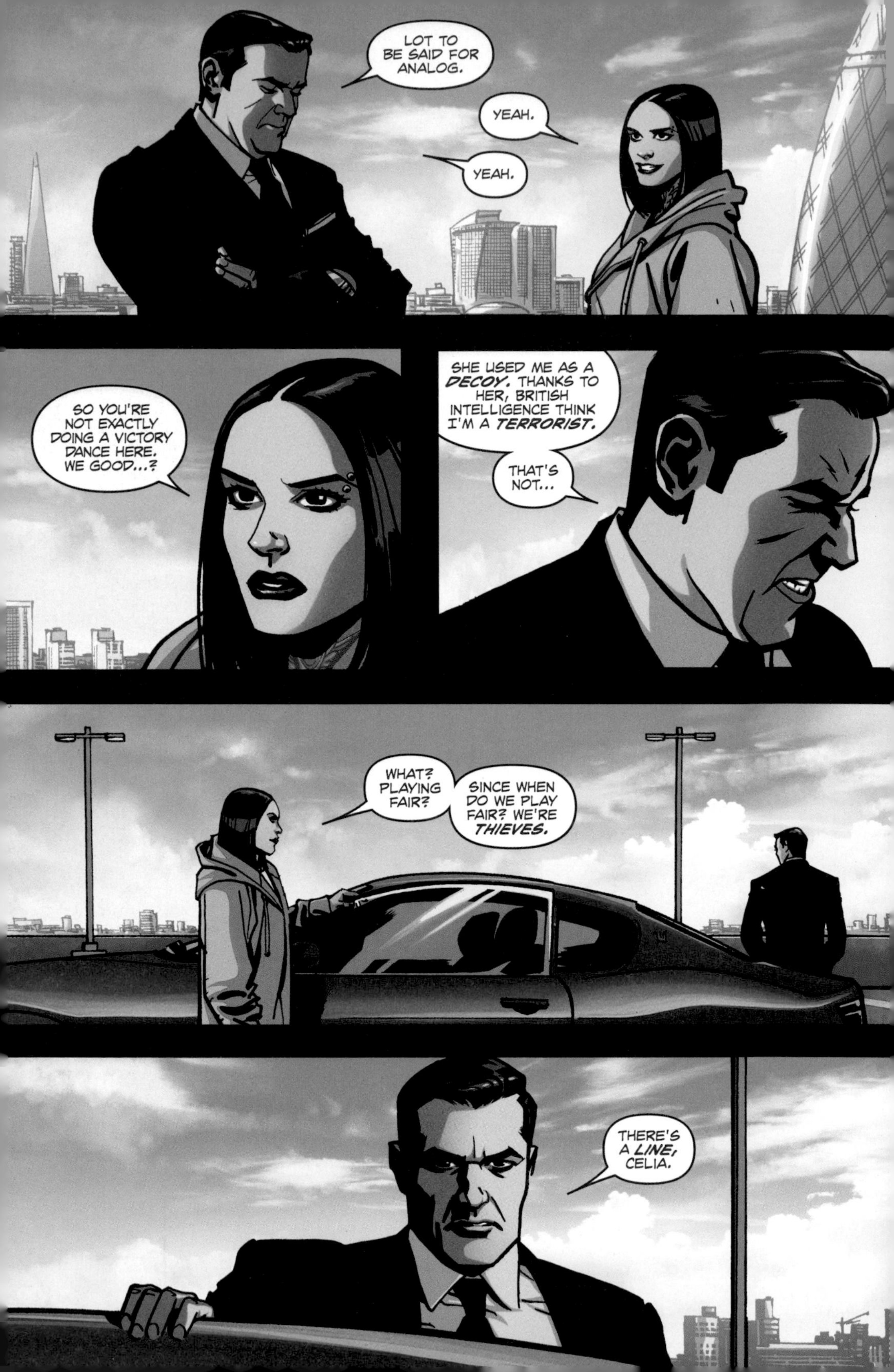
LOT TO BE SAID FOR ANALOG.
YEAH.
YEAH.
SO YOU'RE NOT EXACTLY DOING A VICTORY DANCE HERE. WE GOOD...?
SHE USED ME AS A *DECOY.* THANKS TO HER, BRITISH INTELLIGENCE THINK I'M A *TERRORIST.*
THAT'S NOT...
WHAT? PLAYING FAIR?
SINCE WHEN DO WE PLAY FAIR? WE'RE *THIEVES.*
THERE'S A *LINE,* CELIA.

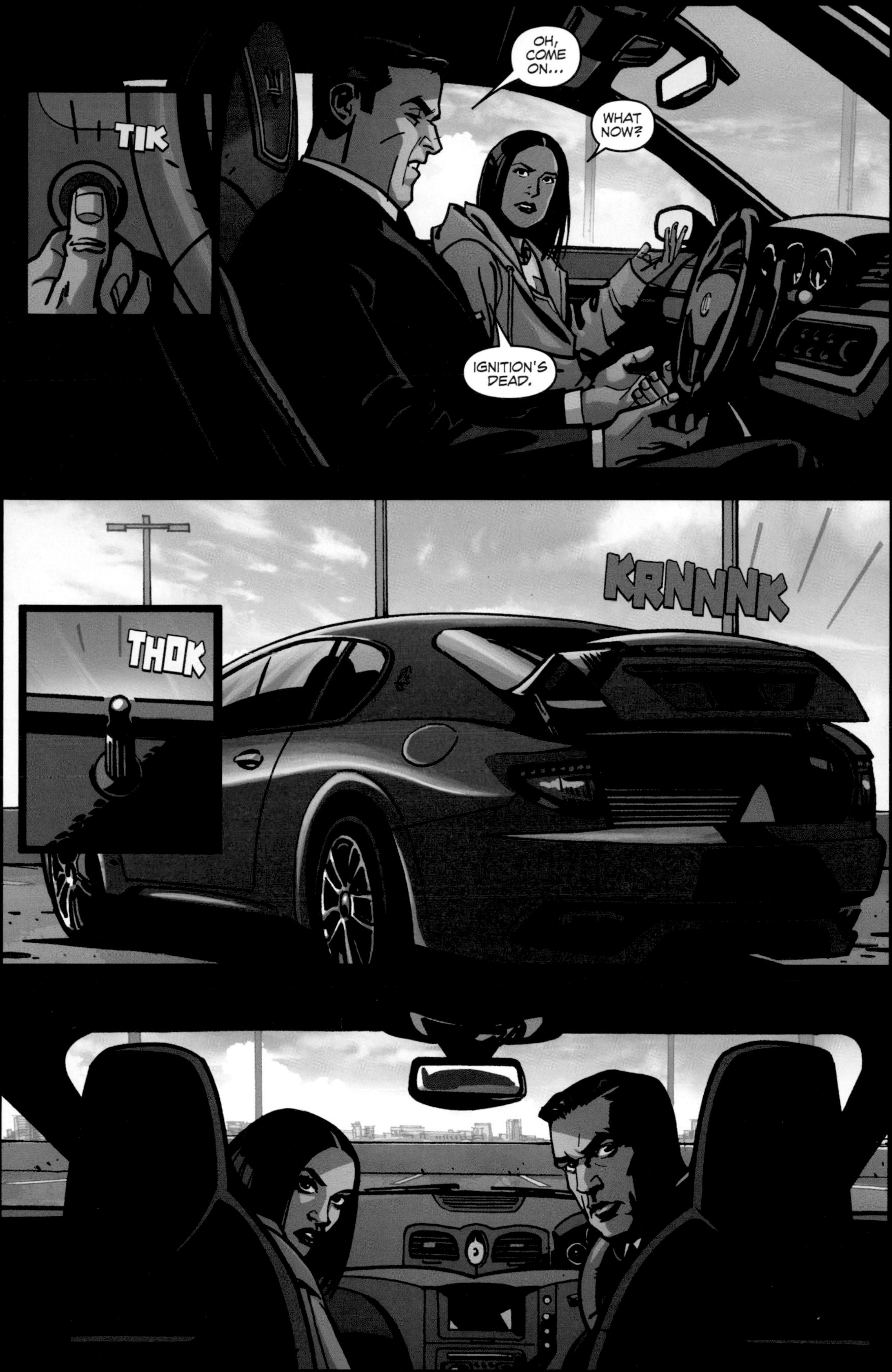
TIK
OH, COME ON...
WHAT NOW?
IGNITION'S DEAD.
THOK
KRNNNK

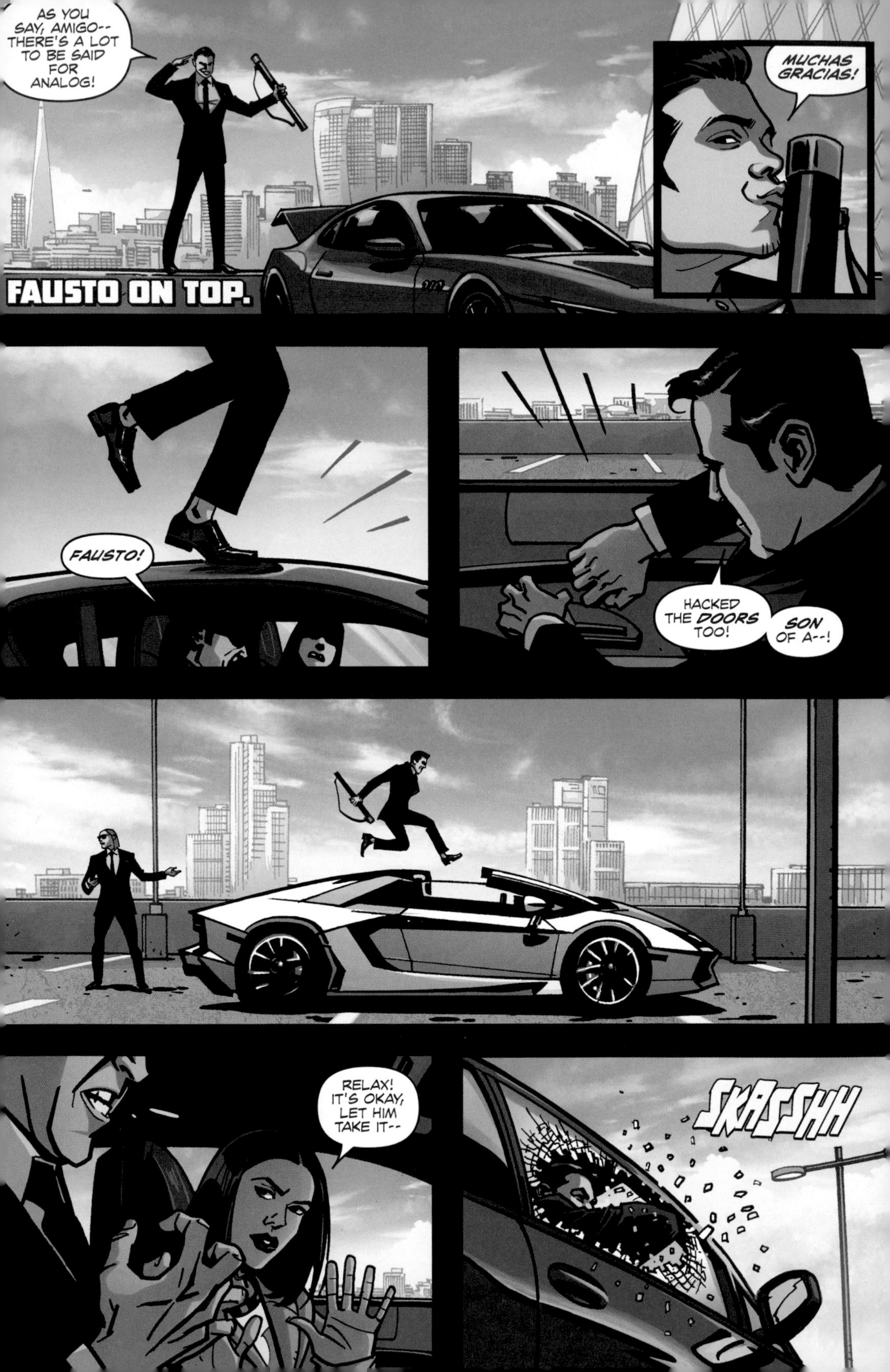
AS YOU SAY, AMIGO-- THERE'S A LOT TO BE SAID FOR ANALOG!
FAUSTO ON TOP.
MUCHAS GRACIAS!
FAUSTO!
HACKED THE DOORS TOO!
SON OF A--!
RELAX! IT'S OKAY, LET HIM TAKE IT--
SKASSHH

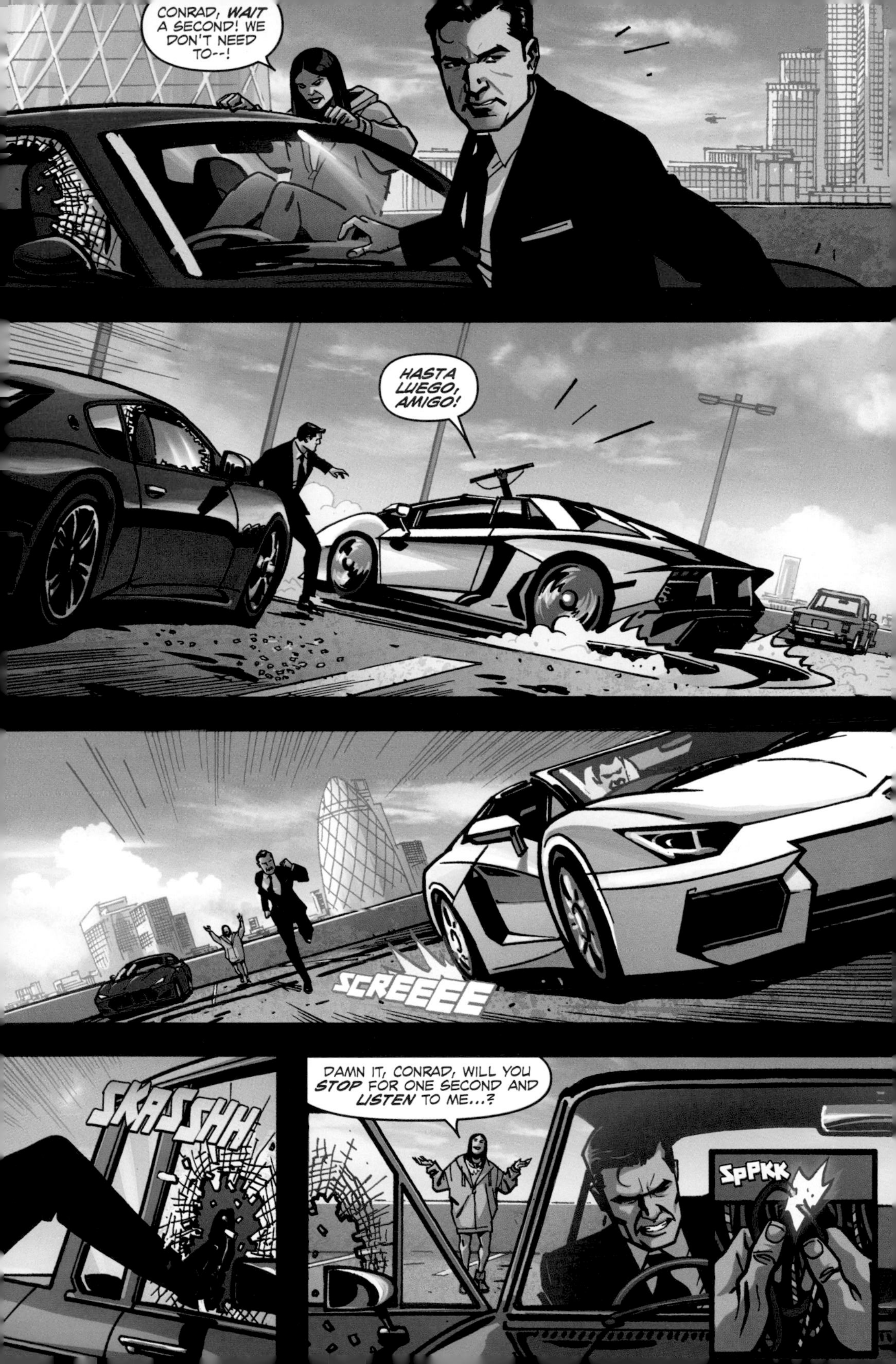
CONRAD, WAIT A SECOND! WE DON'T NEED TO--!
HASTA LUEGO, AMIGO!
SCREEEEE
SKASSHH
DAMN IT, CONRAD, WILL YOU STOP FOR ONE SECOND AND LISTEN TO ME...?
SPPKK

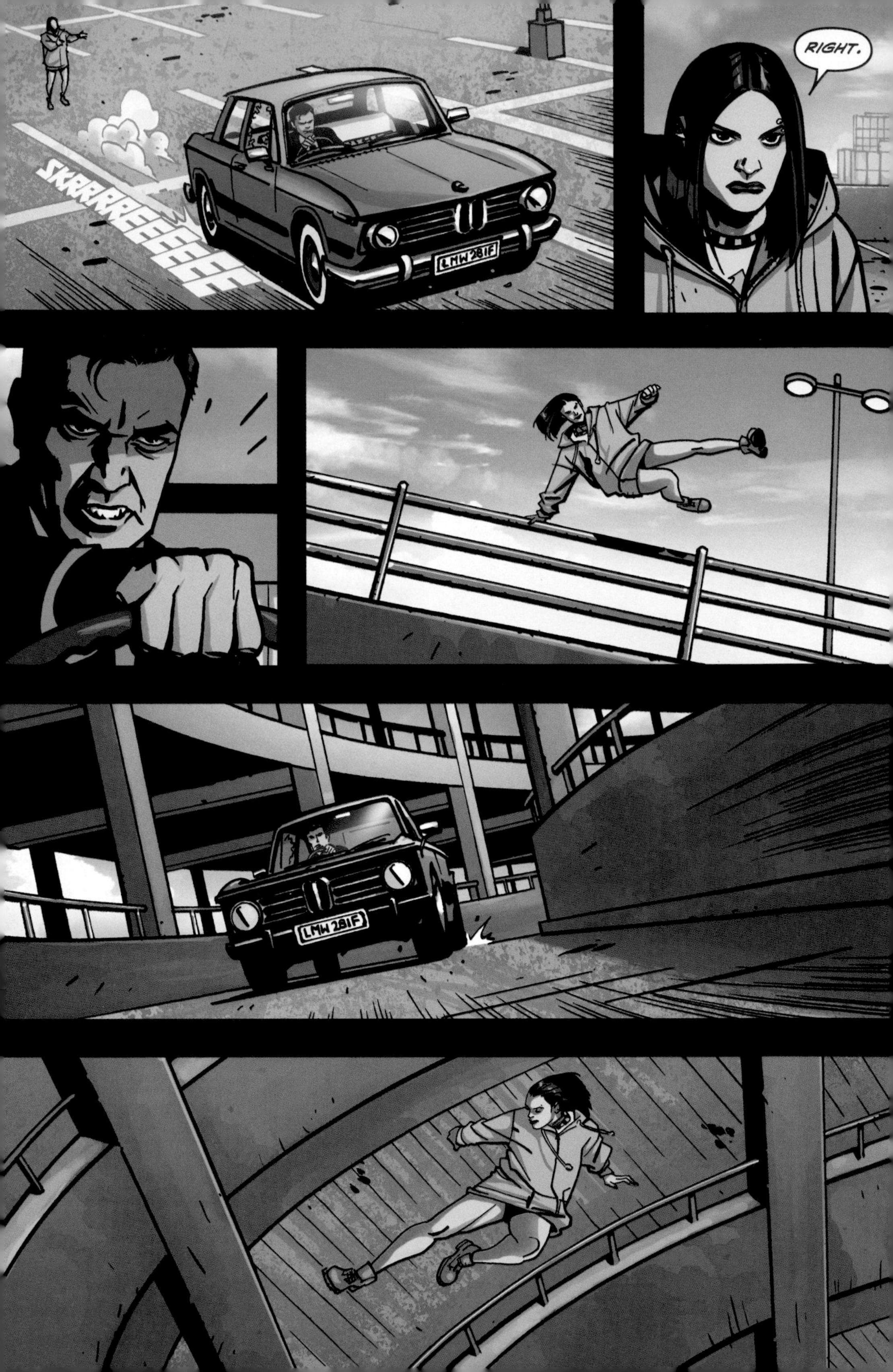
SKRRRREEEEEEE
LMW 281F
RIGHT.
LMW 281F

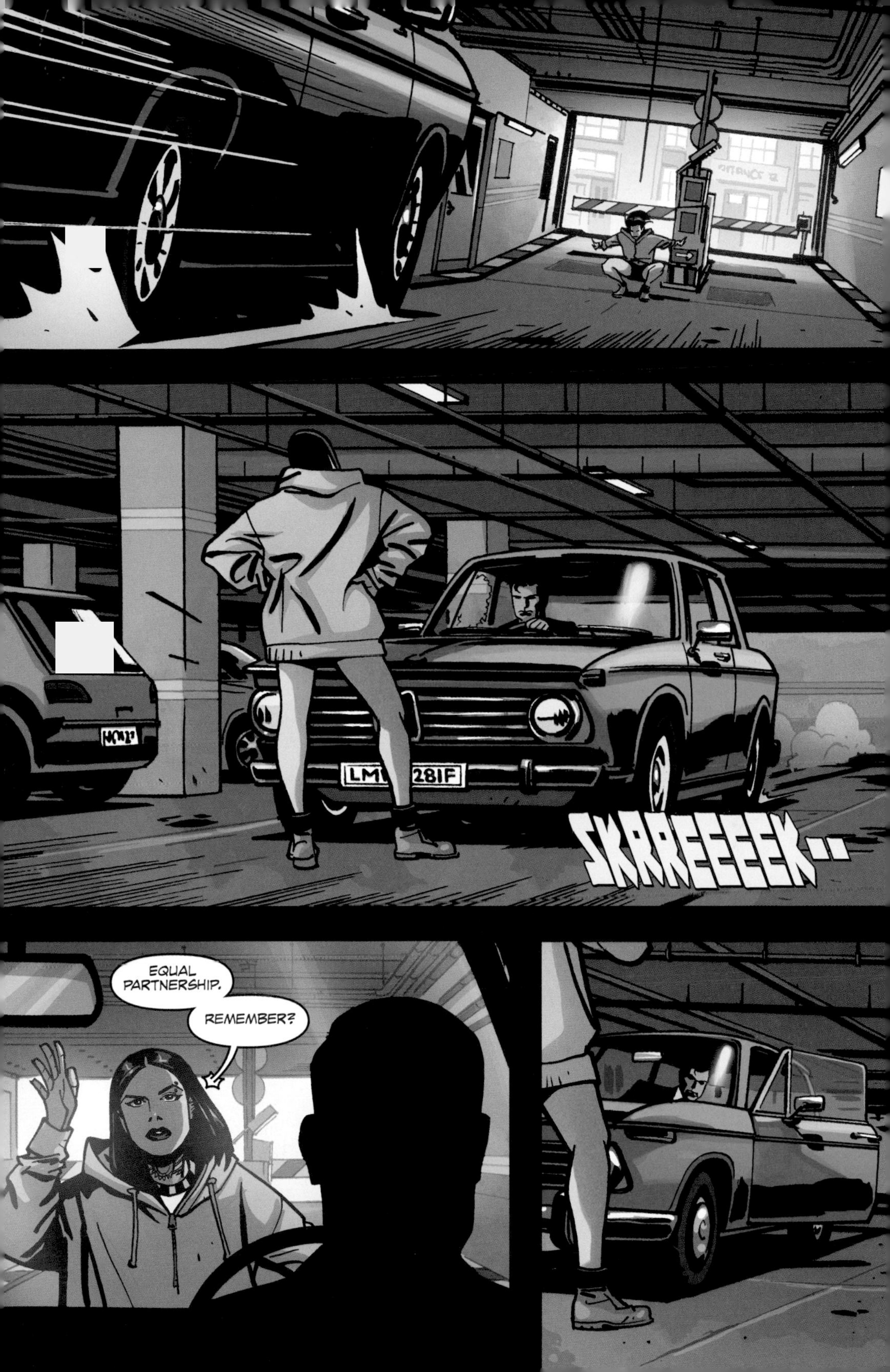
SKRREEEEEK..
EQUAL PARTNERSHIP.
REMEMBER?

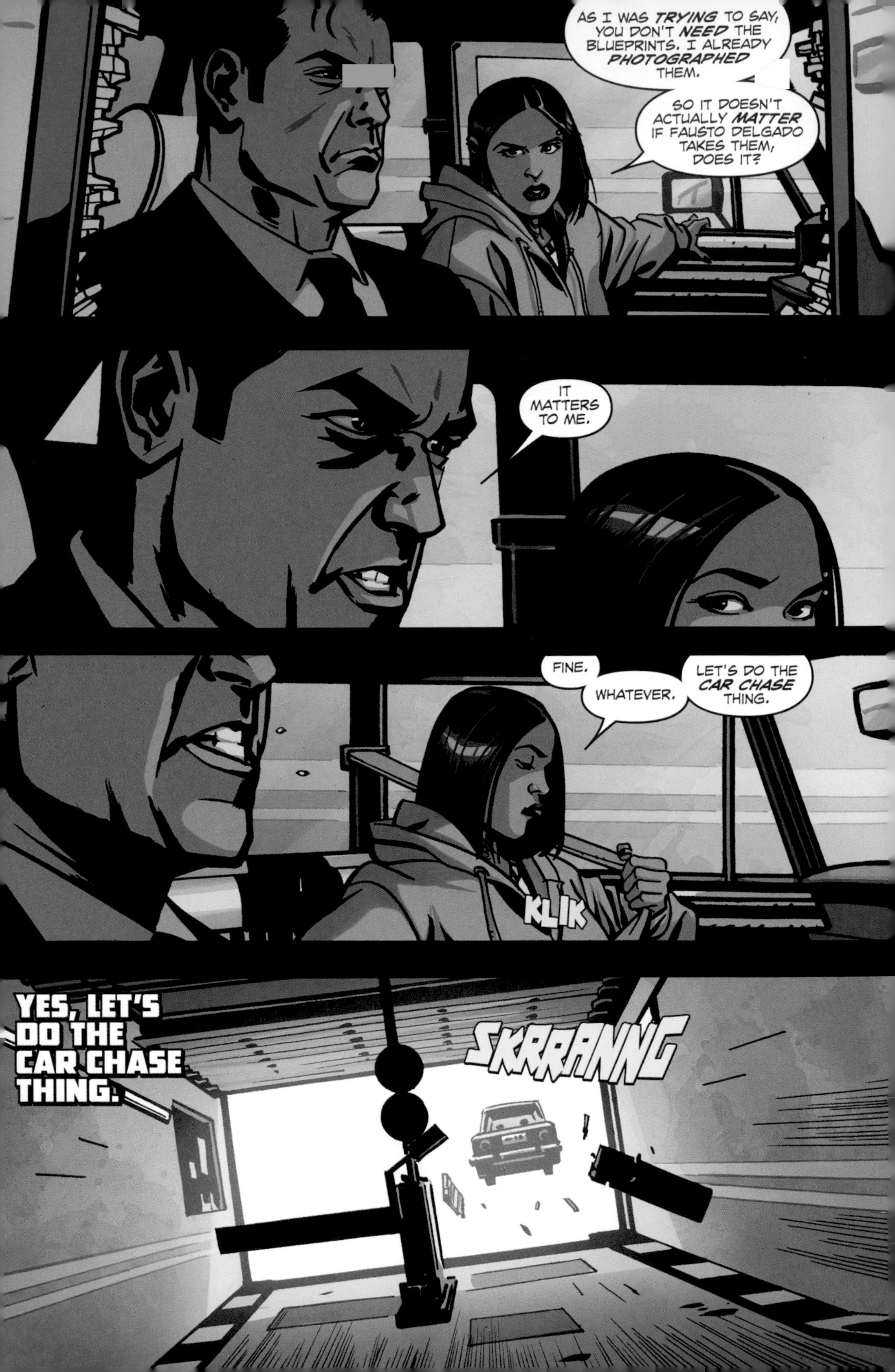

AS I WAS TRYING TO SAY, YOU DON'T NEED THE BLUEPRINTS. I ALREADY PHOTOGRAPHED THEM.
SO IT DOESN'T ACTUALLY MATTER IF FAUSTO DELGADO TAKES THEM, DOES IT?
IT MATTERS TO ME.
FINE.
WHATEVER.
LET'S DO THE CAR CHASE THING.
KLIK
YES, LET'S DO THE CAR CHASE THING.
SKRRANNG

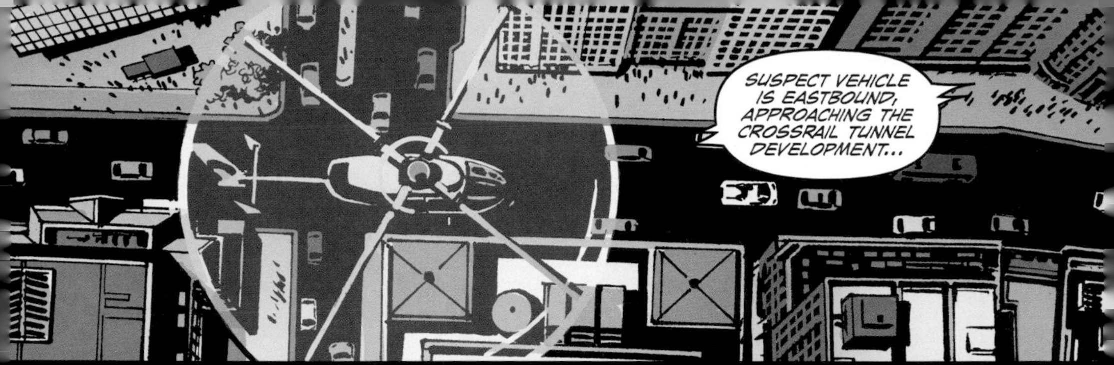
SUSPECT VEHICLE IS EASTBOUND, APPROACHING THE CROSSRAIL TUNNEL DEVELOPMENT...

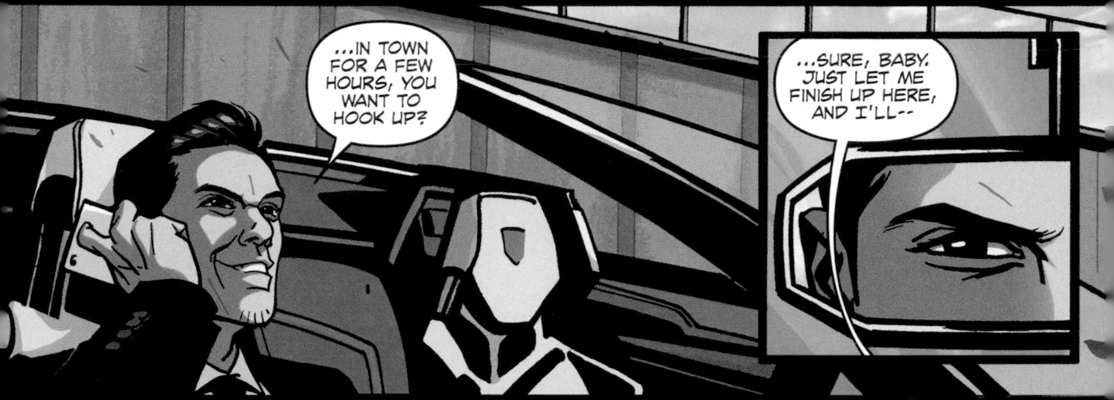
...IN TOWN FOR A FEW HOURS, YOU WANT TO HOOK UP?
...SURE, BABY. JUST LET ME FINISH UP HERE, AND I'LL--

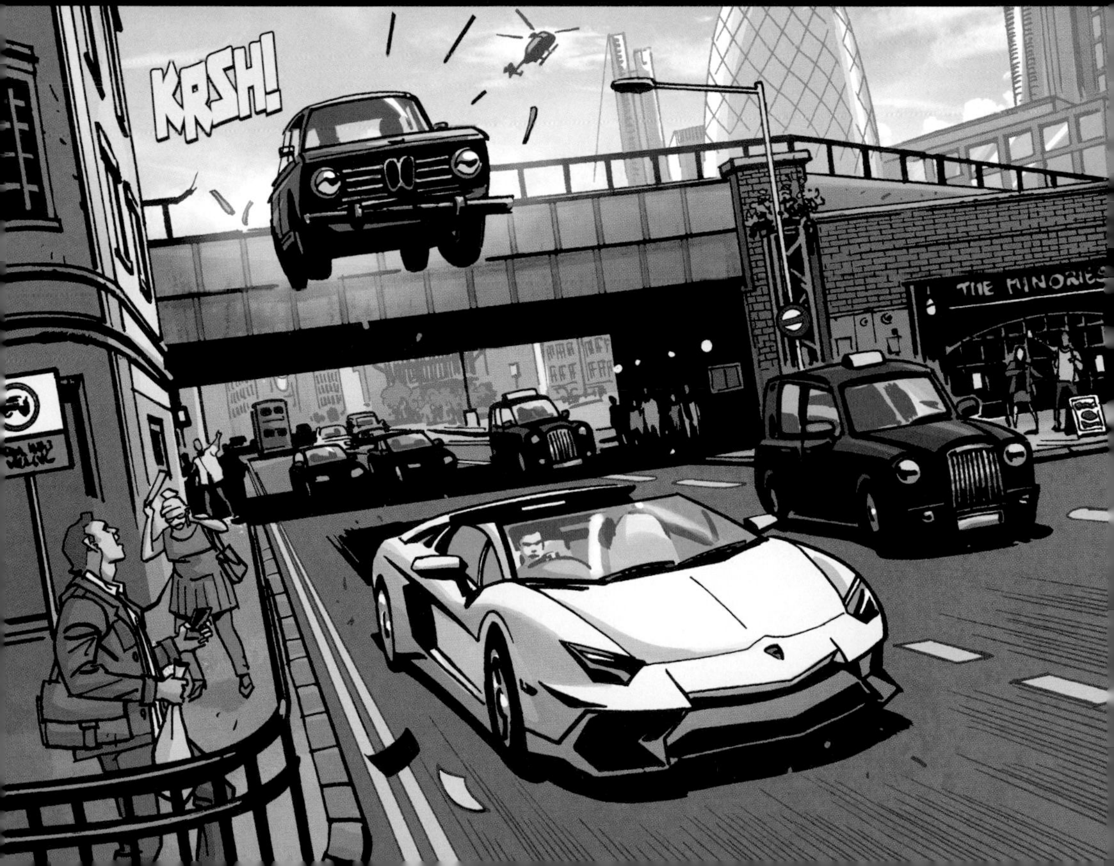
KRSH!
THE MINORIES

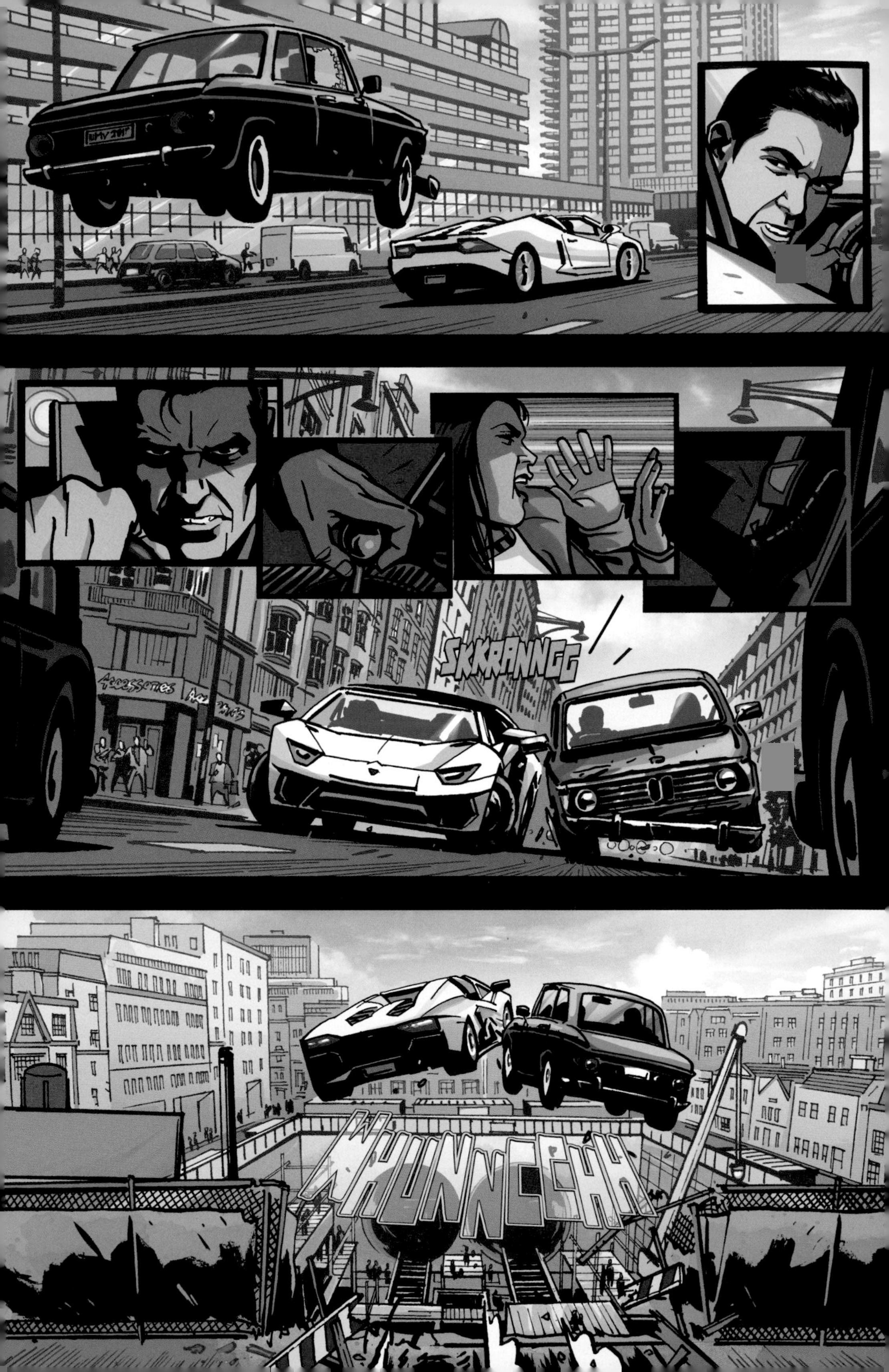
Accessories
SKKRANNGG
WHUNNCEHH

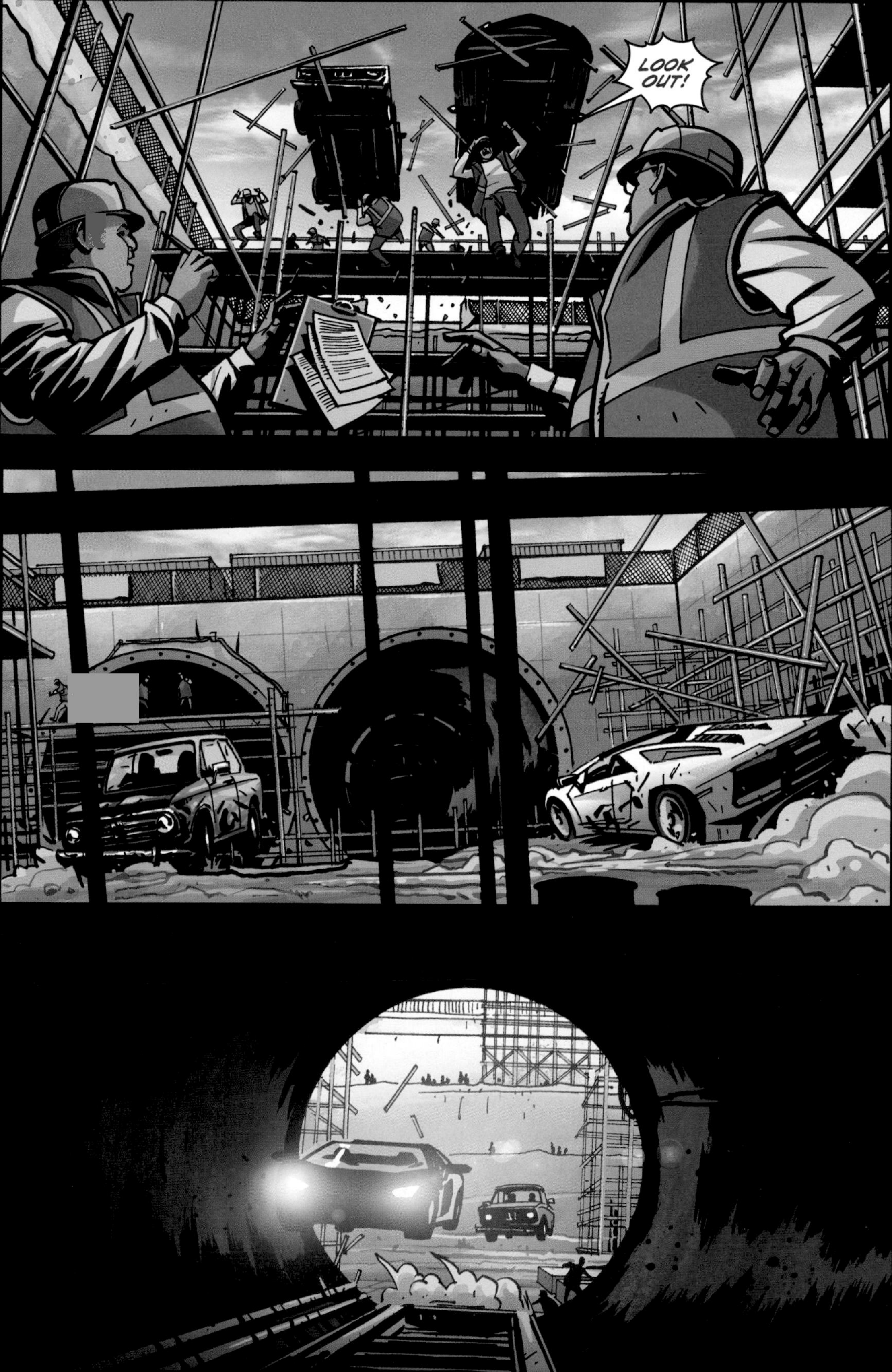
LOOK OUT!

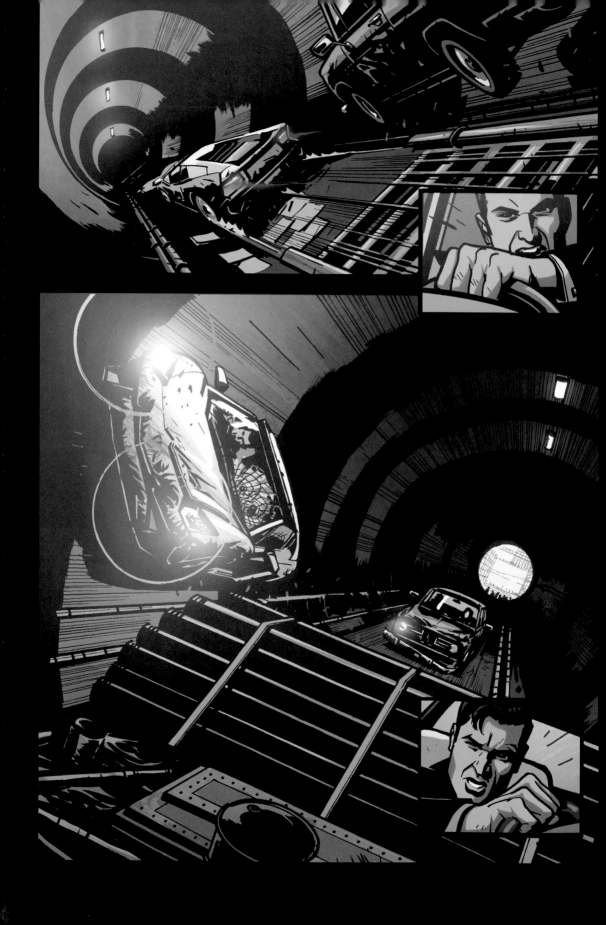

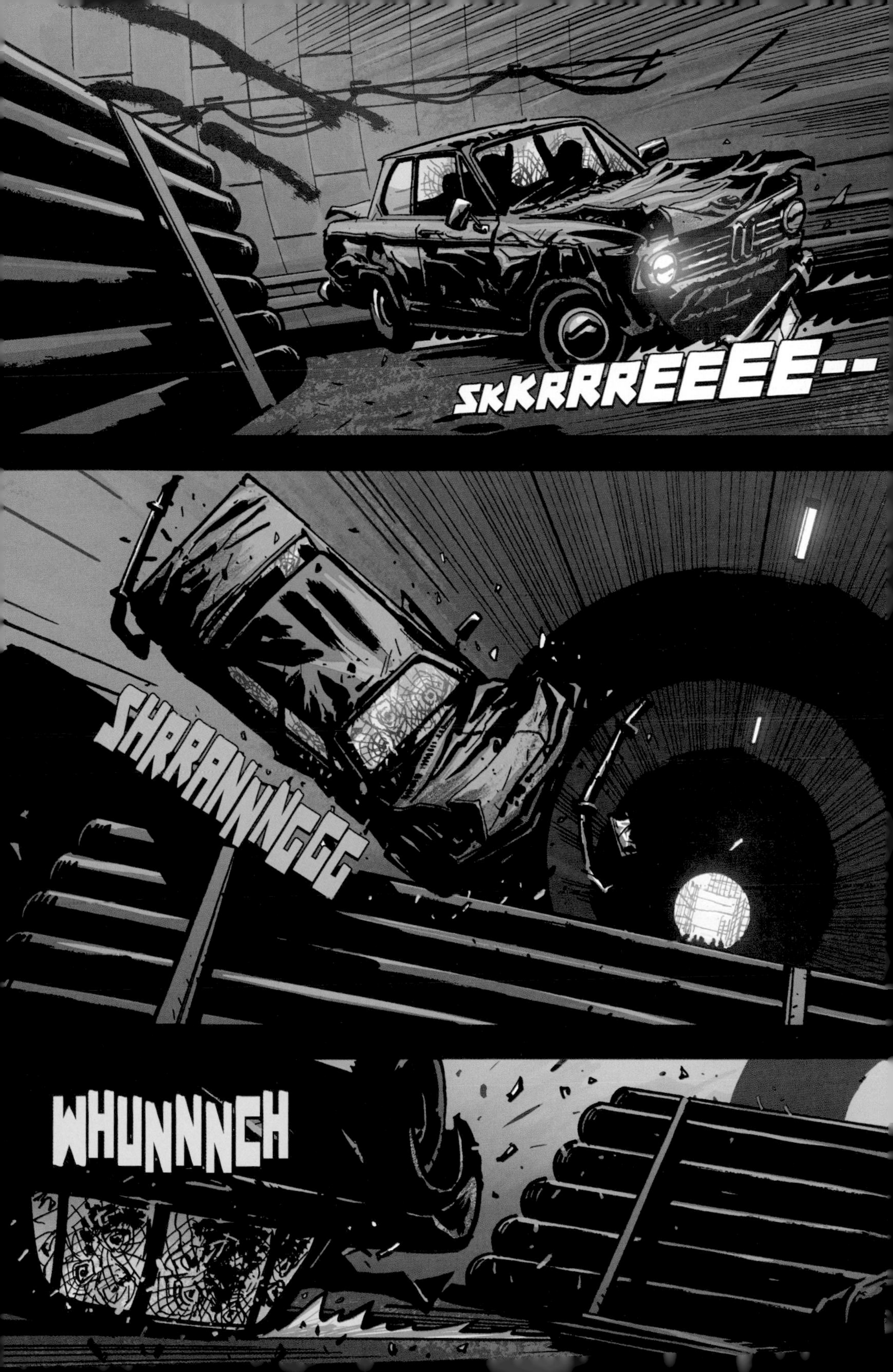
SKKRRREEEE--
SHRRANNNNGGG
WHUNNNCH

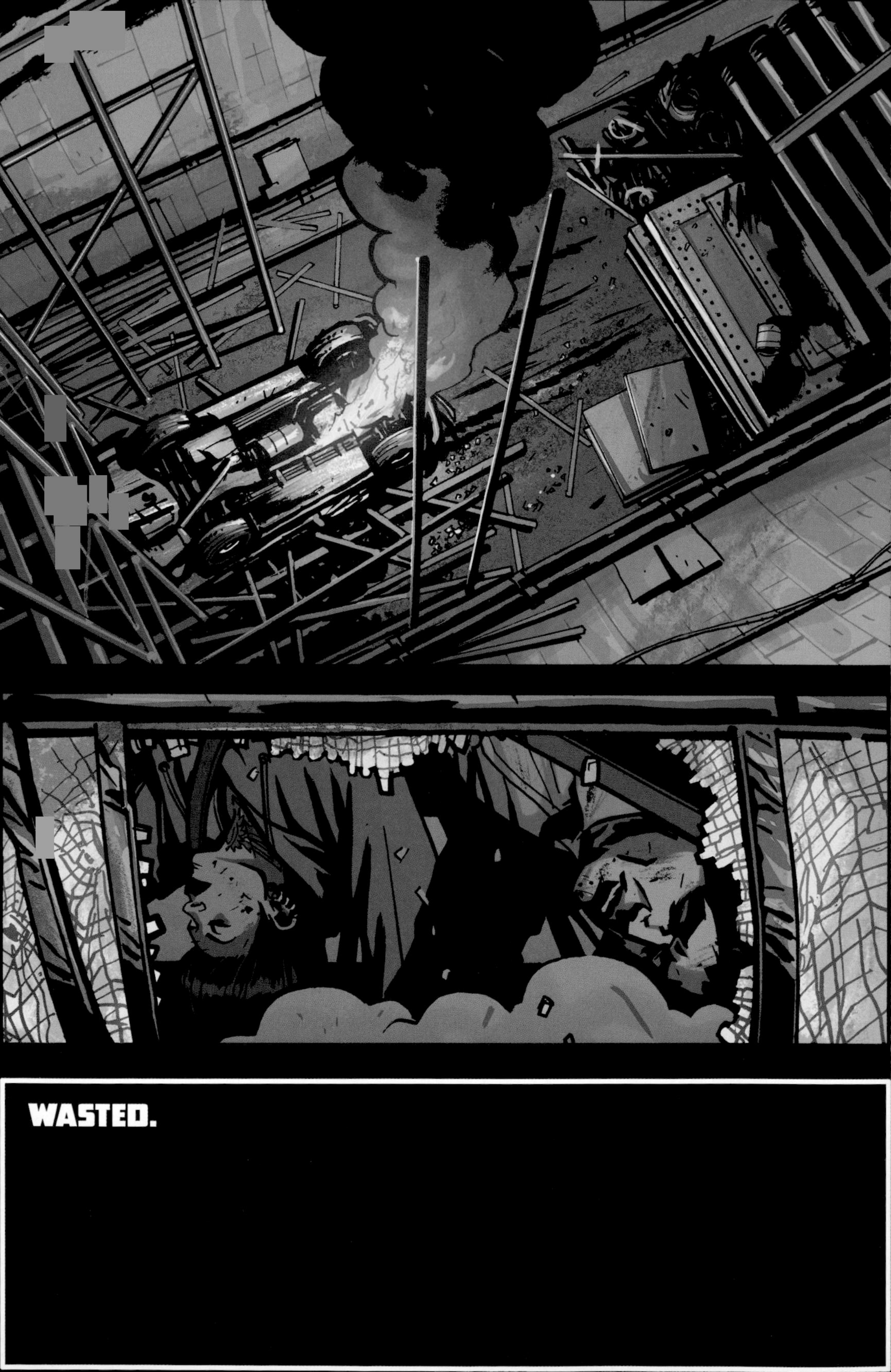
WASTED.

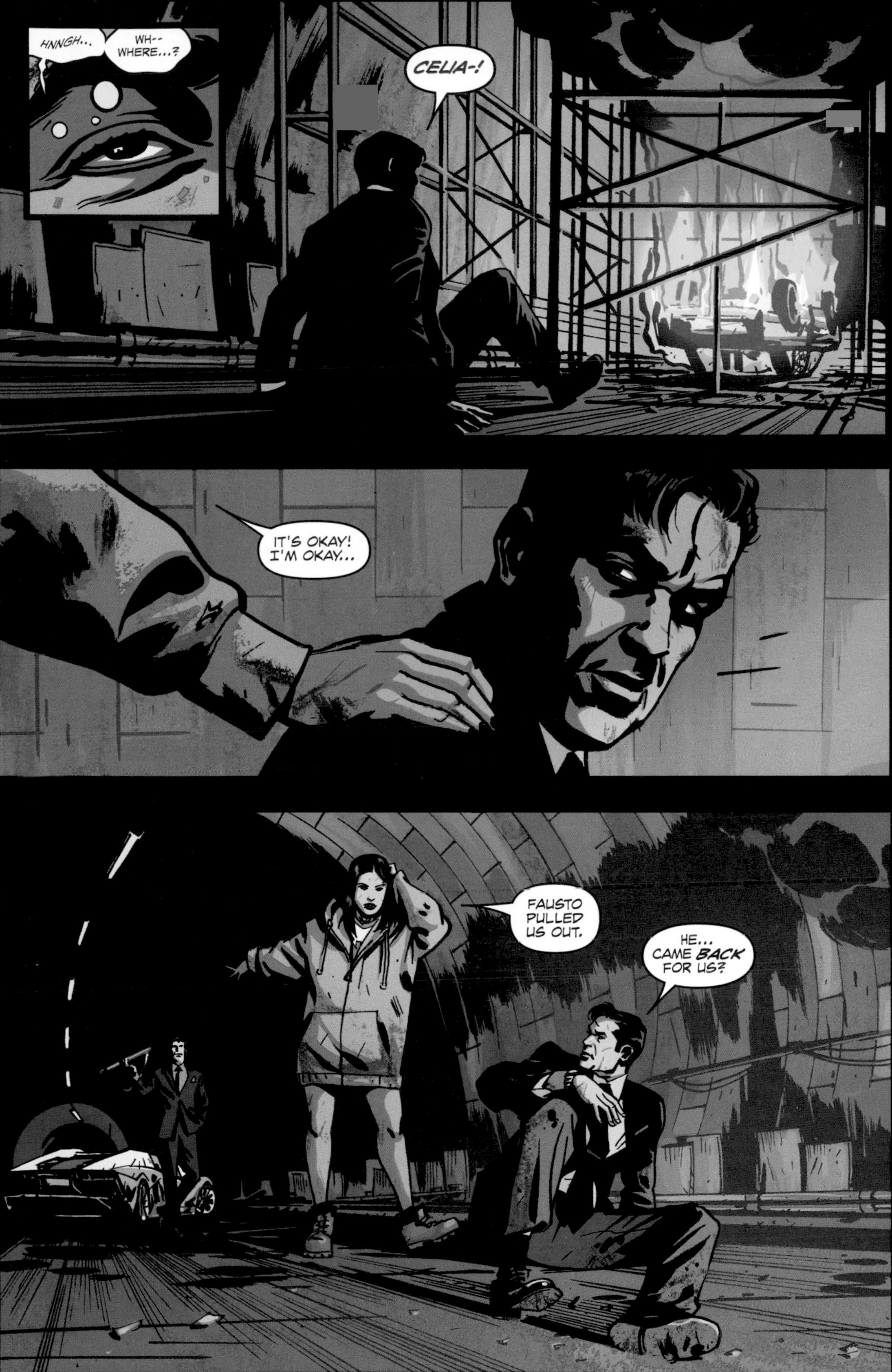
HNNGH...
WH-- WHERE...?
CELIA-!
IT'S OKAY! I'M OKAY...
FAUSTO PULLED US OUT.
HE... CAME BACK FOR US?

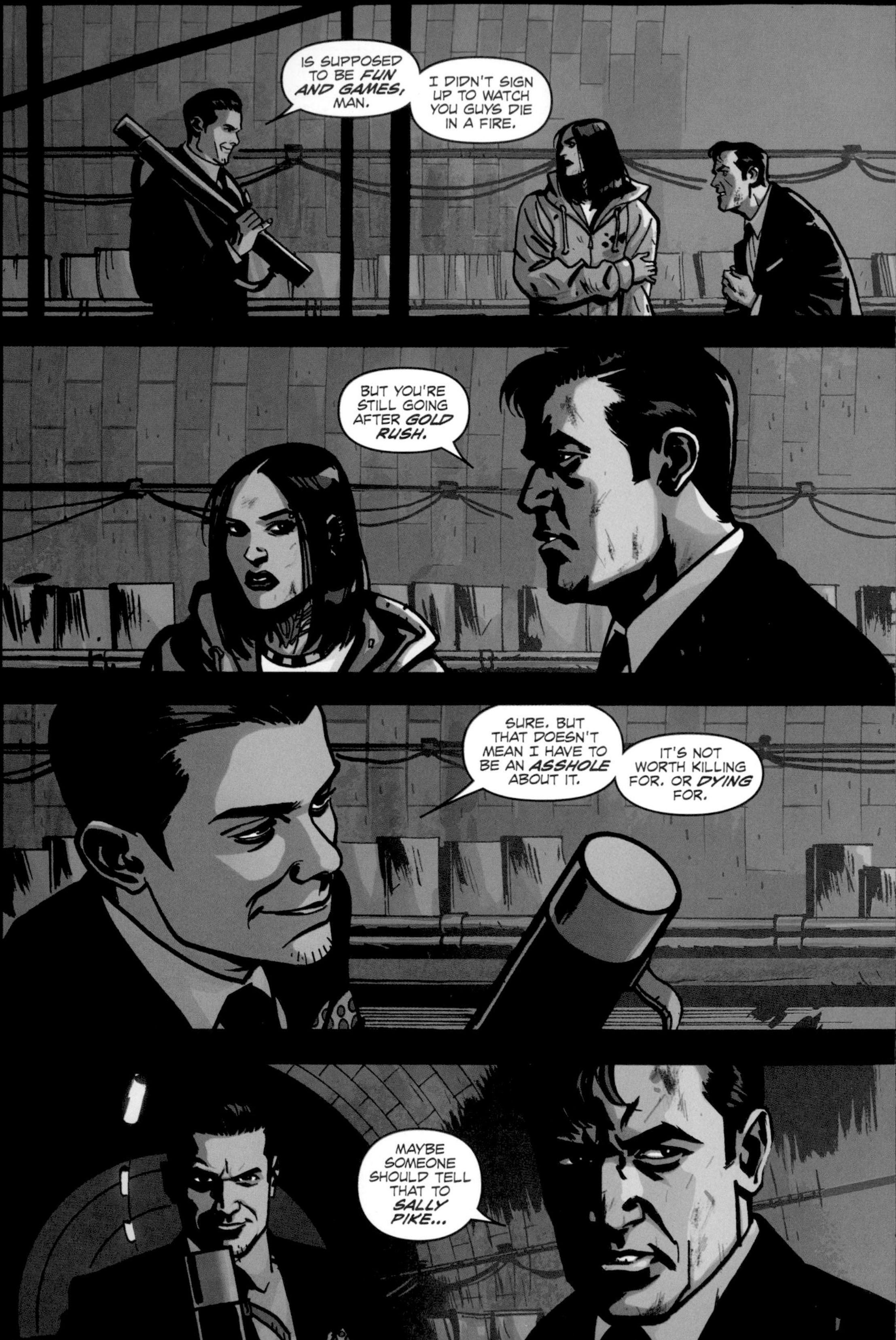
IS SUPPOSED TO BE FUN AND GAMES, MAN.
I DIDN'T SIGN UP TO WATCH YOU GUYS DIE IN A FIRE.
BUT YOU'RE STILL GOING AFTER GOLD RUSH.
SURE. BUT THAT DOESN'T MEAN I HAVE TO BE AN ASSHOLE ABOUT IT.
IT'S NOT WORTH KILLING FOR. OR DYING FOR.
MAYBE SOMEONE SHOULD TELL THAT TO SALLY PIKE...

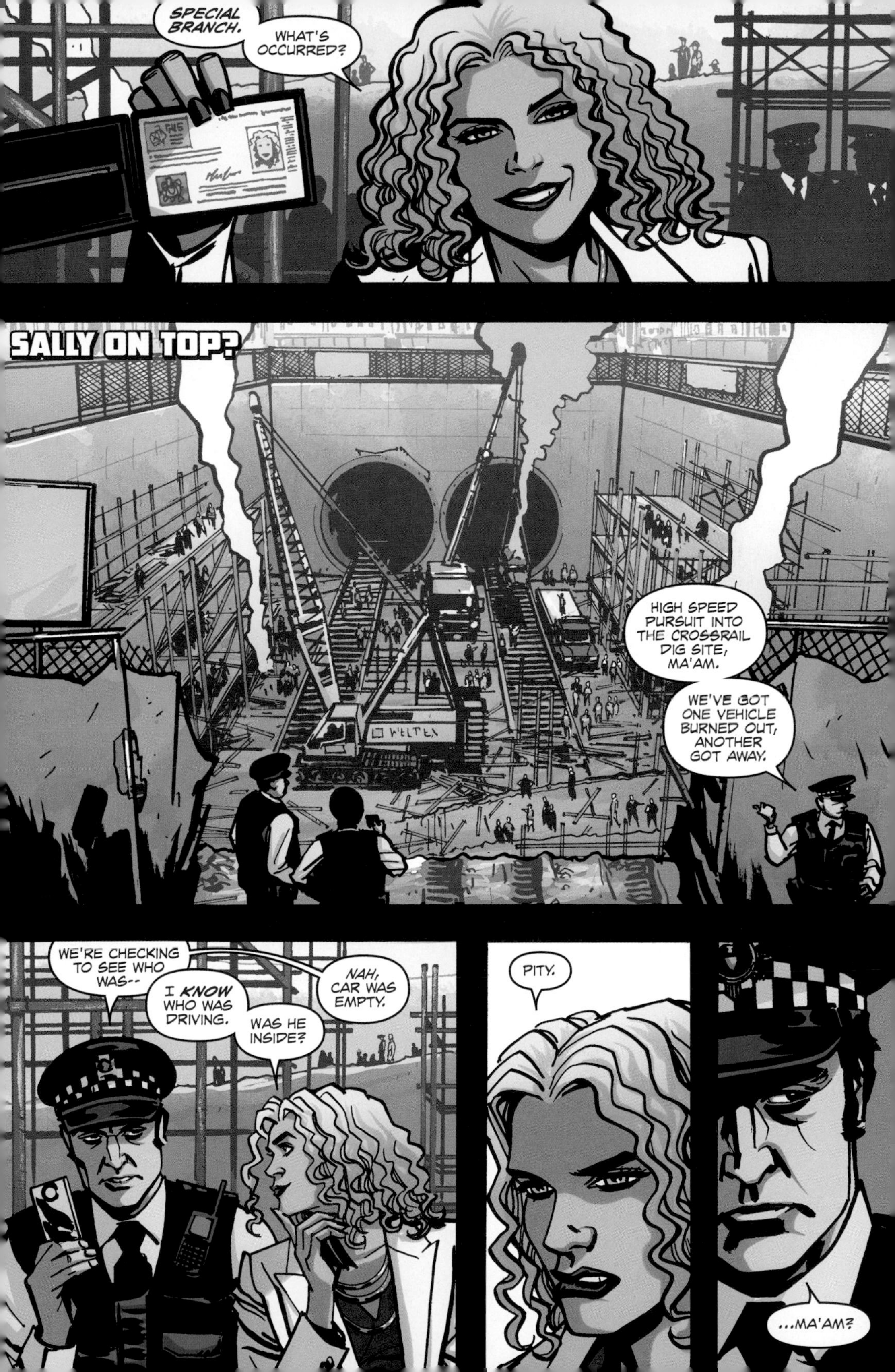
SPECIAL BRANCH.
WHAT'S OCCURRED?
SALLY ON TOP?
HIGH SPEED PURSUIT INTO THE CROSSRAIL DIG SITE, MA'AM.
WE'VE GOT ONE VEHICLE BURNED OUT, ANOTHER GOT AWAY.
WE'RE CHECKING TO SEE WHO WAS--
I KNOW WHO WAS DRIVING.
NAH, CAR WAS EMPTY.
WAS HE INSIDE?
PITY.
...MA'AM?

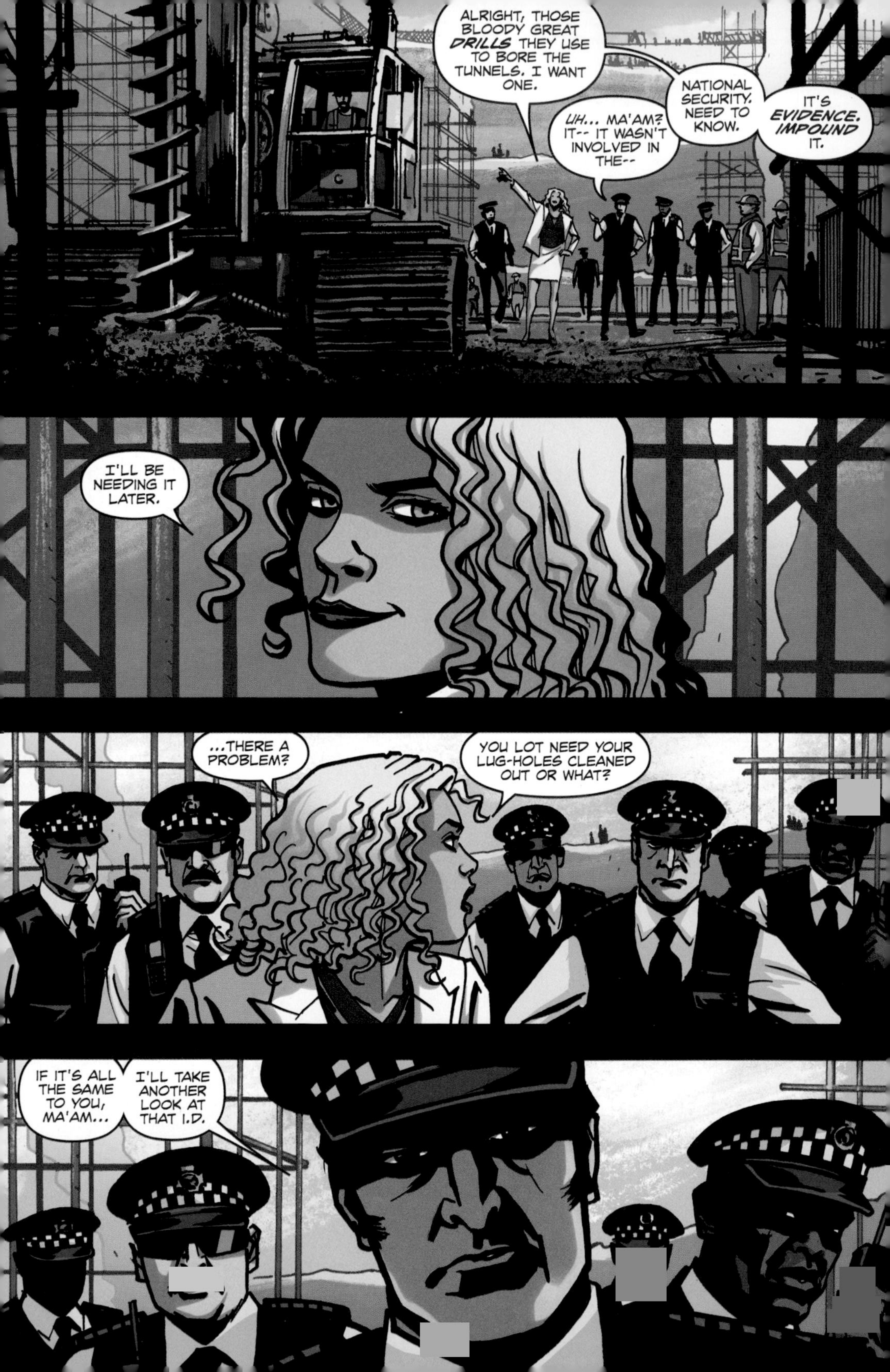
ALRIGHT, THOSE BLOODY GREAT *DRILLS* THEY USE TO BORE THE TUNNELS. I WANT ONE.
UH... MA'AM? IT-- IT WASN'T INVOLVED IN THE--
NATIONAL SECURITY. NEED TO KNOW.
IT'S ***EVIDENCE. IMPOUND*** IT.
I'LL BE NEEDING IT LATER.
...THERE A PROBLEM?
YOU LOT NEED YOUR LUG-HOLES CLEANED OUT OR WHAT?
IF IT'S ALL THE SAME TO YOU, MA'AM...
I'LL TAKE ANOTHER LOOK AT THAT I.D.

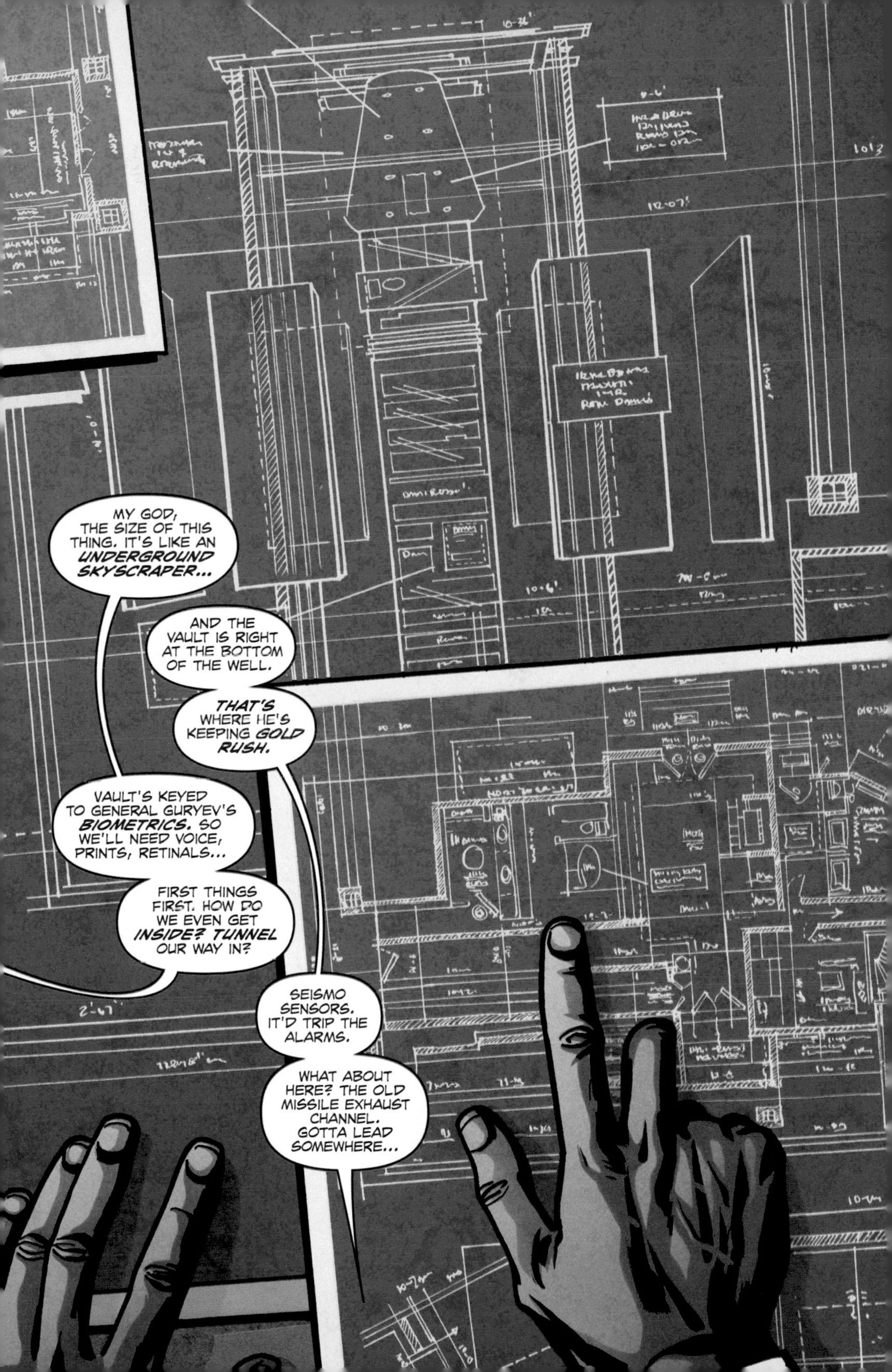
MY GOD, THE SIZE OF THIS THING. IT'S LIKE AN *UNDERGROUND SKYSCRAPER...*
AND THE VAULT IS RIGHT AT THE BOTTOM OF THE WELL.
THAT'S WHERE HE'S KEEPING *GOLD RUSH.*
VAULT'S KEYED TO GENERAL GURYEV'S *BIOMETRICS.* SO WE'LL NEED VOICE, PRINTS, RETINALS...
FIRST THINGS FIRST. HOW DO WE EVEN GET *INSIDE? TUNNEL* OUR WAY IN?
SEISMO SENSORS. IT'D TRIP THE ALARMS.
WHAT ABOUT HERE? THE OLD MISSILE EXHAUST CHANNEL. GOTTA LEAD SOMEWHERE...

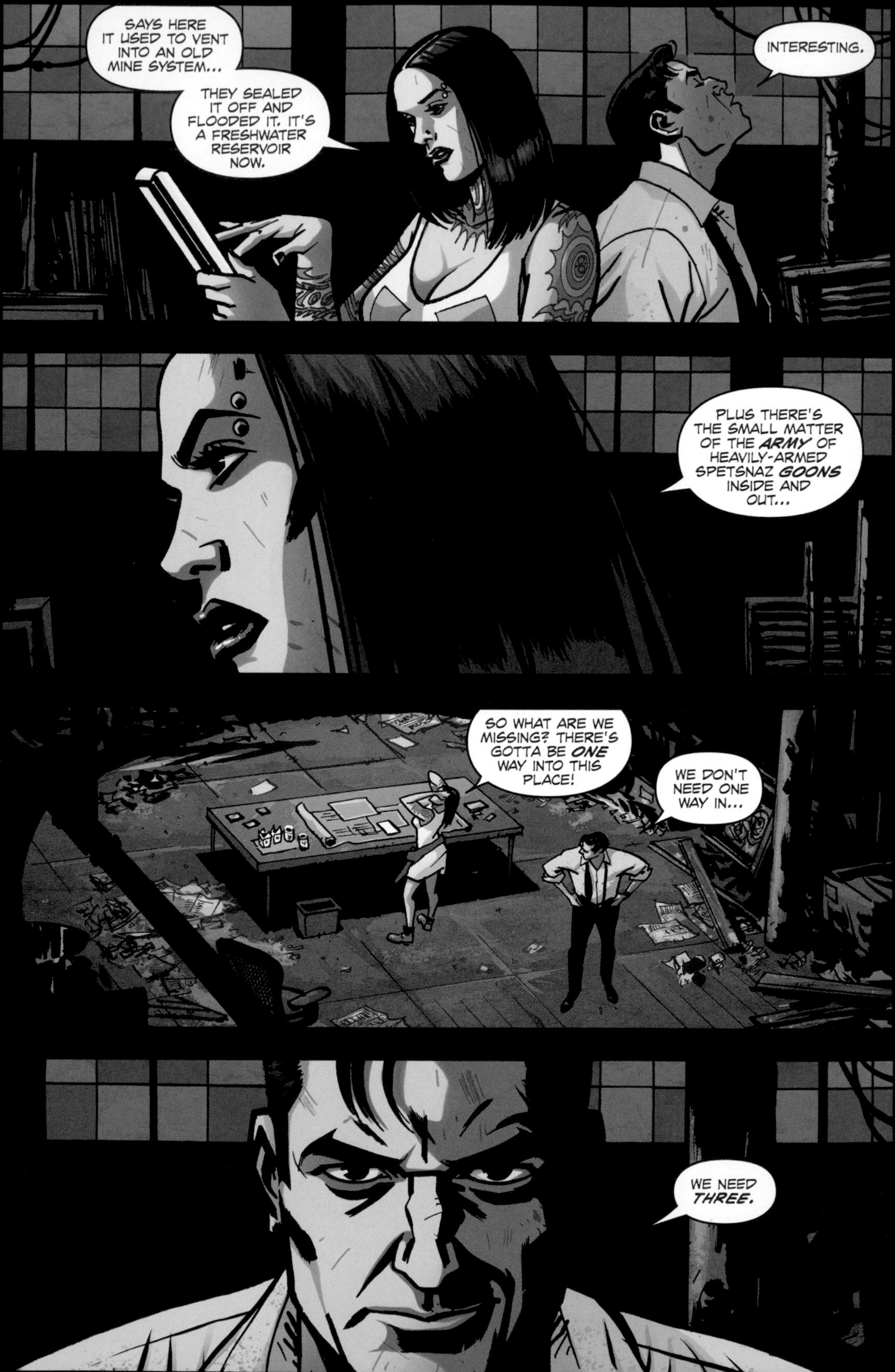
SAYS HERE IT USED TO VENT INTO AN OLD MINE SYSTEM...
THEY SEALED IT OFF AND FLOODED IT. IT'S A FRESHWATER RESERVOIR NOW.
INTERESTING.
PLUS THERE'S THE SMALL MATTER OF THE ARMY OF HEAVILY-ARMED SPETSNAZ GOONS INSIDE AND OUT...
SO WHAT ARE WE MISSING? THERE'S GOTTA BE ONE WAY INTO THIS PLACE!
WE DON'T NEED ONE WAY IN...
WE NEED THREE.

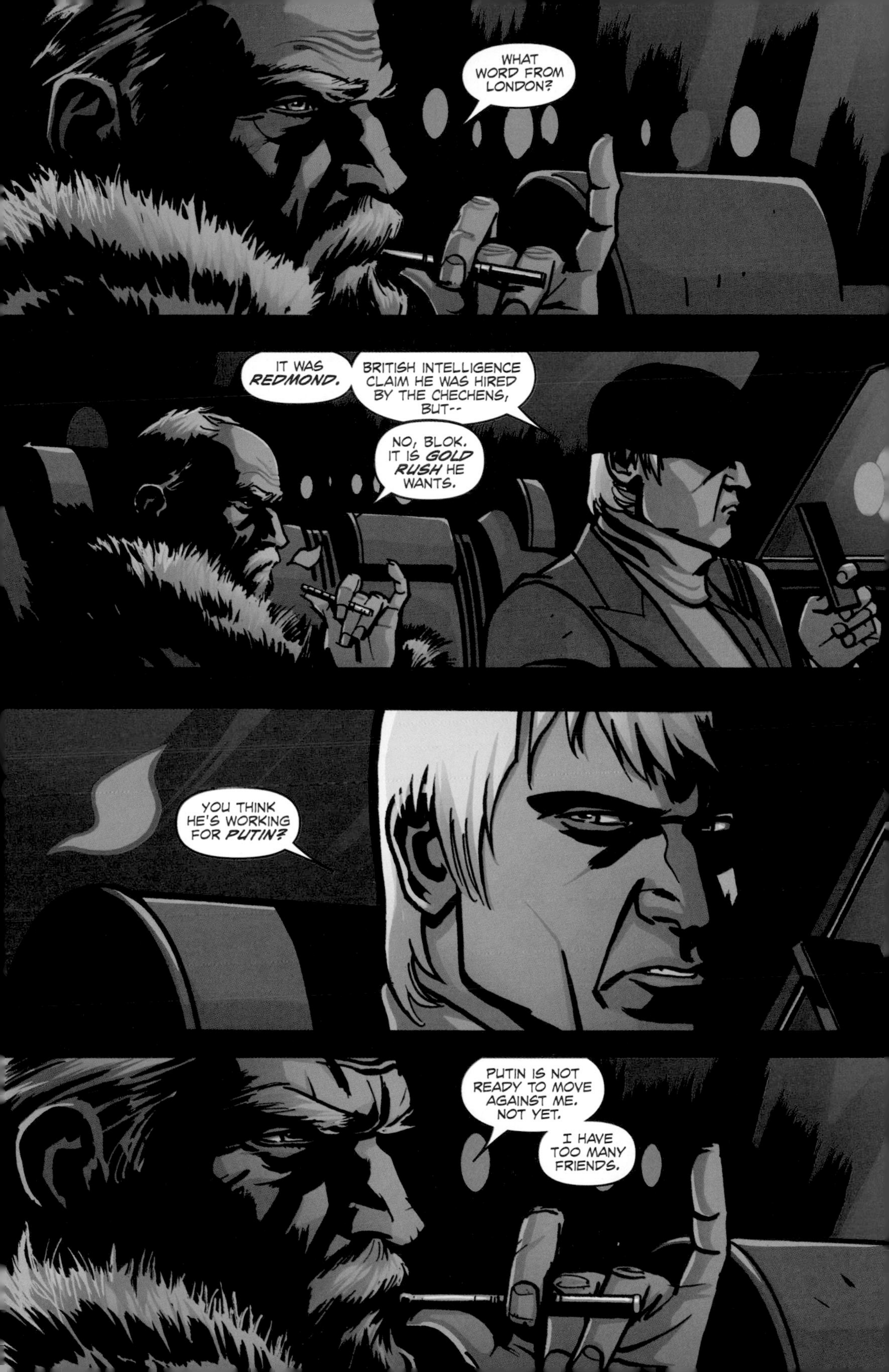
WHAT WORD FROM LONDON?
IT WAS REDMOND.
BRITISH INTELLIGENCE CLAIM HE WAS HIRED BY THE CHECHENS, BUT--
NO, BLOK. IT IS GOLD RUSH HE WANTS.
YOU THINK HE'S WORKING FOR PUTIN?
PUTIN IS NOT READY TO MOVE AGAINST ME. NOT YET.
I HAVE TOO MANY FRIENDS.

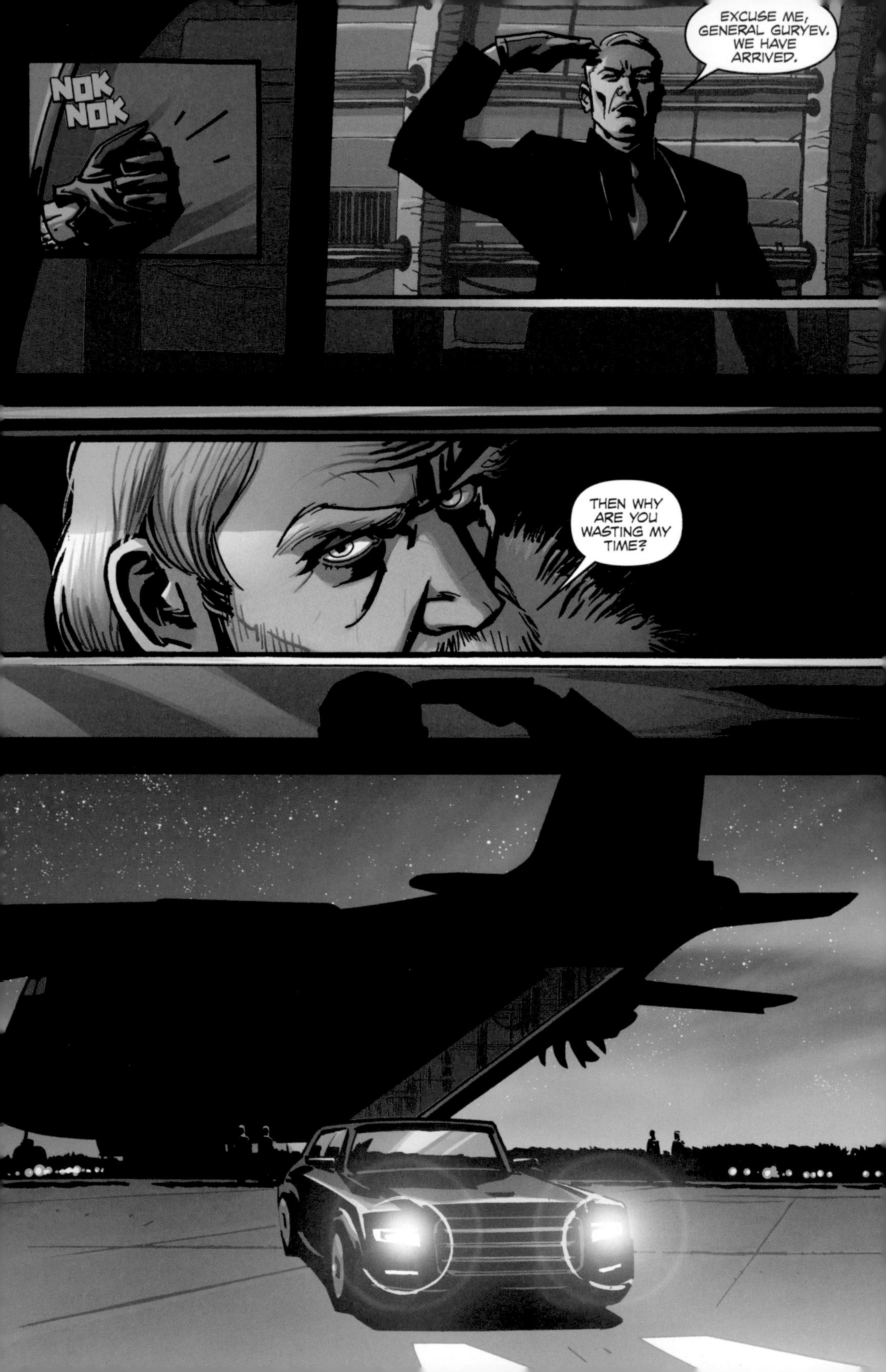
NOK NOK
EXCUSE ME, GENERAL GURYEV. WE HAVE ARRIVED.
THEN WHY ARE YOU WASTING MY TIME?

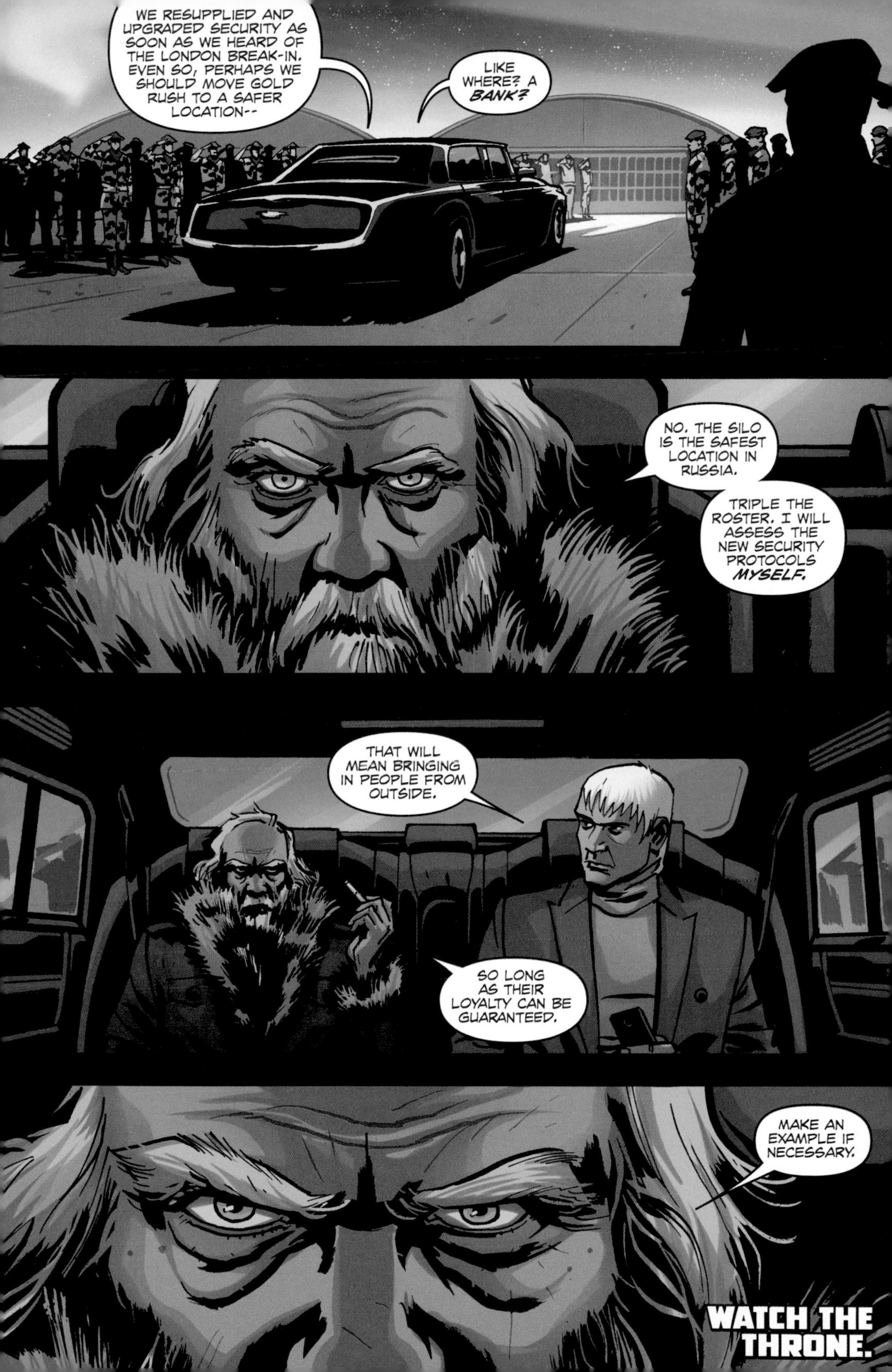
WE RESUPPLIED AND UPGRADED SECURITY AS SOON AS WE HEARD OF THE LONDON BREAK-IN. EVEN SO, PERHAPS WE SHOULD MOVE GOLD RUSH TO A SAFER LOCATION--
LIKE WHERE? A *BANK?*
NO. THE SILO IS THE SAFEST LOCATION IN RUSSIA.
TRIPLE THE ROSTER. I WILL ASSESS THE NEW SECURITY PROTOCOLS *MYSELF.*
THAT WILL MEAN BRINGING IN PEOPLE FROM OUTSIDE.
SO LONG AS THEIR LOYALTY CAN BE GUARANTEED.
MAKE AN EXAMPLE IF NECESSARY.
WATCH THE THRONE.

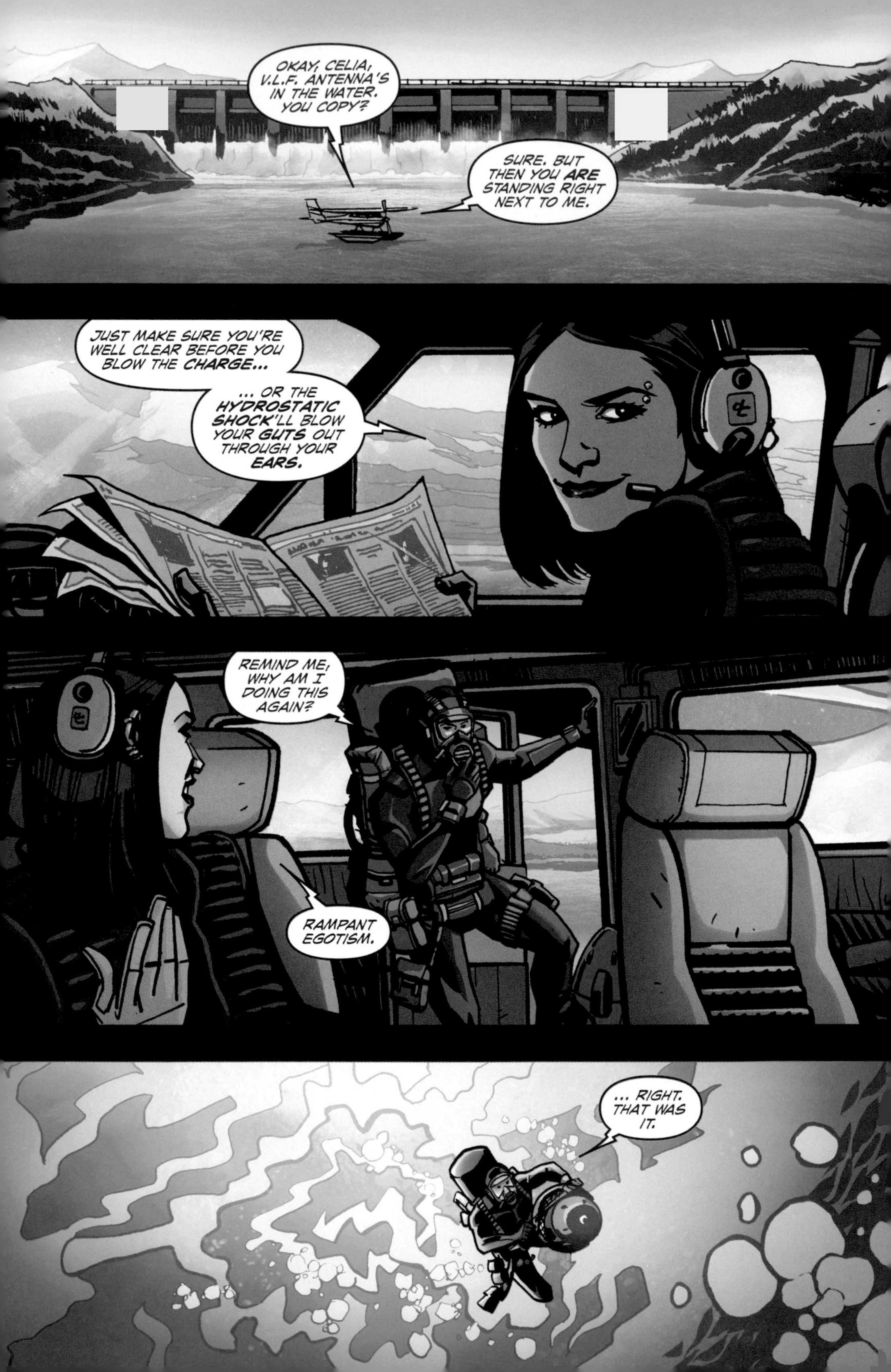
OKAY, CELIA, V.L.F. ANTENNA'S IN THE WATER. YOU COPY?
SURE. BUT THEN YOU ARE STANDING RIGHT NEXT TO ME.
JUST MAKE SURE YOU'RE WELL CLEAR BEFORE YOU BLOW THE CHARGE...
... OR THE HYDROSTATIC SHOCK'LL BLOW YOUR GUTS OUT THROUGH YOUR EARS.
REMIND ME, WHY AM I DOING THIS AGAIN?
RAMPANT EGOTISM.
... RIGHT. THAT WAS IT.

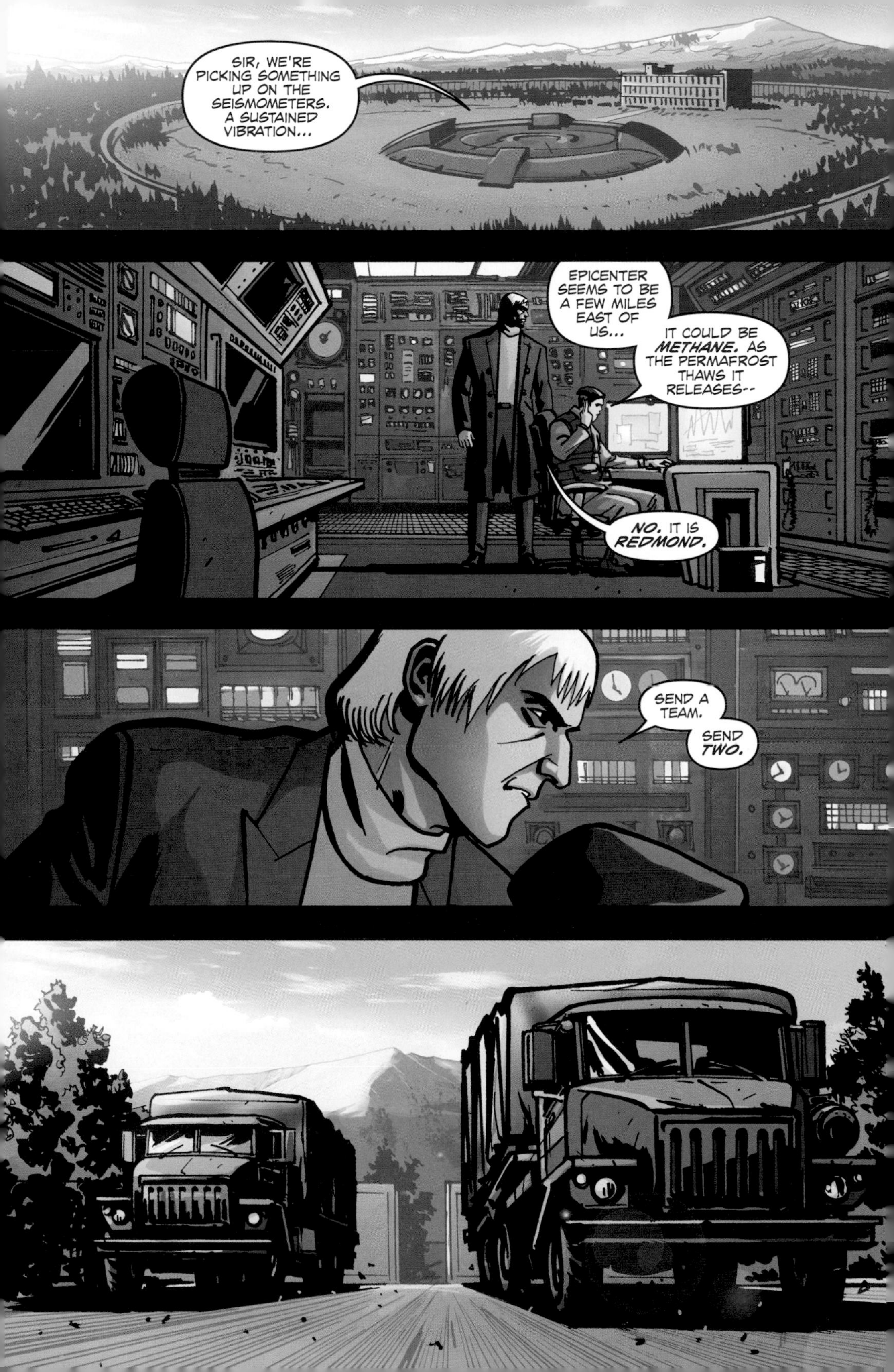
SIR, WE'RE PICKING SOMETHING UP ON THE SEISMOMETERS. A SUSTAINED VIBRATION...
EPICENTER SEEMS TO BE A FEW MILES EAST OF US...
IT COULD BE METHANE. AS THE PERMAFROST THAWS IT RELEASES--
NO. IT IS REDMOND.
SEND A TEAM.
SEND TWO.

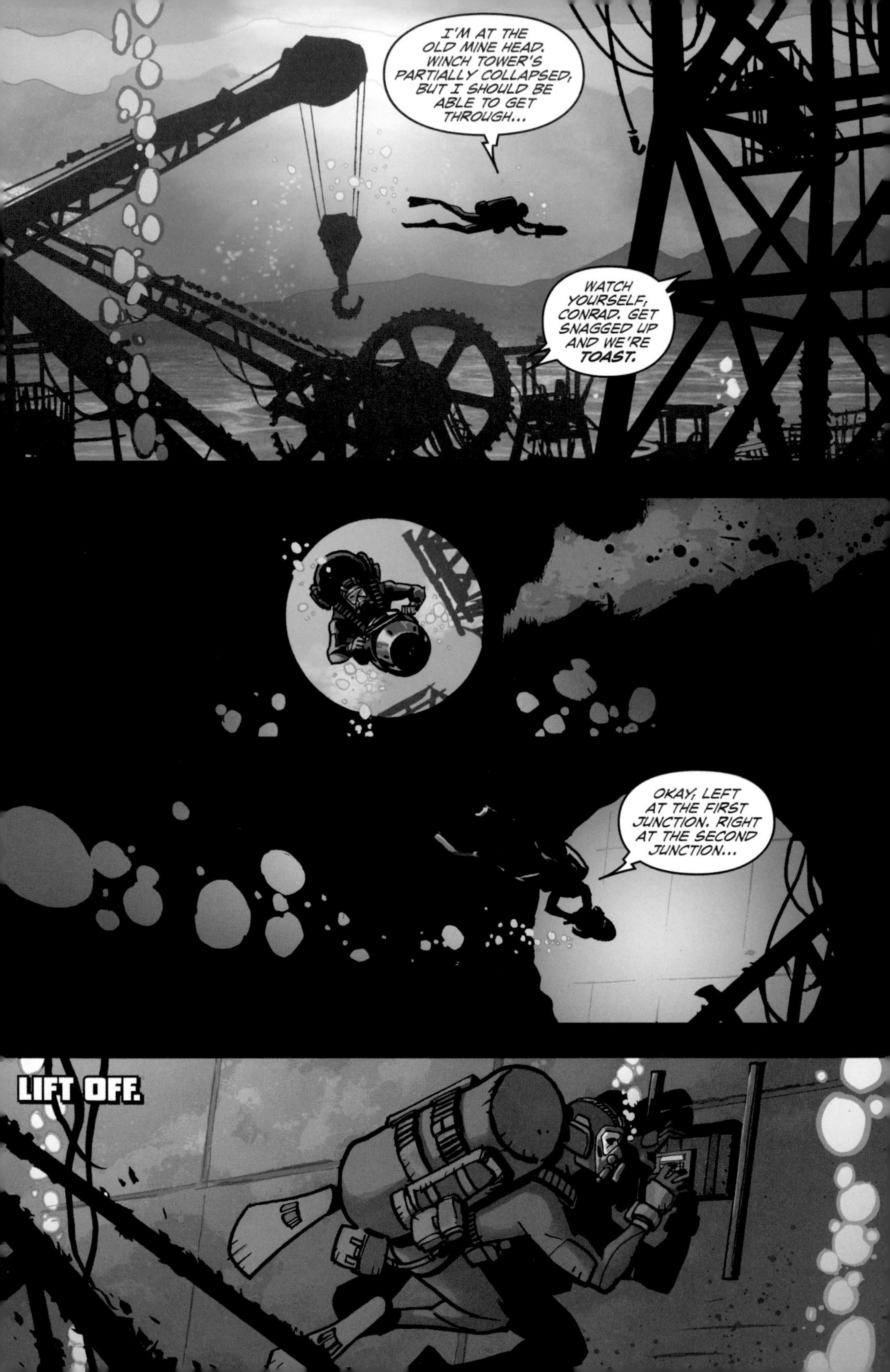
I'M AT THE OLD MINE HEAD. WINCH TOWER'S PARTIALLY COLLAPSED, BUT I SHOULD BE ABLE TO GET THROUGH...
WATCH YOURSELF, CONRAD. GET SNAGGED UP AND WE'RE **TOAST.**
OKAY, LEFT AT THE FIRST JUNCTION. RIGHT AT THE SECOND JUNCTION...
LIFT OFF.

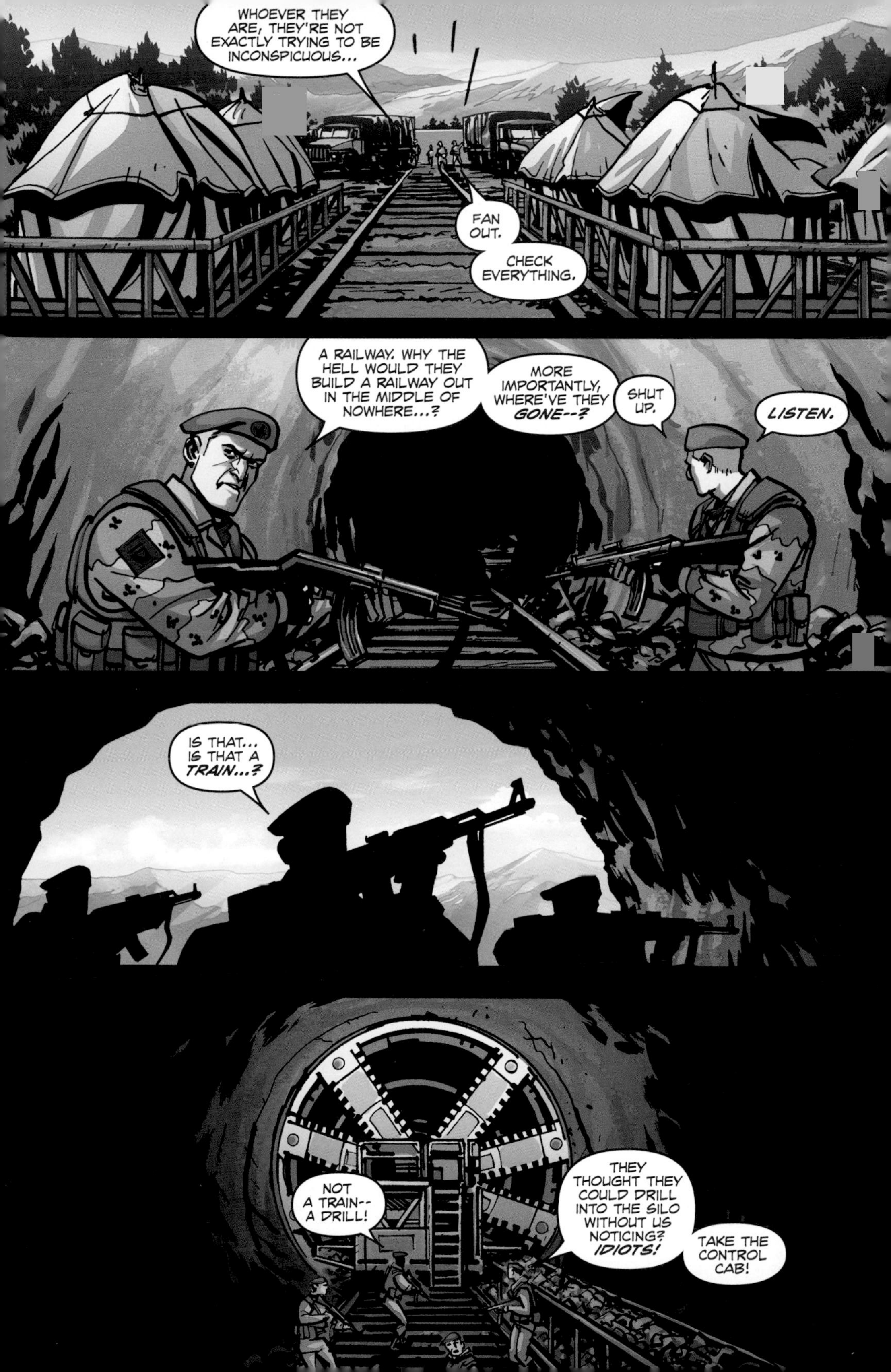
WHOEVER THEY ARE, THEY'RE NOT EXACTLY TRYING TO BE INCONSPICUOUS...
FAN OUT.
CHECK EVERYTHING.
A RAILWAY. WHY THE HELL WOULD THEY BUILD A RAILWAY OUT IN THE MIDDLE OF NOWHERE...?
MORE IMPORTANTLY, WHERE'VE THEY *GONE--?*
SHUT UP.
LISTEN.
IS THAT... IS THAT A *TRAIN...?*
NOT A TRAIN-- A DRILL!
THEY THOUGHT THEY COULD DRILL INTO THE SILO WITHOUT US NOTICING? *IDIOTS!*
TAKE THE CONTROL CAB!

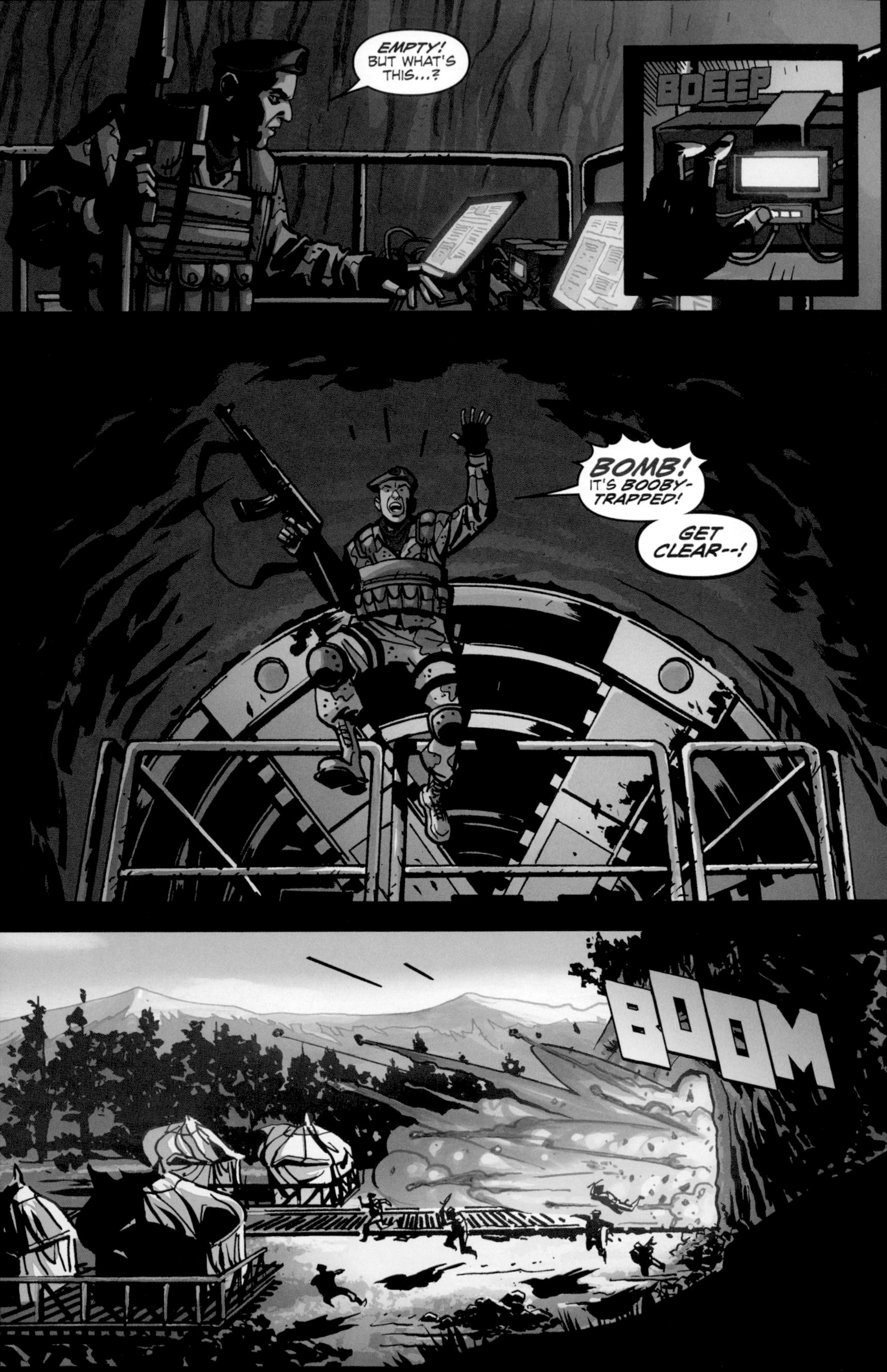
EMPTY! BUT WHAT'S THIS...?
BOEEP
BOMB! IT'S BOOBY-TRAPPED!
GET CLEAR--!
BOOM

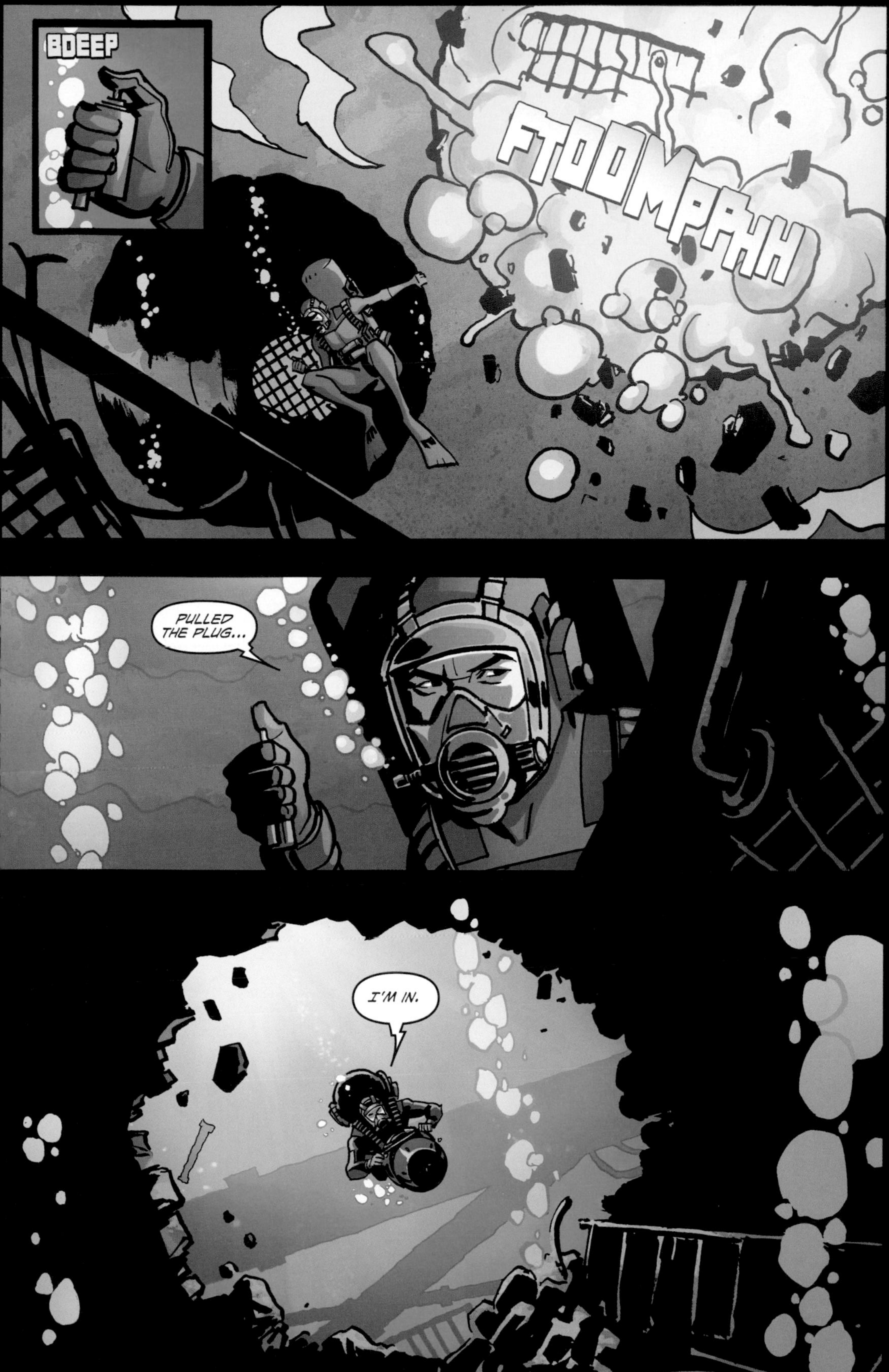
BDEEP
FTOOMPPHH
PULLED THE PLUG...
I'M IN.

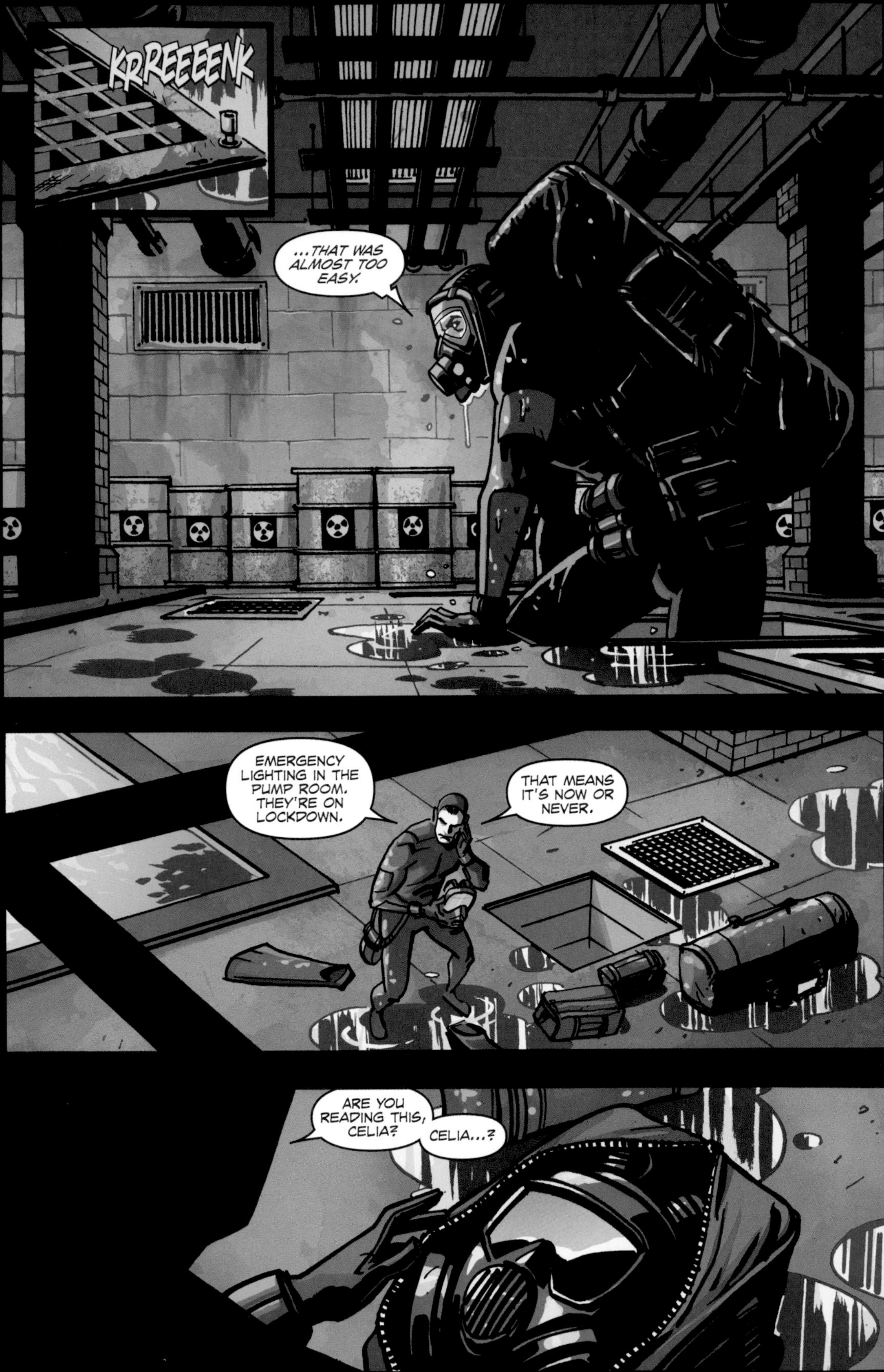
KRREEEENK
...THAT WAS ALMOST TOO EASY.
EMERGENCY LIGHTING IN THE PUMP ROOM. THEY'RE ON LOCKDOWN.
THAT MEANS IT'S NOW OR NEVER.
ARE YOU READING THIS, CELIA?
CELIA...?

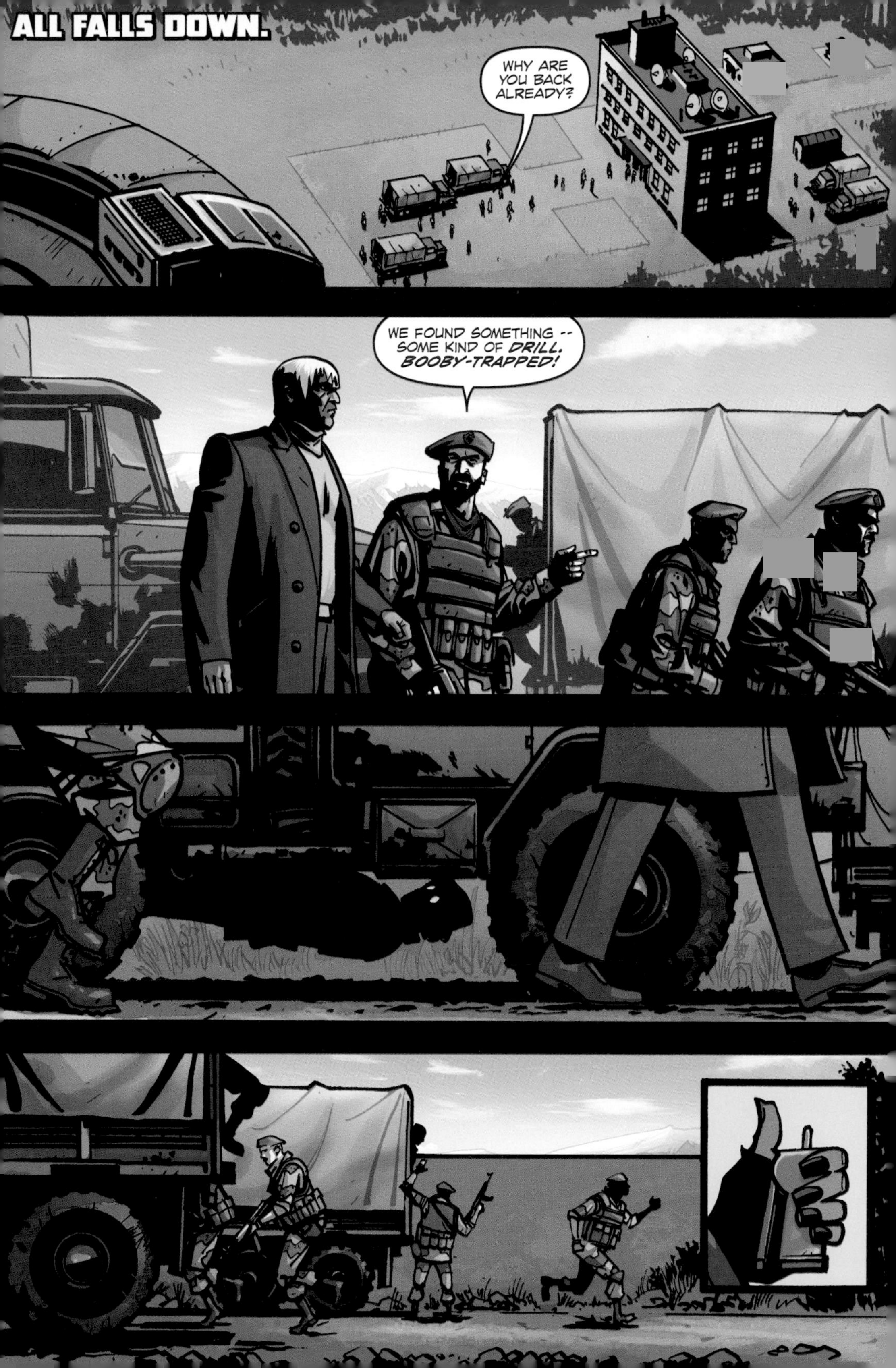
ALL FALLS DOWN.
WHY ARE YOU BACK ALREADY?
WE FOUND SOMETHING -- SOME KIND OF *DRILL. BOOBY-TRAPPED!*

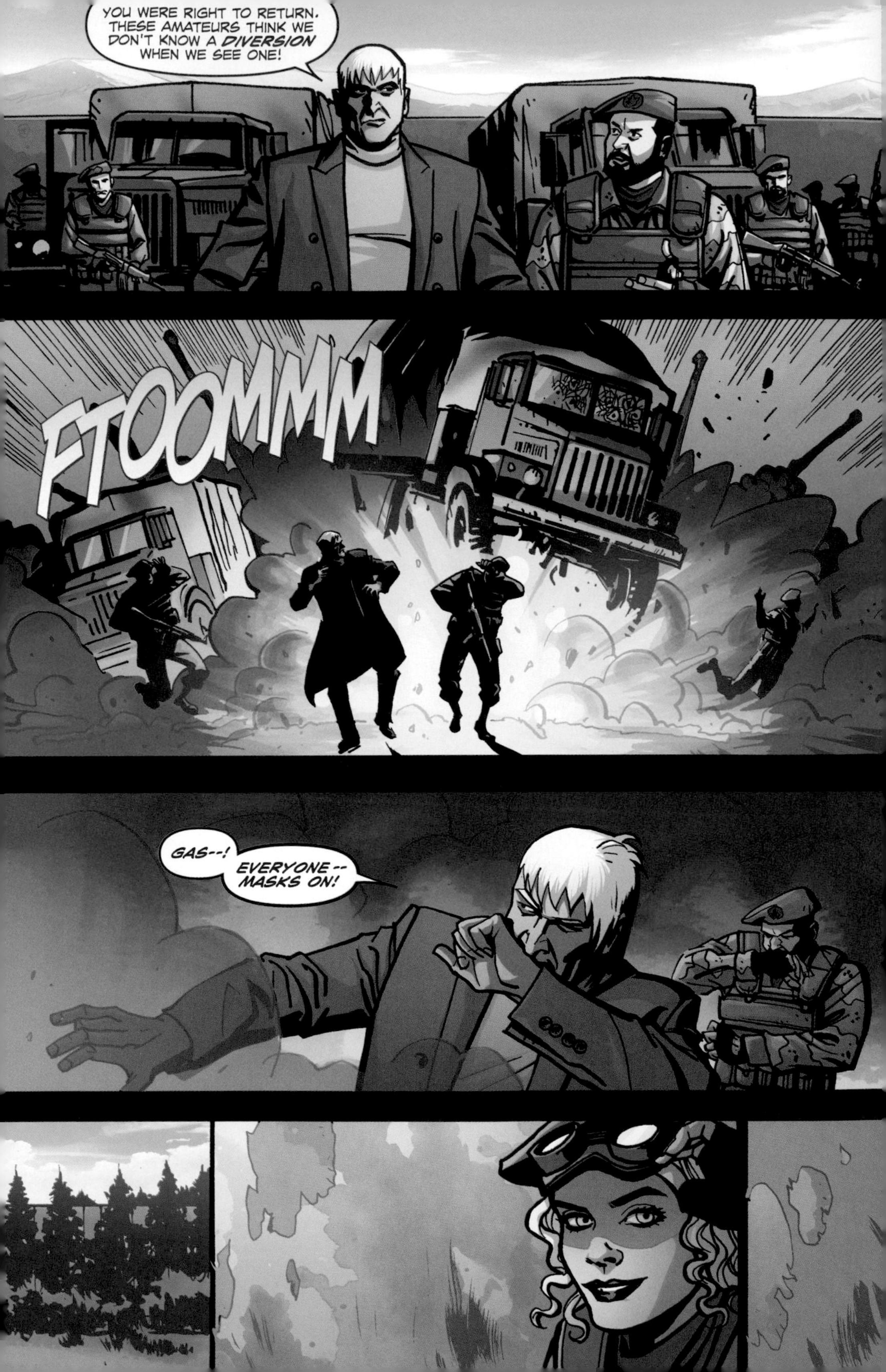
YOU WERE RIGHT TO RETURN. THESE AMATEURS THINK WE DON'T KNOW A *DIVERSION* WHEN WE SEE ONE!
FTOOMMM
GAS--!
EVERYONE-- MASKS ON!

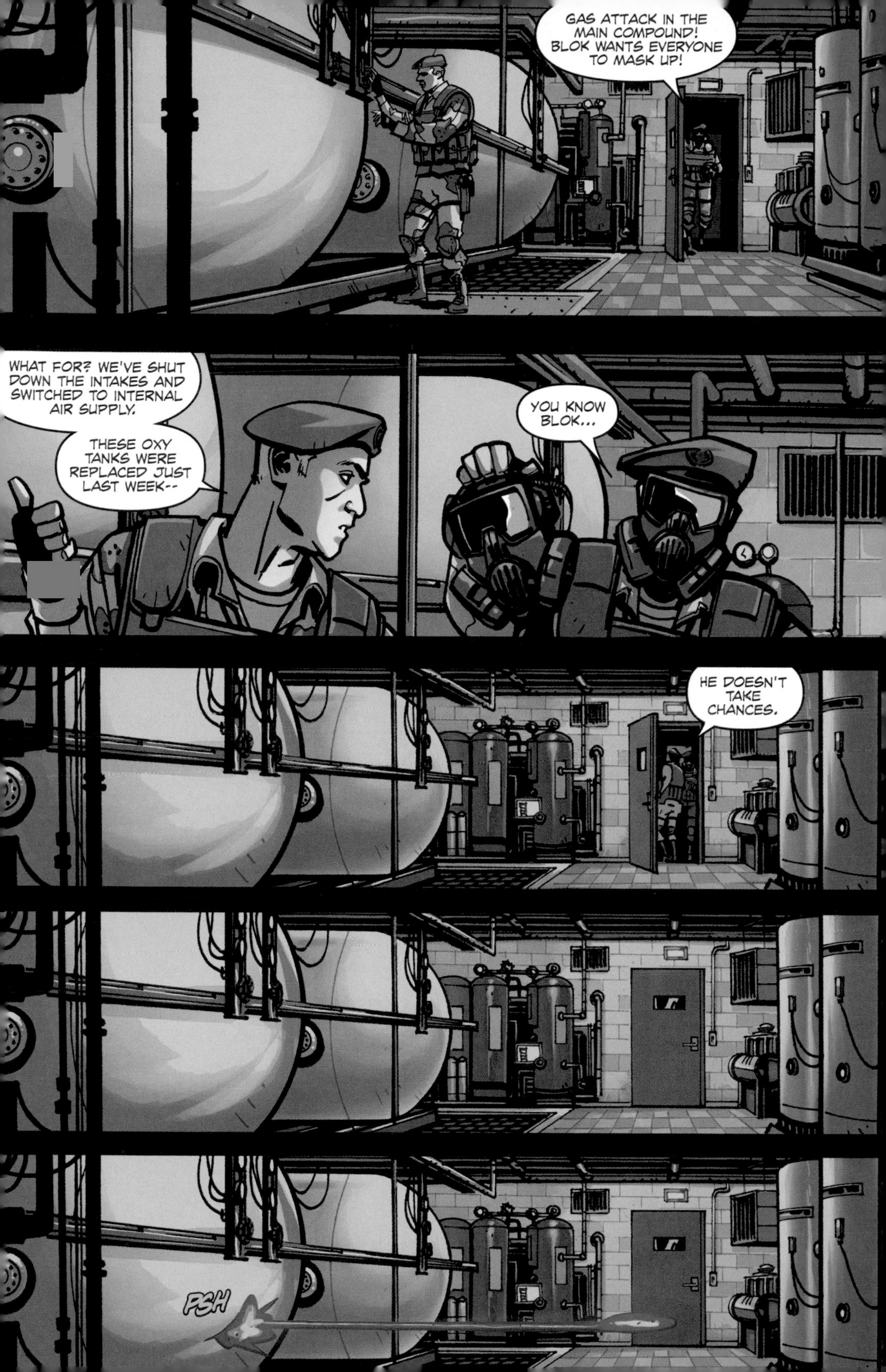
GAS ATTACK IN THE MAIN COMPOUND! BLOK WANTS EVERYONE TO MASK UP!
WHAT FOR? WE'VE SHUT DOWN THE INTAKES AND SWITCHED TO INTERNAL AIR SUPPLY.
THESE OXY TANKS WERE REPLACED JUST LAST WEEK--
YOU KNOW BLOK...
HE DOESN'T TAKE CHANCES.
PSH

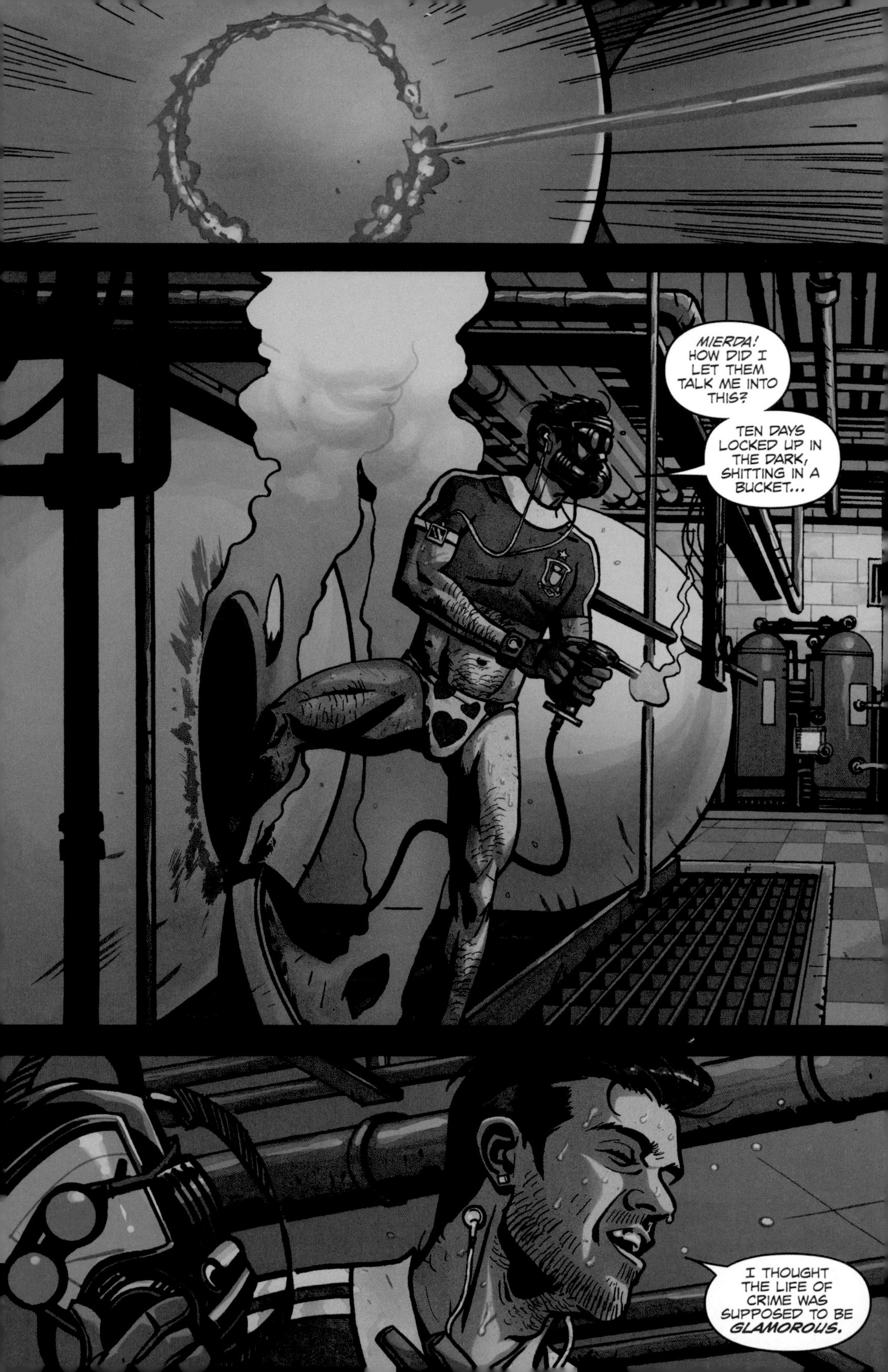
MIERDA! HOW DID I LET THEM TALK ME INTO THIS?
TEN DAYS LOCKED UP IN THE DARK, SHITTING IN A BUCKET...
I THOUGHT THE LIFE OF CRIME WAS SUPPOSED TO BE GLAMOROUS.

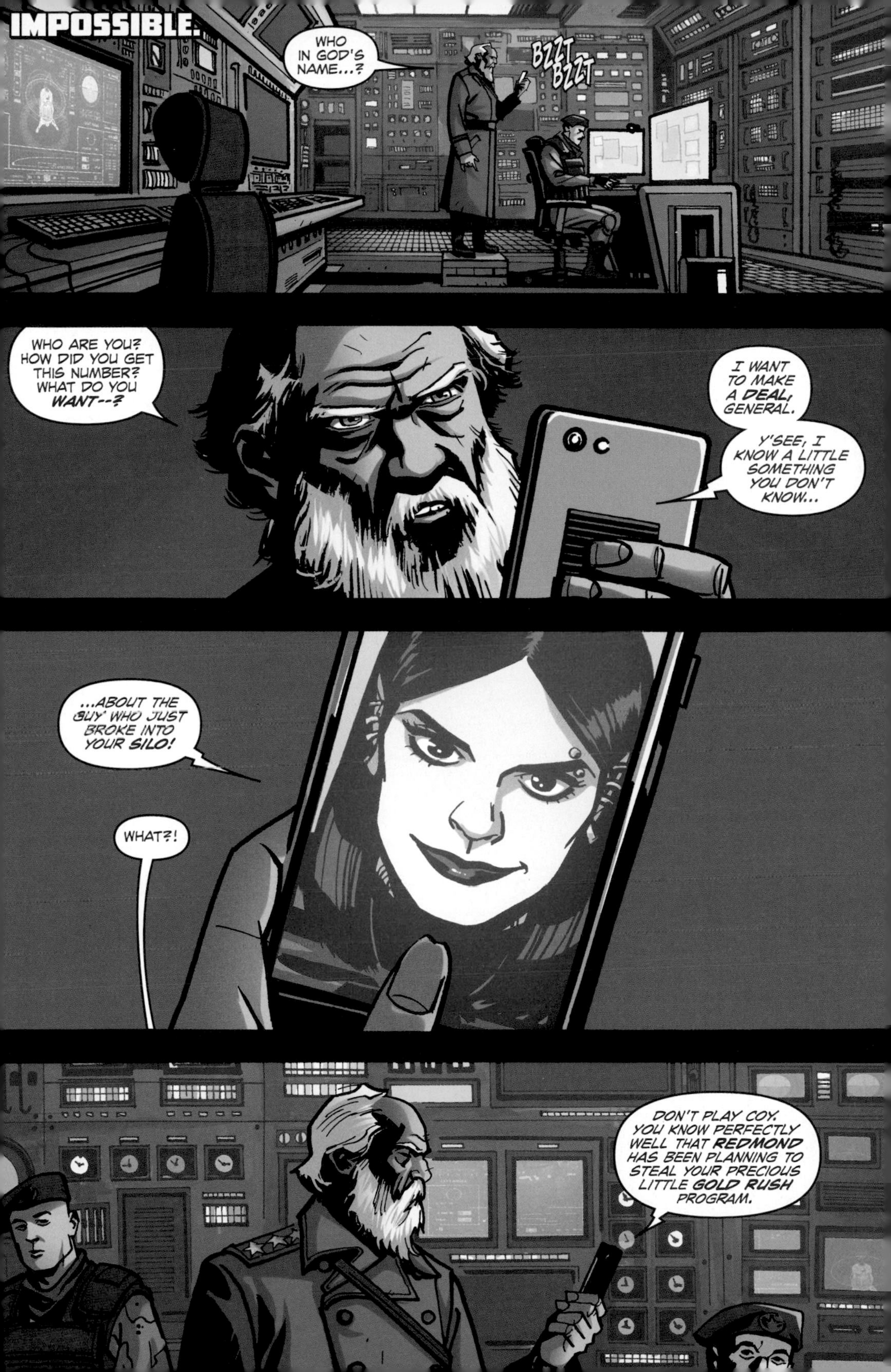
IMPOSSIBLE.
WHO IN GOD'S NAME...?
BZZT BZZT
WHO ARE YOU? HOW DID YOU GET THIS NUMBER? WHAT DO YOU WANT--?
I WANT TO MAKE A DEAL, GENERAL.
Y'SEE, I KNOW A LITTLE SOMETHING YOU DON'T KNOW...
...ABOUT THE GUY WHO JUST BROKE INTO YOUR SILO!
WHAT?!
DON'T PLAY COY. YOU KNOW PERFECTLY WELL THAT REDMOND HAS BEEN PLANNING TO STEAL YOUR PRECIOUS LITTLE GOLD RUSH PROGRAM.

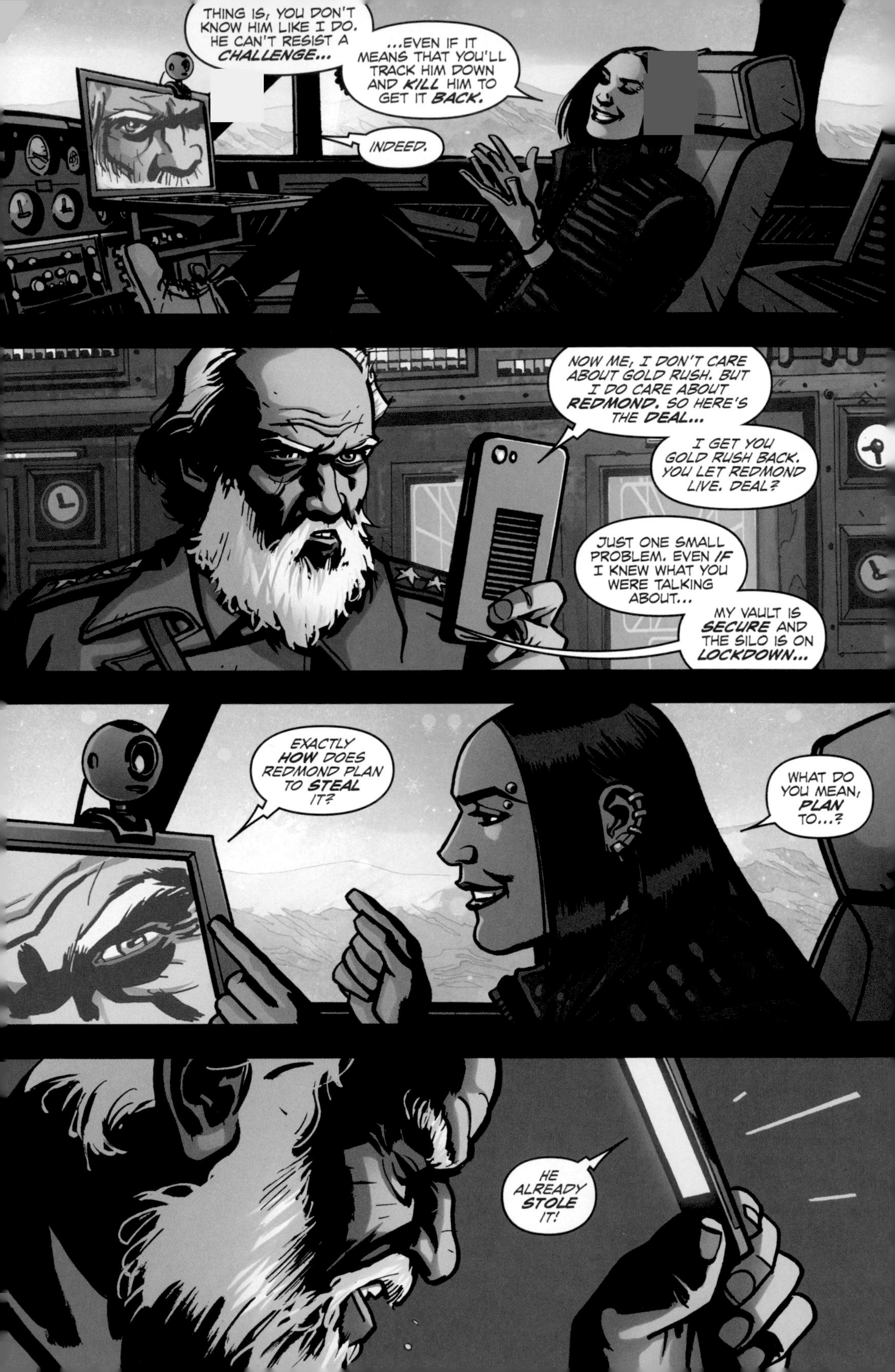
THING IS, YOU DON'T KNOW HIM LIKE I DO. HE CAN'T RESIST A CHALLENGE...
...EVEN IF IT MEANS THAT YOU'LL TRACK HIM DOWN AND KILL HIM TO GET IT BACK.
INDEED.
NOW ME, I DON'T CARE ABOUT GOLD RUSH. BUT I DO CARE ABOUT REDMOND. SO HERE'S THE DEAL...
I GET YOU GOLD RUSH BACK. YOU LET REDMOND LIVE. DEAL?
JUST ONE SMALL PROBLEM. EVEN IF I KNEW WHAT YOU WERE TALKING ABOUT...
MY VAULT IS SECURE AND THE SILO IS ON LOCKDOWN...
EXACTLY HOW DOES REDMOND PLAN TO STEAL IT?
WHAT DO YOU MEAN, PLAN TO...?
HE ALREADY STOLE IT!

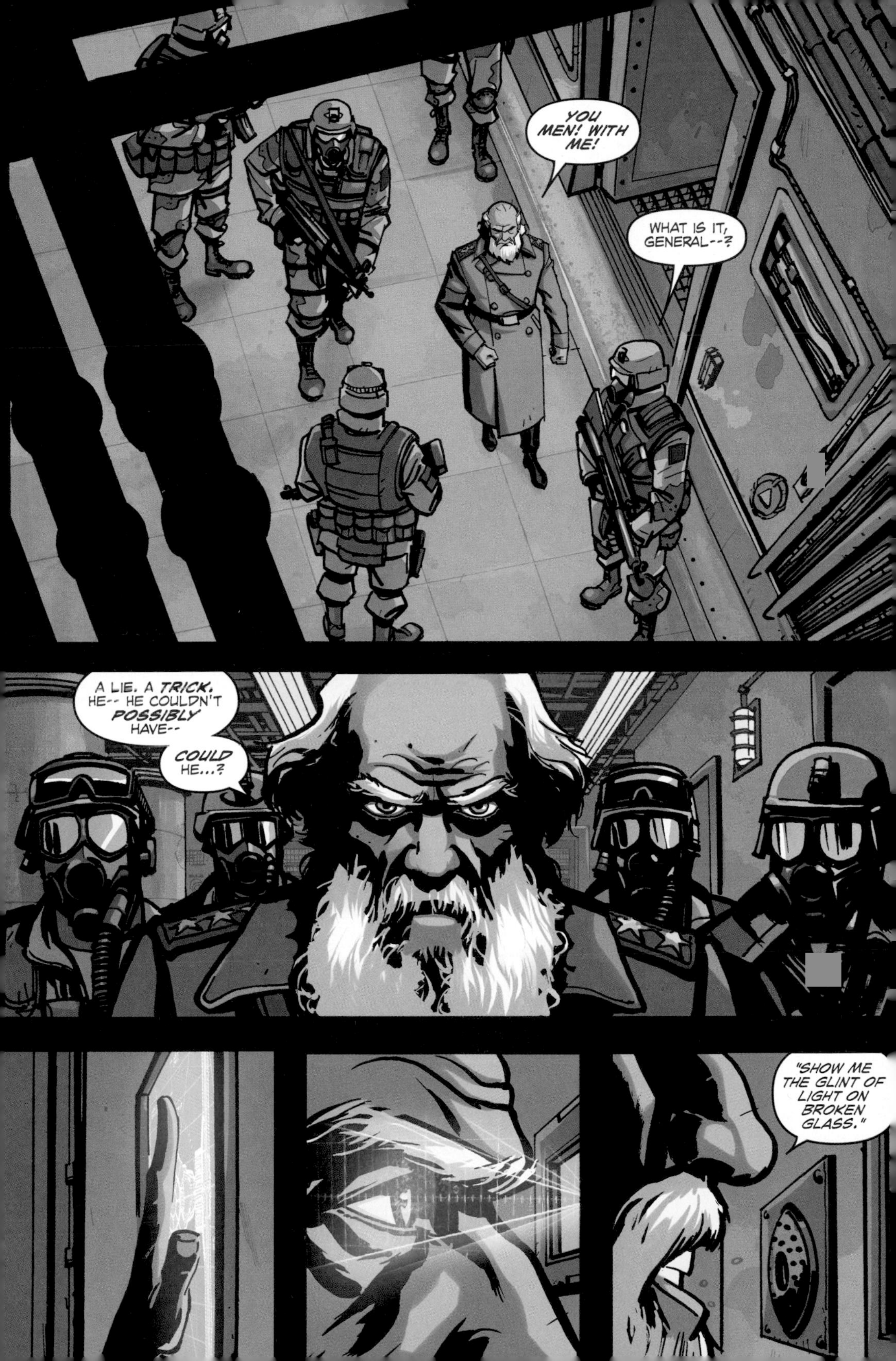
YOU MEN! WITH ME!
WHAT IS IT, GENERAL--?
A LIE. A TRICK. HE-- HE COULDN'T POSSIBLY HAVE--
COULD HE...?
"SHOW ME THE GLINT OF LIGHT ON BROKEN GLASS."

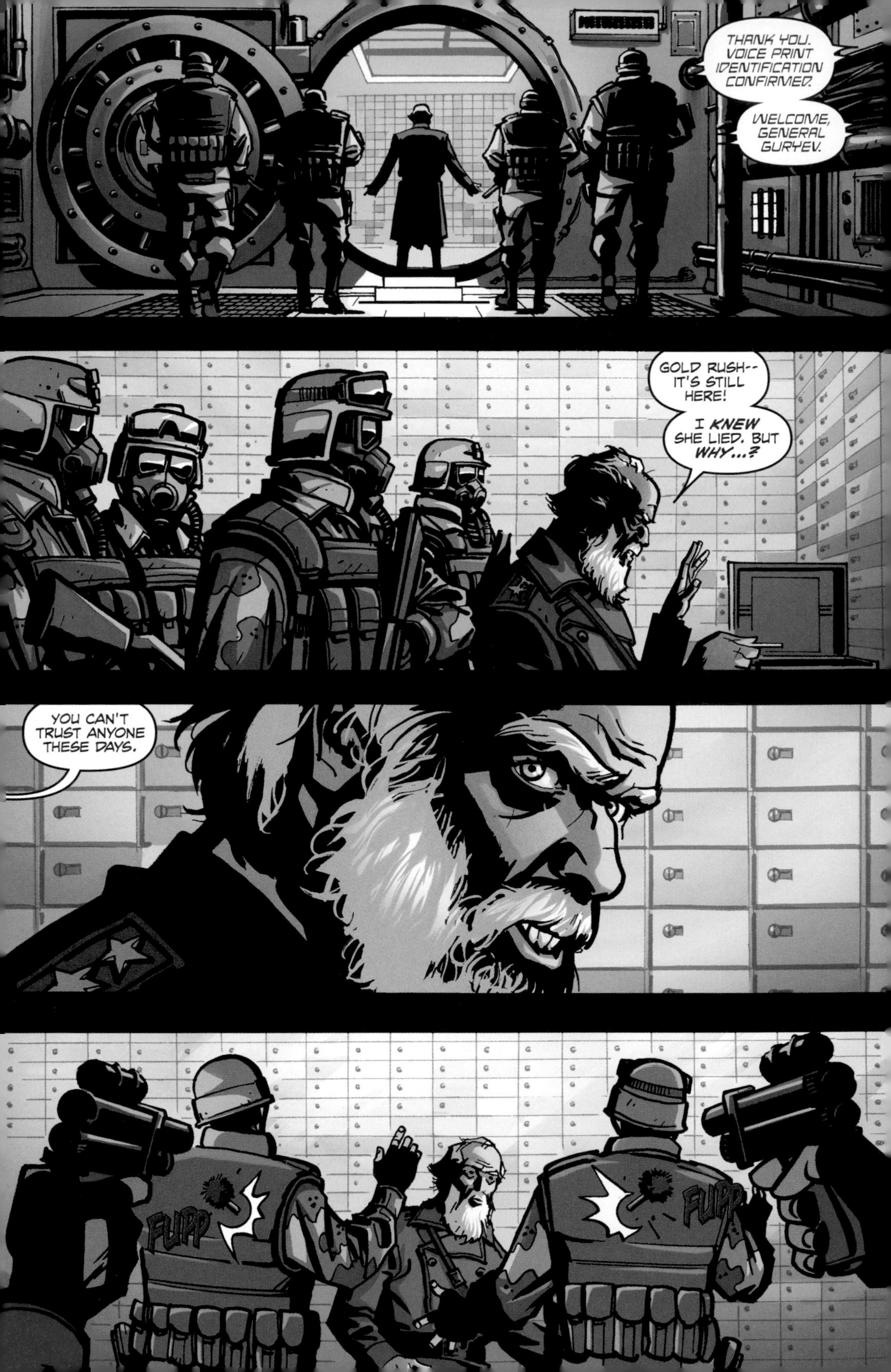
THANK YOU. VOICE PRINT IDENTIFICATION CONFIRMED.
WELCOME, GENERAL GURYEV.
GOLD RUSH-- IT'S STILL HERE!
I KNEW SHE LIED. BUT WHY...?
YOU CAN'T TRUST ANYONE THESE DAYS.
FUPP
FUPP

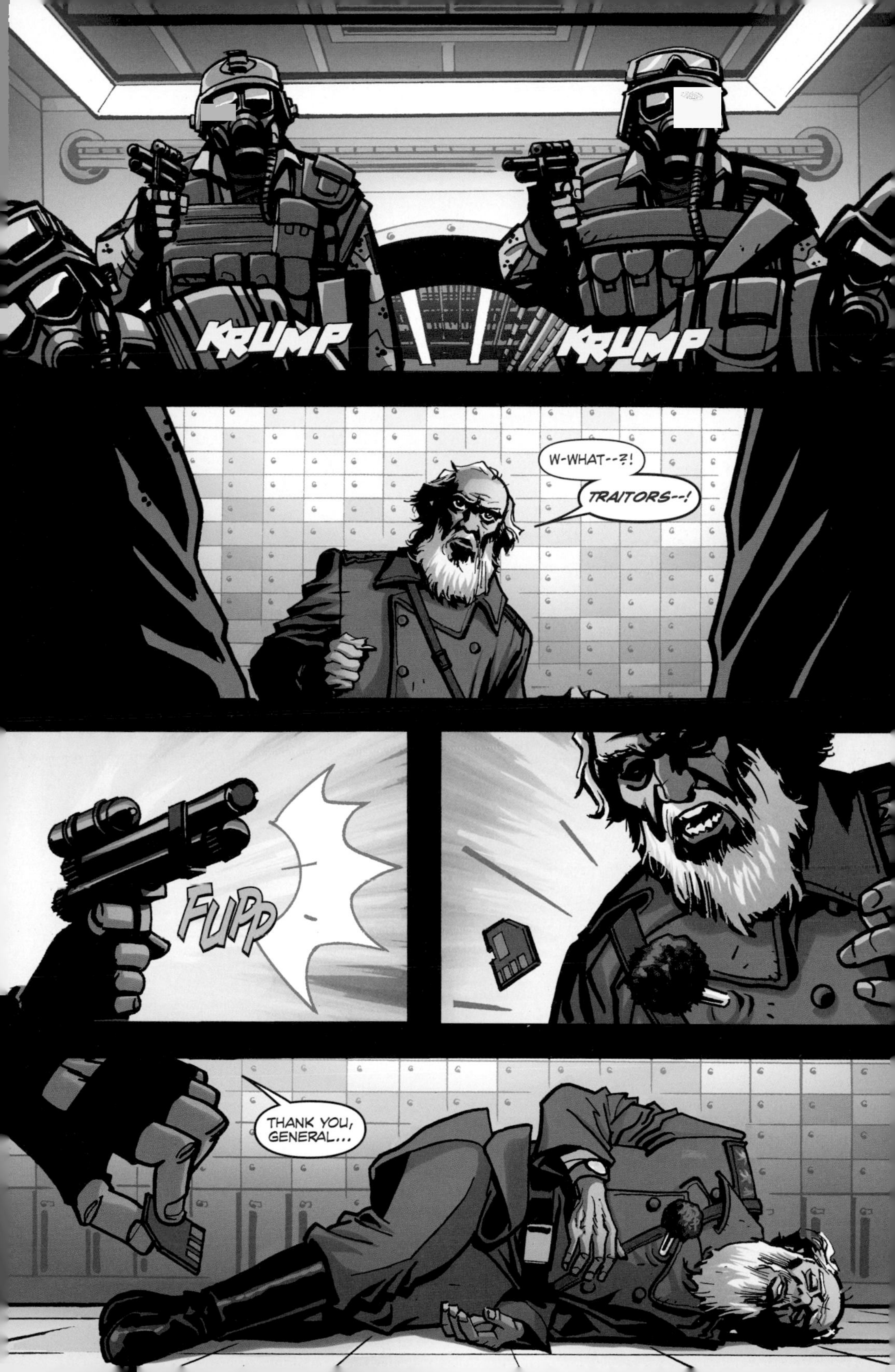
KRUMP
KRUMP
W-WHAT--?!
TRAITORS--!
FUPP
THANK YOU, GENERAL...

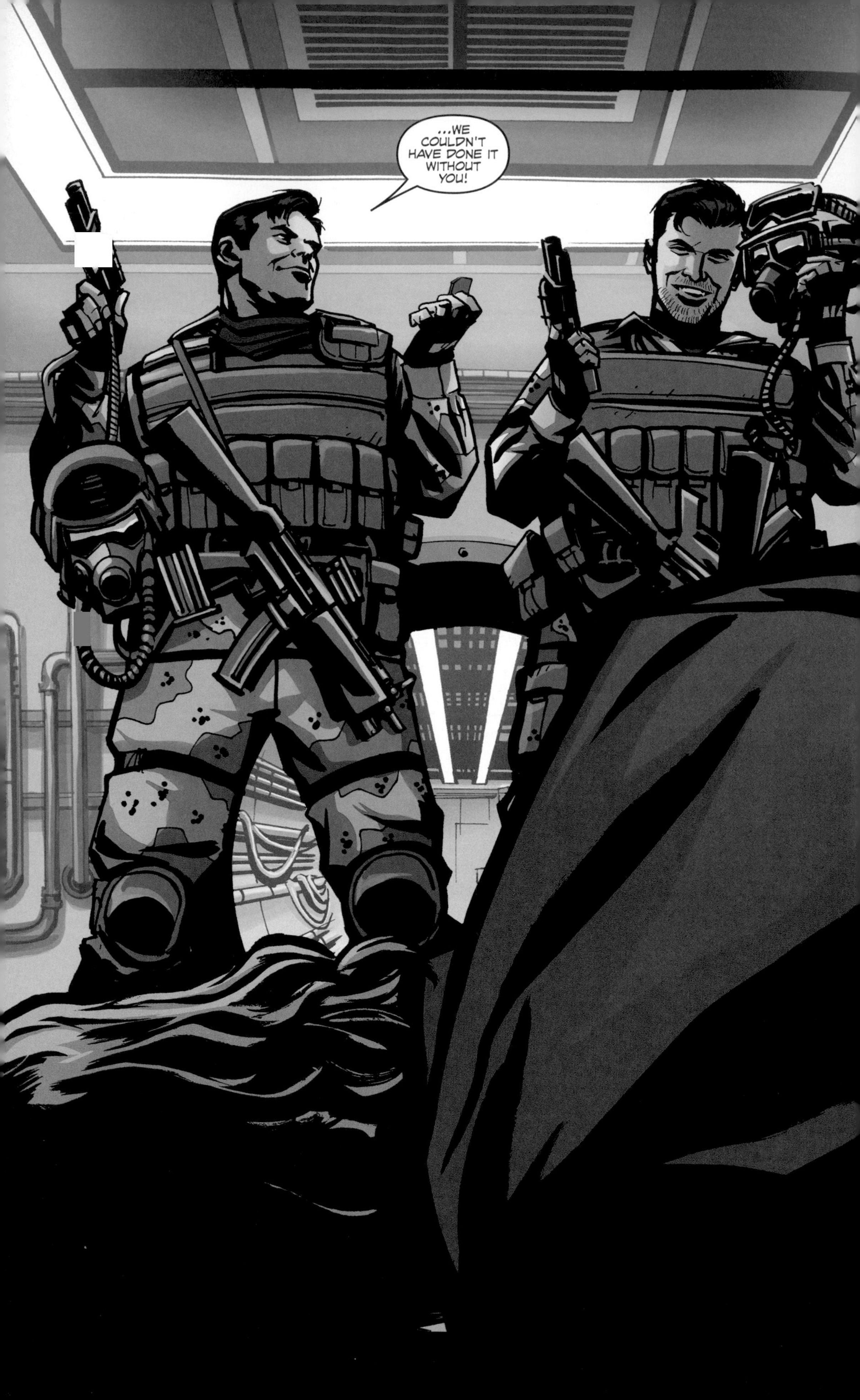
...WE COULDN'T HAVE DONE IT WITHOUT YOU!

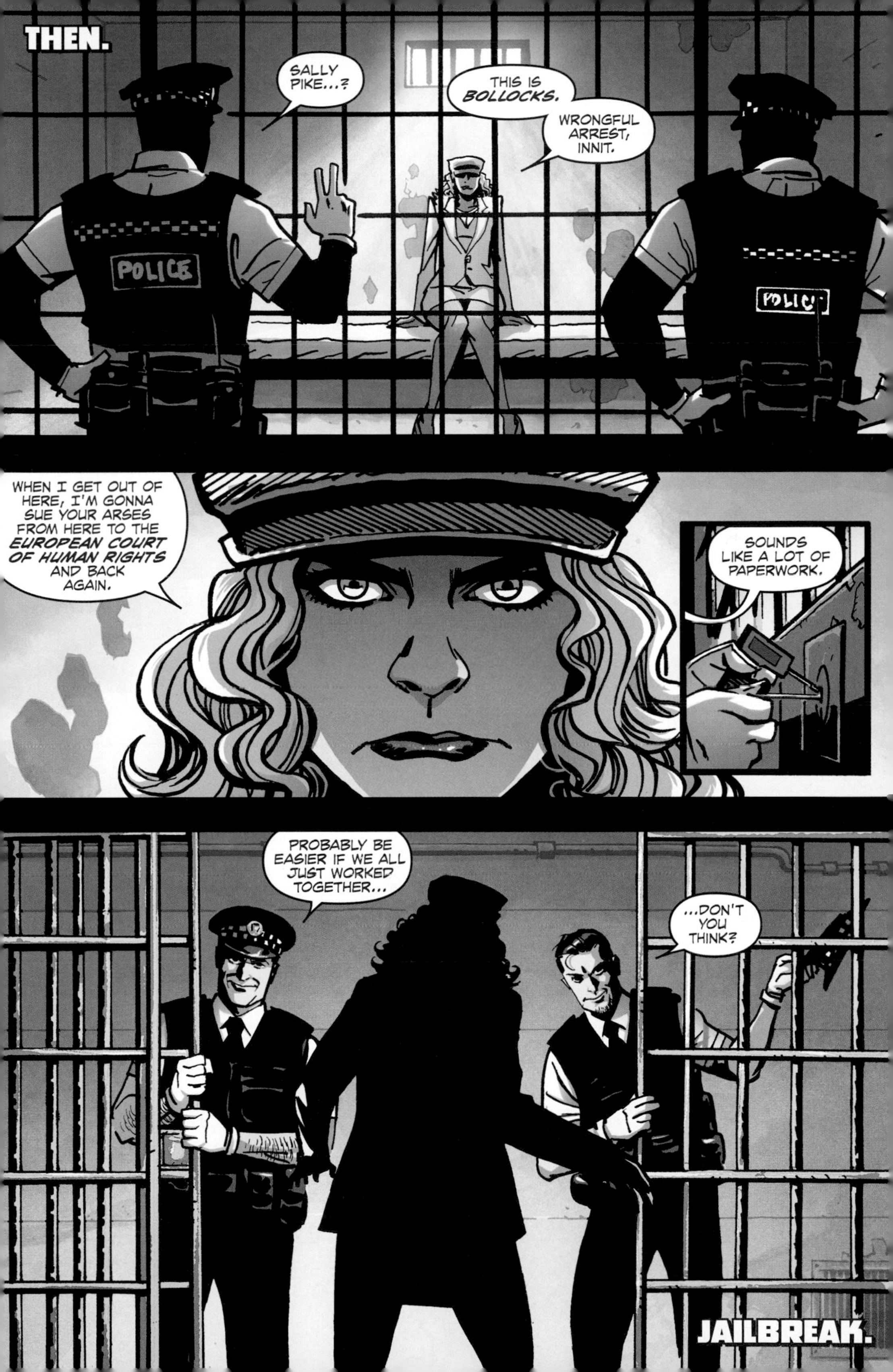
THEN.
SALLY PIKE...?
THIS IS BOLLOCKS.
WRONGFUL ARREST, INNIT.
POLICE
POLICE
WHEN I GET OUT OF HERE, I'M GONNA SUE YOUR ARSES FROM HERE TO THE EUROPEAN COURT OF HUMAN RIGHTS AND BACK AGAIN.
SOUNDS LIKE A LOT OF PAPERWORK.
PROBABLY BE EASIER IF WE ALL JUST WORKED TOGETHER...
...DON'T YOU THINK?
JAILBREAK.

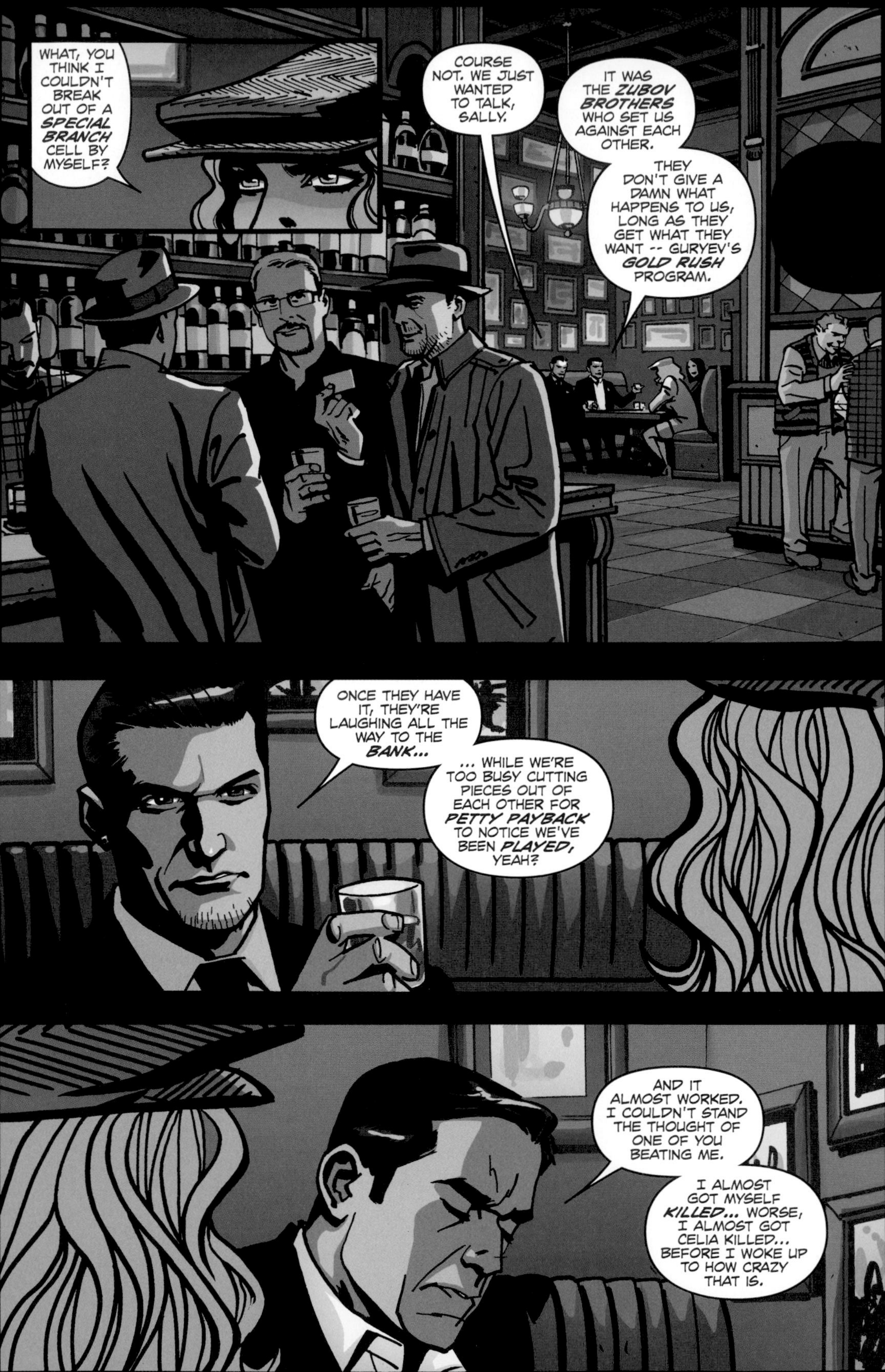
WHAT, YOU THINK I COULDN'T BREAK OUT OF A SPECIAL BRANCH CELL BY MYSELF?
COURSE NOT. WE JUST WANTED TO TALK, SALLY.
IT WAS THE ZUBOV BROTHERS WHO SET US AGAINST EACH OTHER.
THEY DON'T GIVE A DAMN WHAT HAPPENS TO US, LONG AS THEY GET WHAT THEY WANT -- GURYEV'S GOLD RUSH PROGRAM.
ONCE THEY HAVE IT, THEY'RE LAUGHING ALL THE WAY TO THE BANK...
... WHILE WE'RE TOO BUSY CUTTING PIECES OUT OF EACH OTHER FOR PETTY PAYBACK TO NOTICE WE'VE BEEN PLAYED, YEAH?
AND IT ALMOST WORKED. I COULDN'T STAND THE THOUGHT OF ONE OF YOU BEATING ME.
I ALMOST GOT MYSELF KILLED... WORSE, I ALMOST GOT CELIA KILLED... BEFORE I WOKE UP TO HOW CRAZY THAT IS.

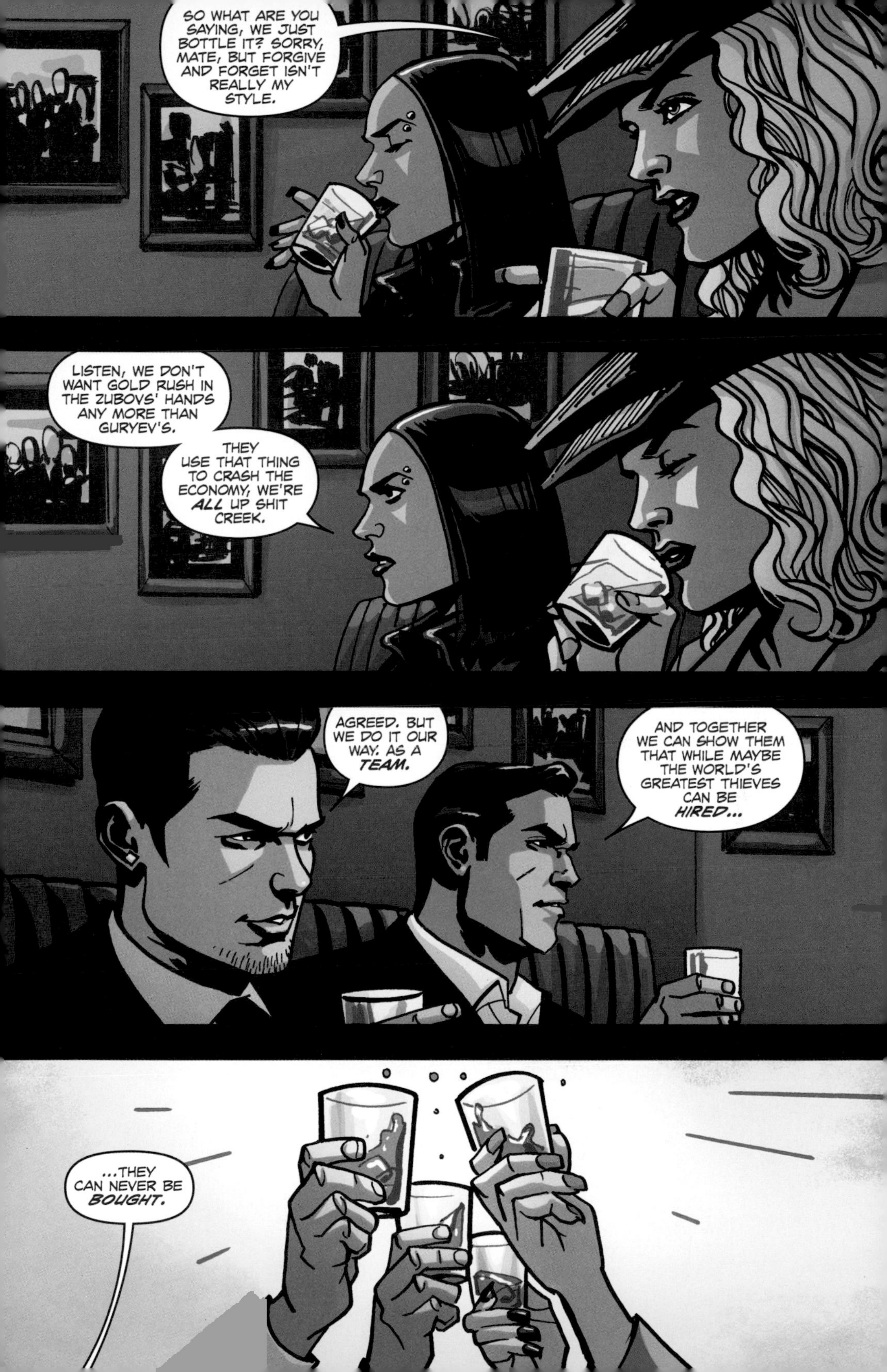
SO WHAT ARE YOU SAYING, WE JUST BOTTLE IT? SORRY, MATE, BUT FORGIVE AND FORGET ISN'T REALLY MY STYLE.
LISTEN, WE DON'T WANT GOLD RUSH IN THE ZUBOVS' HANDS ANY MORE THAN GURYEV'S.
THEY USE THAT THING TO CRASH THE ECONOMY, WE'RE ALL UP SHIT CREEK.
AGREED. BUT WE DO IT OUR WAY. AS A TEAM.
AND TOGETHER WE CAN SHOW THEM THAT WHILE MAYBE THE WORLD'S GREATEST THIEVES CAN BE HIRED...
...THEY CAN NEVER BE BOUGHT.

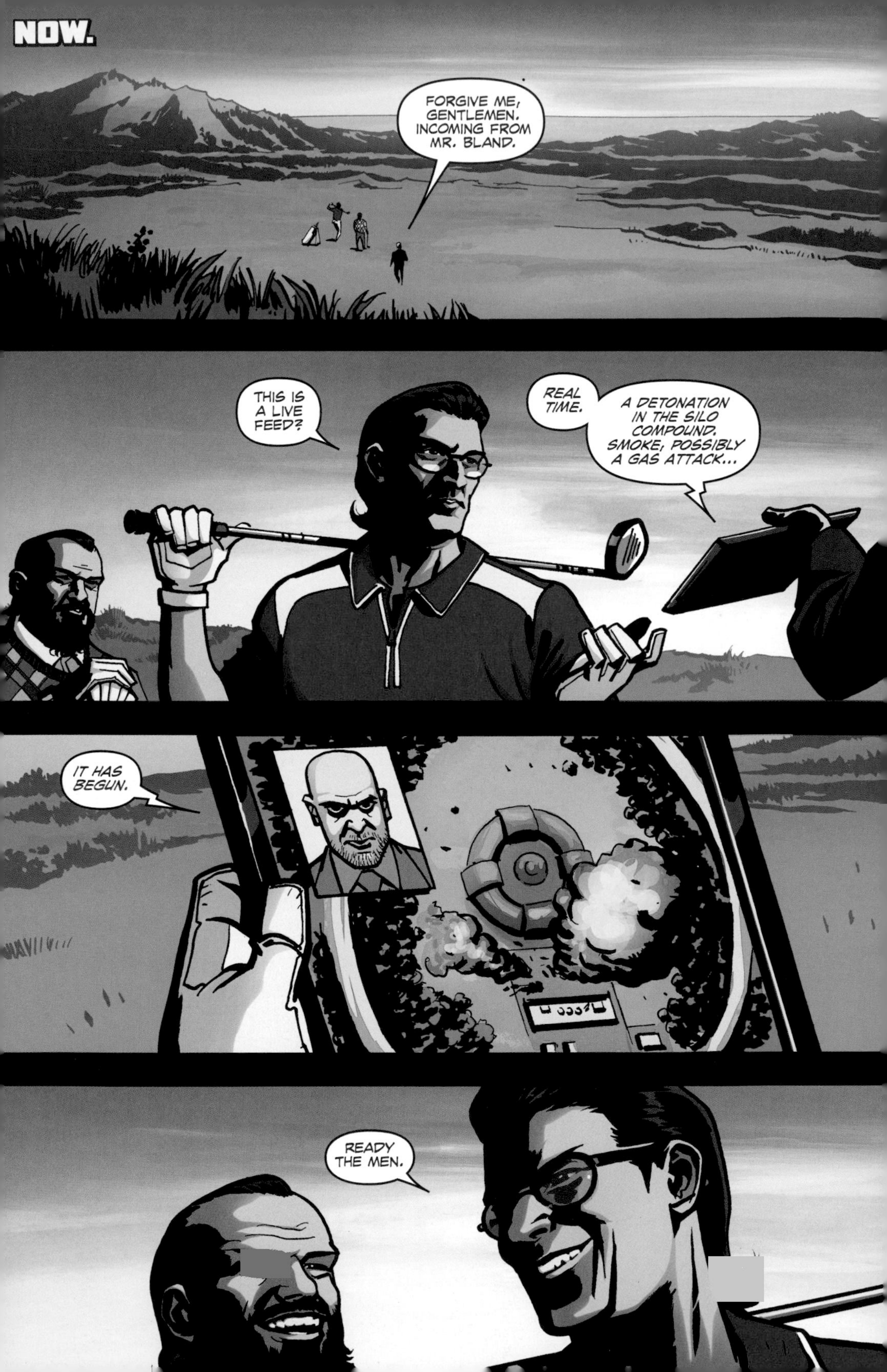
NOW.
FORGIVE ME, GENTLEMEN. INCOMING FROM MR. BLAND.
THIS IS A LIVE FEED?
REAL TIME.
A DETONATION IN THE SILO COMPOUND. SMOKE, POSSIBLY A GAS ATTACK...
IT HAS BEGUN.
READY THE MEN.

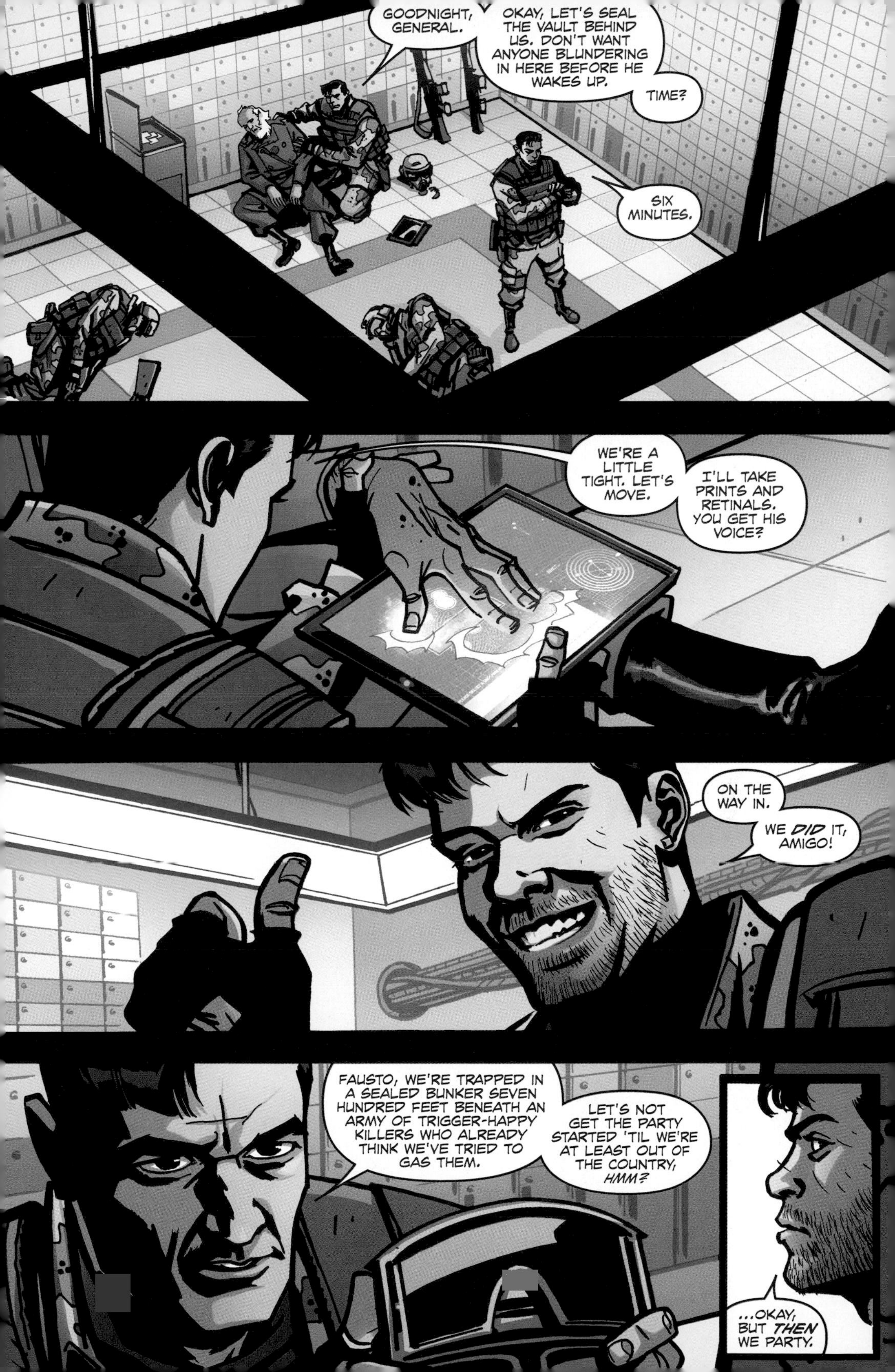
GOODNIGHT, GENERAL.
OKAY, LET'S SEAL THE VAULT BEHIND US. DON'T WANT ANYONE BLUNDERING IN HERE BEFORE HE WAKES UP.
TIME?
SIX MINUTES.
WE'RE A LITTLE TIGHT. LET'S MOVE.
I'LL TAKE PRINTS AND RETINALS. YOU GET HIS VOICE?
ON THE WAY IN.
WE *DID* IT, AMIGO!
FAUSTO, WE'RE TRAPPED IN A SEALED BUNKER SEVEN HUNDRED FEET BENEATH AN ARMY OF TRIGGER-HAPPY KILLERS WHO ALREADY THINK WE'VE TRIED TO GAS THEM.
LET'S NOT GET THE PARTY STARTED 'TIL WE'RE AT LEAST OUT OF THE COUNTRY, *HMM?*
...OKAY, BUT *THEN* WE PARTY.

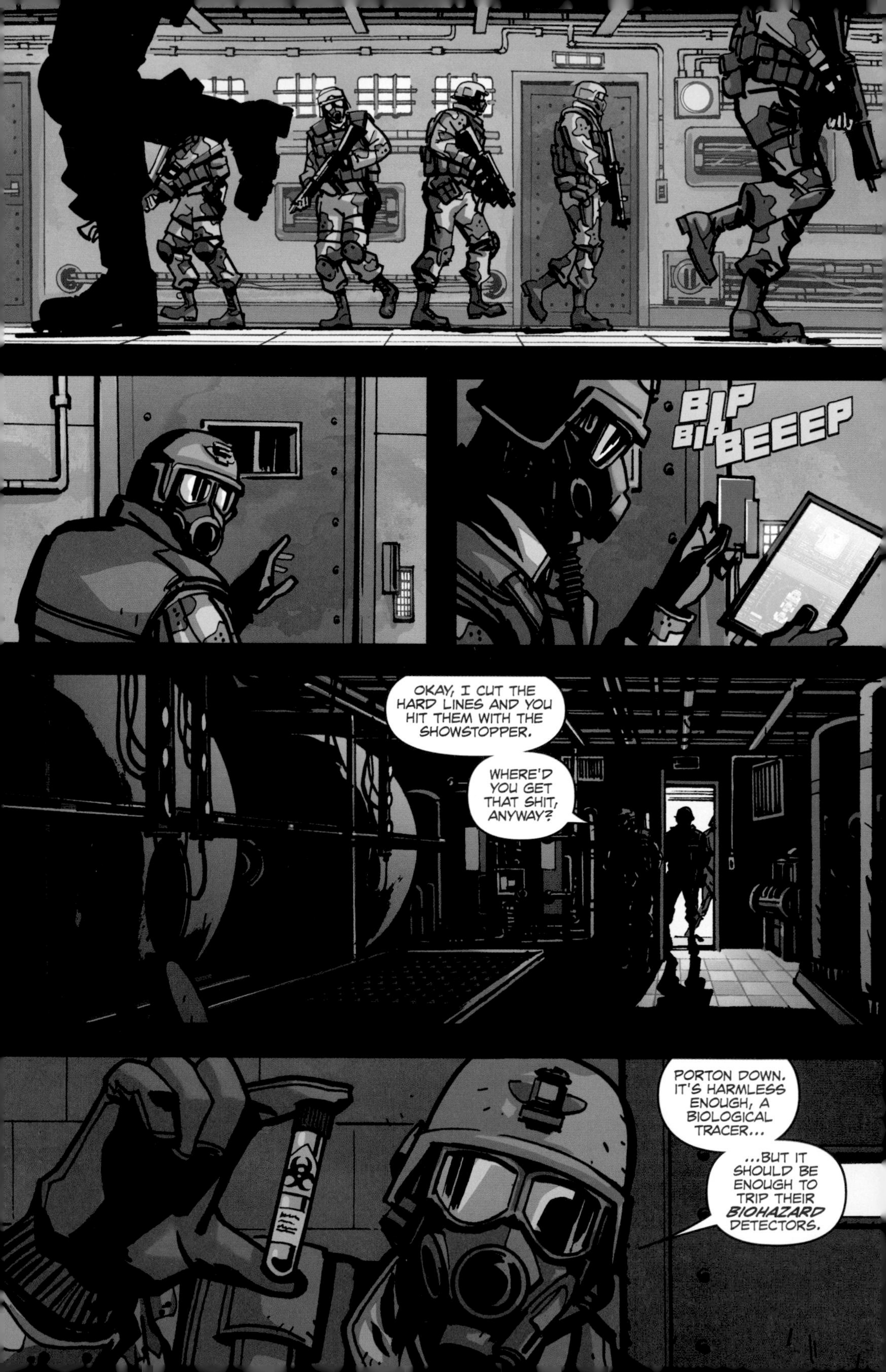
BIP
BIP BEEEP
OKAY, I CUT THE HARD LINES AND YOU HIT THEM WITH THE SHOWSTOPPER.
WHERE'D YOU GET THAT SHIT, ANYWAY?
PORTON DOWN. IT'S HARMLESS ENOUGH, A BIOLOGICAL TRACER...
...BUT IT SHOULD BE ENOUGH TO TRIP THEIR *BIOHAZARD* DETECTORS.

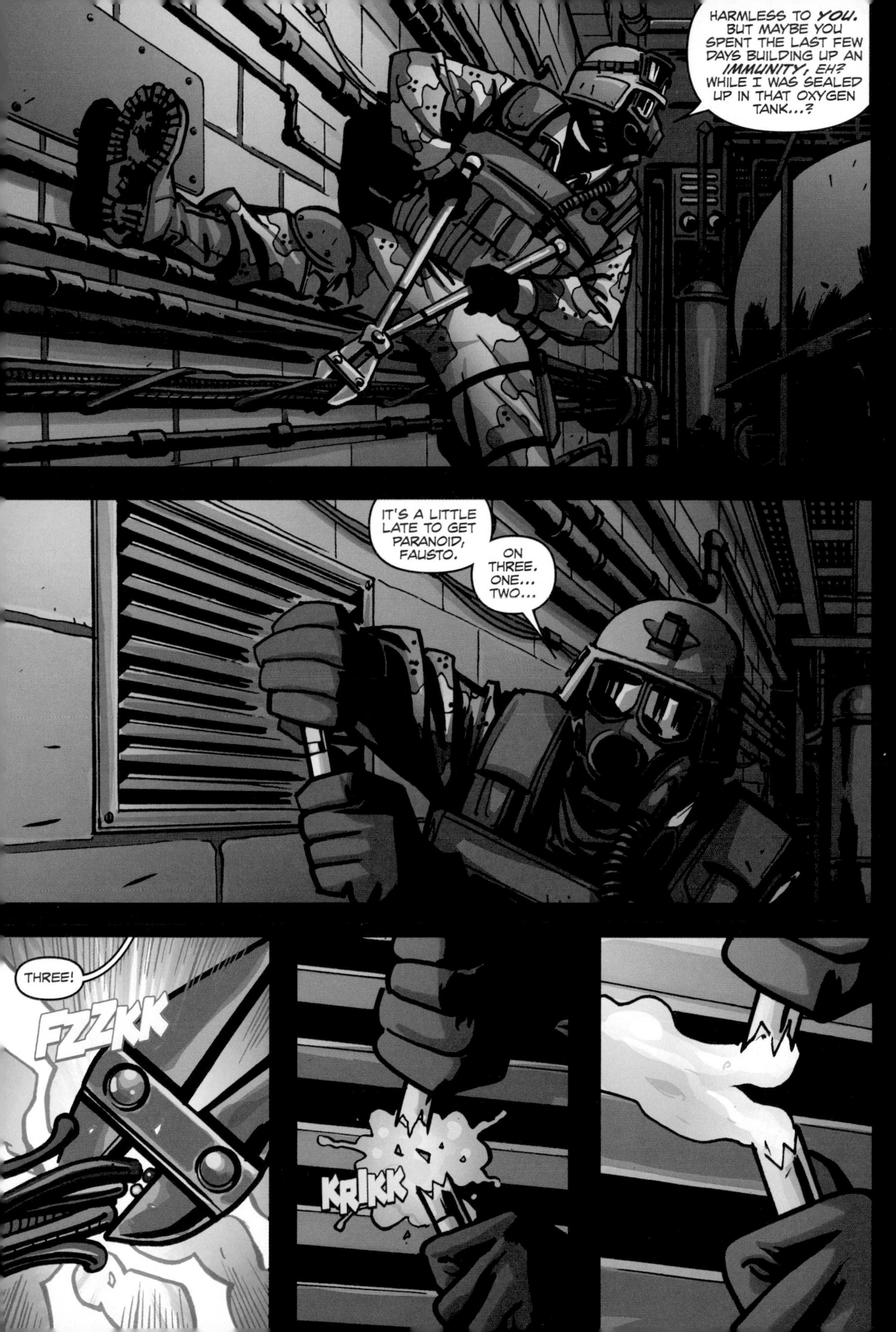
HARMLESS TO *YOU.* BUT MAYBE YOU SPENT THE LAST FEW DAYS BUILDING UP AN *IMMUNITY*, EH? WHILE I WAS SEALED UP IN THAT OXYGEN TANK...?
IT'S A LITTLE LATE TO GET PARANOID, FAUSTO.
ON THREE. ONE... TWO...
THREE!
FZZKK
KRIKK

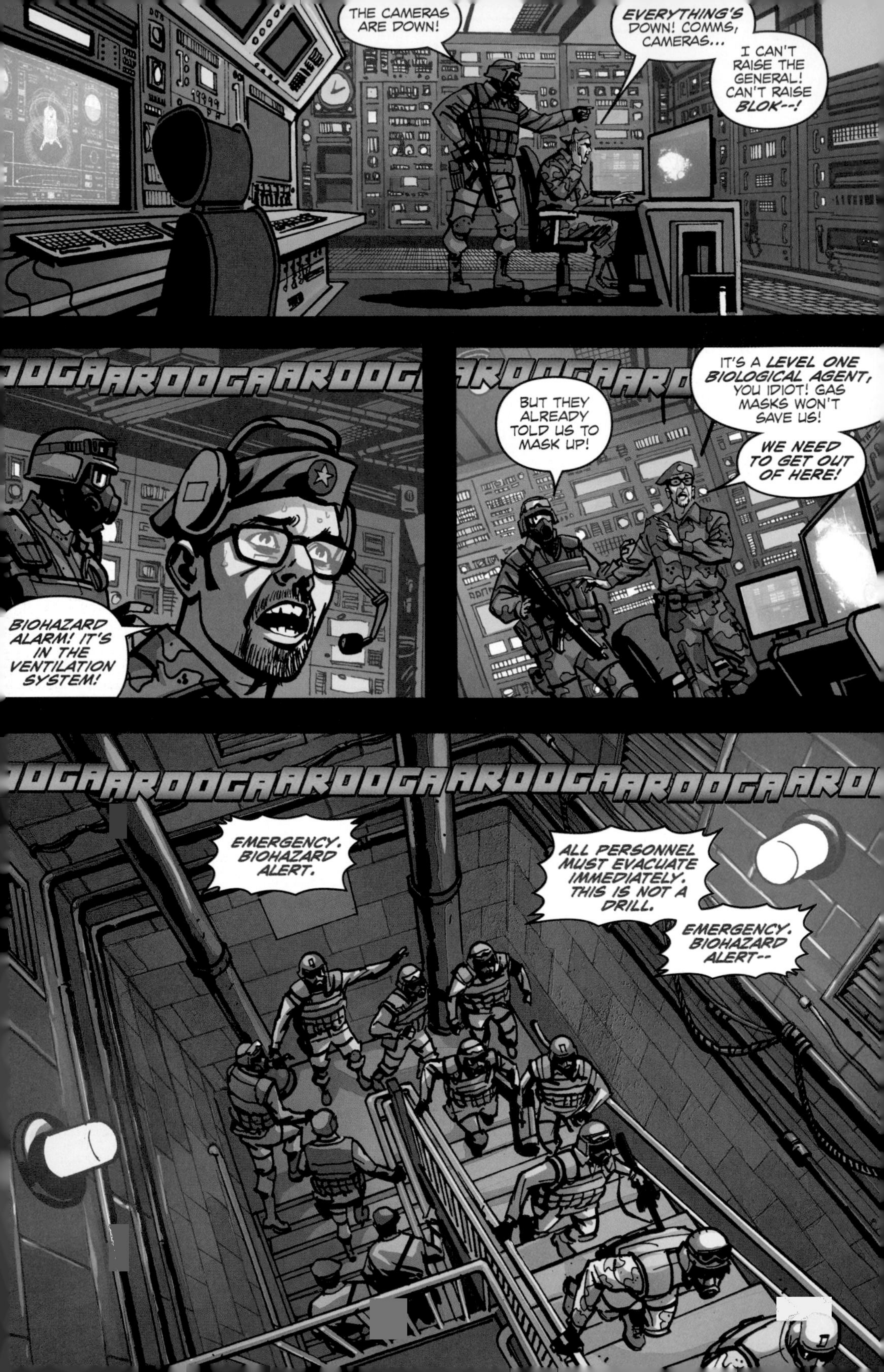

THE CAMERAS ARE DOWN!
EVERYTHING'S DOWN! COMMS, CAMERAS...
I CAN'T RAISE THE GENERAL! CAN'T RAISE BLOK--!
OOGAAROOGAAROOG
BIOHAZARD ALARM! IT'S IN THE VENTILATION SYSTEM!
AROOGAARO
BUT THEY ALREADY TOLD US TO MASK UP!
IT'S A LEVEL ONE BIOLOGICAL AGENT, YOU IDIOT! GAS MASKS WON'T SAVE US!
WE NEED TO GET OUT OF HERE!
OOGAAROOGAAROOGAAROOGAAROOGAARO
EMERGENCY. BIOHAZARD ALERT.
ALL PERSONNEL MUST EVACUATE IMMEDIATELY. THIS IS NOT A DRILL.
EMERGENCY. BIOHAZARD ALERT--

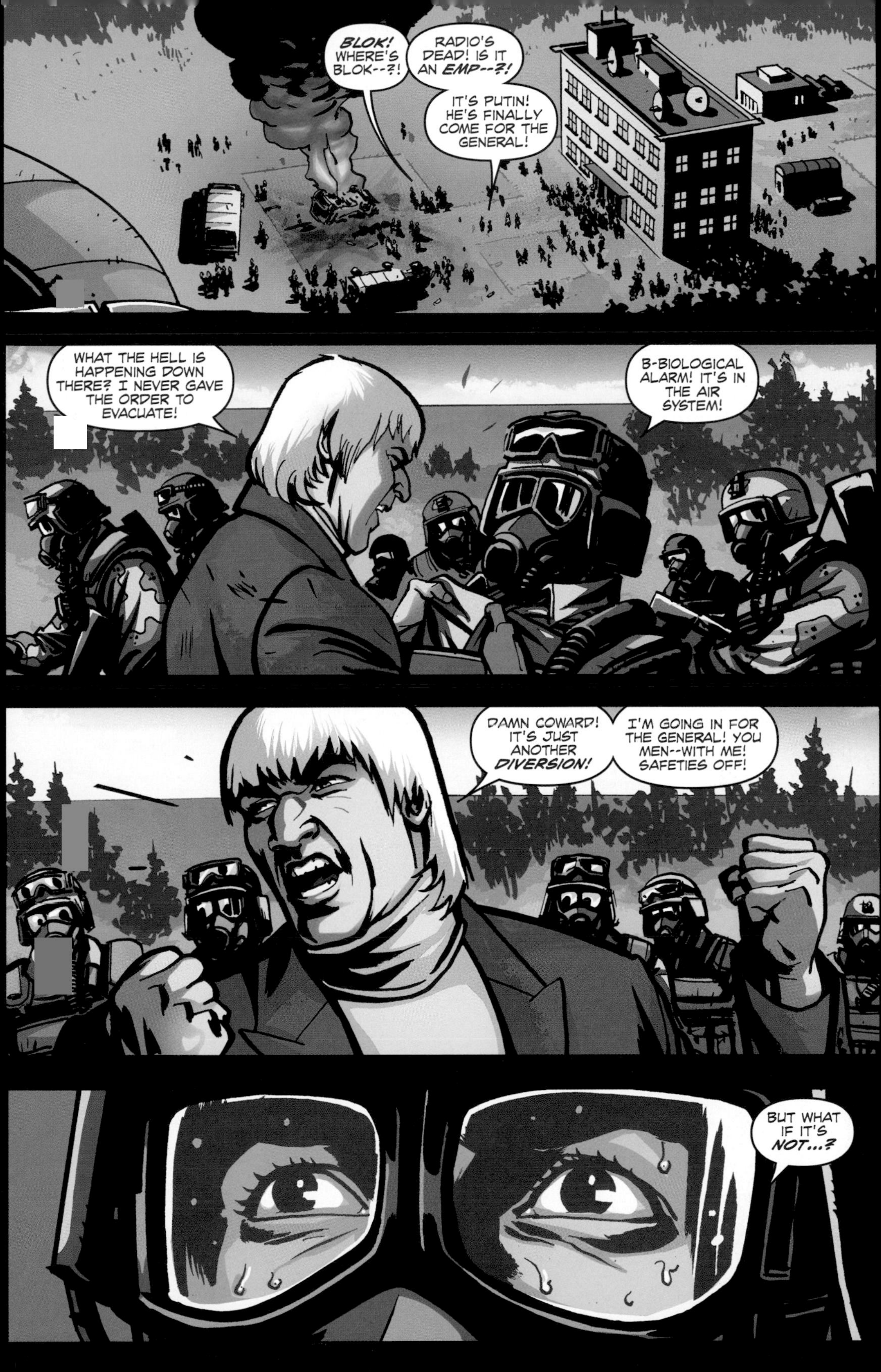
BLOK! WHERE'S BLOK--?!
RADIO'S DEAD! IS IT AN EMP--?!
IT'S PUTIN! HE'S FINALLY COME FOR THE GENERAL!
WHAT THE HELL IS HAPPENING DOWN THERE? I NEVER GAVE THE ORDER TO EVACUATE!
B-BIOLOGICAL ALARM! IT'S IN THE AIR SYSTEM!
DAMN COWARD! IT'S JUST ANOTHER DIVERSION!
I'M GOING IN FOR THE GENERAL! YOU MEN--WITH ME! SAFETIES OFF!
BUT WHAT IF IT'S NOT...?

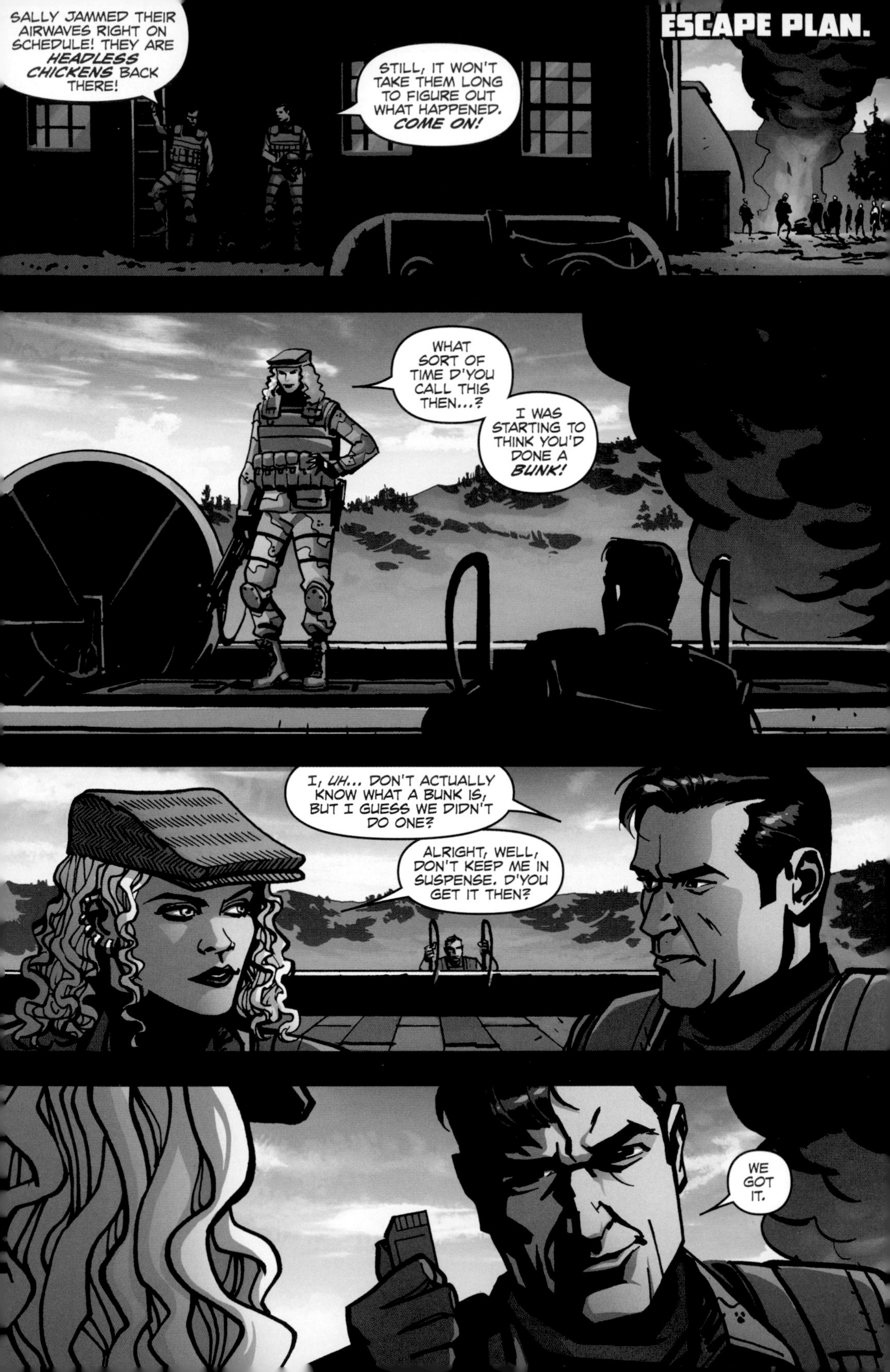
ESCAPE PLAN.
SALLY JAMMED THEIR AIRWAVES RIGHT ON SCHEDULE! THEY ARE HEADLESS CHICKENS BACK THERE!
STILL, IT WON'T TAKE THEM LONG TO FIGURE OUT WHAT HAPPENED. COME ON!
WHAT SORT OF TIME D'YOU CALL THIS THEN...?
I WAS STARTING TO THINK YOU'D DONE A BUNK!
I, UH... DON'T ACTUALLY KNOW WHAT A BUNK IS, BUT I GUESS WE DIDN'T DO ONE?
ALRIGHT, WELL, DON'T KEEP ME IN SUSPENSE. D'YOU GET IT THEN?
WE GOT IT.

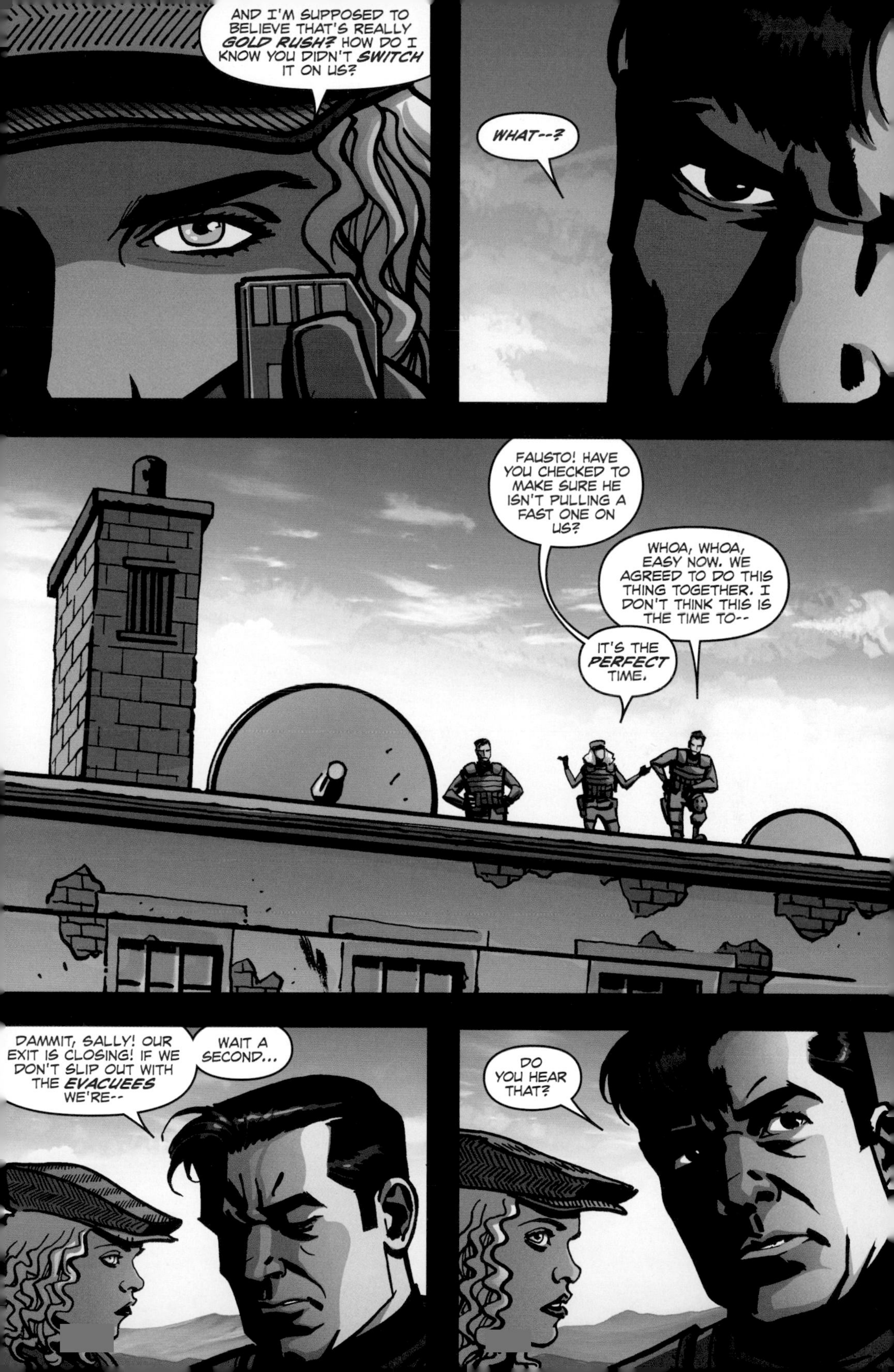
AND I'M SUPPOSED TO BELIEVE THAT'S REALLY GOLD RUSH? HOW DO I KNOW YOU DIDN'T SWITCH IT ON US?
WHAT--?
FAUSTO! HAVE YOU CHECKED TO MAKE SURE HE ISN'T PULLING A FAST ONE ON US?
WHOA, WHOA, EASY NOW. WE AGREED TO DO THIS THING TOGETHER. I DON'T THINK THIS IS THE TIME TO--
IT'S THE PERFECT TIME.
DAMMIT, SALLY! OUR EXIT IS CLOSING! IF WE DON'T SLIP OUT WITH THE EVACUEES WE'RE--
WAIT A SECOND...
DO YOU HEAR THAT?

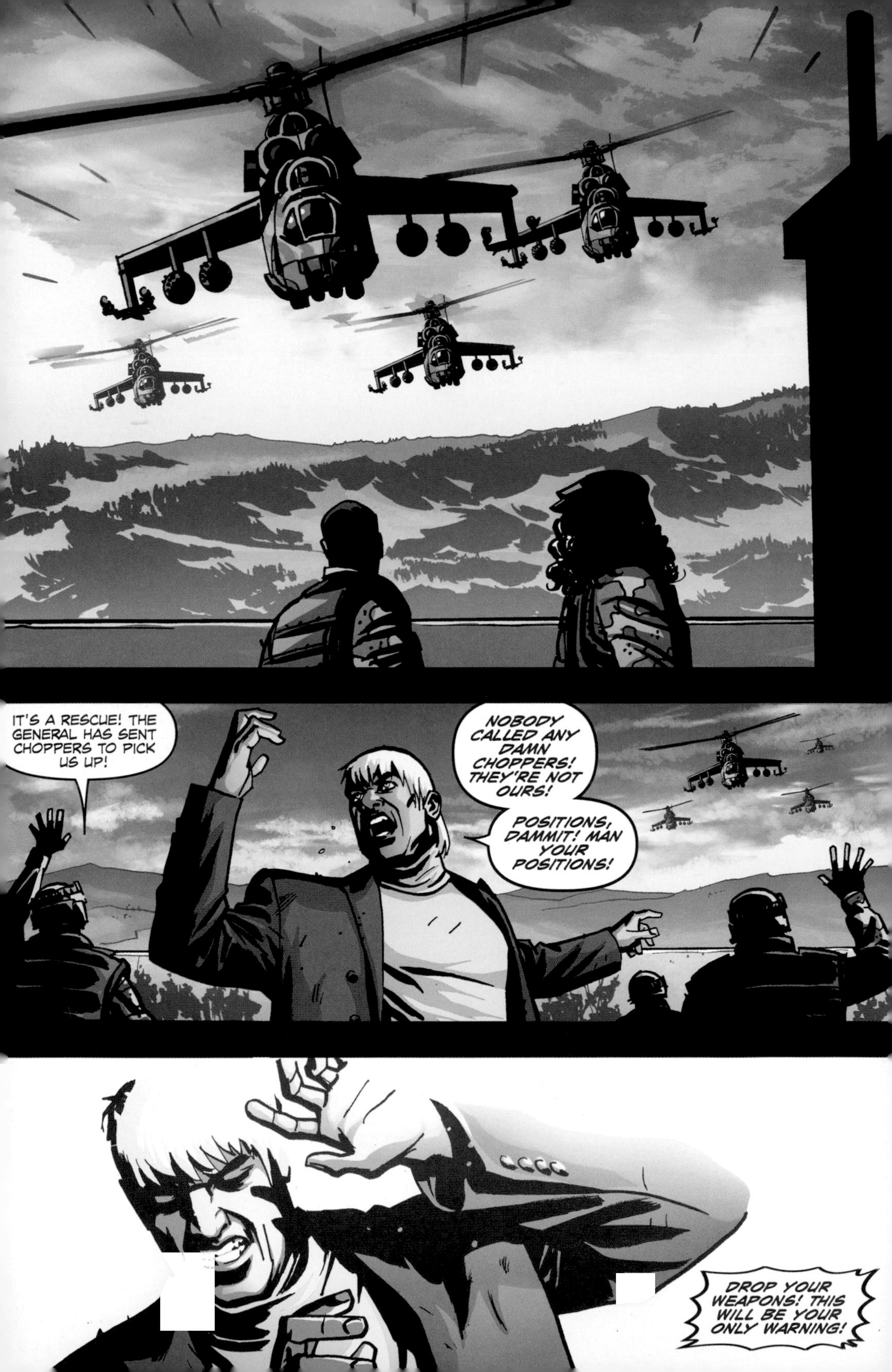
IT'S A RESCUE! THE GENERAL HAS SENT CHOPPERS TO PICK US UP!
NOBODY CALLED ANY DAMN CHOPPERS! THEY'RE NOT OURS!
POSITIONS, DAMMIT! MAN YOUR POSITIONS!
DROP YOUR WEAPONS! THIS WILL BE YOUR ONLY WARNING!

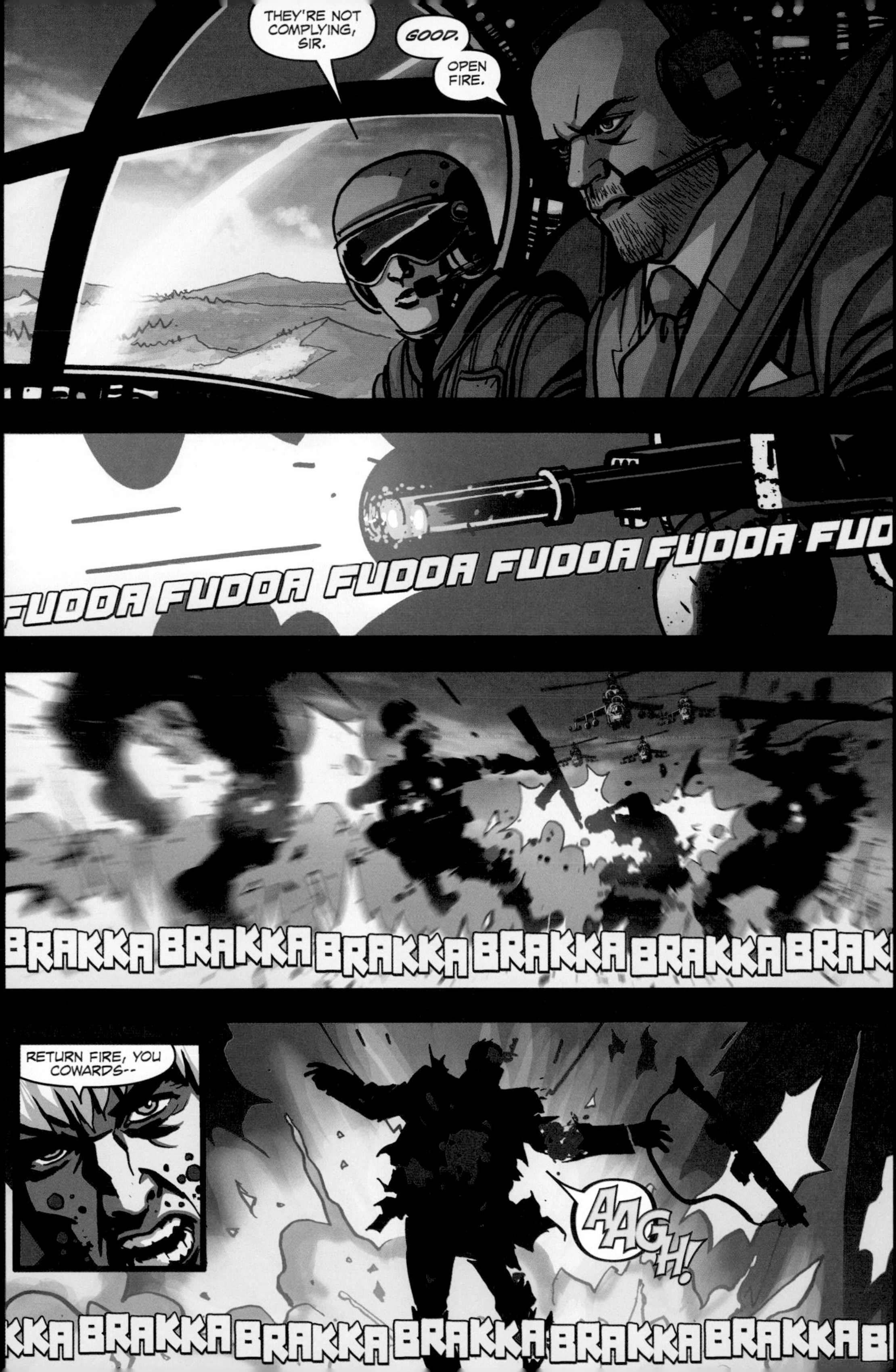

THEY'RE NOT COMPLYING, SIR.
GOOD.
OPEN FIRE.
FUDDA FUDDA FUDDA FUDDA FUDDA FUD
BRAKKA BRAKKA BRAKKA BRAKKA BRAKKA BRAK
RETURN FIRE, YOU COWARDS--
AAGH!
KKA BRAKKA BRAKKA BRAKKA BRAKKA BRAKKA B

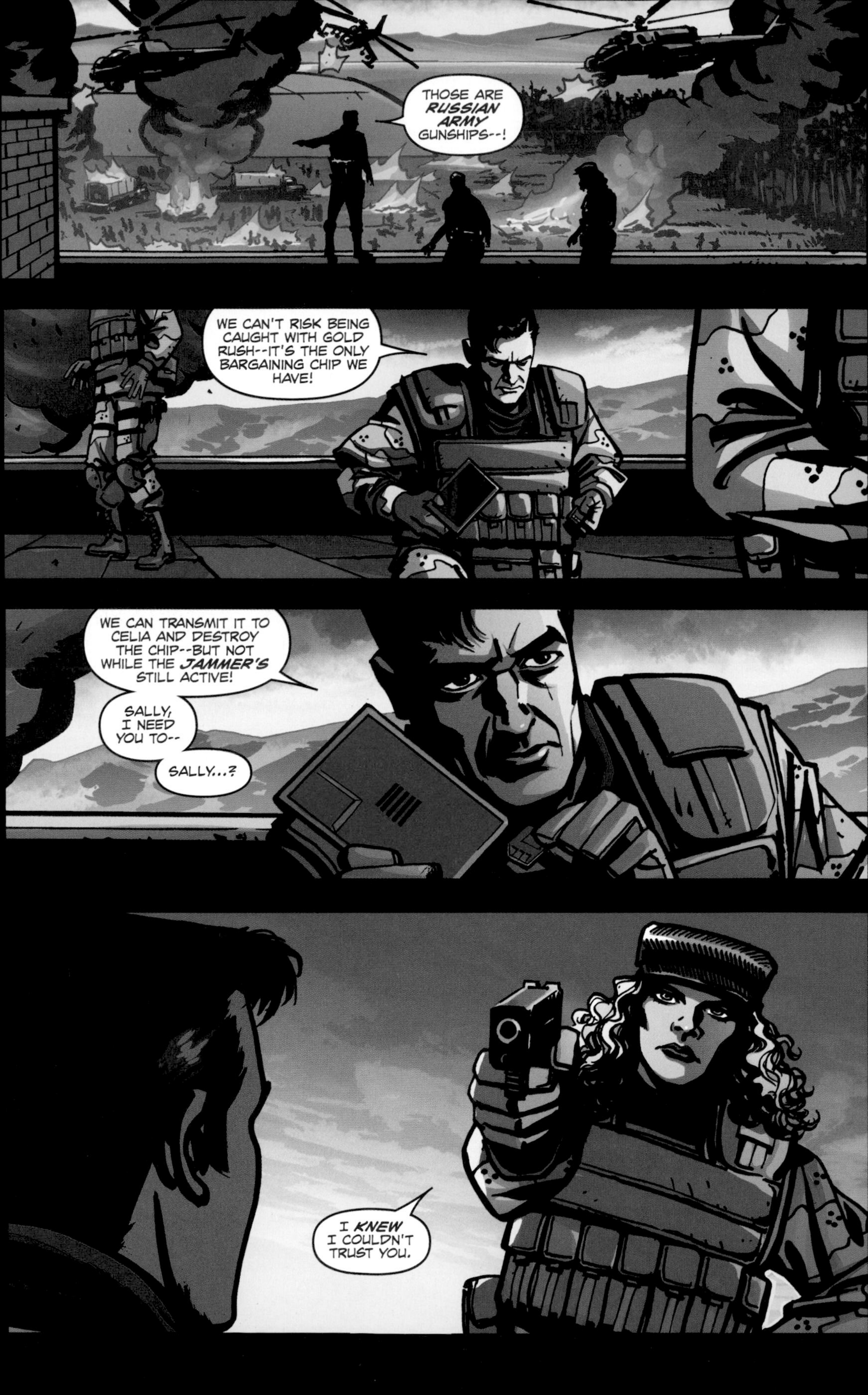
THOSE ARE *RUSSIAN ARMY* GUNSHIPS--!
WE CAN'T RISK BEING CAUGHT WITH GOLD RUSH--IT'S THE ONLY BARGAINING CHIP WE HAVE!
WE CAN TRANSMIT IT TO CELIA AND DESTROY THE CHIP--BUT NOT WHILE THE *JAMMER'S* STILL ACTIVE!
SALLY, I NEED YOU TO--
SALLY...?
I *KNEW* I COULDN'T TRUST YOU.

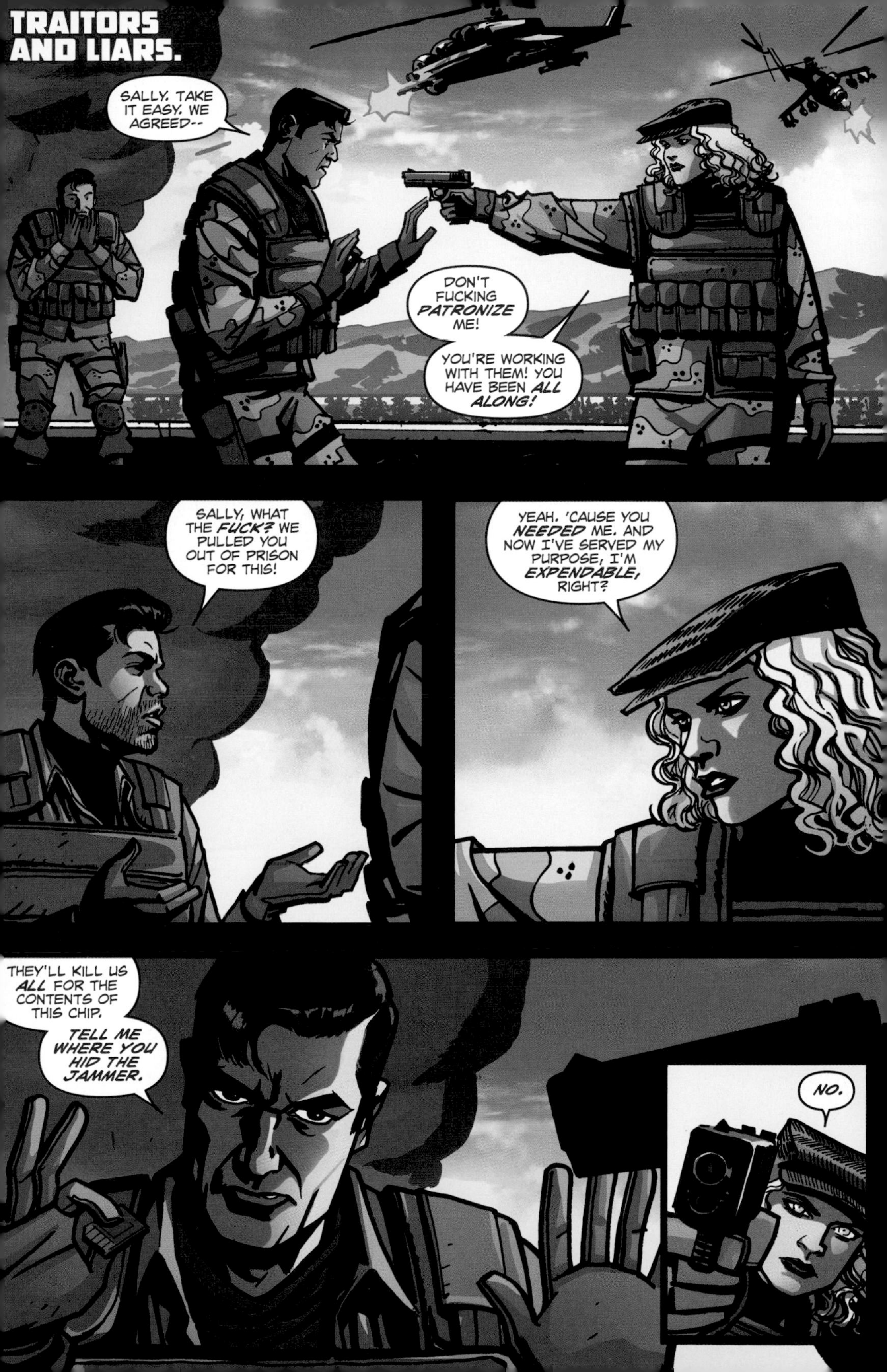
TRAITORS AND LIARS.
SALLY. TAKE IT EASY. WE AGREED--
DON'T FUCKING PATRONIZE ME!
YOU'RE WORKING WITH THEM! YOU HAVE BEEN ALL ALONG!
SALLY, WHAT THE FUCK? WE PULLED YOU OUT OF PRISON FOR THIS!
YEAH. 'CAUSE YOU NEEDED ME. AND NOW I'VE SERVED MY PURPOSE, I'M EXPENDABLE, RIGHT?
THEY'LL KILL US ALL FOR THE CONTENTS OF THIS CHIP.
TELL ME WHERE YOU HID THE JAMMER.
NO.

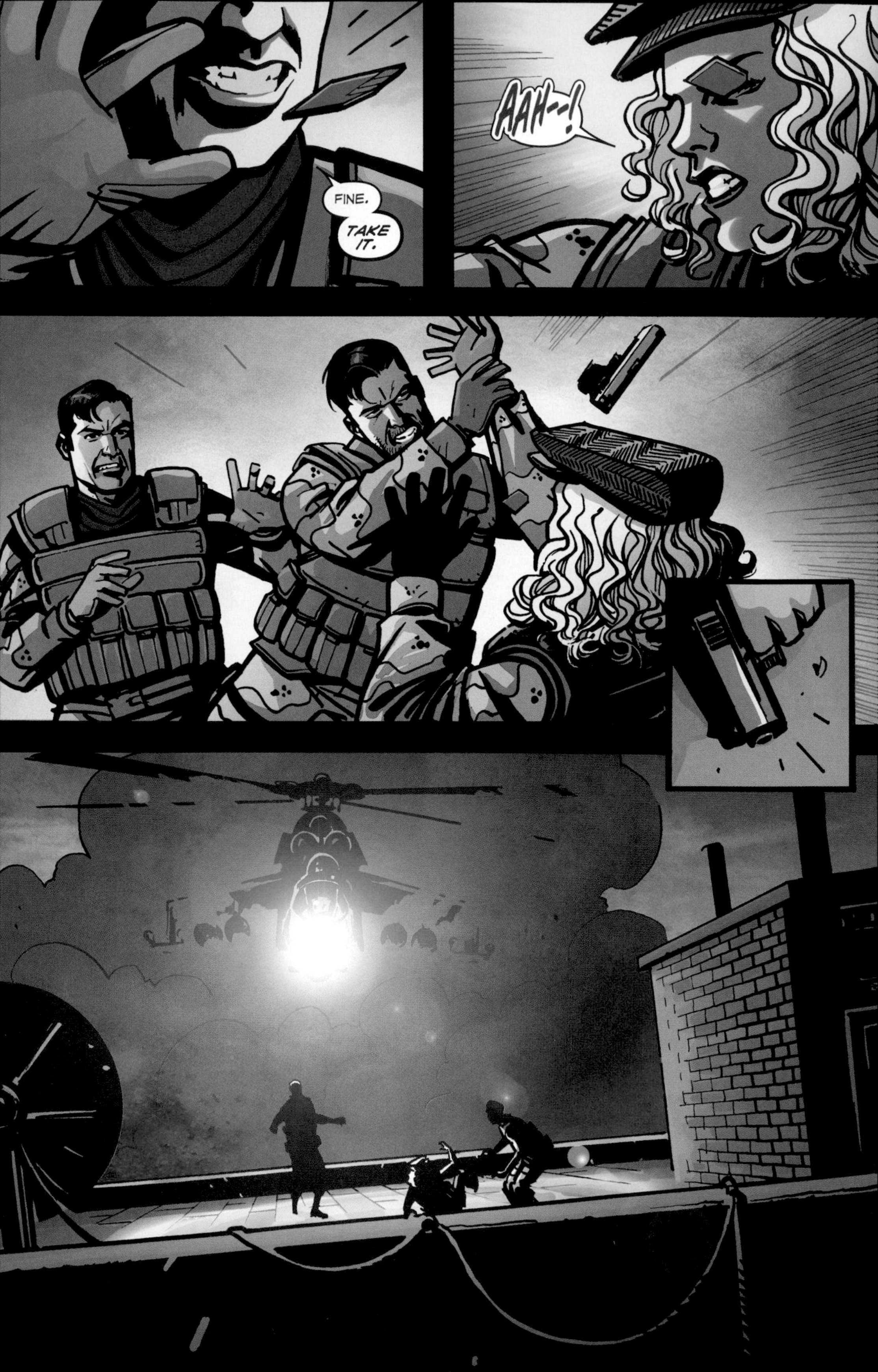
FINE.
TAKE IT.
AAH--!

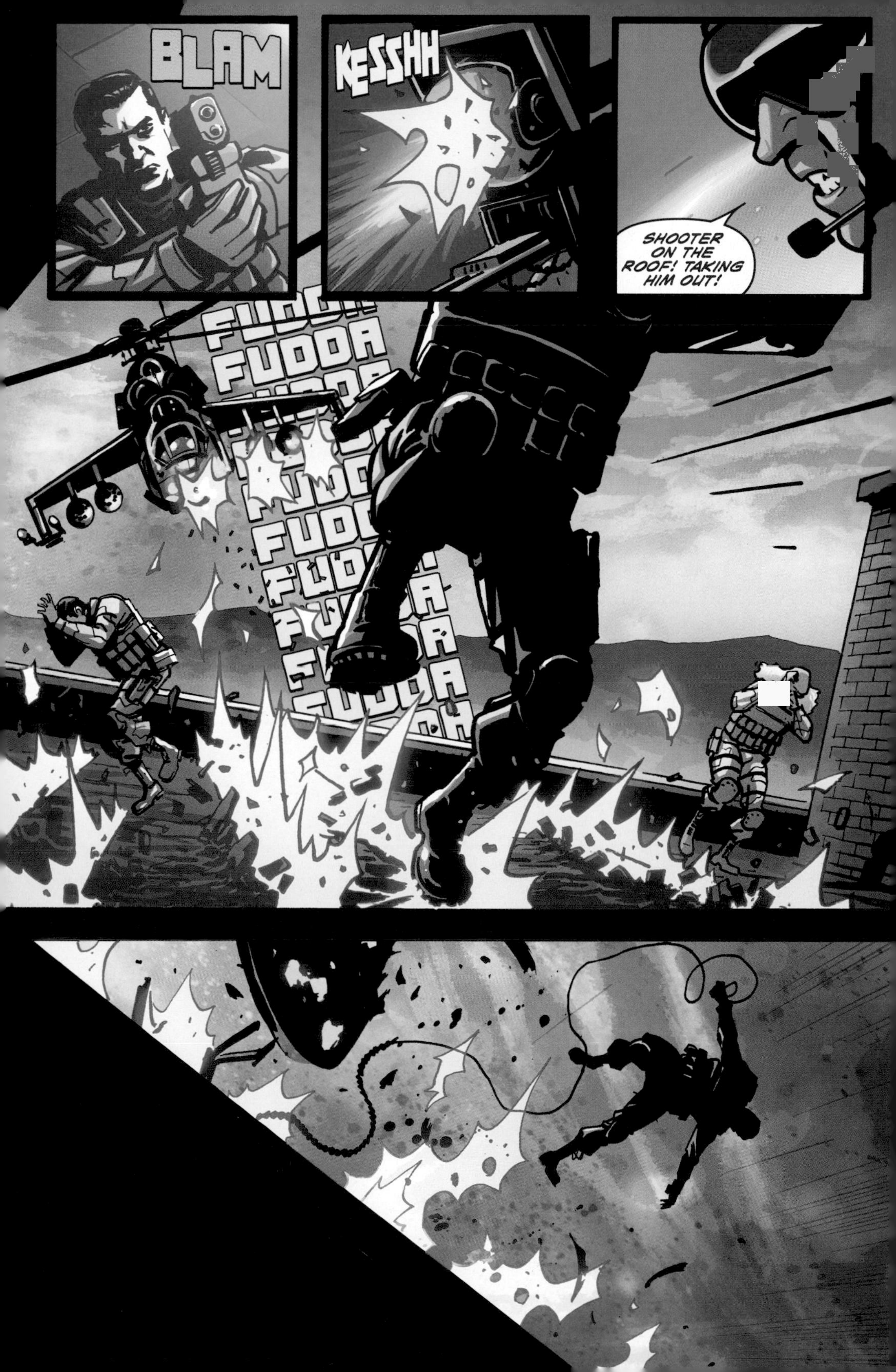
BLAM
KESSHH
SHOOTER ON THE ROOF! TAKING HIM OUT!
FUDDA
FUDDA
FUDDA

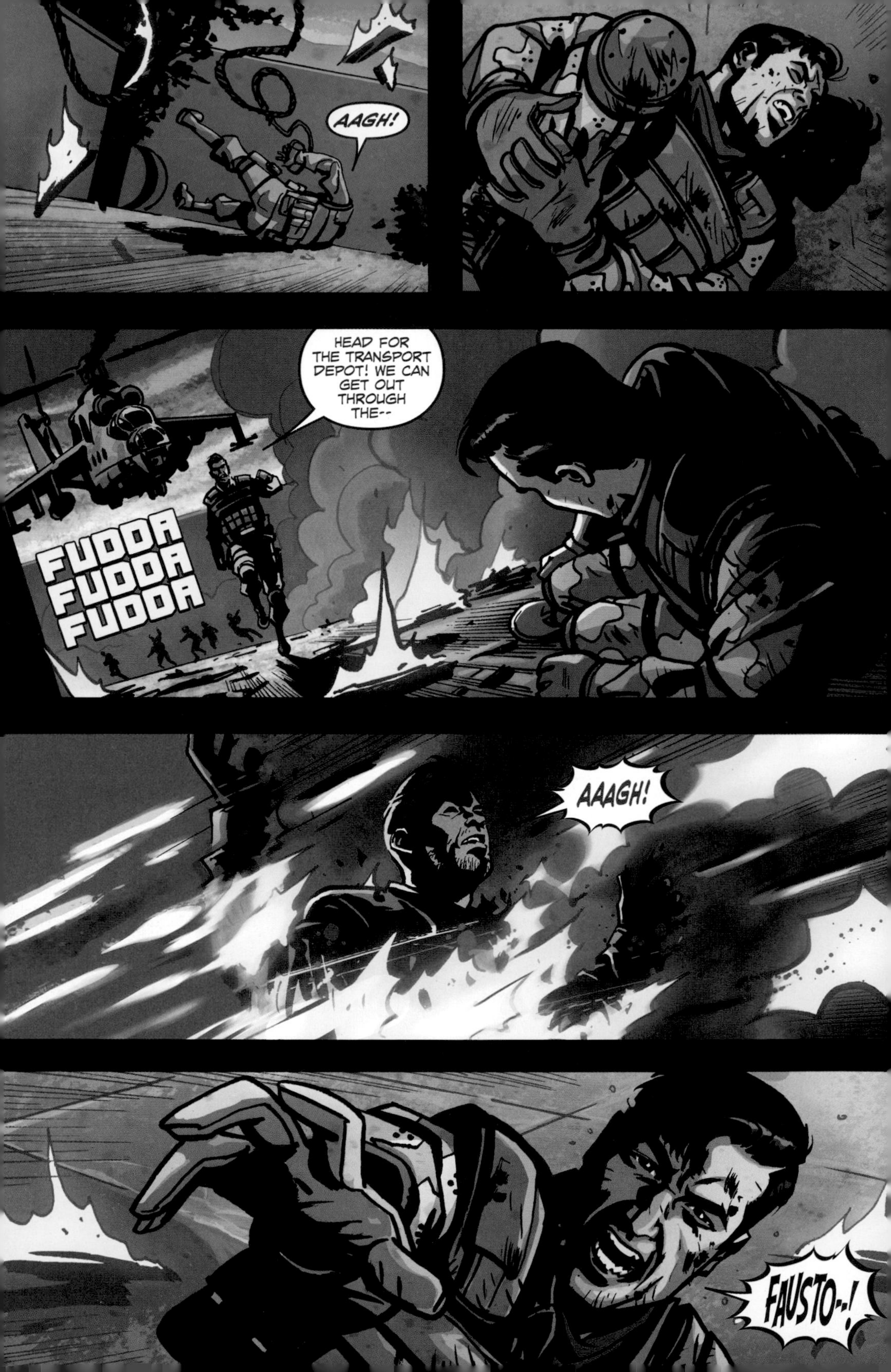
AAGH!
HEAD FOR THE TRANSPORT DEPOT! WE CAN GET OUT THROUGH THE--
FUDDA FUDDA FUDDA
AAAGH!
FAUSTO--!

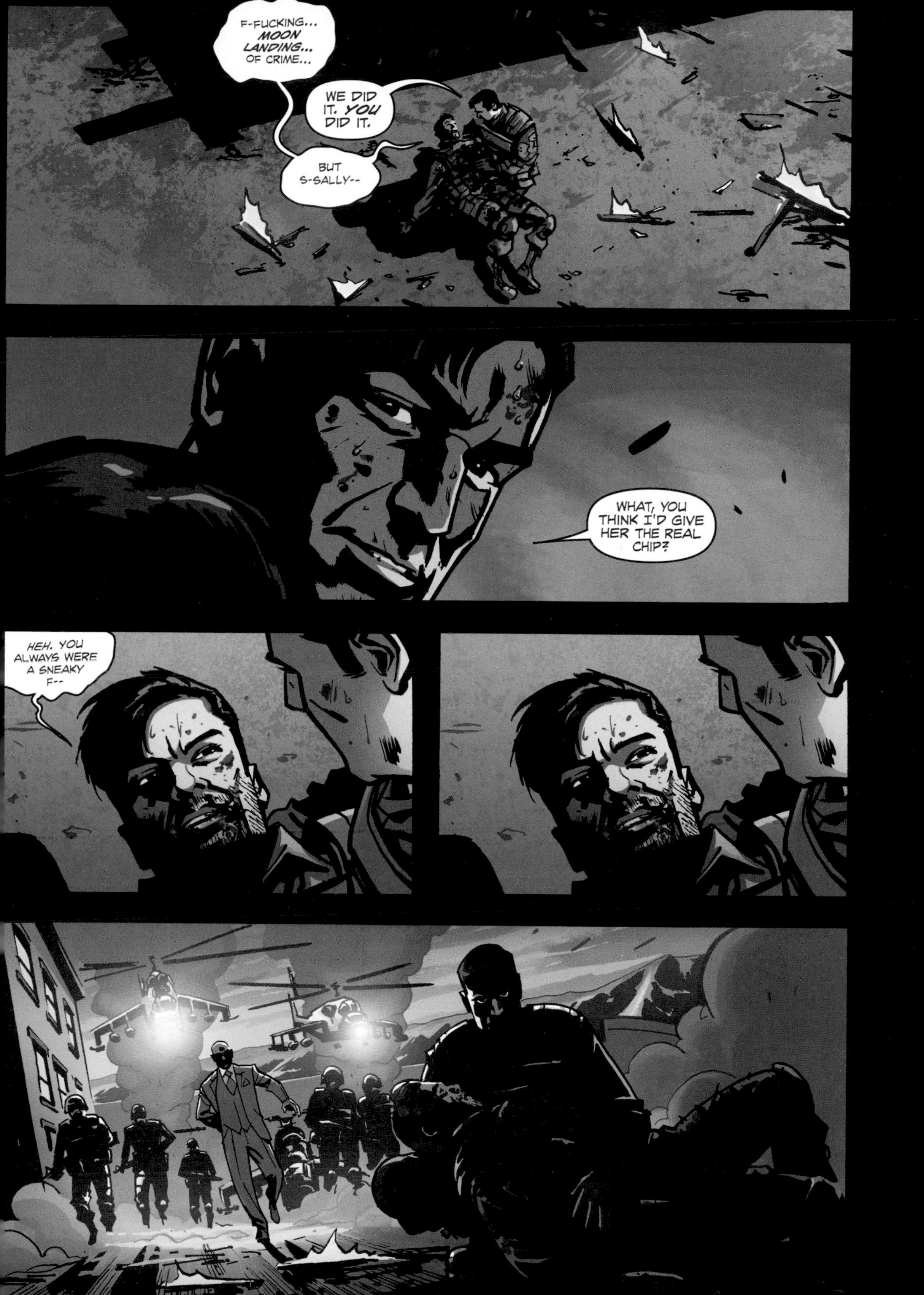

F-FUCKING... MOON LANDING... OF CRIME...
WE DID IT. YOU DID IT.
BUT S-SALLY--
WHAT, YOU THINK I'D GIVE HER THE REAL CHIP?
HEH. YOU ALWAYS WERE A SNEAKY F--

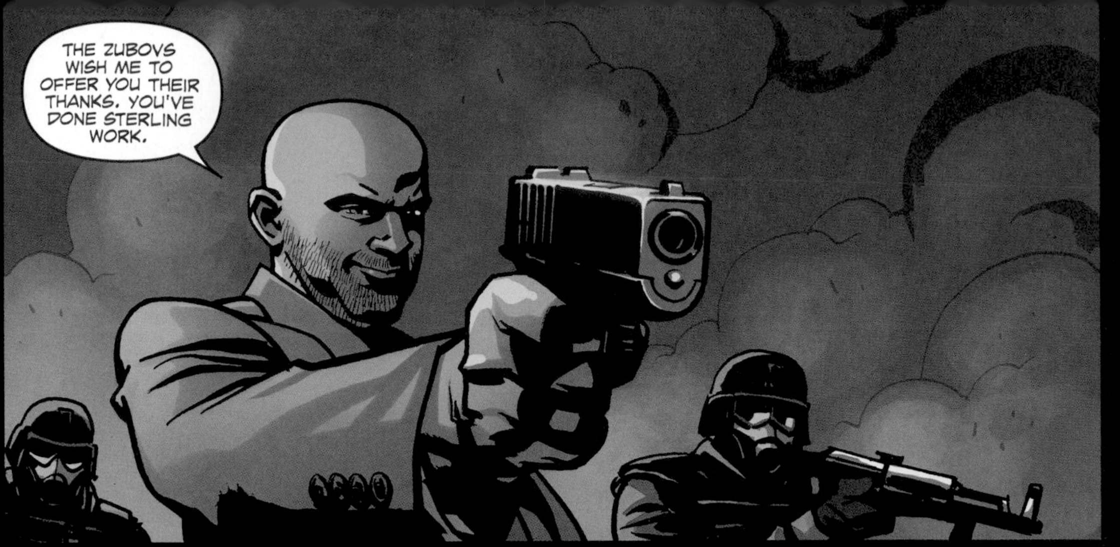
THE ZUBOVS WISH ME TO OFFER YOU THEIR THANKS. YOU'VE DONE STERLING WORK.

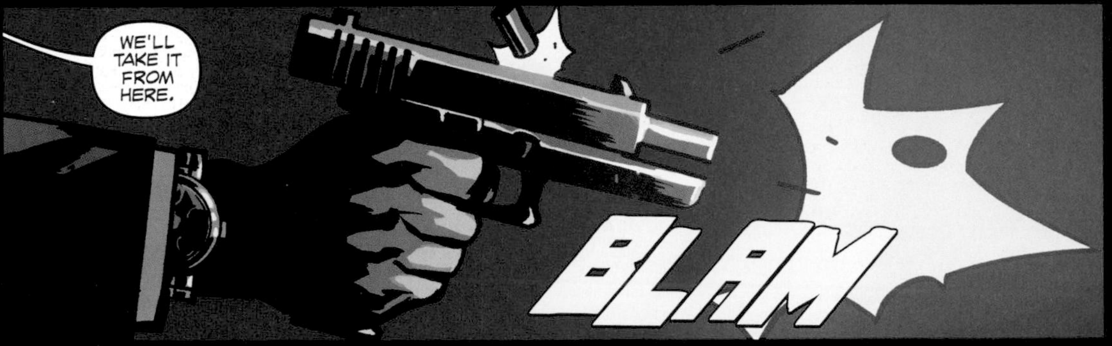
WE'LL TAKE IT FROM HERE.
BLAM

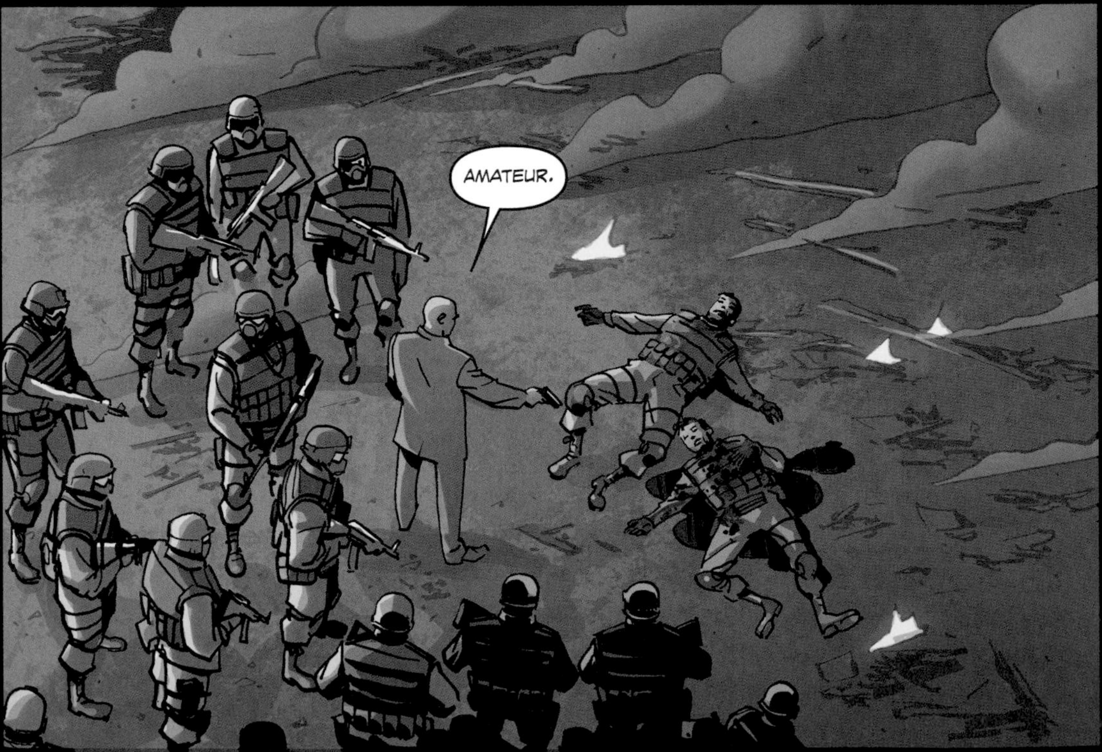
AMATEUR.

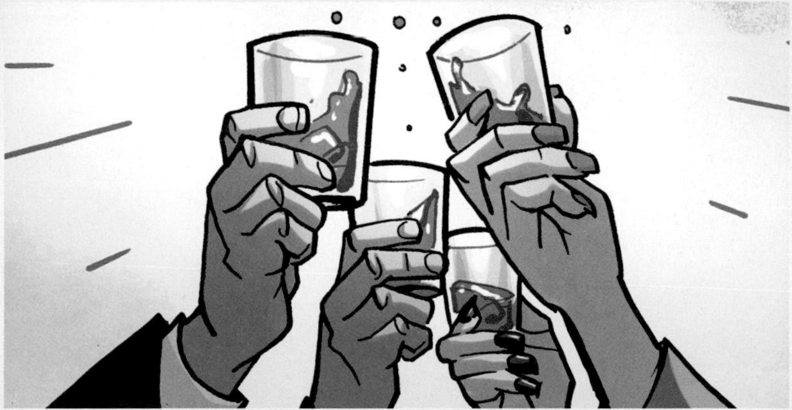

TO BE CONTINUED...

FOR MORE TALES FROM
ROBERT KIRKMAN AND SKYBOUND

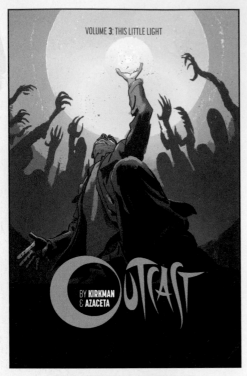

VOLUME 3: THIS LITTLE LIGHT

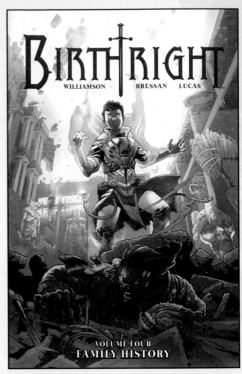

VOL. 1: A DARKNESS SURROUNDS HIM TP
ISBN: 978-1-63215-053-0
$9.99

VOL. 2: A VAST AND UNENDING RUIN TP
ISBN: 978-1-63215-448-4
$14.99

VOL. 3: THIS LITTLE LIGHT TP
ISBN: 978-1-63215-693-8
$14.99

VOL. 1: HOMECOMING TP
ISBN: 978-1-63215-231-2
$9.99

VOL. 2: CALL TO ADVENTURE TP
ISBN: 978-1-63215-446-0
$12.99

VOL. 3: ALLIES AND ENEMIES TP
ISBN: 978-1-63215-683-9
$12.99

VOL. 4: FAMILY HISTORY TP
ISBN: 978-1-63215-871-0
$12.99

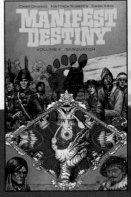

VOL. 1: FIRST GENERATION TP
ISBN: 978-1-60706-683-5
$12.99

VOL. 2: SECOND GENERATION TP
ISBN: 978-1-60706-830-3
$12.99

VOL. 3: THIRD GENERATION TP
ISBN: 978-1-60706-939-3
$12.99

VOL. 4: FOURTH GENERATION TP
ISBN: 978-1-63215-036-3
$12.99

VOL. 1: HAUNTED HEIST TP
ISBN: 978-1-60706-836-5
$9.99

VOL. 2: BOOKS OF THE DEAD TP
ISBN: 978-1-63215-046-2
$12.99

VOL. 3: DEATH WISH TP
ISBN: 978-1-63215-051-6
$12.99

VOL. 4: GHOST TOWN TP
ISBN: 978-1-63215-317-3
$12.99

VOL. 1: UNDER THE KNIFE TP
ISBN: 978-1-60706-441-1
$12.99

VOL. 2: MAL PRACTICE TP
ISBN: 978-1-60706-693-4
$14.99

VOL. 1: FLORA & FAUNA TP
ISBN: 978-1-60706-982-9
$9.99

VOL. 2: AMPHIBIA & INSECTA TP
ISBN: 978-1-63215-052-3
$14.99

**VOL. 3: CHIROPTERA &
CARNIFORMAVES TP**
ISBN: 978-1-63215-397-5
$14.99

VOL. 4: SASQUATCH TP
ISBN: 978-1-63215-890-1
$14.99

OR MORE OF THE WALKING DEAD

ROBERT KIRKMAN TONY MOORE
THE WALKING DEAD
VOLUME 1
DAYS GONE BYE

VOL. 1: DAYS GONE BYE TP
ISBN: 978-1-58240-672-5
$14.99
VOL. 2: MILES BEHIND US TP
ISBN: 978-1-58240-775-3
$14.99
VOL. 3: SAFETY BEHIND BARS TP
ISBN: 978-1-58240-805-7
$14.99
VOL. 4: THE HEART'S DESIRE TP
ISBN: 978-1-58240-530-8
$14.99
VOL. 5: THE BEST DEFENSE TP
ISBN: 978-1-58240-612-1
$14.99
VOL. 6: THIS SORROWFUL LIFE TP
ISBN: 978-1-58240-684-8
$14.99
VOL. 7: THE CALM BEFORE TP
ISBN: 978-1-58240-828-6
$14.99
VOL. 8: MADE TO SUFFER TP
ISBN: 978-1-58240-883-5
$14.99
VOL. 9: HERE WE REMAIN TP
ISBN: 978-1-60706-022-2
$14.99
VOL. 10: WHAT WE BECOME TP
ISBN: 978-1-60706-075-8
$14.99
VOL. 11: FEAR THE HUNTERS TP
ISBN: 978-1-60706-181-6
$14.99
VOL. 12: LIFE AMONG THEM TP
ISBN: 978-1-60706-254-7
$14.99
VOL. 13: TOO FAR GONE TP
ISBN: 978-1-60706-329-2
$14.99
VOL. 14: NO WAY OUT TP
ISBN: 978-1-60706-392-6
$14.99
VOL. 15: WE FIND OURSELVES TP
ISBN: 978-1-60706-440-4
$14.99
VOL. 16: A LARGER WORLD TP
ISBN: 978-1-60706-559-3
$14.99
VOL. 17: SOMETHING TO FEAR TP
ISBN: 978-1-60706-615-6
$14.99
VOL. 18: WHAT COMES AFTER TP
ISBN: 978-1-60706-687-3
$14.99
VOL. 19: MARCH TO WAR TP
ISBN: 978-1-60706-818-1
$14.99
VOL. 20: ALL OUT WAR PART ONE TP
ISBN: 978-1-60706-882-2
$14.99
VOL. 21: ALL OUT WAR PART TWO TP
ISBN: 978-1-63215-030-1
$14.99
VOL. 22: A NEW BEGINNING TP
ISBN: 978-1-63215-041-7
$14.99
VOL. 23: WHISPERS INTO SCREAMS TP
ISBN: 978-1-63215-258-9
$14.99
VOL. 24: LIFE AND DEATH TP
ISBN: 978-1-63215-402-6
$14.99
VOL. 25: NO TURNING BACK TP
ISBN: 978-1-63215-612-9
$14.99
VOL. 26: CALL TO ARMS TP
ISBN: 978-1-63215-917-5
$14.99
VOL. 1: SPANISH EDITION TP
ISBN: 978-1-60706-797-9
$14.99
VOL. 2: SPANISH EDITION TP
ISBN: 978-1-60706-845-7
$14.99
VOL. 3: SPANISH EDITION TP
ISBN: 978-1-60706-883-9
$14.99
VOL. 4: SPANISH EDITION TP
ISBN: 978-1-63215-035-6
$14.99

THE WALKING DEAD
BOOK ONE
a continuing story of survival horror.

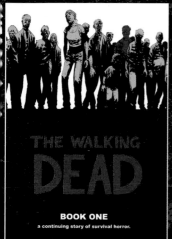

BOOK ONE HC
ISBN: 978-1-58240-619-0
$34.99
BOOK TWO HC
ISBN: 978-1-58240-698-5
$34.99
BOOK THREE HC
ISBN: 978-1 58240-825-5
$34.99
BOOK FOUR HC
ISBN: 978-1-60706-000-0
$34.99
BOOK FIVE HC
ISBN: 978-1-60706-171-7
$34.99
BOOK SIX HC
ISBN: 978-1-60706-327-8
$34.99
BOOK SEVEN HC
ISBN: 978-1-60706-439-8
$34.99
BOOK EIGHT HC
ISBN: 978-1-60706-593-7
$34.99
BOOK NINE HC
ISBN: 978-1-60706-798-6
$34.99
BOOK TEN HC
ISBN: 978-1-63215-034-9
$34.99
BOOK ELEVEN HC
ISBN: 978-1-63215-271-8
$34.99
BOOK TWELVE HC
ISBN: 978-1-63215-451-4
$34.99
BOOK THIRTEEN HC
ISBN: 978-1-63215-916-8
$34.99

COMPENDIUMS

The ultimate edition of The New York Times bestseller!
THE WALKING DEAD
COMPENDIUM ONE
Robert Kirkman • Charlie Adlard • Tony Moore • Cliff Rathburn

COMPENDIUM TP, VOL. 1
ISBN: 978-1-60706-076-5
$59.99
COMPENDIUM TP, VOL. 2
ISBN: 978-1-60706-596-8
$59.99
COMPENDIUM TP, VOL. 3
ISBN: 978-1-63215-456-9
$59.99

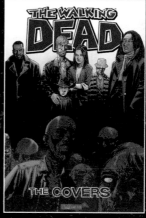

SPECIALTY BOOKS

THE WALKING DEAD
THE COVERS

THE WALKING DEAD: THE COVERS, VOL. 1 HC
ISBN: 978-1-60706-002-4
$24.99
THE WALKING DEAD: ALL OUT WAR HC
ISBN: 978-1-63215-038-7
$34.99
THE WALKING DEAD COLORING BOOK
ISBN: 978-1-63215-774-4
$14.99
THE WALKING DEAD RICK GRIMES COLORING BOOK
ISBN: 978-1-5343-0003-3
$14.99

OMNIBUS

THE WALKING DEAD

OMNIBUS, VOL. 1
ISBN: 978-1-60706-503-6
$100.00
OMNIBUS, VOL. 2
ISBN: 978-1-60706-515-9
$100.00
OMNIBUS, VOL. 3
ISBN: 978-1-60706-330-8
$100.00
OMNIBUS, VOL. 4
ISBN: 978-1-60706-616-3
$100.00
OMNIBUS, VOL. 5
ISBN: 978-1-63215-042-4
$100.00
OMNIBUS, VOL. 6
ISBN: 978-1-63215-521-4
$100.00

FOR MORE OF INVINCIBLE

TRADEPAPERBACKS

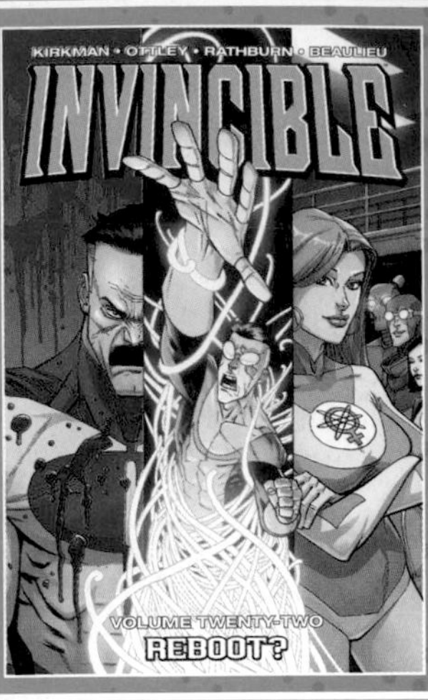
KIRKMAN • OTTLEY • RATHBURN • BEAULIEU
INVINCIBLE
VOLUME TWENTY-TWO
REBOOT?

VOL. 1: FAMILY MATTERS TP
ISBN: 978-1-58240-711-1
$12.99
VOL. 2: EIGHT IS ENOUGH TP
ISBN: 978-1-58240-347-2
$12.99
VOL. 3: PERFECT STRANGERS TP
ISBN: 978-1-58240-793-7
$12.99
VOL. 4: HEAD OF THE CLASS TP
ISBN: 978-1-58240-778-4
$14.99
VOL. 5: THE FACTS OF LIFE TP
ISBN: 978-1-58240-554-4
$14.99
VOL. 6: A DIFFERENT WORLD TP
ISBN: 978-1-58240-579-7
$14.99
VOL. 7: THREE'S COMPANY TP
ISBN: 978-1-58240-656-5
$14.99
VOL. 8: MY FAVORITE MARTIAN TP
ISBN: 978-1-58240-683-1
$16.99
VOL. 9: OUT OF THIS WORLD TP
ISBN: 978-1-58240-827-9
$14.99

VOL. 10: WHO'S THE BOSS TP
ISBN: 978-1-60706-013-0
$16.99
VOL. 11: HAPPY DAYS TP
ISBN: 978-1-60706-062-8
$16.99
VOL. 12: STILL STANDING TP
ISBN: 978-1-60706-166-3
$16.99
VOL. 13: GROWING PAINS TP
ISBN: 978-1-60706-251-6
$16.99
VOL. 14: THE VILTRUMITE WAR TP
ISBN: 978-1-60706-367-4
$19.99
VOL. 15: GET SMART TP
ISBN: 978-1-60706-498-5
$16.99
VOL. 16: FAMILY TIES TP
ISBN: 978-1-60706-579-1
$16.99
VOL. 17: WHAT'S HAPPENING TP
ISBN: 978-1-60706-662-0
$16.99
VOL. 18: DEATH OF EVERYONE TP
ISBN: 978-1-60706-762-7
$16.99

VOL. 19: THE WAR AT HOME TP
ISBN: 978-1-60706-856-3
$16.99
VOL. 20: FRIENDS TP
ISBN: 978-1-63215-043-1
$16.99
VOL. 21: MODERN FAMILY TP
ISBN: 978-1-63215-318-0
$16.99
VOL. 22: REBOOT? TP
ISBN: 978-1-63215-626-6
$16.99

THE OFFICIAL HANDBOOK OF
THE INVINCIBLE UNIVERSE TP
ISBN: 978-1-58240-831-6
$12.99
INVINCIBLE PRESENTS,
VOL. 1: ATOM EVE & REX SPLODE TP
ISBN: 978-1-60706-255-4
$14.99

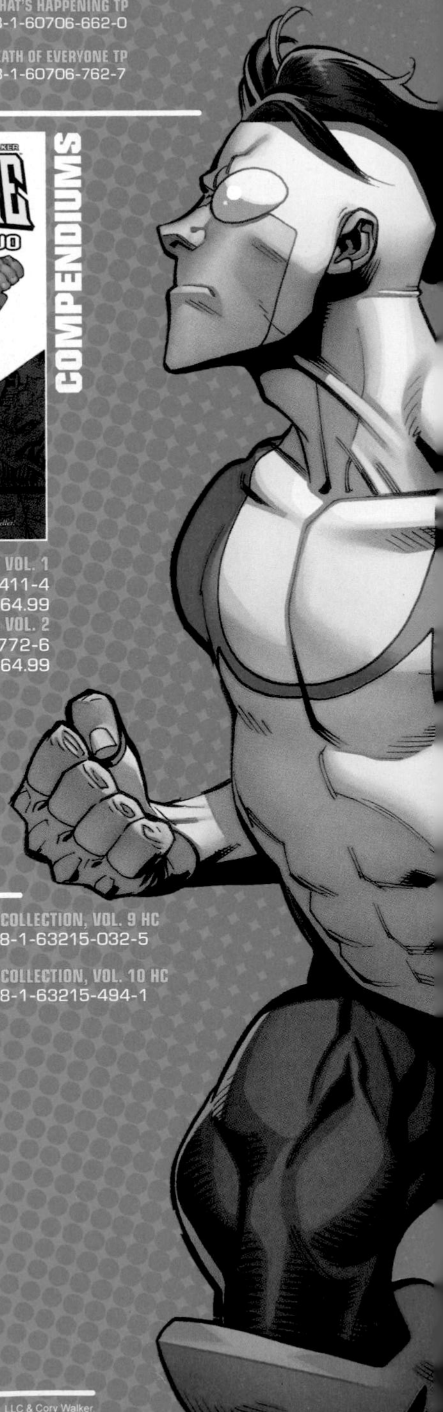

COMPLETE LIBRARY

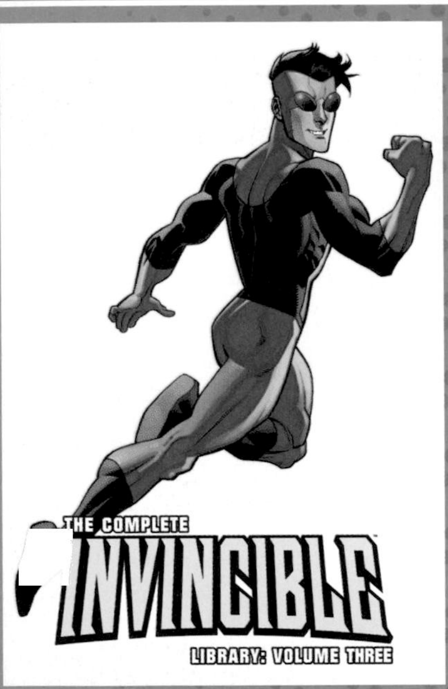
THE COMPLETE
INVINCIBLE
LIBRARY: VOLUME THREE

THE COMPLETE INVINCIBLE LIBRARY, VOL. 2 HC
ISBN: 978-1-60706-112-0
$125.00
THE COMPLETE INVINCIBLE LIBRARY, VOL. 3 HC
ISBN: 978-1-60706-421-3
$125.00

COMPENDIUMS

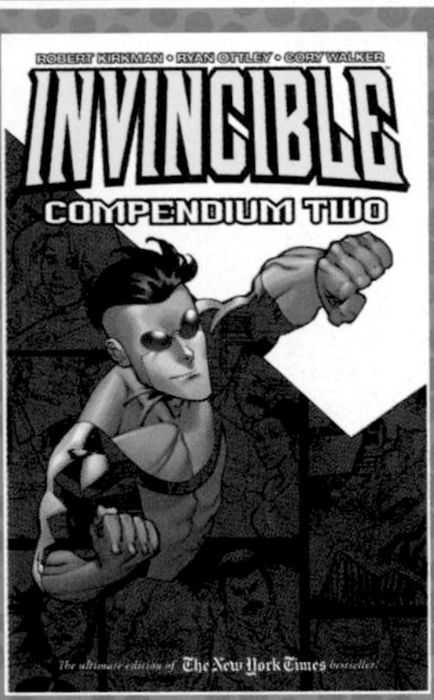
ROBERT KIRKMAN • RYAN OTTLEY • CORY WALKER
INVINCIBLE
COMPENDIUM TWO
The ultimate edition of The New York Times bestseller!

COMPENDIUM VOL. 1
ISBN: 978-1-60706-411-4
$64.99
COMPENDIUM VOL. 2
ISBN: 978-1-60706-772-6
$64.99

ULTIMATE COLLECTIONS

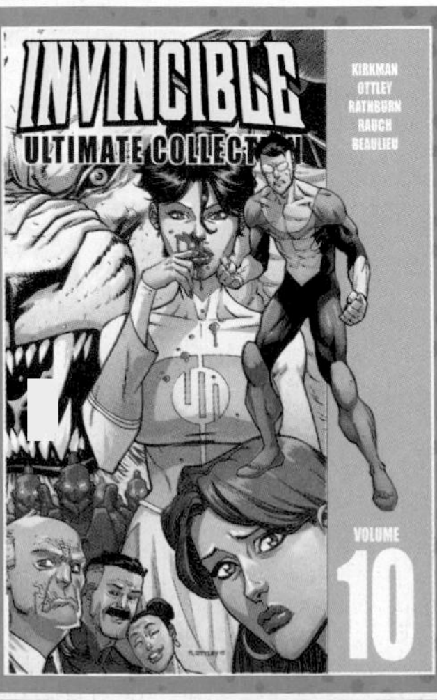
INVINCIBLE
KIRKMAN
OTTLEY
RATHBURN
RAUCH
BEAULIEU
VOLUME
10

ULTIMATE COLLECTION, VOL. 1 HC
ISBN 978-1-58240-500-1
$34.99
ULTIMATE COLLECTION, VOL. 2 HC
ISBN: 978-1-58240-594-0
$34.99
ULTIMATE COLLECTION, VOL. 3 HC
ISBN: 978-1-58240-763-0
$34.99
ULTIMATE COLLECTION, VOL. 4 HC
ISBN: 978-1-58240-989-4
$34.99
ULTIMATE COLLECTION, VOL. 5 HC
ISBN: 978-1-60706-116-8
$34.99
ULTIMATE COLLECTION, VOL. 6 HC
ISBN: 978-1-60706-360-5
$34.99
ULTIMATE COLLECTION, VOL. 7 HC
ISBN: 978-1-60706-509-8
$39.99
ULTIMATE COLLECTION, VOL. 8 HC
ISBN: 978-1-60706-680-4
$39.99

ULTIMATE COLLECTION, VOL. 9 HC
ISBN: 978-1-63215-032-5
$39.99
ULTIMATE COLLECTION, VOL. 10 HC
ISBN: 978-1-63215-494-1
$39.99

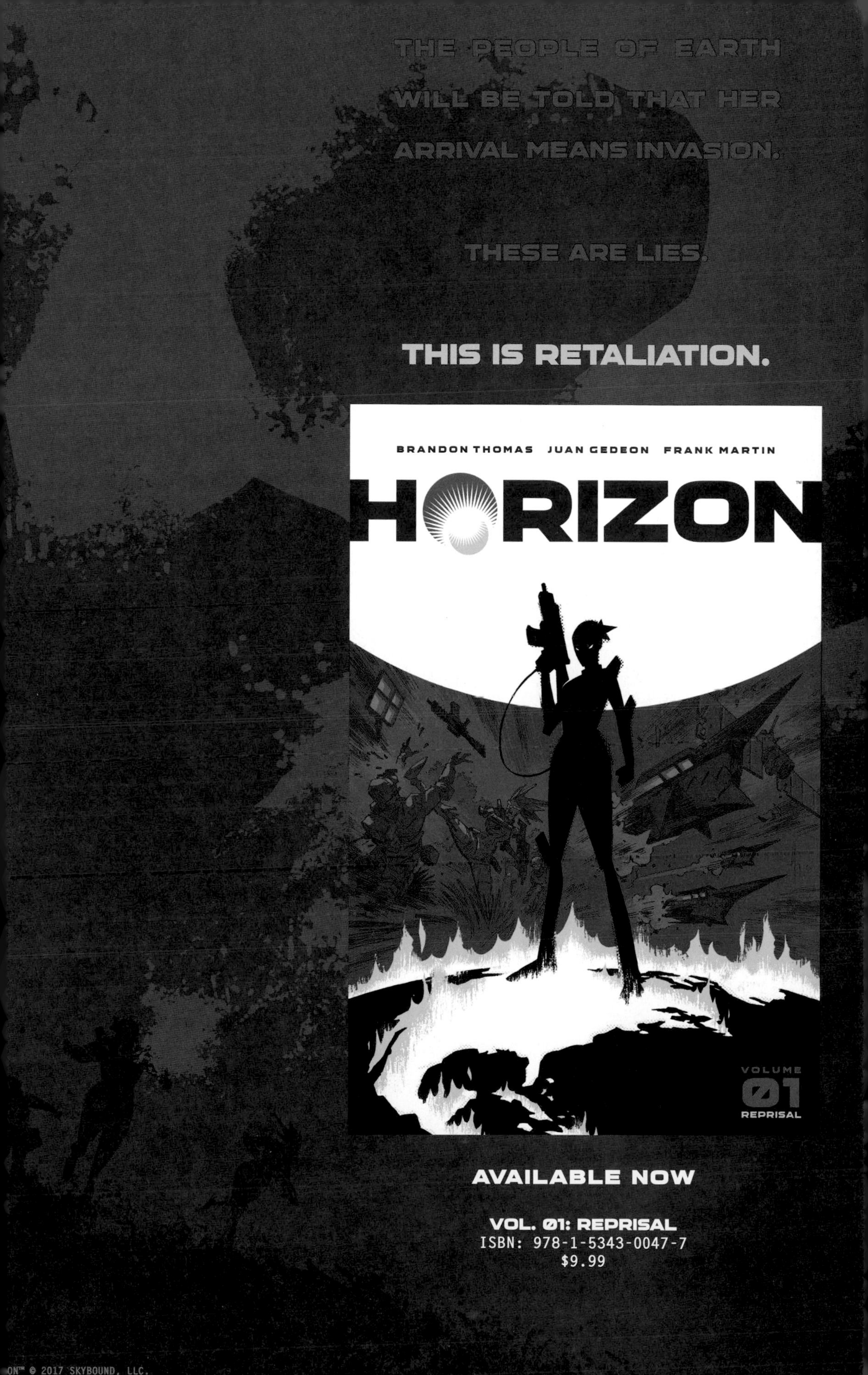
THE PEOPLE OF EARTH
WILL BE TOLD THAT HER
ARRIVAL MEANS INVASION.
THESE ARE LIES.
THIS IS RETALIATION.
BRANDON THOMAS JUAN GEDEON FRANK MARTIN
HORIZON™
VOLUME 01 REPRISAL
AVAILABLE NOW
VOL. 01: REPRISAL
ISBN: 978-1-5343-0047-7
$9.99